Who hasn't thought Pride and Prejudice could use more dragons?

Praise for Maria Grace

"Maria Grace did a wonderful job spinning a tale that's enjoyable for Austen lovers who do and who don't typically delve into the fantasy genre because she does a great job balancing the dragon world she has created alongside Austen's characters." ***Just Jane 1813***

"Grace has quickly become one of my favorite authors of Austen-inspired fiction. Her love of Austen's characters and the Regency era shine through in all of her novels." ***Diary of an Eccentric***

"Maria Grace is stunning and emotional, and readers will be blown away by the uniqueness of her plot and characterization" ***Savvy Wit and Verse***

"I believe that this is what Maria Grace does best, blend old and new together to create a story that has the framework of Austen and her characters, but contains enough new and exciting content to keep me turning the pages. … Grace's style is not to be missed."
From the desk of Kimberly Denny-Ryder

Netherfield: Rogue Dragon

Maria Grace

White Soup Press

Published by: White Soup Press

Netherfield: Rogue Dragon
Copyright © 2018 Maria Grace

All rights reserved including the right to reproduce this book, or portions thereof, in any format whatsoever.

The characters and events portrayed in this book are fictitious or are used fictitiously. Any similarity to actual persons, living or dead, events or locales is entirely coincidental and not intended by the author.

For information, address
author.MariaGrace@gmail.com

ISBN-13: **978-0-9980937-7-2** (White Soup Press)

Author's Website: RandomBitsofFaascination.com
Email address: Author.MariaGrace@gmail.com

Dedication

For my husband and sons.
You have always believed in me.

Chapter 1

"What will you do?"

Elizabeth shrugged. "The same thing I usually do—think like a dragon and act accordingly.

NIPPY MARCH AIR scoured Elizabeth's face as the mews' uneven paving stones assaulted her feet in her dash to Darcy's carriage. She pulled her green cloak tighter around her shoulders, her fairy dragon, April, safely nestled amongst her hood's folds. The sun's first rosy rays barely peeked over the horizon, not yet having their warming influence on the day.

Saying her goodbyes to Georgiana and Pemberley in the cellar dragon lair below Darcy's London townhouse had been the right decision. Forcing everyone to endure the morning nipping at ears and noses, fighting tears and melancholy, would have not made their parting any easier. Poor dears. Who was more distraught: Georgiana, for the loss of the sister she had just claimed, or Pemberley, now bereft of both her Keepers?

The two would be in good hands with Barwines Chudleigh, Lady Astrid, and the rest of the Blue Order officers taking them under their—sometimes literal — wings. There should be comfort in that. But still—to be asked to walk away after only just becoming acquainted with them and the new sense of family they brought, even for the critical work the Order demanded! Beastly unfair. Even so, Georgiana and Pemberley maintained brave faces and did not cry; she would do the same—at least while in their company.

The driver handed her into the plush carriage and shut the door. The entire coach smelled of him—his shaving oil, his soap, his own particular scent. Him. She blinked the burning from her eyes. Beastly unfair.

Warm bricks smoothed the edge off the chill, and a toasty lap rug lifted her to the heights of indulgence. Not that it was a far stretch to get there in Darcy's well-appointed coach. Thick squabs with supple leather covers, a table of sorts that pulled down from the sidewall, gleaming hardware—not so long ago she would never have imagined traveling in such luxury.

This would be her lot as Mrs. Darcy. How easy it would be to become accustomed to excellent equipage and a refined home filled with minor dragons, not to mention another Dragon Keeper determined to do right by his Dragon Mates. Truly, what more could she dream of?

Perhaps not to feel guilty for her good fortune.

Still though, one issue haunted her. Would Mr.

Netherfield: Rogue Dragon

Darcy be as determined and devoted toward his wife as to the dragons? Papa certainly was not. But then again, none would suggest that a fair comparison.

"You are fretting again," April whispered, snuggling closer into her neck. Fluffy blue feather-scales tickled Elizabeth's ear.

"Are you cold? You can come under the lap rug if you like."

"You are warm enough for me. There are times—occasionally—that it must be nice to be a warm-blood." April tucked the tip of her beaky nose under her tail.

Elizabeth laughed and stroked April's head. "I suppose you are right."

"But you should not fret. All is as it should be now."

"You have a most peculiar notion of how things should be. You do realize we are in search of a rogue dragon. My youngest sister has gone off with a man trying to make himself a Deaf Speaker. And my other sister is currently betrothed to a tentatively-approved Deaf Speaker, a man generally loathed by man and dragon alike. None of that seems exactly desirable to me." Elizabeth threw her head back into the squabs. Described like that, their situation had all the hallmarks of a Gothic tale in the making.

April nipped her ear softly. "You forget you are betrothed to an excellent Keeper, away from that horrid, jealous Longbourn, and Keeper to an infant vikontes who will someday be a tremendous influence in the Dragon Conclave. I am entirely content."

"You have very decided opinions, my Friend."

"And you ignore too many correct opinions." April snorted, tickling the side of Elizabeth's jaw.

She made it all sound simple, but then dragons

tended to overlook what was inconvenient to their particular agenda. Unfortunately, April's insistence did not change the difficult realities, no matter how much either of them wanted it. Elizabeth wrapped one arm tightly around her waist.

The carriage turned into the mews behind the Gardiners' house. They stopped at the back door near a laden luggage cart, Uncle Gardiner's horse tied to its side. Was it insurance he would have transport in case Papa became angry with him again?

She winced. Uncle should not have to think that way about Papa. But truly, was it surprising he did?

Rustle and Cait landed on the carriage roof. The driver greeted them in muffled tones. According to Darcy, the driver heard dragons but had no Dragon Friend. It seemed odd that one who heard dragons might not want to live with one, but apparently not everyone found draconic company appealing.

Before Elizabeth could leave the coach's warmth, Uncle helped Mary and Heather slide in beside her. Heather climbed inside Mary's generous furry muff, tucked her tail over her nose, and snored a musical fairy dragon snore—adorable, like most things concerning fairy dragons.

"Do you think Longbourn will have already told Papa the news?" Mary glanced over her shoulder as though looking for one of them.

"Since the majority is not in his favor, I somehow doubt it. I expect the duty will fall to you and Uncle Gardiner."

"I wish you would talk to him." Mary plucked at a tuft of silky brown muff fur.

Really, that is what worried her? Elizabeth grimaced and clenched her teeth. Sharp words and sarcasm would not improve matters. "I hardly think that possible, considering I am now a stranger to Longbourn estate."

Mary clapped her hands to her cheeks. "Oh, Elizabeth, I am sorry! I cannot believe I forgot—"

"Well, I suppose it is a good thing I have not lest Longbourn become enraged over the trespass."

"You need not sound so angry with me. I meant no offense."

"Considering you gained what you most wanted whilst I have lost just as much and perhaps a great deal more, is it too much to ask that you would remember my situation? If for no other reason, as Longbourn's Keeper, it behooves you to pay attention to those things that affect your dragon." So much for avoiding sharp words.

"You need not sound so bitter. It is not as though you are without home or dragon. Are you not betrothed to a man of consequence both in the Blue Order and in London society?" Mary turned her face aside.

Was it possible Mary was jealous? She got everything she desired, and yet she still resented Elizabeth?

"You sought Mr. Collins. I had never considered Mr. Darcy until we stood in the Dragon Conclave, and I had little choice. That may not mean much to you, but it is material to me." Elizabeth knotted her fist under her cloak, relishing the cut of her fingernails against her palm.

Heather stirred and opened one eye. "You are not being very kind."

Gracious! Heather had never criticized Mary before.

"She is right." April poked her head out of Elizabeth's hood. "Who are you to criticize if you are less perfect than her?"

"That is all we need to hear on the matter." Elizabeth covered April with her palm.

Mr. Collins clambered in, Uncle Gardiner close behind, the coach rocking and swaying with their shifting weight.

Uncle pulled the door shut and rapped on the roof. The carriage lurched as the horses set into motion. "With such an early start, we may well be at Longbourn before the family makes it down to breakfast."

"Remember, Papa is apt to be cranky before he has had his first willow bark tea and coffee." Elizabeth avoided looking at Mary.

"Then I shall not offer any news of importance until he is well dosed with his morning libations." Uncle winked. Though he smiled and seemed cheerful, something about the way he carried his shoulders—but why would he not be tense, all things considered?

Elizabeth turned to Collins. "How did you find your audience with Lady Astrid?"

He still wore a wide-eyed look that might be permanent; at least the pallor had finally left his countenance, though. Probably a good thing. Watching him faint dead away yet again would not improve their journey.

The edge of his mouth pulled back in an expression faintly resembling a sneer. So much for any hope of a pleasing conversation. "I must say, there is a great deal to accustom oneself to. So much intrigue and so many secrets within this Order of yours. A great deal of subterfuge is being practiced at all levels of society."

Already casting judgments and aspersions about the Blue Order? Surely the man was intent upon getting himself eaten by judicial decree. "I suppose that is one way to look at matters. But I would argue it is in the best interest of both species that it continues. Prior to the Pendragon Treaty, we all tottered at the brink of destruction. When most of those who cannot hear are not able to accept the presence of dragons, much less live peaceably with them, what else can be done?"

Collins braced his feet on the floor boards and pressed into the squabs. "I suppose that is the case. Certainly the need for secrecy has been impressed upon me—and the dire consequences of violating it."

Uncle reprimanded him with a glance.

"Do not get the wrong idea. As I said, I understand the need for it all." He harrumphed softly and tucked his chin to his chest. "Though, the standards are not equally imposed."

The hairs on the back of Elizabeth's neck prickled.

April crept out of Elizabeth's hood and perched on her forearm, prickly toes piercing her sleeve. "The dumb one's implications are dangerous."

Mary glowered at April.

"He is deaf, dear, not dumb," Elizabeth whispered.

"No, he is dumb." April sent Collins an ear-nipping look.

"What is it saying? I do not like it growling at me." Collins nudged Mary with his heel.

"'She', not 'it,' and I would counsel you to remember basic etiquette whilst dealing with dragons. You might not be able to properly hear their voices, but they can perfectly comprehend yours. They take offence easily and are often not apt to forgive." Elizabeth restrained the urge to step on Collins' foot.

"Of course, forgive me. What is she saying?" Oh, if he were not careful, April would peck that condescending smile right off!

"She does not like what you imply, sir. Nor do I."

"I am not surprised," he muttered to his waistcoat.

April's toes tightened on Elizabeth's arm. Any tighter, and they might draw blood.

"What am I to make of that remark?"

"Simply that I am confused about how the Blue Order applies its regulations." His chest puffed a bit—just like a dragon vying for dominance. He probably would not appreciate the comparison.

So self-satisfied and self-important … horrid man! "It would behoove you to speak plainly, sir."

April growled, hackles rising. On the other hand, perhaps the best thing he could do was to stop speaking altogether.

"If secrecy is so valued, why have you not been reprimanded for allowing those outside the Order to hear those stories you were telling the Gardiner children? That seems a breach of all the secrecy directives, does it not?" He carefully kept his face turned away from Uncle Gardiner.

Elizabeth's jaw dropped. April chittered so fast not even she could make it out. Heather peeked out from Mary's muff and joined in much more softly.

"Mr. Collins!" Uncle stomped. "You are hardly in any place to offer criticism when your own understanding is so meager."

"How can I perfect my information without asking questions?"

"There is a difference, sir, between a question and an accusation," Uncle hissed like an angry cockatrice.

"Elizabeth cannot possibly be at fault—in anything?" Bitterness fairly dripped from Mary's words. "She has always been such a favorite—"

Uncle slapped the squab beside him. "You will cease this line of conversation and stop commenting

Netherfield: Rogue Dragon

on what you clearly do not comprehend. The unmitigated gall—you have been tolerated—not accepted mind you, but tolerated—by the Order for less than forty-eight hours, and already you see fit to condemn? And you Mary—you may have been Junior Keeper to Longbourn, but you were as happy as your father to drop everything upon your sister's shoulders and leave her to bear the brunt of Longbourn's care—and his tempers—on her own. You claimed it was Longbourn's preferences, but it was as much your own laziness as anything else."

Elizabeth winced. Perhaps she could take Uncle's horse the rest of the way.

Mary's face colored, and she stared at her hands. "I fulfilled everything Papa asked of me."

"This amounted to nearly nothing. Examples of the kind of effort you should have put forth abounded. Despite your father's lackadaisical Dragon Keeping, he still provided you an excellent role model of devotion to the Order and Dragonkind, or did you even notice the time he spent in study and research?"

"He never tried to teach me—"

"Were you a willing pupil? Did you attempt to truly apply yourself, or did you make yourself difficult to instruct?"

Elizabeth pressed into the side of the carriage. No wonder the Gardiner boys were careful not to anger their father.

"I know enough—"

"—to do what? To be accepted by the Order? Yes, you know that much. But what could you possibly accomplish on your own? Could you meet a cockatrix on her own terms and come out the dominant female? Or introduce two cockatrice and keep them from killing one another? Can you soothe an amphithere's grief without her saying a word as to what troubled her or gain the loyalty much less the cooperation of a tatzelwurm? Would you risk your very life to save a wild-hatched firedrake on the slim chance it might imprint? Would you have known to call for a tatzelwurm to tend the wounds you received in the process? You may be a full-fledged Keeper now, Mary, but you are not Elizabeth's equal in ways you cannot begin to understand."

"So, that is all that matters—dragons and nothing else? What of the people who Keep them and those who must live unknowingly around them? Do they count for nothing?" Mary's voice turned sharp and thin as it did when she was near tears.

"What are you saying?" The words barely escaped Elizabeth's tight throat.

"It seems the Blue Order gives little thought to people, particularly those who are, through no fault of their own, caught up in the dragon world. Has anyone ever considered how Mama's life has been manipulated by dragons and how little choice she has in the matter?"

Elizabeth pinched her temples. "She would not be mistress of an estate apart from Longbourn. The Bennets are only landed because the current Longbourn's brood mother chose them as Keepers to the estate. We are who we are because of the dragons."

"Not all estates have dragons. Consider Netherfield Park …" Mary clapped her hands to her face. "Heavens, what is going to happen to Jane and Bingley? If there is indeed a rogue dragon there, but neither can hear it …" She fell back into the sidewall.

"I am going to Netherfield to see nothing untoward happens to them."

"What will you do?"

Netherfield: Rogue Dragon

Elizabeth shrugged. "The same thing I usually do—think like a dragon and act accordingly."

"What exactly does that look like?"

"I never know until I am in the middle of it. It depends on so many things, starting with the dragon's species, age, the relationships with Keepers or Friends, other dragons or even animals in the vicinity, hunger, dominance, is there hoarding involved, has the dragon's territory been violated in any way…" Elizabeth raised open hands.

Mary's jaw dropped.

"Now you see." Uncle crossed his arms over his chest and sat back, self-satisfied.

How should one feel about what he had just done? On the one hand, his vocal support was gratifying, especially when Papa had never offered as much. On the other, how much would Mary—and Mr. Collins—resent Uncle's set down? Mary had shown a surprising amount of bitterness just now.

Was it really resentment, though, or the voice of the tremendous pressure of the last few days? After all, worrying that the man one wanted to marry might be eaten by a dragon in a judicial action would be rather anxiety-provoking.

Elizabeth giggled.

"What is so funny?" Mary's eyes bulged.

Elizabeth shook her head. "A rather draconic joke, I am afraid. Not one most warm-bloods would find amusing."

Was it telling that her own sense of humor had become positively cold-blooded? And if so, what did it mean?

Mary rolled her eyes and turned aside to the side glass where the outskirts of Meryton appeared on the horizon.

It seemed only a few moments later the carriage stopped at the border of Longbourn estate.

"Elizabeth cannot cross into Longbourn's territory." Uncle opened the door and jumped out. "You and Collins may walk to the house from here or ride the luggage cart if you wish. I will accompany Elizabeth to Netherfield and take my horse back to Longbourn."

Collins' brows wrinkled, definitely less than pleased, but he wisely chose not to remark as he ducked out of the coach.

Mary paused, staring at the carriage floor. "I … I …"

Elizabeth touched her arm. "It is a difficult time for us all. None of us is currently at our best."

"No, I suppose we are not. I hope …"

"So do I." Now was not the time for draconic bluntness. Diplomacy had its uses.

Uncle handed Mary down and made room for her on the luggage cart. He tied his horse to the back of the carriage and climbed inside with Elizabeth, signaling the driver to continue. "I hope their pettiness has not upset you."

"I have long suspected those sentiments in Mary, so I am not surprised. I hardly count anything Mr. Collins says as significant. Even before he was aware of dragons, he rarely said anything sensible. Why would I expect that to be any different now?"

Uncle snickered. "Mary appears able to manage him well enough. Perhaps, between her and your father, they will be able to shape him into something the Order will accept."

"He seems anxious to please—so I think it likely, especially since he is not clever enough to form designs upon the dragons. By all appearances, he only is concerned with the condition and convenience of his own skin."

"At least that assists us in motivating him." Uncle dragged his fist across his mouth. "In all seriousness, though, have you a plan once you arrive at Netherfield?"

"No, I have nothing specifically in mind, but a great many options. It all depends on the dragon and his—or her—temperament. I imagine this one is cunning, being able to steer clear of Longbourn to avoid a territorial war. Similarly, it cannot be a dominant dragon, or it would have tried to fight Longbourn for his territory. So, I do not expect it to be aggressive toward me—it is unlikely it would chance upsetting Longbourn by harming me. On the whole, lindwurms are not very active dragons."

"And you are certain this is a lindwurm?"

"Few species have the dexterity to write, and fewer are able to paint. Lindwurms are often capable of both. Lady Astrid sent me off with several tomes on the species to study, so I shall spend some of my time doing that whilst I explore the nooks and crannies of Netherfield—and the cellars."

"Do you not fear there may be more poisoned rooms?"

April popped her head up. "One of the wyverns at Barwines Chudleigh's salon taught me how to smell for it. I will watch over her."

"You see, I will be well protected." She patted April.

Pray Uncle would not remark upon the wisdom of counting upon a fairy dragon for anything, much less protection.

Uncle harrumphed. "I will send Rustle to you daily.

Keep me abreast of everything. And if there is information you need from your father—"

"I shall not hesitate to seek help obtaining it. I promise. However, I do not expect that sort of problem. He will not permit his resentment to threaten his devotion to the Order or dragonkind."

Uncle did not look convinced.

Nicholls met them at Netherfield's front door. Tucked under a frilly white cap, her totally white hair made it difficult to detect where her hair ended and the cap began. She was young for her hair to have lost all the color but wore it as a badge of authority that none in her domain dared question. Of average height and build, she might be easily overlooked except for the efficient way she carried herself encouraged everyone to get out of her way and allow her to carry on with her business unquestioned.

She ushered Elizabeth and Uncle Gardiner inside, clearly uncomfortable. Did Mr. and Mrs. Bingley expect them? They had not sent word. How long would they be staying? Would Miss Elizabeth be returning to Longbourn? Were they there because of Miss Lydia's sudden departure?

One could hardly fault her many questions, but they needed to be addressed quickly before she formed opinions too strong to be persuaded out of. Still in the vestibule, Elizabeth, Uncle Gardiner, and April offered the official explanation, carefully crafted by the Blue Order.

Lydia had been called away to attend a sick relation. Elizabeth had been sent in her place to assist in preparing the house for its new mistress. Rooms must be cleaned and inventoried by Elizabeth herself with the staff to assist as she required.

Nicholls hesitated to accept that part of the story. Who could blame her? No one who knew Jane would believe she could be so exacting a mistress. Dragon persuasions could only go so far with most people.

Finally April—ingenious little soul that she was—suggested it would be a gift for Jane to return to a home already arranged to her preferences. Moreover, Elizabeth was a most considerate and loving sister to attempt giving a gift on such a grand scale. Uncle Gardiner added his support to the notion, and their subterfuge was complete.

Thank heavens! But perhaps Mary did have a point about dragons imposing unfairly upon those who had no say in dragon affairs.

Uncle Gardner took his leave, and Nicholls showed Elizabeth to her chambers—a lovely large room in the family wing. Her previous stay at Netherfield had been as a guest of questionable welcome, so she had not been in this part of the house, except fleetingly, in search of maps that might have led them to Pemberley's egg. Today she could stop and take in her surroundings.

Morning sunlight streamed through a pair of tall windows, flanked by damask drapes in golds and blues, flooding all the nooks and corners with light. Subdued dragon imagery filled the spacious chamber and the attached dressing room, the kind that could easily be overlooked by the dragon-deaf, but stood out to anyone acquainted with the Blue Order. The feathers on the paper hangings in both rooms were not peacock, but amphithere. The paintings, landscapes like those hanging in the drawing room, contained tantalizing hints of draconic influence. Mahogany dragon claws clutched balls on the furniture's feet, resting on a burgundy carpet bearing subtle, swirling dragon silhouettes.

One piece might have been a coincidence, perhaps even two, but no one acquired so much dragon-inspired decoration without doing so intentionally.

Moreover, this décor was not the work of a single generation. At one time Netherfield must have been a dragon estate. But what happened to its dragon? There had to be some record of it somewhere. Why did Papa not know? Or did he know and simply never saw reason to mention it? Why would he keep it to himself, though?

Alone in the roomy chambers, the weight of the last se'nnight descended upon her, slowly forcing her to the floor. A rogue dragon might well be slithering in the cellar below her, one with the potential to destroy the fragile fabric of dragon society. If the country fell into dragon war, everyone had so very much to lose. She wrapped her arms around her knees and rested her forehead on them. It all fell to her to find a way to resolve the matter without bloodshed—warm or cold. How was she to accomplish that?

April nestled against her cheek and trilled softly, the song soothing the edge of her angst. "Darcy should be here with you. He would not have permitted them to speak to you so."

"Darcy is doing what he must. And Mary ... she just does not know any better." But April was right—it would have been nice to have Darcy there with them. Very nice. He might not know what to do better than she, but he would make her feel like she had a chance

Netherfield: Rogue Dragon

at figuring it out.

"She should, and she will. I will have a talk with Heather. She cannot permit her Friend to act so inappropriately."

Elizabeth swallowed back a giggle. "Do you really think Heather capable of such a thing?"

April tossed her head in the fairy dragon equivalent of an eye roll. "You listen to me."

"I suppose you have a point." Elizabeth pushed up from the floor. The weight was still there, making it difficult to move, but what choice was there? "But we should set all that aside for now and find some place to begin."

April flittered to the bed post. "We should ask the Netherfield dragons what they know."

"Netherfield dragons?" There were local dragons whom she did not know?

"The local fairy dragons are too twitterpated to be of any real use. But there are several minor wyrms—wild ones—who live in the woods near the folly, and there is a shy puck living near the garden. If there has been a major dragon about, they are likely to know."

"So near the house? Does not that seem rather close for a wild dragon?"

"She is not wild. She was Friend to a tenant who lived on the estate some time ago—perhaps in your grandfather's day. After her death, she chose to stay but did not find another Friend. She is very timid." April landed on the windowsill and pointed toward the garden with her wing.

"Do you know if there is anything the puck particularly likes?"

"You mean does she have a hoard? Yes, pucks always have a hoard. Her Friend was a seamstress. She loves yarns and threads of all sorts. The wild fairy dragons often try to steal from her to make their nests. She is not fond of my kind."

"Well, who could blame her? There is hardly a greater offense to such a dragon than to steal from their stash. Might she like some of the pretty cherry-colored twist I have in my work bag?" Elizabeth rummaged through her work bag and held up the twist. April chirruped. "Then lead me to our shy friend, and we will see what she has to say."

Nicholls might be a meticulous housekeeper, but the kitchen garden was nothing short of a disgrace. Rabbits—a great many of them, it seemed—had the run of it. April led her to the edge of the woods near the garden. Several rabbits bounded out of the underbrush and into a hole concealed by a tall spiky holly bush.

"Here." April hovered over the holly.

"Are you certain? Did you not see those rabbits?"

April snorted. "She is a peculiar dragon."

That was not saying very much. Most dragons had distinct peculiarities. "In what way?"

"She is a puck; they are all a bit odd." April landed carefully on the uppermost holly branch, daintily avoiding the prickles.

"If you mean they hoard valueless things, I have come prepared."

"That is not the only way in which she is odd." April pulled a prickly leaf from between her long toes. "It is the rabbits. She likes rabbits."

"Likes rabbits? Like Pemberley and her dogs?"

"At least the dogs live in her dragon lair."

Elizabeth crouched and peered into the hole. "You

mean the puck lives in the warren with the rabbits? Pucks are house dragons—unless she has been mistreated, why would she—"

"She is peculiar, just as I said. She protects her rabbits from foxes and the like. Considering the state of the garden, the warren seems to be doing very well under her care."

Elizabeth headed back to the house.

April flew after her. "Are you giving up already? That is not like you. What is wrong?"

"I am not giving up, only realizing we must take a different approach. I scared the rabbits back into their holes, so it is unlikely she will come out and talk to me, at least not today. So I must smooth the way for a proper introduction." She shoved the kitchen door open. "Help me convince the cook to provide me with some vegetables."

April cheeped her skepticism but assisted in persuading the cook it was the most natural thing in the world to offer Elizabeth carrot tops, broccoli trimmings, cauliflower leaves, and a few apple slices—and not question why.

Elizabeth brought the kitchen castoffs to the holly bush and arranged them prettily on an old, slightly battered tin plate. She added the cherry-colored twist at the front edge of the offerings and pushed it close to the rabbit hole.

"Now we wait." She stood and dusted off her hands. "Do you think you can persuade Cook to regularly prepare such a plate?"

"The woman is quite a gudgeon. It will not be a problem, especially since she has little taste for vegetables herself. Do not ask her to part with anything sweet though. That would have her balking very quickly."

"I will keep that in mind." It was not surprising the puck would not be personable and ready to talk, but it still was a bit disappointing. Where were creatures with Lydia's personality when she really needed them?

The folly of that thought became evident a few minutes later when April introduced her to the wild wyrms living in the deeply shaded woods, near a broken-down folly. Though the weather-worn look might be considered fashionable, in this case it appeared more a matter of neglect than intent. The roof had caved in, and the trim around the doorway dangled from a single nail. A strong storm might bring the entire structure down. At least the nearby mossy stone bench remained solid enough for her to sit on while talking with the pair of forest wyrms that appeared out of the leafy floor litter at April's first call.

And talk they did! Heavens above, did those wyrms chatter.

Unusually friendly for wild dragons, they curled up their long scaly bodies at her feet. Dark and dappled, they blended into the dead leaves and loam.

The dominant one, a male, dared rub his furry leonine face against her ankles, almost like a cat. Such an audacious move, trying to mark her as his own territory. April dove at him, pecking at his head until he kept a respectful distance. The smaller female proved less apt to claim territory but far more vocal.

In furry-purry voices they talked over one another, offering their observations on any and everything above ground. They spoke so fast, it was hard to make out most of what they said.

Most Dragon Mates thought fairy dragons were brainless dolts—those people had never tried to talk to wild wyrms. But when Elizabeth asked about the night of the Netherfield Ball, they became very, very quiet, staring at her with wide almost frightened eyes.

"Have you heard any dragon voices that are new to the territory?" She leaned down close to hear them.

The smaller one turned on her tail and disappeared.

The male rose up like a cobra ready to strike, his mane extended like a hood, and hissed. He wove back and forth, hypnotic in his rhythm. "Not a safe question. Do not ask again. You do not want to know such things. You do not want to know."

Elizabeth allowed her eyes to glaze over, and she nodded blankly—exactly as the wyrm would have expected. No point in allowing him to realize she was immune to his efforts, at least not now.

He shoved his head under her hand. "Scratch ears."

April chittered overhead whilst Elizabeth scratched behind his ears.

"Come back and bring us chicken feet." He slithered away.

April flew after him, scolding.

Elizabeth leaned back and chewed her lip. For having told her nothing, the wyrms had implied a great deal.

"The nerve of that creature, expecting you to bring them treats after they have been so utterly presumptuous and unhelpful." April landed on her shoulder, feather-scales puffed.

She scratched under April's chin. "He overstepped himself, but we have only just met. It is hardly surprising he should be testing the waters."

"You have lived here all your life. He well knows your reputation. Why else would they be demanding chicken feet?"

"It was hardly a demand, dearling. I have not taken

offense, and neither should you. If you think about it, it was rather considerate of them to have told me how to motivate their assistance in the future."

"You are far too forgiving of their rudeness."

"They confirmed the presence of a lindwurm here."

"They said nothing of the sort."

"Considering the male was driven to persuade me away from my questions, I take that as an indication of a lindwurm's presence. They are bullying fellows toward smaller wyrms."

April harrumphed. "It seems odd to celebrate the discovery of what we already knew."

"We also know this lindwurm desires secrecy—so he must not be especially aggressive. Moreover, knowing it can read and write, I expect we are dealing with a scholarly dragon, not one interested in dominating a territory. So we should be able to reason with it."

April hovered in front of Elizabeth's nose. "You liked all those arguments with Chudleigh's friends at her salon?"

"They did get a mite heated to be sure, but I still find it preferable to discuss issues rather than worry about being eaten in a fit of pique."

"I suppose there is that."

Upon their return to the house, Nicholls met Elizabeth with household books in hand and invited her to the housekeeper's office. Neat and snug, it resembled Hill's office at Longbourn with shelves of linens and china lining one wall and stores of the more expensive food stuffs along another. Near the windows, a utilitarian table doubled as Nicholls' writing desk. Plain, white walls made the space bright and emphasized the lack of decorations—and dragons—in the room. Unlike

Darcy House whose staff was largely, if not exclusively Dragon Friends, it seemed the Netherfield servants were not.

Nicholls opened her books and set to work, efficient and businesslike as the best housekeepers were. With Elizabeth in residence, meals must be considered. The regular laundry day was approaching; would the new Mrs. Bingley desire that schedule be kept, or would she rather the task wait until she returned? Would Miss Elizabeth prefer the maids cleaned the rooms as she inventoried them, or should they proceed on their own?

The meeting required several hours and far more quick thinking than Elizabeth preferred. Running a household was her last priority, but since it was the guise she used for being here, somehow she had to find the wherewithal to pretend it was her only purpose. Exactly the sort of subterfuge Mr. Collins found distasteful.

"What do you wish done with Miss Lydia's things, Miss?" Nicholls shut her book—did that mean she was finally finished?—and looked at Elizabeth expectantly. "She left quite a bit in her chamber. I am surprised she did not take it all with her. Perhaps she was expecting to be back soon? Do you think she will want it sent along to her?"

"I am not sure. Perhaps it would be best to let me pack it up. I should be able to sort out what to do with it."

"I will take you to her room."

Lydia had been ensconced in the guest wing, near a servants' passage. Not a high-status room, but according to Nicholls, it was what she wanted. And of course,

Lydia nearly always got what she wanted. But why would she deviate so far from her usual demand for the best?

With a quick curtsey, Nicholls trundled off. April launched from Elizabeth's shoulder and buzzed about the narrow chamber.

Though relatively small, two windows brought sunshine into the bedroom, making it cheery and bright. Clearly it had been decorated with young female guests in mind. Gauzy blue drapes fluttered in the slight breeze that slipped through the edges of the windows. Dainty floral paper hangings matched the bed curtains and coverlet. Fairy dragons that looked a great deal like little birds hovered over the flowers on the paper hanging. Yet another landscape hung over the little bed. Subtle carvings of wyrms coiled around the legs of the oak dressing table. Even here, dragons influenced the décor.

So much Lydia had left behind! That was not like her; she preferred to bring far more than she needed on any trip. Even if they were walking to town, she somehow contrived to bring an extra-large reticule with who-knew-what inside.

Two trunks remained in the room. The closet was full of gowns—why did she think she would need a ball gown and an evening dress to manage the house whilst Jane was away? Several morning dresses and day dresses were there as well. It seemed she might have only taken one of each with her? How strange.

Elizabeth opened the smaller of the two trunks. One stocking and one glove lay crumpled within. Careless girl! No doubt she would miss those. What chance their mates were tossed in the press near the closet? She tugged open the sticky drawers.

Of course, with no one to watch over her, Lydia had not bothered to fold her body linen; it was shoved in the drawers. It would serve Lydia right if Elizabeth tossed it carelessly into the trunk, but no, she had been taught far too well. Mama would be lecturing in her head for weeks if she did such a thing.

April cheeped a little laugh as Elizabeth roughly folded the linen and packed the trunk. Not as neat as Mama would have liked, but enough that she need not feel guilty about it. So very much left behind. What was Lydia doing without all her clothes?

None of this made sense.

What was that? Elizabeth withdrew a slim mustard-yellow book from between two petticoats. Did Lydia actually keep a commonplace book? She sat on the edge of the bed in a sliver of sunbeam and flipped it open. A journal? Who would have believed Lydia had the patience to record her thoughts in a journal?

Once again Mary's voice rang in her ears. She had no right to read Lydia's private meditations. One more compromise of human courtesy in favor of dragon-kind! But no, this was about more than the dragons; it was also about Lydia's safety and protecting the family reputation. Those reasons demanded she read the journal.

She tucked the nagging guilt into a relatively harmless corner of her mind and turned the page. Typical Lydiaesque ramblings, pages and pages of it. Much like her conversation—effusions of fancy which said very little. She skipped several pages.

Wait, what was that? Suddenly everything was different. Lydia's enthusiastic scrawl was replaced by an odd, cryptic mix of numbers, letters and symbols. A cipher? Why would Lydia be using a cipher in her journal?

She turned back a few pages until she found the place where the writing had changed and read the entries just prior.

A new game Wickham was teaching her: to play like British spies. In that way they could write letters to one another, and no one would know to accuse them of impropriety. Heavens, what subterfuge! What utter disrespect toward her parents, toward society in general!

This was the sort of thing Mr. Collins should be concerned about, not judging the efforts of the Blue Order!

Had Mr. Darcy not already disabused her compassion toward Mr. Wickham, these entries would surely have accomplished it. She forced her eyes back to the page. Apparently, learning the code was difficult for Lydia. Wickham became impatient with her mistakes. What better way than to practice in her journal? And so the gibberish began.

She scanned the remaining pages, but no helpful key to the encryption existed. Perhaps it was elsewhere … the shelves and drawers, between the mattresses, under the bed, even the undersides of all the furniture and drawers. Nothing.

Why? Why did the key have to be the one single thing the feather-pate would choose to bring with her? Elizabeth shut the trunks with a bit more force than necessary.

At least she would have a puzzle to keep her occupied when she could not sleep—which seemed highly likely.

Chapter 2

DARCY PUSHED THE sticky window open, its panes grimy and smudged. Another night spent in a roadside inn. At least this one was tolerable. Yesterday, they had billeted in an abandoned barn when Fitzwilliam deemed the inn unsafe. Given Fitzwilliam's tolerance for uncivilized conditions, that pronouncement was one not to be ignored.

Tonight's room was little more than a closet, like the other inns, but a modicum cleaner. A bed shoved into one corner of the room bore linens that did not appear too stained. The two upholstered chairs and something that barely qualified as a table occupied most of the space near the fireplace. Barely enough space to walk between them, but it was an improvement over several of the places they had stayed.

Walker should arrive soon. Hopefully he would bring better news than had come out of Brighton. For one as prone to talk as Wickham was, it was suspicious that none—human nor dragon—had any inkling of his intentions or his whereabouts. He always boasted of his plans and how he would never get caught. Always. How was this the only time he managed to keep his mouth shut? A man did not change his stripes any more than a dragon changed his scales. What was afoot?

Walker swooped in, bypassing the window sill altogether and alighting on the back of Fitzwilliam's chair. He turned his back toward Darcy, a signal to release the satchel straps. Darcy quickly removed the bag and scratched between Walker's wings as Elizabeth had taught him.

Walker shot him an appreciative I-am-glad-you-finally-learned look.

Fitzwilliam poured a small glass of brandy and placed it near a plate of cold meat on the table. "When you are ready."

Walker flapped to the table and swallowed the topmost piece of meat whole. Not an attractive sight, watching the large lump slide down his gullet.

"You can stop to chew. We will not have to leave this place in haste. It is not like the last inn we tried to stop at." Fitzwilliam slapped Darcy's back.

Walker glared, more for show than anything else, but chewed the next slice.

"What has you so anxious?" Darcy poured two more glasses.

Walker gulped his brandy without spilling a drop—quite an accomplishment for a creature with a sharp curved beak. "The minor dragons of the countryside have gotten word of a wandering rogue dragon, not governed by the Blue Order."

"How? From where?"

"Who knows? It could have come direct from the Conclave—such news would be difficult to keep quiet. Even if the major dragons said nothing, all it would take is a single talkative fairy dragon or a wyrm of some sort." Walker tossed a small slice of meat into the air, catching and swallowing it in a single movement. "The general unrest grows as word spreads, despite the Court's assurances that the rogue was clearly limited to Hertfordshire. The major dragons I have encountered are reassuring their Keeps that the Blue Order still maintains the peace among dragonkind. But the disquiet among the minor dragons still unsettles them. If the major dragons lose faith that all the other large dragons will honor the peace established by the articles of the Pendragon Accords, I fear it may not be long before a botched greeting or an unexpected visitor sets off aggression that could escalate quickly."

"Bloody hell and damnation!" Fitzwilliam slapped the arm of his chair. "Sir Patrick, the Minister of International Dragon Relations, has been working with Vice Chancellor Torrington for the better part of a year to coordinate the visit from a representative of the Eastern Dragon Federation. They worked out the details of the travel three months ago. The envoy is traveling the underground tunnels, meeting our agents at designated checkpoints. So far all is well, but if there is anything certain about dealing with international politics—"

"—and dragons— it is that nothing is simple." Darcy dragged his hand down his face. "Dare I ask—how do you know this?"

"Father thought with my army experience I might be of use to Sir Patrick. I think he is trying to groom me for the office eventually." Fitzwilliam's expression suggested there was a great deal remaining unsaid.

Darcy blew out a breath through puffed cheeks. "A lovely, simple plan with so many possible wrong turns."

"In the literal sense." Fitzwilliam clutched his temples. "I will write to Sir Patrick tonight."

"I will take it to him directly." Walker paced along the edge of the table. "Only because these are unusual days, mind you. Do not get in the habit of thinking of me as some messenger bird."

"You saw Cait at Longbourn?" Darcy sat near Walker.

"Yes, and she is as well as can be expected. I am sure Lady Elizabeth has said something to that effect in her letter. But the strain of dealing with that fool Collins is wearing on Cait's temper. Longbourn is not helping either, cranky lizard. He tried to stop me from entering his territory."

Darcy winced. "Did you inflict too much damage?"

"There was no blood shed, but you will find a few of his head scales in the satchel. Keep them in case you need to remind him of your dominance."

"You took his head scales?"

Walker snorted something that sounded much like a snicker. "He was too angry to be in good form. Cait assisted me. She was delighted to take out her vexations on such an appropriate target."

Darcy covered his eyes with his hand and shook his head. "Everything is dominance with dragons."

"We are not unlike men in that. You simply choose to demonstrate it in a warm-blooded way. We are much quicker the point." Walker smirked, no doubt still enjoying his supremacy over Longbourn. "Enough talk. I need to eat. Pour me more brandy and read your letters."

Fitzwilliam saluted and refilled Walker's cup. Darcy sorted the messages and handed Fitzwilliam several, taking his own to a stained, overstuffed chair in the darkest corner of the room. It stank of the last sweat-soaked person who had sat there, but it was the closest thing to privacy to be had tonight.

Best deal with Lord Matlock's letter first.

Lovely. Now, in addition to seeking out Wickham, the Chancellor of the Order expected him and Fitzwilliam to visit all the Dragon Estates along the way and quell rumors of rogue dragons attacking the countryside whilst quietly gathering news of any discontent regarding the recent Dragon Conclave. What were they? Blue Order spies? He pinched his temples hard. At least Matlock had not demanded they deviate from their planned journey to do his bidding. That was something.

But why was he worried over the response to the Dragon Conclave? Was it Pemberley that caused him concern or Collins? Perhaps it was the test of the new marriage articles that resulted in two essentially ordered betrothals? Or something else entirely?

Gah! Now was not the time to speculate on the state of the Dragon State. Focus on the task at hand and deal with the rest as it came.

He cracked open the blue sealing wax on Elizabeth's thick letter. The penmanship was firm and feminine, strong, but evocative of feeling. Just like her.

My dear sir,

No doubt you are aware that we have made it safely to Hertfordshire. Uncle Gardiner, Mary and Mr. Collins are welcome guests at Longbourn house, but I am not. I have taken up residence at Netherfield. Longbourn himself is displeased that I am in the area at all and continues to refuse to allow me in his territory, as is his right. My mother and Kitty have been successfully persuaded that it is right and proper that I take over at Netherfield for Lydia who is now visiting an ill relation.

I never realized how convenient it might be to have a wealth of relatives in ill-health.

He chuckled. She probably quirked a brow with a wry little smile as she wrote that.

I was able to attend holy services on Sunday to hear Mary and Mr. Collins' banns read. No objections were raised, thankfully, but after that, things became rather interesting.

Apparently, Lord Matlock wrote to my father with instructions that our banns be read both at my family's parish and at the Kympton parish near Pemberley. So, whether we were ready for it or not, our betrothal is now part of the public record. It took me entirely by surprise as my father had not deigned to warn me. April and Rustle are pleased with the turn of events though. I hope you are not too disquieted by them.

Naturally, my mother was delighted at the announcement, though somewhat vexed that she only learned the news with the rest of the parish. She has taken every effort to enjoy her success as she has called upon her friends this week. Whether that means you will become her favorite son, I cannot say. She is very fond of Bingley, and Collins has the advantage of allowing her to live out her days at Longbourn. Still though, Netherfield is merely leased whilst Pemberley has been in your family for generations, and that is decidedly in your favor.

Surely that provoked another arched eyebrow as she wrote it. Would that he could see it for himself.

He dragged his hand down his face. Their betrothal—and he was not even there to hear it for himself, to sit beside her and see her blush as their names were called, to see Mrs. Bennet congratulated on the spectacular match made by her daughter when it was in fact he who had made the better match. It would be difficult to forgive Matlock for his interference.

But then again, it was a subtle way of announcing to any who had not attended the Conclave that all was well with Pemberley—both the dragon and the estate. Probably a necessary precaution considering the current climate.

At least Elizabeth gave no indication she was put out by it all. Would she tell him, though, if she were? Probably. She did possess draconic directness in spades. Not that he would dare complain about it. It was one of her most remarkable, and even endearing, traits.

Cait visits me regularly as much I think to get away from the chaos that is my ancestral home as for me to monitor her progress. Her gravidity is obvious now, and flying great distances is demanding for her, so the fact that she comes to see me speaks volumes.

In addition to my other tasks, I have acquired, with my uncle's help, a book from Papa's library on eggs and egg laying, penned some one hundred years ago. It was tucked away on one of the upper shelves in a dark, cobwebby corner that Papa rarely consults. While old, it is the only thing I have, so I shall study it carefully. Do not tell Walker, but I also have arranged to talk to a nearby poulterer and a falconer to see what I might glean from them. I know he and Cait might be offended. I am aware they are not birds, but I am just searching for anything that might allow me to assist her most effectively when the time comes. There are, after all, no dragon midwives available.

He guffawed—a dragon midwife! Had anyone ever considered such a profession for a species that laid eggs? But somehow it seemed only natural that she would. No wonder Walker wanted Cait to remain near her.

Hopefully, I will have better success in that endeavor than I have had with the reasons I am here in the first place. The Netherfield dragon has kept steadfastly hidden from me although I have heard rustling in the cellars which I am certain is dragon-based. The local forest wyrms avoid all discussion of the creature, but they do not appear in fear of their lives which suggests the dragon is not unduly aggressive and has an ample supply of food. I am not sure what he is eating, though, which is no small source of concern.

The Netherfield puck still remains shy and unwilling to talk to me despite the regular offerings I leave for her and her friends. While these sorts of meetings often require time and patience, I fear I may run short of both.

Lydia left a great deal behind at Netherfield, which I find puzzling. But the greatest puzzle is her journal in which she has begun to write using a cipher provided by Mr. Wickham. I am having little luck deciphering it, but I have included a faithful copy of several pages in the hopes that you or perhaps F will have better success with it. I do not know that it will offer useful information, but for now it is the best that I have available.

He pulled out the copied pages. It would be too much to ask for them to be immediately decipherable—nothing could be so easy. But she was right; Fitzwilliam might be able to make sense of them. At the very least, it would be something to do before they ran mad with all their failures.

I hope your trust in me has not been misplaced as I have accomplished very little. I warn you, April has scolded several times about how she thinks you should be here—with us—instead of on the road so far away. When you make your way back to us, I fear your ears may be at risk, so you may want to consider investing in a hat with solid earflaps before you arrive.

While I have assured her of the legitimacy of your travels, at times I think she is right. Your company would be very welcome.

Ever yours, E

She would welcome his company! He glanced over his shoulder. He was probably grinning like a fool, and neither of his companions would fail to notice and remark on it. No, it was not a declaration of deepest love, but it was certainly a positive sentiment, one he would appreciate and relish for what it was.

"So what news have you? Is it too much to expect your betrothed has already subdued the rogue dragon and is bringing him into the Blue Order?" Fitzwilliam wandered over and leaned against the arm of Darcy's chair.

Walker snorted from the other side of the room. "I would have told you directly had that been the case."

"So then, what has your fair one to say?"

Darcy refolded her letter. "As expected, our rogue is a shy creature and not yet ready to communicate openly. But there are signs that he is not looking for a territory battle, nor is he in danger of resorting to starvation hunting."

"Good news to be certain. I expect my father will be impatient for more than that, but it is a start."

"And she sends work for you to keep you out of

trouble." He handed Fitzwilliam the cryptic pages. "She found her sister's journal. Recently Lydia began writing in a cipher that was given to her by Wickham. Probably to send her covert messages under the family's noses. In any case, Elizabeth cannot make anything of it but thinks you might. There might be nothing there—"

Fitzwilliam snatched up the pages and brought them to the closest candle. "But it is certainly worth investigating." He rubbed his hands briskly, his expression shifting to a subtle relish. Even more than Darcy, Fitzwilliam hated, loathed, despised being idle, moreover he had been complaining bitterly of exactly that for several days.

"So, oh great officer of the King's army, what say you? Is all abundantly clear and easily revealed?"

Fitzwilliam's upper lip curled back. "It is similar to several ciphers that we used on the continent, but not exactly the same. I should be able to sort this out, given a little time. I cannot imagine Wickham would suggest something complicated to that Bennet sister."

"She is a silly bit of fluff, to be sure, but do not underestimate her intelligence." Walker muttered through a large mouthful.

"Indeed?" They both stared at the cockatrice.

"Just because she did not demonstrate it to you does not mean she is unintelligent. Silliness and intelligence are not mutually exclusive. Remember, her family actively encouraged her ridiculous behavior. An intelligent girl could easily work that to her benefit—and I think she did."

Darcy scrubbed his face with his palms. "The last thing we need is a clever woman working with Wickham. He is bad enough on his own. With a crafty partner, I shudder to think what he might be able to accomplish."

Fitzwilliam turned from the ciphers and grunted under his breath. "This is not your fault, Darcy. A rogue dragon in Hertfordshire has nothing to do with you or what happened to Pemberley."

"I grant you that much, however—"

Fitzwilliam rolled his eyes and shook his head.

"Do not look at me that way! You know it is true. Had I been more diligent in dealing with Wickham's treachery in the first place—"

"How many times do we have to go over this? It is not your fault. You packed him into the militia just as my father told you, without hesitation. What more could you have done?"

"I should have realized sooner what he was about."

"That would have meant you would have had to stand against your father who found Wickham entirely agreeable. Honestly, Darcy, neither you nor I have the fortitude to stand up to our fathers—both formidable men not prone to brooking opposition. Had you insisted your father give up Wickham, you might well have found yourself on very thin terms with him—banished to London, away from Georgiana. You might well have been unable to protect her from eloping with Wickham. Where would we be then? Torment yourself all you like. You will get no support from me in that endeavor. I am convinced that no man could have prevented the egg from being stolen, and no others but you and Miss Elizabeth could have managed to rescue an already-hatched drakling from the unthinkable." Fitzwilliam harrumphed and turned his shoulder toward Darcy, focusing on the coded pages.

Darcy leaned back in his chair and stifled a sigh. No

point in giving Fitzwilliam more to critique. It was not that Fitzwilliam's arguments were utterly baseless. He had made several excellent points, especially about the likelihood that Wickham's elopement plans would have succeeded. But still …

Little would make Fitzwilliam understand. Perhaps if he had a dragon to whom he was connected. Then he might—the connection changed the way the world looked in subtle but real ways.

Perhaps he might befriend one of Cait's clutch—if the timing could be worked out. If only he might be a Keeper though—he would make an excellent Keeper, far better than his brother who was already destined for the position.

Although Darcy suspected Cownt Matlock preferred Fitzwilliam to his brother, that alone was not grounds to overthrow inheritance laws. There were many men—and women—who would make better Keepers than those who held the role—the image of Anne de Bourgh flashed in his mind—and would never have the opportunity. Perhaps England would be better off finding a way to intentionally assign Keepers to their Dragon, but not without disturbing the entire order of society. Inheriting their Keepers was a compromise the dragons made for the sake of peace.

And none of this brought them any closer to finding Wickham and Lydia, or the rogue dragon, or reuniting him with Elizabeth. That could not happen any too soon.

Elizabeth pushed up from the narrow cellar steps. Sitting hunched on cramped stairs that offered no padding encouraged the damp cold to sink into her joints, leaving her bones aching like an old woman's. How many hours had she stared at the boxes and barrels and trunks piled along the dark, dank walls, hoping the stubborn dragon would reveal himself? Far too many.

Without April's help in persuading Nicholls otherwise, the housekeeper would be thinking Elizabeth well on her way to becoming daft by now.

Perhaps she was. Stubborn old lizard.

She stretched her back and shoulders and trudged upstairs. Sleep. It was dark and late and sleep was the only thing left to do for now.

At least her room was warm and the featherbeds were soft. She slipped under the blankets and dreamt of dragons.

"Wake up, but be still," a sweet voice whispered in her ear. Elizabeth stopped herself just in time and leaned into April just a little bit.

"Open your eyes, but do not move otherwise. On the dressing table, near the window."

Elizabeth's heart raced, but she held her breath, trying to remain as still as possible. Slowly, carefully, she peeked her eyelids open, turning only her eyes toward the window.

Silhouetted in the moonlight, a beagle-sized dragon stood on the dressing table between the mirror and water jug. Clearly female, the four-legged, long-tailed dragon sported a frilled hood, half-extended, ready to help her appear larger if startled. She turned her head this way and that, examining, considering the situation.

April rested her chin on Elizabeth's cheek, trilling softly. "You are welcome. Pray come in." Sometimes her song had the same effect on dragons that it did on people.

The puck's hood relaxed a mite.

"We have some dried meat you might share with us if you come closer." April flitted to a closed box on the bedside table between the bed and the dressing table. She lifted the lid with her long toes.

The puck raised her snout and took a deep breath. Her long tongue flashed out and licked her lips.

"I would like to share with you." Elizabeth pressed into the featherbed and turned her head just slightly toward the shy dragon, the bed linens rustling softly.

The puck jumped back, her hood flaring to full spread. Moonlight shone through the thin membrane, giving the impression of a large lace veil.

"You are quite lovely like that." Elizabeth whispered, rolling to her shoulder, but keeping her head on the pillow.

"Share with us." April plucked up a sliver of dried meat and tossed it to the dressing table.

The puck gobbled it up with a flick of her long tongue and smacked her lips.

"There is more if you come closer."

She crept to the edge of the dressing table, and April threw her another sliver.

"More?" What a soft, silky voice the puck had.

April hopped a piece of meat to Elizabeth's hand, and she tossed it, trying not to move too much or too suddenly. The treat bounced against the dressing table stool—the intended target—and hit the floor.

The puck chased it down and swallowed it whole.

Elizabeth threw another piece, closer to the bed and rose on her elbow.

In a single movement, the puck scooped up the

tidbit and scrambled onto the bedside table. Nearly eye-to-eye with Elizabeth, she jumped back hissing slightly, hood flaring again.

April hopped to the table and handed a shard of meat directly to the puck. "I am April, Friend to Elizabeth. She has been leaving the plate for your furry friends and the silk twists for you. She is safe."

"I am not blind. I know." The puck gobbled down another sliver of meat.

"Would you tell us your name?" Elizabeth asked, April trilling softly in the background.

Moonlight shimmered off the puck's bright eyes. She sat and scratched a wing nub with her hind foot. "I am Talia."

"I am pleased to make your acquaintance, Talia." Elizabeth nodded, not enough to concede dominance, but sufficient to make clear she was no threat. "I understand you were once Friend to a seamstress who lived nearby."

"I was. She died."

April offered another shaving of meat, but Talia was slower to take it.

"And she had no kin to take you in?"

"Her daughters could not hear, and they did not like the furry hoppers she kept, either."

"So you took over their care—for your Friend?"

Talia bobbed her head, her hood relaxing.

"That is a very noble thing for you to do, worthy of a great Friend."

"I like them. They are warm and quiet and soft."

"Indeed they are. And their noses are very cute when they twitch. Do their whiskers tickle as much as they look like they do?" Elizabeth sat up very slowly.

"Not so very much once one becomes used to

them."

"You protect them, I imagine? There are many enemies about, dogs, foxes, stoats …"

Talia shuddered. "Yes. Too many creatures find them satisfying to eat."

"Do you need to protect them from other dragons as well?"

Talia leaned back and hissed. "You want to know if the blue one wants to eat them?"

"Blue one? Is he a large dragon?" A blue lindwurm—those were rare in England, usually from the continent. But that made little sense.

"Too large to be bothered with my furry hoppers." Talia glanced toward the meat box.

"That is good to hear. Has he been about for a long time?"

"He does not like you very much."

April withdrew more meat and set it near Talia.

"I had no idea. I have never met him. How can he already dislike me?" Elizabeth moderated her tone carefully. It would not do to have the puck think her angry.

"Every dragon in the county knows you have made Longbourn very irritated."

"Longbourn has been very disagreeable?"

Talia swallowed the meat with a little shiver. "Horrid. He has been taking his temper out on us all."

"I am very sorry to hear that. It is wrong of him to behave so."

"It is wrong of you to upset him. Anyone with sense would know that."

"Sometimes dragons are wrong."

Talia snorted, poking her nose into the box and pulled out a large piece of meat.

Netherfield: Rogue Dragon

"Is the blue one afraid of Longbourn?"

"Don't know." Talia muttered through a mouthful. "The blue one does not like to fight, though. He has a special way to keep peace with an angry neighbor."

"When you see the blue one again, would you give him a message from me?"

Talia skittered back, hood flaring a little. "I will not tell him anything that will make him angry with me."

"I would never ask you to do such a thing. I just hope you would tell him that I am not as terrible as Longbourn makes me out to be. I would very much like to have a conversation with him."

"I might."

"If I continue to put out plates for your furry hoppers and perhaps a little colorful twist for your hoard, might it be more likely?"

Talia turned her back but cocked her head as though in thought. "Worsted wool."

"You want wool?"

"To line my nest. It helps keep my hoppers warm."

"Then I shall endeavor to acquire you a whole ball of worsted wool."

"I might talk to him."

April laid another piece of meat at Talia's feet. She gulped it down and scurried away into the darkness.

"That was interesting." Elizabeth wrapped her arms around her knees and laid her chin on them.

They were dealing with a large blue lindwurm, possibly from the continent, who did not like to fight and was cowed by Longbourn's temper, but was creative enough to find some way to placate him. Much of that was good news. She sighed—full-out dragon war was a little less likely, but she still needed to talk to the lindwurm. Perhaps little Talia would help. It would certainly be worth a trip into town later this morning for worsted wool.

The next day after breakfast, she placed a plate heaped with vegetable trimmings, a ball of green worsted wool, and a bobbin of blue thread under the holly bush. Hopefully Talia would appreciate the offerings and would not become greedy at her good fortune. It was difficult to tell with pucks, but she seemed to be a largely retiring and agreeable sort, so that boded well.

The garden and warm sunshine were a pleasant change of scenery. Far too many hours had been spent combing through dark, dusty rooms, servants' passages, and sitting in the cellar. Not that those had been entirely unprofitable endeavors. She now had a wealth of paintings to study, some very modern-looking, a large scroll in rather messy dragon script to decipher, and a deeper appreciation for the draconic lineage of Netherfield itself.

A book hidden away on the upper shelf in one of the small libraries had proven quite interesting. Apparently, the estate had been named in some of the original Pendragon documents that drew up the territory boundaries for the original English dragon population. A rather powerful drake had been the first Netherfield. He had served as the county's leading dragon. But all traces and records of him disappeared about two hundred years ago. What had happened, and why had his duties never been transferred to another dragon but left to fall by the wayside? Perhaps one of Papa's forefathers had recorded something in the Longbourn records about it. But it was not terribly likely, for only Papa and his father had been meticulous record keepers.

She would need to talk to Papa, but he seemed indifferent to her presence. None of her family had paid her much notice. Mama and Kitty were easy enough to forgive, subject as they would be to Longbourn's persuasions, but Mary and Papa were another matter.

No, now was not the time to become maudlin. No point would be served by that.

"Miss Bennet!"

Elizabeth looked over her shoulder.

One of the scullery maids scurried toward her. "Nicholls said you would want this directly." She handed Elizabeth a thick folded letter, barely stopping as she rushed to her next task. Nicholls did not believe in allowing the girls free time to get into mischief.

Was that her style of management or a suggestion from the lindwurm so as to reduce the likelihood of discovery? Likely as not, it was a combination of both. Embracing draconic suggestions happened far more readily when it was in line with one's own inclinations.

Mary's precise and regular handwriting graced the neatly-folded missive. She closed her eyes and exhaled heavily. Was it wrong to feel a bit of dread? Mary's unpleasantness was totally understandable, but it was exhausting. Staring at it was not going to make it any easier—may as well face the dragon quickly.

The wedding is Monday, March 23 at 9 o'clock. Pray come. Walker asked that I send this along to you. He is with Cait right now but will see you before he returns to Darcy.
M.

She was invited to the wedding. That was more than she had expected. But did Mary actually want her there, or was it a matter of preventing questions as to why her sister, who was so close by, would not be at the wedding? Perhaps being at the wedding would make it easier to explain why she was not at the wedding breakfast. Oh, that definitely was uncharitable and not a worthy thought at all.

Even if the frustrations—and all told, the loneliness—were eating away at her, it did not behoove her to indulge in that kind of thinking. Besides, folded within Mary's note was a thick letter from Darcy. She smiled in spite of herself, a little of the lonesomeness fading.

She hurried to the maze—ironically where she had overheard Miss Bingley and Darcy talking all those months ago—and found a stone bench in a sunbeam under a white wood arch. She curled up on the bench and leaned against the now bare lattice, the warmth of the bench sinking into her joints—or was that the warmth of knowing the letter was from him?

He had written in ink this time. Hopefully that meant his accommodations were better and he was less hurried this time.

My dear Elizabeth,

Since you inquired directly in your last letter, I am pleased to say, we are warm, fed and dry, and reasonably comfortable this time. I cannot pretend to be displeased that this segment of our journey has taken us past establishments that F deems safe enough for us to stay in. Although I loathe saying it, I am glad you are not with us presently. None of these places are fit for you. It gives me peace of mind to know you are safely at Netherfield. Somehow the thought of a rogue dragon there seems less dangerous than the ruffians we must rub shoulders with here. I realize that must sound a bit odd, all told, but I feel certain that you would agree.

He was right. She pressed the letter to her chest. Had anyone else ever understood her so well?

I regret I have nothing in the way of good news to report from our efforts. Wickham and Miss Lydia seem to have disappeared without a trace. Neither man nor dragon has encountered them. It is unusual for Wickham to be so discreet in his movements. If nothing else, his typical failure to pay his debts usually makes him easy to trace.

F is beginning to suspect that they did not make their way to Gretna Green after all. But we shall continue our efforts in this part of the country for a little longer to be absolutely certain.

Lord Matlock is making sure he gets the most out of our labors by having us visit the dragon estates along the way to keep a watch on the increasing concerns over the rogue dragon. Despite all pains to let people know that it is definitely contained in Hertfordshire (and pray tell me that I am correct in that assumption!), the very notion causes so much unrest that I am not sure we are believed.

Had Papa any idea how dangerous the situation had become? Perhaps if he did, he would be more forthcoming with assistance. At the very least, Uncle Gardiner needed to be made aware of these changes.

F has made a little progress in translating the pages you sent. He says the cipher appears to be based on one used in the army. I have included his partial translations as well as what he has deduced so far in terms of breaking the cipher. I am afraid that what he has gathered from your sister's journal is mostly concerning ribbons and hats and of little application to the current situation. Still, I am hopeful that you will be able to put what I have enclosed to good use.

Have you been able to make contact with the Netherfield dragon yet? I had a thought in that regard. It may be a very bad one, but I trust in your graciousness not to laugh at me for it. There is evidence that the dragon is able to read and write. Have you considered perhaps leaving a written message for him rather than simply hoping he will grant you an audience? As I write this, it does sound ridiculous and perhaps it is, but I thought it worth sharing the notion with you.

He went on to discuss the sorts of things that people wrote of in regular letters. News of shared acquaintances and loved ones, in this case, dragons and Keepers. Georgiana and Pemberley were doing well. Though Pemberley missed them, the letters they had sent her were keeping her spirits up. She was making progress under the Blue Order tutelage in London, and now able to hold a pencil which was the first step in being able to write. In fact, the little drakling had insisted on making her mark on Georgiana's last letter. Perhaps it was not so normal to have a dragon signing a letter. But Dragon Keepers were hardly typical. Still though, the conversation was welcome … and warm and rather witty. He expressed himself very well on paper, even if he did not do so in person.

She set the letter aside and turned her face to the sun, eyes closed.

His idea about leaving a written message for the lindwurm was unconventional, but it was a good one. Since she had made no other headway, there was little to lose by trying it. The cellar floor was covered in soft dirt in which she could scratch a bit of dragon script that no one would recognize as a message. Much safer than chancing that a piece of paper might be picked up. Yes, she would try that tonight.

She ought to write to Darcy immediately and let him know. It would probably make him smile. His letter sounded so tense and yet so concerned for her. It would be good to send him some pleasing news, especially since there was so little to be had.

Chapter 3

MONDAY MORNING PROVED to be a cool, refined sort of morning that did not call attention to itself for what it was, exactly what one wanted for a wedding day. Elizabeth executed her toilette with particular care, not that anyone would especially notice, but it made her feel better. One's sister did not get married every day. She had missed Jane's wedding, so she needed to enjoy Mary's—what little of it she could participate in—twice as much to make up for the loss.

She pulled her green cloak around her shoulders, and April settled into the hood. The little church was not so far away as to necessitate calling the carriage. If she used it, Mama would doubtless make a fuss over the fine coach and what a very fine thing it was that Elizabeth would be Mrs. Darcy. While it was expected that Mama should exult in her daughter's success in the marriage mart as it were, it was not fair to distract from Mary's day.

She steeled herself during her brisk walk, the chill fading as she warmed from the exercise. It returned, though, when she saw the church in the distance, the family coach nearby.

Perhaps this was a bad idea. If she turned back now, none would be the wiser.

But no, Mary had invited her, and she needed to be there. With an especially deep breath, she made her way toward the chapel door.

"Elizabeth!" Kitty, in her second-best green lawn gown, greeted her and took her hands. "You look so very well. I am sorry you have missed all the excitement at the house. I know you have been ever so busy at Netherfield making things ready for Jane, but still it would have been nice to see you just once."

"Indeed she is right," Mama cut in. "Missing Jane's wedding was indeed a sadness, but you do not need to make up for it by slighting Mary as well."

"She has more than made up for it by getting Mr. Darcy. He will be by far the richest and best connected of your sons. And the handsomest," April twittered softly.

Elizabeth cast a warning glance at her shoulder. It was not wise to push a persuasion too far.

Mama looked a little startled and stared at Elizabeth as though remembering something she had forgotten. Her expression softened and a very pleased, even self-satisfied air crept over her. "But then, I am sure you are quite caught up in your own wedding planning. Do not forget you have a mother and sister quite willing to help you with that. Just think, you are to be Mrs. Darcy! What a fine, important lady you will be—the wedding clothes you will need!"

"I have planned nothing yet, Mama. Mr. Darcy is

away on business right now, and we will not plan the wedding until after that is complete."

"We have hardly had time to order Mary's, you know. Just two weeks to prepare. I imagine we shall go to London yet to your uncle's warehouses, not that she will need as much as you to be sure. A vicar's wife can hardly compare to what—"

The vicar emerged from the door and beckoned them inside. Mama harrumphed softly and rearranged the collar of her pelisse. Kitty hurried to take her place near the front of the church with Uncle Gardiner who was serving as groomsman.

The little chapel looked exactly as it usually did. Plain white walls, with matching windows on each side, it smelled of age and damp and dust. Worn, dark wooden pews in two columns flanked the walls like soldiers waiting to march. The simple hexagonal pulpit would hold the vicar several steps up above the congregants. A completely unremarkable church.

Somehow that was disappointing, even heartbreakingly so. Should not a place look remarkable on a day as life-changing as a wedding? Mary had said she, Kitty and Lydia had adorned the church with flowers when Jane wed Bingley. Did Mary not want them, or was she being overlooked once again?

Papa grunted at her as he walked past her toward the back of the church, not even making eye contact. Was that his own preference or Longbourn's? Did the difference even matter?

She sat near Mama.

Mary approached the front of the church on Papa's arm, and the wedding proceeded exactly as the Book of Common Prayer set out that it should, completely ordinary and proper. Exactly as Mr. Collins—and probably Mary—would have it.

What would her wedding with Mr. Darcy be like? Surely Pemberley would have to be present—for the wedding breakfast at least if not the ceremony itself. The little dear would never accept being absent for the event that insured she would have her two Keepers permanently.

Elizabeth pressed her lips hard—it was difficult to say what was more entertaining, the idea of the drakling throwing a tantrum in order to be allowed to attend the wedding, or figuring out how to bring a major dragon into the church. There was a chapel in the underground offices of the Blue Order—perhaps it would do for the wedding. What would Mr. Darcy say to such a notion?

She tried to imagine him being disagreeable about it, but the image would not coalesce. It was simply impossible to see him so. He would not be the one to deny the baby something she so dearly desired—and honestly, he probably would not deny Elizabeth, either—even if it meant he had to procure a special license, the services of a Blue Order bishop, and they would be married in Pemberley's dragon lair. She pressed her hand to her chest. Yes, he really was the sort of man who would do that for her. Absolutely nothing like the dragon-deaf dolt who stood beside Mary.

April cuddled her cheek as though she could sense Elizabeth's thoughts and approved most heartily.

The vicar declared Mary and Collins man and wife, and they disappeared into the vestry to sign the marriage lines. Papa hovered near the chapel door, glancing alternately at the vestry door and at Mama as she trundled out toward the coach. This might be the only opportunity Elizabeth had to ask him about

Netherfield. She slipped out of the pew and hurried to him.

He grunted at her. Lovely.

"Pray, have you any records on the history of Netherfield? I am quite certain it was a dragon estate at one time. Is it possible that there might be yet another dragon lurking about with a claim to the territory?" She stood beside him, not quite looking at him.

His expressions shifted subtly, from something like disapproval to budding interest. Of course, dragon lore would draw him out when nothing else could.

"There was no major dragon in residence during my grandfather's lifetime, but the last resident owner was a Dragon Friend. I have several centuries of county records among my library holdings, though. I will examine them immediately and send you word of what I find."

"If that is too much trouble, you could have Uncle bring the books to me, and I can search them."

"They are part of the estate, and Longbourn will not approve of them being placed in your care."

She held her breath to hold back her sigh. He was willing to help her; that should be enough, even though it was not.

Mr. and Mrs. Collins emerged from the vestry, her arm in his. He looked satisfied—with himself and with the proceedings. Heather perched in Mary's bonnet, a fluffy pink ornament that accented the pale pink of her best gown. Mary's cheeks glowed, by all appearances genuinely happy.

How ironic. After all her bitter complaining, did she realize that she was marrying the man she had hoped for because of draconic interference and that her wedding would likely never have happened without it?

Now was probably not an appropriate time to mention it.

Mr. Collins slipped away to speak to Papa.

"Heather and I are glad you have come," Mary said softly.

"I hope you shall be very happy together and your marriage is all you have hoped for."

"I expect it will be. Even more, now that he is becoming aware of the true nature of the estate he will inherit." Mary glanced over her shoulder toward Collins.

"Has Longbourn officially acknowledged him yet?"

"No. Papa wants to bring him to the lair for a formal introduction soon. With Cait's help, I am sure it will not be long. I have every hope that once that chore has been accomplished, things will settle down and be much easier for us all." Mary's eyes lost a little of their smile.

"Longbourn has been cross and cranky with you?" Elizabeth touched Mary's elbow. "Is there something I can do to help? I know a few things that tend to soothe his moods."

"Let us not talk of such things on my wedding day." Mary looked away as though Elizabeth had suddenly sprouted a large wart on her nose.

"You are invited to Netherfield should you ever wish to speak of it."

"Thank you for the invitation." She may as well have said she would never darken Netherfield's door.

April leaned very close and whispered, "She is not like herself—perhaps her resentment has been suggested."

Was that possible? But by whom? Would Longbourn attempt such a persuasion? He had tried to persuade Elizabeth to marry Collins. If he would stoop to that, then he was certainly not beyond this. But why? Given that persuading a Keeper was forbidden in the first place, it seemed odd at best that Longbourn should go to the trouble of doing so just to get back at Elizabeth. No, that made no sense.

Mr. Collins collected Mary without so much as a word to Elizabeth, and the wedding party took their leave of the church, leaving Elizabeth to walk back to Netherfield, alone.

A swath of Netherfield's woods bordered Longbourn's. It would be as close to Mary's wedding breakfast as she would be able to go. Though it made precious little sense, she turned down along the wooded path.

"Darcy should be here," April chittered and flapped. "I am going to tell Walker that he must remedy this situation immediately."

The woods' shadows welcomed them along the cool path between the trees. Branches arched up overhead to form a skeletal canopy—it would be full and green soon, but now it was only a promise of what was to come. The forest floor likewise remained dry and crunchy, waiting for the full advent of spring to soften it with rains and new growth.

"You are unhappy." April hovered near Elizabeth's face.

"He has work to do. Besides, I do not need Mr. Darcy to be happy." Perhaps not, but it would not hurt.

"Yes, you do. You should be happy. Longbourn is a bully and just plain mean. A disgrace to his kind. The Blue Order really ought to bring him under better regulation." April landed on Elizabeth's shoulder.

"I know you have very decided opinions, but

Netherfield: Rogue Dragon

perhaps, just perhaps, it is not good to share them so near to his territory. He does have an awful propensity—"

A roar just softer than dragon thunder rattled branches overhead and crashing footsteps approached.

"—to appear when one voices such things." Elizabeth squeezed her eyes shut and forced herself to draw in long deep breaths. But her heart still fluttered and her belly pinched, especially when the first whiff of dragon musk mixed with the distinct odor of wyvern wafted on the breeze.

"I do not want you in my territory." Huge stomping footfalls punctuated the declaration.

"Good day to you too, Longbourn." She flashed a false smile and curtsied.

"Get out of my woods." He leaned down toward her face, extending his tail for balance.

"I am on Netherfield territory not yours."

"These are my woods." He edged closer, breath hot and putrid on her face.

Mary really needed to take better care of his teeth or he would soon be in need of a tooth key himself.

"Do not attempt to poach territory that is not yours. You know that is against the Accords—even if there is no dragon assigned to the land." She folded her arms across her chest and pulled her shoulders back. How would he respond if she spread her cloak and flapped to make herself large? Probably not well, but it was a thought.

"I do not want you here."

April buzzed toward him and pecked between his eyes, not that he could feel it much through his thick hide.

"I am very sorry for you then. I hate to suspend any

pleasure of yours. But I am entirely within my right to be here, and I will enjoy my walk since you are determined to keep me from my family's celebration."

"You should not have been at the wedding. I told them both I did not want you there. They went against my wishes."

"I am sorry you are so selfish and small-minded that you should wish to keep me from my own sister's wedding. But since it occurred outside of your territory, you have no control in the matter. They were within their rights to allow me to be present. You should be satisfied that you have prevented me from attending the wedding breakfast. I am feeling that deeply. Is that not enough for you?"

He huffed acrid breath in her face. "This is not my fault. It is your choice."

"How exactly is this my fault?"

"You abandoned your place as Keeper." He thumped the tip of his tail. A large branch snapped and sent a shower of debris against Elizabeth's skirt.

"Because you tried to persuade me. Now you are trying to use persuasion to make Mary cross with me."

"She has enough to be cross about; she does not need my help."

"What is that supposed to mean?"

"She has to manage Collins, who is an idiot, and Cait who is the very picture of a shrew, not to mention your feather-pated mother, and she has been neglecting me. Of course, she is short-tempered. No persuasion is needed to accomplish that." He wrinkled his nose, sending April flying backwards.

"So you have then considered it?"

"I am not persuading her or anyone else! Why can you not accept that?"

She glared at him through narrowed eyes. "Why did you threaten me and leave me in fear for my life?"

"That again? Why must you take that so personally? You made me angry—"

"And that makes it all acceptable? You lost your temper. That is not my fault. The very least you could do is apologize for what you did and for what you tried to do."

He rose to full height, towering over her. "I am a dragon. I do not need to apologize for anything. You need to come to your senses and stop accusing me—"

"There is no point to continuing this conversation. Bring me proof that you did not attempt persuasion, and I will immediately recant and apologize."

Longbourn's eyes brightened, eye ridges lifting high. "And you will return to your position as my Keeper?"

"You know I cannot. The Blue Order has already ruled that Mary is Keeper here now. I cannot overturn that."

"You would rather be Keeper to that clumsy baby than me." Longbourn growled deep enough to shake the nearby branches.

"I have been assigned as Pemberley's Keeper by decree of the Order. That is beyond my power to alter. But I will most willingly apologize—"

"What good is an apology then, if it changes nothing?"

"Why must you be so stubborn? We could at least enjoy the time I have here. I would be pleased to visit you and do all the things—"

"Then you would turn around and leave me. No, that is not acceptable." He stomped, raining dry leaves over them.

"I do not want to be at odds with you."

He stared at her with huge, sad eyes—not angry, but sad—and turned away, slinking off into the forest, pouting.

She leaned against a large tree and covered her eyes with her arm. When did it all go so arsy-versy?

"He is selfish and jealous and far too accustomed to having his own way." April worked her way back into Elizabeth's hood.

"Large dragons generally have their way for good reason, you know. Few can stop them."

"You did, though."

"I wonder if that was a good idea."

April cuddled the side of Elizabeth's jaw. "Only because he is making you feel guilty right now. You cannot look at Pemberley's face and tell me it is not right for you to be her Keeper. A firedrake as powerful as she will be must be set upon the right path very early. It will probably take both you and Darcy to make certain that happens."

She scratched April's chin. "You make a very compelling point, my Friend." A point her head understood, but her heart struggled to embrace. "I am getting chilled. Let us return to Netherfield."

Just after dinner, which Elizabeth took in her room whilst she studied one of the tomes on lindwurms, Cait pecked at the window, obviously offended that it had not been left open for her. Elizabeth threw it open and helped her manage her tail feathers, arranging them all safely as she landed on the top edge of the dressing table's mirror. A message satchel was strapped to her back, nearly obscured by the lush feathers of her nearly-black ruff.

"I am glad to see you, but I did not expect Papa to send you with messages." She pointed to the satchel. Cait turned to make it easier to reach.

"He meant to send Rustle, but after all those people calling today, I simply had to get out! Oh, it was dreadful." Cait shook out her feathers in a well-practiced, elegant movement.

"What do you mean?"

"That shallow pate Collins! I may yet tear his eyes out. No one would find fault with me for doing so." Silhouetted against the waning sunlight, Cait was still in fine form, though her belly showed obvious—to Elizabeth—signs of her condition.

"What happened?"

"One of the guests caught sight of me and instead of allowing Heather to persuade her away from bothering me, Collins decided he should show off the fancy bird that was now staying at Longbourn—as if I were some credit to him! The unmitigated gall of the man! If it were up to me, the court should have ordered him eaten so none of us would have to deal with him. I still think they should and would happily testify so."

Elizabeth extended a hand to offer a scratch which Cait accepted. "I am sure it is all made so much worse because you are not far from laying your clutch."

"They have no idea what it is like—and your sister is little help. She has no sympathy for what I suffer. Your father offers sympathy but little more. It cannot be too soon that the Order finds another to take my place. If Collins shows me off as a fancy piece of livestock again, I swear, I shall bite off his little finger. I am no parrot and certainly no chicken!"

Elizabeth smoothed her ruff. "I quite understand; it is insulting. I will write to my father and inform him he needs to teach Collins better."

Cait tossed her head. "He is not the only one in need of reform. Why are you accusing Longbourn of persuading Mary?"

"Are you suggesting Mary could work up so much resentment on her own? She seems to have grown far worse since she has come to Longbourn, despite the fact she should be satisfied with all the outcomes. Mary has been known to be a bit contrary at times, I grant you, but this is entirely out of character."

"I am saying it is not Longbourn."

Elizabeth pinched the bridge of her nose. "You believe him when he claims that? I do not."

"You are clearly as stupid as the rest of your family." Cait tossed her spectacular ruff and spread her tail as though her beauty was reason enough to trust anything she said.

Best let that insult go unrecognized. "Do you have an idea who is persuading Mary then?"

"You are seeking a rogue dragon, are you not?"

"He is trying to persuade Mary? I suppose you would have me believe he was also the voice I heard at Longbourn trying to get me to accept Collins."

Oh, the look Cait cast her way!

"That is utterly ridiculous. Why would he do such a thing? How would he get into the Longbourn cellars in the first place? You know Longbourn would not tolerate another major dragon in his territory, much less in the house! He barely tolerates you as it is."

"Jealous, crusty lizard." She snorted and picked at her wing. "I cannot speak as to why. Why does a major dragon do anything? They have their own reasons. Would he not have won Longbourn's appreciation if he had succeeded? Nonetheless, you should look past the end of your own nose and consider what ought to have been one of your first thoughts."

Elizabeth rolled her eyes. "I will give the notion due consideration."

"You had best do that before it is too late, and you miss an opportunity you need." Cait shook out her wings. "I need a dust bath."

"April has found a pleasant spot in the rose garden. She can show you if you like."

April cheeped and flew off with Cait close behind. She had been taking a lot of dust baths recently. Fairy dragons did that when preparing to join—or attempt to join—a harem.

How long would it be before April left? Best not dwell on that now.

Elizabeth fell heavily into the overstuffed chair near the fire. Could Cait possibly be right? The Netherfield dragon trying to persuade Longbourn's Keepers? No, that hardly made sense at all. It was simply not possible.

But it might be a point of conversation, one arousing enough to draw the lindwurm out to speak with her. Since nothing else had worked yet, it was worth the effort.

She pulled her shawl around her shoulders and took up the fireplace poker. The cellar was dark and cold, but the dirt was soft enough for her to write with the poker:

Why are you persuading Mary to be cross?

—⁂—

Darcy sank back into the large, soft and very clean chair near the fireplace in a room easily twice the size of any he had seen for at least a fortnight. Bright white linens—he had actually checked after the rigors of recent days—covered the tall bed surrounded by bed curtains not tattered and torn. Both a closet and a chest of drawers accepted his luggage—all free from any sign of vermin or dust. The very definition of luxury.

Mr. Thomas Powlett's invitation to stay at Birchcaster Heath, though he claimed the accommodations to be modest, was far more welcome than he knew. This was the first time in weeks that Darcy had a room to himself. In the quiet, his thoughts finally turned settled and well-ordered, almost like the pain of a lingering headache receding.

His meeting with the drake, Birchcaster, had been quite satisfying. It seemed he shared the easy-going temperament of his Keeper and welcomed the Blue Order assurances that there was no need for alarm. Far better than the reception they received at the last estate whose resident wyrm, Overport, was not averse to calling them liars and threatening to run them off his land himself. Matlock would soon receive a letter suggesting the need for some Order oversight on that estate.

Just how many more estates of that ilk dotted the English countryside? What did that mean for the actual state of the Blue Order and their influence over the Dragon State? He raked his hands through his hair, pulling slightly. He had never wanted to become involved in the administration of dragon affairs. Father had managed to keep clear of the duty, arguing on more than one occasion with Uncle Matlock on the matter. He had kept himself to Pemberley and been done with it all. But with the death of Old Pemberley and the birth of little Pemberley, everything changed.

How melodramatic that sounded, but she would be

the first firedrake to be raised in the modern era. Instructing her and shaping her understanding would be crucial for the future of England and the Blue Order.

Thank heavens Miss Elizabeth would be at his side through it all. It was tempting to think that Pemberley somehow recognized that her situation would need more than he alone could offer. But that was imbuing a baby dragon with sage wisdom, and even he realized that was crediting her with a bit too much. Still though, it was fortunate.

Walker pecked the French door that opened onto the balcony, and it swung open. He hopped in and closed it behind him. "I had nearly forgotten how pleasant it was to come into lodgings designed to accommodate my kind." He flapped his wings slightly.

"It does feel a bit like the return to civilization, does it not?" Darcy laughed and reached for the buckles on the satchel. "I wonder that you will be able to fly anywhere without this in place once we are done with this affair. I have become so used to seeing you with it. You look quite naked without."

Walker snapped his beak in a warning that was not entirely playful. "Nakedness is a warm-blooded convention that I would thank you to keep to yourself."

"How did you find Cait this visit?"

"Big, broody, and balky. She hates nearly everyone and everything right now." Walker picked something invisible from between his toes.

"Rather like she was the last time she clutched?"

Walker hopped to a small tabletop. "Precisely, so I am not overly concerned. I suppose it is an advantage that I am only able to make short visits, so she rather welcomes my arrival. She does detest Collins though. The Order needs to provide another translator soon, or she may peck his eyes out."

"He is such a dullard?" Darcy rubbed his forehead hard.

"Worse. He is a dullard with opinions. It seems he has decided it is his right as a warm-blood—which by the way, he thinks makes him the superior partner in the relationship—to have opinions on all matters related to dragons and the Blue Order. Opinions which he unfortunately thinks are correct. He borders on quite unteachable."

"Bennet will have his work cut out for him, molding Collins into an appropriate candidate for membership into the Order. Perhaps Collins has forgotten what it will mean for him if he continues to be so opinionated. Do you think it would be helpful if I wrote to remind him of his very precarious position?"

"I know Cait would be grateful for it."

Darcy leaned forward on his elbow. "Grateful enough that she might permit Fitzwilliam to try to befriend one of her clutch?"

"If he listens to you, she might befriend you herself."

"Thank you for that honor, but no." Darcy guffawed. Cait in his household? But then again, Elizabeth had already asserted dominance over her ... No, it was a very bad idea.

"Good. There is a reason cockatrice only live together for brief periods." Walker scanned the room, probably looking for a plate.

"The kitchen sent up a bowl for you just an hour ago. There, on the dressing table."

Walker found it and tore into the raw meat. Darcy turned to his letter.

My dear Mr. Darcy,

Thank you for sending along Georgiana's latest letter. It is delightful to see how much of a change her time with Lady Astrid is making. It is difficult to believe she was once so reticent about dragons.

Have you considered that Barnwines Chudleigh's continuing favor might well put her in a way of meeting an eligible Keeper? No, I do not think Chudleigh is inclined to bother with matchmaking directly, but she is a very social creature. With all her salons and parties, I am certain many introductions are being made. So you may wish to steel yourself for the possibility of yet another wedding in the near future.

After having just attended Mary's, I realized that there might be special circumstances surrounding our own. You might think me silly to suppose it, but it seems likely that there may be dragons among those who wish to attend our wedding breakfast. I have no idea how one plans a wedding breakfast to include dragons—the very idea boggles the mind, but then again, so much of what is going on right now does as well. Perhaps if we both give the matter some thought, we might come up with something that will suit all parties.

He reread the paragraph twice, chuckling each time. Dragons at a wedding breakfast—the very thought! But she was right; it was entirely possible. At the very least it would not hurt to be prepared for such an event. What was more, she was thinking about their wedding, and in—what must be for her—positive terms.

Bless it all, if his betrothed wanted dragons at her wedding breakfast, then by Jove there would be dragons. It would no doubt be the most talked about wedding the Blue Order would ever know—not at all what he would desire, but for her, it would be worth it.

April has taken to spending time with Cait. She—April, not Cait—has been short-tempered, and my ears bear witness to the degree of her irritation. The broodiness will only grow worse until she finds a proper mate. Fairy dragons are native to the Longbourn woods, so I doubt she will have difficulty finding a harem to join. She is—well, you quite know her personality—she will have no trouble in exerting dominance over the other females. I expect she will have a clutch of her own before summer.

I am glad for her, but—and I have spoken of this to no one—I am concerned that she may decide to lay her clutch in the wild and remain with them to protect the eggs. She has more sense than the average fairy dragon and will be diligent in seeing them hatch safely. I do not know if she will decide to return to me after that, though. She has never been my prisoner, but I have also never considered what would happen should she decide to leave. It has never been a possibility before.

I do not wish to sound maudlin or melancholy, but without the company of my family, Netherfield has been lonely. So much so, I would swear to you I heard giggling in the hall last night, much like my sisters', but there was no one there. Not even the maids. I wonder that I may be going daft.

I pray this does not sound overly sentimental, but how much longer do you think your journey will take? I find myself impatient for your arrival at Netherfield.

He traced the last several words as though it would bring her closer. She missed his company, wanted him there with her. If that was not tantamount to a declaration of love, what was?

Longbourn will not be pleased to have a second broody female nearby. As I understand, he and Cait have already had words on multiple occasions. I encountered him just after Mary's wedding. He is little changed since we last saw him—except perhaps he is more agitated over Collins.

I am convinced that Cait will need assistance in laying her clutch. The advice from the poulterer and the falconer has been much more helpful than I imagined, and between them and the book from Papa, I believe I have assembled a sound strategy to assist her. Perhaps the Order might name me the first dragon midwife.

If anyone could aspire to such a title, it would be Elizabeth. He dropped his chin to his chest, chuckling at the image of her hurrying out from Pemberley in the middle of the night to attend a dragon laying.

I have learned a little more about the paintings that bear so many draconic evidences. Talia, the puck who lives in the garden (By the way, when you come, could you perhaps bring with you a variety of threads and yarn, the more colorful the better. And wool! She is a great lover of a warm nest.) has proven a great wealth of knowledge (assisted by her fondness for dried meat.) She has been a resident at Netherfield for many years now and says the Netherfield dragon is a relatively recent arrival. Likewise, the paintings are fairly new.

Apparently, every few months a new painting arrives on the doorstep, wrapped in brown paper, with instructions to Nicholls to see it appropriately hung in the house. In exchange for her rabbit warren remaining undisturbed (I will explain that when you arrive,) Talia encourages Nicholls to think the paintings souvenirs of Mr. Bascombe's travels to the continent and beyond.

Needless to say, it seems reasonable to assume that they are the work of our rogue dragon and having them hang in the house suits his vanity. I have been studying the paintings at length, and many seem to repeat the theme of escape and sanctuary with many dragon types represented. What I do not know is if these themes are to be taken literally or metaphorically, or perhaps our painter lacks imagination and cannot think of anything else to render on canvas.

I took your suggestion and scratched a message to the Netherfield Dragon in the soft cellar dirt, asking him why he was persuading Mary to be disagreeable.

He wrote back to me: Because I do not like you.

I am not sure which surprised me more, that he responded at all, or that he claims not to like me without having even met me. Needless to say, I asked him why, and I currently await his response.

In my idle moments I have been continuing to work at deciphering Lydia's journal. Without Fitzwilliam's expertise and experience, I have enjoyed less success than he. But I did come across a phrase that is potentially concerning. I have included both the encrypted characters and my attempt at translating them. I do not know what to make of it, but it does seem significant.

Pray let me know your thoughts and when you might make your way to Netherfield. And me.

Yours, EB

Darcy's hands trembled just a bit, for so many very good reasons, but those had to wait. He forced himself to turn the page over and stare at the passages from Lydia's journal. The sheet full of coded characters made no sense, but below one phrase Elizabeth wrote: *introduce him to my secret friend.*

His hands turned cold as he read the words twice, thrice. Secret friend. He bolted next door to Fitzwilliam's room and barged in.

"What the devil has gotten into you, Darcy?" Fitzwilliam jumped from his chair, knocking an empty glass to the floor.

"Word from Elizabeth." He held out the missive.

"She has deciphered—"

"Not very much, but see for yourself." He turned the letter to the coded passage.

Fitzwilliam scanned the page, his finger tracing as he went. "Introduce ... special not secret, special friend? Get me my portfolio."

Darcy fetched the portfolio from the closet. Fitzwilliam had already spread the paper out on the table in direct sunlight. He pulled notes and a pencil from his portfolio and spent the next half an hour scribbling across the ciphered characters.

"Bloody hell, that girl's head is filled with fluff and nonsense."

"Be careful—"

"Not Elizabeth you idiot, her sister. I can only make out enough to be certain that I am not certain of anything. She refers to a special friend, but who that might be is anyone's guess, much less whom she wishes to introduce to him. I have deciphered that it is a him at least. And that he is tall and handsome."

"She wishes to introduce someone to Wickham?"

"Or it is possible she means that she wishes to introduce Wickham to someone. I do not know. Lord, I wish I did, but I do not." He scribbled something out further down the page and wrote something else in its place. "This strongly suggests that she wished to make the introduction near Netherfield, and the date is not long before she disappeared. It is quite possible she never actually left Hertfordshire."

Darcy's eyes bulged, and his jaw gaped. "What? She is well-known in the area. How could she possibly remain hidden there?"

"Humor this old army spy for a moment." Fitzwilliam raised an open hand.

"Spy?"

Fitzwilliam flashed a lean smile and nodded once. Darcy gulped. What else did he not know about his cousin?

"You told me the terrain around Hertfordshire was largely karst, no?"

Darcy slapped his forehead hard. "Caverns. So many damnable caverns!"

"Quite so. You searched a great number of them looking for Pemberley, as I recall. Some of them, if your descriptions were accurate, would be large enough to house a couple. If properly stocked, they could remain there for quite some time. Wickham could easily acquire supplies in the next village over and never show his face in Meryton."

"We have been on a goose chase whilst Wickham and Lydia have been at arm's length from Elizabeth all this time?" Darcy clenched his fists until they trembled.

"Considering we have found no trace of them on the road, and as Wickham has never been good at covering his tracks, it seems highly likely to me."

"That could explain the giggling in the hall and why he said he did not like her."

"What are you talking about?"

"Elizabeth made contact with the dragon—they have left notes for one another, and his last said that he did not like her very well."

"There is no telling what Wickham could have told him! The dragon could think her very dangerous, indeed." Tight lines became visible along Fitzwilliam's eyes.

"We leave for Hertfordshire at dawn then. I will send Walker immediately to warn her of our concerns."

Dear God, let the warning not be too late! With the current state of dragon affairs, if any blood was shed, war might well be inevitable.

Elizabeth sat on the bottom step of the dark cellar stairs, her face in her hands. The air smelt of cold damp rock, similar to a dragon lair—perhaps that was why the lindwurm came here. Perhaps not, but it was as good a reason as any. Would that he had never come here at all.

She peeked up, but the wispy script in the dusty floor did not change: *Because you are arrogant, selfish and insensitive to others.* Dragons were known to be direct, and apparently this one was no different.

Talia scurried out of a small hole in the far wall. She circled the marks and stared at the words. "What is that? It makes you unhappy."

"Netherfield does not like me."

Talia's wing nubs twitched, a dragon shrug, and she approached the stairs. "My Friend's daughters did not like me. It happens." She edged closer for a scratch between her shoulders.

Elizabeth obliged. Talia leaned into her, contented guttural sounds rumbling in her throat.

At least the little dragon approved of her.

Elizabeth turned aside and blinked rapidly. Perhaps Talia was right. It did happen. But not to Elizabeth, at least not where dragons were concerned. Certainly some had been less personable than others; that was only to be expected. But outright dislike? That she had never experienced before.

Moreover, it made no sense. Why would he have taken a dislike to her when she had no interaction with him, ever? She wrapped her arms around her waist, rocking slightly. Talia pressed against her leg, wrapping her tail around Elizabeth's ankle.

How was she to respond to such an accusation? She stood and scratched out the offending words with her foot, leaving the ground smooth and clean. Best not scribble something in haste. He could wait for a well-thought-out response. If it caused him a little discomfort—and to perhaps rethink his own reply—then so much the better.

Talia scampered off, and Elizabeth dragged herself up the stairs. As she closed the cellar behind her, the longcase clock in the parlor chimed eleven.

It was time to meet with Papa. Finally. He had refused to see her at Netherfield—he did not dare offend Longbourn by crossing him so directly. She shaded her face with her hand and rolled her eyes. He had, though, agreed they might happen upon each other at the crossroad between the Netherfield and Longbourn estates. It was outside Longbourn's territory, but not within the boundaries of Netherfield Park. Stubborn, vexing, contrary man!

At least he had consented to meet with her; that was the material thing and what she needed to remember.

She went to her rooms for her bonnet and shawl. Her cloak hung in the closet—it was odd not to reach for it. But April had been away three days now. What need was there to wear it? April did not need a place to conceal herself, and Elizabeth was not going to meet any major dragons today—at least not a literal one.

She tied the bonnet under her chin, tight enough that it would stay in place should April suddenly land on it. But that was not likely to happen. April was probably with a fairy dragon harem right now, showing the male who could fly the highest and had the sweetest song, two contests she had to win if she was to gain enough of the local cock's attention to be able to mate.

She yanked a handkerchief from the drawer, muttering as she dabbed her eyes. Yes, April was just a little fairy dragon—an incredibly annoying and snippy one at that. But—Elizabeth swallowed hard—it was difficult to be without her constant companion of eleven years now.

What would she do without her faithful Friend?

She tucked the handkerchief up her sleeve as she made her way down the grand stairs, her drab skirts whispering across the marble. Best not think about that now. Meeting with Papa would be difficult enough. Melancholy thoughts would not make it better.

The late morning sun peeked through low clouds, hinting that, just perhaps, it might not rain on the empty fields this afternoon. Green shoots should be appearing soon. A light breeze carried a touch of warmth upon it, enough that it might not make Papa's joints ache quite so much. Spring was always a most welcome season.

Not far off, Papa leaned heavily against the fingerpost that stood askew at the cross road. Rustle perched at the top of the post, leaning a little drunkenly with it. It would be laughable, except that cockatrice did not appreciate being laughed at. Even lesser members of the species, like Rustle, had their pride.

No doubt the walk from Longbourn had left Papa in serious pain. That would not help his mood. But this was his suggestion. Had she her druthers, they would have met in a place comfortable for him, at the very least, one near a bench where he could sit.

"Good day, Papa."

He grunted something noncommittal.

"Was the walk very difficult for you?"

"Gardiner drove me here in the coach. Rustle will call him back when he is required." He did not meet her eyes. "Where is April?"

"She has joined a harem, I think. Pray let Longbourn know; perhaps even suggest he try to be tolerant of them this mating season."

"Why do you not tell him yourself? It seems you have no compunction about approaching him." He shifted his weight to one foot and crossed his arms over his chest.

So that was what was bothering him.

"I did not approach him. He came to me, outside of his territory, as I returned from Mary's wedding. If anyone was out of line, it was he and not me." She squared her shoulders and stood a little straighter. When had she become nearly as tall as Papa?

"He is the estate dragon—"

"Who left his estate. He does not rule beyond his boundaries."

His gnarled hands flew open. "If you would simply stop being so stubborn—"

As if she were the stubborn one! "The Order has named Mary Keeper, and she is married to Collins now. That is not going to change."

He stomped, just a little. It must have hurt. "And you will be married to Darcy without so much as my awareness, much less consent."

"Had you been at the Conclave, you could have given it."

"So now you would criticize how I manage Order affairs? Not to mention you assume my approval—"

She clenched her fists and stepped back. "I came to

talk about Cait."

"You have worked out what to do about her egg binding? Tell me and I shall see that it is done." He reached toward his pocket—was he planning to try and write notes—or have her write them?

"It is not something I can tell you precisely."

"What do you mean?" A particular low note entered his voice, one that usually presaged a bout of temper.

"I am still sorting out all the information and working out how what the poulterer told me might be accomplished for her." She turned aside and braced herself.

"Poulterer? She is a dragon, not a chicken!"

"I am entirely aware of that."

"You cannot apply what one would do with a chicken—"

She sucked in a deep breath and counted to nine. "It is useful information, especially when considered in conjunction with the information in the rather ancient, and I might add, incomplete tome you sent me."

He stomped over to face her directly. "She will be so comforted and pleased to know you think her no different than a chicken."

"Those are your words and attitudes, not mine. I would thank you to keep them to yourself!"

"Because you will hear no contradiction."

She leaned in close to his face, voice barely above a whisper. "Because this is not the first time I have done such a thing! How do you think I came to a solution for Bedlow's teething or worked out how to manage scale mites in the nest? No dragon lore contained that information. I worked it out by looking to other sources."

"Had I known that earlier, I would have put a stop

to it." His face turned florid.

Where did he think her information had come from? From some volume she had access to but he did not?

"And cheated how many dragons out of the comfort they have found? Have you forgotten how much relief Bedford found when I worked with the blacksmith to devise a tooth key to remove his rotten tooth? Had he continued suffering, he might well have done himself or someone around him a serious injury!"

"Might, might, might! It is all speculation." He threw his hands into the air. "You have no idea what would have happened. The tooth might very well have righted itself or fallen out on its own. You do not know. For all we know, you might have interfered with the natural way of things as you did with April's hatching."

Her fists knotted of their own accord, her arms quivering. "Are you suggesting we would be better off had she not hatched at all?"

"I am merely saying you have a propensity to insert yourself into dragon matters without thinking it through thoroughly. What appears to be helpful might actually be harmful. If every clutch of fairy dragons were rescued, England would be up to their noses in the worthless little flitter-bobs."

"So you consider my Friend worthless?"

"Her species is—"

"Is small and helpless and cute—not at all what one might consider a dragon to be. Thus, she is worthless. I am glad to know your feelings on the matter." Disagreeable, short-sighted man! So assured he was right and the only one who could be. If she looked at his face any longer—she turned her back.

"Tell me how to take care of Cait. I cannot stand here much longer."

"No."

"What do you mean, no?" That got his attention.

"If I tell you, you are likely to dismiss a great deal of what I say and try to manage this on your own. Half-knowledge could easily kill her as well as ruin her eggs. I will not provide you with anything that might encourage that."

"So you refuse to help her? That will delight the Order."

"That is not what I said, and you know it. What is more, Rustle has heard the entire conversation." She cupped her hands around her mouth and shouted. "See that Uncle Gardiner knows what has been said and understands that Papa has no knowledge as to how to help Cait."

Rustle nodded and launched from the fingerpost.

"Lizzy! How dare you!"

"You leave me little choice. I will not risk her on your prejudices and ill-informed efforts."

"And you have suddenly become an expert in laying dragons?"

"I have certainly studied far more than you on the matter."

"Impudent girl! I am ashamed of you!! Your time at the Order is making you arrogant. You cannot compare your knowledge to mine."

She walked several steps away, skirt catching in the tall dry grasses on the roadside, each breath dragging, tearing at her throat. "What you know is different to what I know and not what is essential to help Cait right now. Histories will not help her. Rustle will come for me the moment Cait thinks she might begin laying."

"You know Longbourn will not allow you in the house," he called from behind her.

"It is your responsibility to see that he does. Whatever it takes, you must do it, or the life of the translator the Blue Order assigned to your house is on your hands. I would not want to explain to the Order—or to Lady Catherine—that something has gone wrong because I was denied access to her."

"That is going too far. You will not—"

"No, Papa, you have no right to make such demands on me. Have you forgotten? I am—in a large part by your choice—no longer part of your household. Longbourn banished me, and you have made no effort to intervene. I no longer answer to anyone from Longbourn, including you."

"Disrespectful, arrogant—" He stormed toward her.

She turned to face him and stepped backwards, matching him step for step. "You chose this, not I. Now you must live with it. I will go now, but first I should warn you, there is indeed another major dragon nearby. Longbourn needs to be warned, and my sisters and mother watched closely. The entire dragon state is in an uproar, and the slightest incident could spell disaster."

His entire countenance changed, pallor creeping across his face. "Do not interfere in matters you do not understand."

"What is that supposed to mean?"

"Do not interfere."

"Do you know something about the rogue dragon?" It really was not a question. The answer was evident in his every look.

"Do not interfere, Lizzy."

"I am operating under direct instructions from the Order. You must tell me what you know."

"Rogue dragons are dangerous, too dangerous for a woman to deal with. You must not interfere." He turned his back and shuffled toward the road to Longbourn. No doubt Uncle Gardiner would meet him with the coach soon.

What point was there in following? He was such an obstinate man. No amount of pleading would persuade him. So, so stubborn.

She wrapped her arms around her waist and shambled toward Netherfield, her hands numb, her belly roiling, her shoulders aching. Not only had he thrown her away in favor of Longbourn, he thought her efforts to help dragons no more than foolish experimenting, not worthy of respect, despite the results she had achieved.

She was no more than a foolish little girl in his eyes and would never be more than that. She tripped over a fallen branch and landed hard on her knees. Twittering fairy dragons zipped overhead—it must be a local harem. Was that April there in the lead, flying higher than any of them? The color was right, and the way she dipped and wove looked just like April diving through the halls of the Blue Order. It must be her—but she did not stop.

Elizabeth sobbed into her hands. Perhaps Papa was right. She had no business trying to do such work. Maybe it was too much for just a woman to handle, and she should leave it to the trained officers and scholars to manage. What was the Order thinking, sending her on such an errand? What would they do if she failed?

Chapter 4

DARCY STEADIED HIS horse and shaded his eyes, watching Walker cut through the grey-blue sky, just below the clouds, occasionally passing through a sunbeam that glinted off his vaguely metallic feather-scales. It would not likely rain this afternoon, but the sky definitely would not allow them to forget that it was apt to happen in the near future. As if anyone in all of England ever forgot that was a distinct possibility!

Walker squawked and dove. Odd for him to be hunting now. It was not as though he had any reason to be hungry—and that had not been a terror-inducing predatory shriek, the kind that paralyzed prey. What was he about? Walker landed—what was that beside him? Or rather, who?

Walker nudged the huddled woman until she permitted his head under her arm. She threw her arms around the cockatrice, sobbing. The only person whom Walker would permit such intimacies was

Elizabeth.

Darcy jumped off his horse and ran the final few steps, falling to his knees in the field's tall grass beside them. "Elizabeth?"

She turned to stare at him, face tear-streaked, eyes swollen.

He wrapped her in his arms and pulled her close, cradling her head into his shoulder. "Whatever it is, you are not alone."

She sobbed harder, clutching at his jacket, rocking with the force of her cries.

Had he said precisely the wrong thing? It would not be the first time. But it would be nice to understand his error so he did not repeat it. Perhaps he should not say anything. That seemed best, so he pulled her closer and held her tightly until the tears subsided.

"I did not know to expect you. I thought it would be another two days before you came," she whispered into his coat.

"The weather and the roads were very favorable. I hope I have not disappointed."

She giggled, then laughed a little hysterically. "No, not at all. I am glad you are come."

"I cannot tell you how pleased I am to hear that." He pressed his forehead to hers. "Will you tell me what has you here in the middle of the fields?"

"I am just being a silly woman." She lifted her face and blinked at the sky. Had she ever looked so much a damsel in distress as she did now?

"There are few who would dare say that of you. I can only guess you have been in the company of one of them recently? Since I do not smell dragon, I imagine you just encountered one of the warm-blooded variety."

She snickered and sniffled at the same time, hiccoughing.

He handed her a handkerchief. "I can hardly imagine Collins driving you to such a state. So that only leaves one candidate. What did your father have to say?"

She dabbed her eyes and scrubbed her cheeks with the handkerchief. "He is incredibly stubborn and condescending toward what he does not understand."

Foolish old goat!

"Do you wish to tell me about it here, or shall we talk as we walk back to Netherfield?"

She met his gaze with an odd little quirked-brown one of her own. "Do not think I have mistaken it that either way, you expect I shall be telling you about it."

He brushed a stray tear from her cheek with his thumb. If only he could do something more to soothe them away. "If you do not wish to talk about it, I will not force the issue. But since we are partners in this matter, it seems like a reasonable course of action."

"Partners." She leaned her head against his shoulder. "I like the notion of being partners. Yours is a rather uncommon attitude, I do confess."

Walker squawked conversationally, as though it were the commonest thing in the world for him to be privy to, much less participate in, such a tête-à-tête.

"Chalk it up to having a Friend cockatrice who has always insisted that we were equals. It does cause one to think in rather unique ways."

She glanced back at Walker. "I knew there was a reason why I admired him so."

Her eyes suggested she was teasing. Pray it was so, lest he find himself jealous of a cockatrice.

Walker bobbed his head and hop-flapped toward

them.

"As much as I value your company, you should go see Cait. She eschews flying more than necessary right now. If you catch her a fresh meal, I know she would receive you with great favor, but avoid the Netherfield rabbits."

"Excuse me?" Walker turned his head nearly sideways and gawked at her.

Had he any idea of how undignified that expression was?

"The local puck considers them part of her hoard."

Walker chirruped, nodding. That one did not interfere with another dragon's hoard was simply a matter of courtesy—and keeping the peace. He threw himself into the sky and glided toward Longbourn.

"A puck who hoards rabbits? I have never heard of such a thing. I thought they preferred shiny, glittery bits and bobs." Good thing Quincy was far easier to please, or none at Rosings would have any peace from him.

"This one likes fibers as well, especially warm ones. I think that is one of the things she likes about the rabbits, but that is only speculation. I will introduce you. She is a sweet creature, quite unlike the bundle of mischief that is Quincy." No one else in his acquaintance ever used the word "sweet" to describe a dragon—it would sound disingenuous if they did. But from Elizabeth it was perfectly sincere.

He stood and offered her a hand up. She took it, brushing the dirt off her skirt as she rose. He tucked her hand in the crook of his arm. Perhaps that was too bold, but she was his betrothed—and she would let him know clearly if his attentions were unwanted.

She smiled up at him—that special smile of hers

that warmed his heart and stirred his spirit.

"April is still away?"

She pointed to a few distant specks in the sky and nodded, swallowing hard.

He laid his hand over hers as they walked toward the house. "When my father died, Walker was not certain that he wanted to stay with me. I had grown up with him, but he was grieving my father's loss as much as I. Walker left for nearly two months—I still do not know where he went or what he did during those months. Old Pemberley was failing and disliked company, so I could not turn to him. Even with all the other dragons on the estate, it was a very lonely, difficult time."

Her eyes squeezed shut, and she squeaked as tears flowed down her cheeks.

Oh, not again! He stopped and pulled back. "Pray, forgive me. I should not have burdened you."

"No, no, it is not that, not at all." She shook her head violently and clutched his hand. "You understand what it means for her to leave me. No one else does." She crumpled and wept into her hands.

What else was there to do but to wrap arms around her and hold her tight until she regained control? "I suppose when your best friend is a dragon, there are not many who can relate. I wonder if that was why April was so adamant that I should come back soon—she realized what was in the offing."

"You are the only person I have ever known willing to credit my fairy dragon Friend with so much forethought and wisdom." She held his handkerchief to her face.

They walked on, her head leaning against his shoulder. While it was deeply regrettable that April had left, was it wrong to be pleased she had given him these moments with Elizabeth in his arms?

"Our banns have been properly read now." He held his breath. Pray this did not upset her, too.

"I expect the whole of Meryton will be glad to see you here. There has been speculation—"

"That I might not return for you?"

She tried to shrug away the suggestion with a labored smile that looked more miserable than merry. "You know how people are, and I am ... well, considered something of an oddity."

Darcy threw back his head and laughed. "My dearest Elizabeth, if you are odd, then I can hardly imagine how I am regarded."

She looked up at him, brow arched, the edges of her lips curling up just a mite. "I suppose you are correct. It does make us an excellent match, then, does it not?"

"Really? Is that what you think?" He stared straight into her eyes. Dear God, she meant it! "There are some things that need to be said that cannot wait. Is there a place we can sit?"

She led him into a bit of woods and a broken-down folly. "Will this do?"

Dappled shade enveloped them with the sense of a place not quite, but almost entirely forgotten. He sat near the middle of the bench, forcing her to sit near him. Perhaps a bit inelegant, but it did achieve the desired effect.

He rubbed his hands together before his chest. "I realize that I often do not make a good first impression, and in our case, that impression was a lasting one. I am glad you no longer count my separating you from Pemberley as a blemish on my account."

She blushed and dodged his gaze. "I will always

regret having thought that of you. It was impulsive and unfair of me."

It was far easier not to look at her as he spoke. "I admit it was not a difficult conclusion to draw. Had I been more open, more like Bingley or my cousin Fitzwilliam, perhaps it would have been easier for you to believe more rightly of my character, or at least approach me to discuss the matter."

From the corner of his eye, he watched her worry her hands and pick at her apron.

"I do hope though, as we have worked together for Pemberley's well-being, that you have seen a more positive side of me. I may not be the most agreeable of men, or one who speaks easily and clearly, but you cannot doubt my sincerity in matters concerning my dragon's welfare—and yours."

She rubbed her hands along her shoulders, though she did not seem cold. "Indeed I have seen that, perhaps most clearly in the way so many dragons respect and admire you. That speaks volumes for you."

He took one of her hands in his. "I admired you for quite some time before that day in the Dragon Conclave. I had hoped you would have realized it, perhaps understood the regard I had for you. You are so perceptive to the dragons; I thought surely I could not be more difficult to understand than they."

"And you would be very, very wrong." She peeked up at him, the corners of her eyes betraying a hint of amusement.

"So it would seem. I am sorry for that. Especially if it has given you pause to doubt the nature of our betrothal."

"You must agree that it is most unusual, considering the Order just passed new legislation limiting the powers of dragons to decide human marriage, then on its heels they all but order our own betrothal. And Mary and Mr. Collins' as well. Do not forget them." She rolled her eyes. Was that just for Collins or the entire situation?

"I would rather forget him, thank you very much. But their circumstance does not alter the fact that we are to be married." Dare he look into her eyes right now? Would her amusement continue, or would he find a core truth that he would rather not know?

"I grant you, our betrothal was—is—rather peculiar."

"And entirely untoward—without so much as even a declaration of friendship from me, to be pushed into accepting an offer of marriage." He threw his hands up.

She looked away.

Perhaps she did not want to hear more, but if he did not speak now, there might not be another chance. "I was a fool not to listen to Walker. He implored me—on more than one occasion—to tell you explicitly how I felt about you. I deferred, certain that you would not be interested or that it was neither the time nor place for it. Better moments would present themselves. As usual, Walker was right."

"I imagine he is aware of that."

"Yes. And he has not hesitated to let me know in no uncertain terms. He does revel in reminding me of what an idiot I can be." He glanced over his shoulder. It would be like Walker to appear behind him just in time to hear such an admission.

"They enjoy their shows of dominance, do they not?"

"I suppose that is an advantage to having a fairy

dragon as a companion."

"Ha! Is that what you think? Have you noticed the scars on my ears?" She covered both ears with her hands.

"April is the only fairy dragon of my acquaintance to be so bold."

"I suppose you are right. Ladies generally prefer a milder disposition like Heather's. April refused that sort of companion right from the start. She was quite ready to attempt to fend for herself rather than settle for a Friend who did not match her temperament. She thinks very highly of you, though."

He took both her hands and held them close to his chest. "I think very highly of you. I wish I had told you of my ardent admiration well before we stood before the Conclave and agreed to marry. I know you only accepted because of our Friends' assurances and certainty in the match. I wish you could have accepted me on my merits alone."

She laughed. "You really think I would accept a man without the approval of my dragon friends?"

"I have no doubt—you would not. Still, one does not substitute for the other. I would very much like for you to accept me for myself alone." It was probably far too familiar a gesture, but he stroked her cheek with the back of his fingers. So silky and soft.

She smiled, and her eyes glistened. "Would it tell you anything to know that you are the only man April has ever approved of for me?"

"I would still like to know I have your approval as well."

"I believe my chances of happiness, upon entering the marriage state, are at least as good with you as with any other Dragon Keeper, so you will do." There was that playful quirk of her eyebrow again.

"I will accept that, though I admit I was hoping for a bit more." Hopefully he did not look as crestfallen as he felt.

She gasped. "Forgive me! I am apt to resort to levity when I know not what else to say. My feelings are in such turmoil, I hardly know how to express myself. Does it say what you need to know that the days here have been increasingly lonely, and when I have considered what company I would most desire, I have come to the conclusion it is yours?"

"Even above your dragons'? That is indeed a compliment."

"It makes me understand—a little—April's desire to be with her own kind." Her lip quivered as she spoke.

Heaven's above, had she any idea of what that expression—what those words—did to him! No man could be expected to endure such without responding.

Her lips were warm and soft against his as she yielded in his arms, her arms twining around his shoulders. Could she feel his heart ready to beat out of his chest as he pulled her close? So right, so very right. This was where she belonged, where she had always belonged, where she must remain.

Her breath came in short pants, ragged and hot on his cheek. Dragons' Blood! If he did not find some control soon ...

"Chicken feet? Chicken feet!"

They jumped apart.

Two forest wyrms looked up at them expectantly, a bit of drool sliding down the male's leonine fang.

Elizabeth scratched their ears through their manes, still gasping for breath. She probably had no idea of what a picture she was presenting for him as she leaned down to reach them. "I am afraid not; we were not planning to come here today."

Their chins sank to the ground. Manipulative little creatures for sure. Still, the friendship of any local dragon was worth maintaining. Darcy reached into his pocket and removed a large snuffbox enameled with the crest of the Order in gold over blue. He opened the box and held it out to Elizabeth.

Her nose wrinkled. "What is that?"

"It is rather pungent, is it not? Those are the beetles Gardiner imports that made him a Friend of the Order."

The wyrms rose up almost as high as Darcy's knees, sniffing and tasting the air with forked tongues.

"Would these do for you?" He placed a dried beetle in front of each wyrm.

The wyrms sniffed the beetles all around, licked them several times then snatched them up. A little green goo dotted their lips as they crunched down on their prizes. They squealed in delight. No wonder the dragons had named Gardiner a special Friend of the Order.

"More?" The male asked, a beetle leg and antennae hanging from the edge of his mouth.

Darcy reached into the snuff box again, but Elizabeth stayed his hand.

"You may have more, but you must promise to bring us news of the great blue one. Tell him we wish to meet him."

The pair skirted back, undecided. Darcy retrieved a second beetle for each and held them up in their sight.

The female quivered and darted forward, eyes on the crunchy prize. "I will tell him."

Netherfield: Rogue Dragon

Darcy set her treat on the ground before her. One did not risk one's fingers to an unfamiliar dragon, no matter how harmless it might seem.

The male grumbled and hissed. "He comes to the cellar every night waiting for your message. He is not happy you have not written back."

Elizabeth nodded, and Darcy delivered the prize.

"You may tell him that he was very rude. I do not wish to be, so I am carefully considering my reply."

Whether or not the wyrm heard or cared through his beetle-fueled delight was difficult to tell.

"Bring us more information like that and there are beetles and chickens' feet for you." Darcy snapped the snuff box closed. The smaller female wyrm wound herself around his ankles with a sound that was not quite a purr, not quite a growl, but it was friendly whatever it was, then disappeared into the forest loam. The male quickly followed.

Darcy shoved the snuff box back into his pocket. "Does this sort of thing often happen to you? Dragons just showing up out of nowhere ready to answer your questions and throwing themselves at your feet."

"Regularly. For as long as I can remember." She chuckled. "It occurred far more often after April befriended me. My poor father—I think I nearly drove him to distraction—he never knew what sort of dragon I would come across next. Did I ever tell you how I became friendly with a basilisk?"

"They are renowned for their dislike of company. It does not surprise me that you would manage to charm one, though. I suppose these wyrms, and perhaps your basilisk friend as well, will be expecting an invitation to the wedding breakfast."

How her eyes sparkled "Then it must be held at

Pemberley. Who but a dragon-hearing cook could be persuaded to put beetles, chickens' feet, and dried cod on the menu?"

He laughed until tears ran down his cheeks. "Do not forget the bones for Pemberley and her dogs."

"Yes, of course, they must be invited as well. Oh, what an event it will be!" She dabbed her eyes on the edge of her sleeve.

"It cannot come soon enough for me." He pressed his forehead to hers.

"Or for me."

That was the answer he longed for and required another kiss.

Several more.

They both retired early that night. Nicholls returned him to the chambers he used whilst he had stayed there with Bingley. How different the spacious chambers looked now than when he had first come. Every surface evidenced draconic themes.

Carved scales emblazoned the molding near the ceiling. Dragon claws and balls finished all the chairs. Paintings that were probably done by the rogue lindwurm littered the walls while four full lindwurms were carved into the bed posts.

Dragons were everywhere. Had he ever really looked at them the first time he had been here? Subtle and tasteful, most—the paintings were the notable exceptions—were the sort of pieces that might find their way into rooms at Pemberley if the Darcys had felt the need to be reminded of dragons at every turn.

It still puzzled him. What motivated one to put

dragons on every surface? Was it not just easier to welcome them into the house to take their place as part of the resident staff and family? But then, perhaps his perspective was the odd one. Even the Bennet house, as he understood, hosted only one companion dragon until very recently. At least Elizabeth agreed with his view. For now that was all that mattered.

He fell asleep nearly as soon as he pulled the counterpane over his shoulders.

The next morning, he rose early as he always did. Elizabeth was an early riser as well. Would it be too much to hope for that she might be waiting for him, or if not that, soon to look for him in the morning room?

Apparently it was not.

She sat at the large round table, nearest the bay window jutting out into sunshine. Opposite her, a mahogany sideboard—with dragon-claw-and-ball feet—held a breakfast spread. Apparently Elizabeth shared his preference to eat early, too. The kippers, though, he would leave for Walker. Their scent was a mite off-putting.

"Good morning, Mr. Darcy." She rose and curtsied. A jumble of books lay open in front of her, and no less than half a dozen paintings leaned against the wall behind. The morning room was beginning to resemble Bennet's study—but perhaps that was not an appropriate thing to say.

"It seems you have already been up for quite some time. I feel quite the lay-abed." He sat beside her. How comfortable and easy that was now.

"You may lay aside such judgements of yourself. I have only just arrived here. Nicholls humors me, permitting me to leave my morning work here so I may pick up each day where I have left off."

"I can only imagine the persuasion that requires. I have met few housekeepers who can tolerate this level of ... ah ..."

"Disorder? Chaos?"

"... as you say ... they are usually very particular about the public rooms of the house."

"Hill certainly is. It has taken ever so long to convince her to stay out of Papa's study. I have had the sole cleaning of it for many years. I expect that it has not been dusted in months now. I imagine I shall soon have to call upon Rumblkins to help me strengthen Nicholls' persuasion." A bit of a shadow crossed her face. She raised her cup toward him. "The coffee is very good, very bracing for the day."

"Have you already planned a full schedule? A course of study, art appreciation and perhaps riding for a bit of exercise to round out the day?"

"If you wish to think of it that way, yes. I am indeed a demanding task-mistress." Her right eye twitched in a bit of a wink.

Was every morning with her to be so entirely engaging? If this was a foretaste of what his marriage would be, none could be more fortunate. He refilled her cup and poured one for himself.

She added a bit of cream and sugar and sipped it thoughtfully. "I did not think to ask yesterday, but where is Fitzwilliam? Is everything all right?"

"He stopped in London to meet with his father, among others. Apparently, the Eastern Dragon envoy failed to cross a planned checkpoint. There is concern."

She gasped and pressed the back of her hand to her mouth. "Pray tell me, the envoy was not supposed to come near Hertfordshire."

"No, not at all. The planned route was to approach London directly from the south. I know of no way to reach Hertfordshire except to go through London. There are sentries posted at all the tunnel intersections along the way, watching for the emissary."

"Of whom we know nothing, of course, not even a name?"

"We do know the representative is an Eastern dragon."

She slapped her forehead and dragged her hand down her face. "You are aware there are multiple varieties of Eastern dragon and that the number of toes they have is related to their ranking in society which profoundly influences how they should be greeted."

Darcy clutched his forehead. "No, I had no idea. Hopefully though, the Order does and will provide adequate information. The important issue is that we do not need to worry about that, at least not for now. We can rest assured that business shall not mix with our own."

Elizabeth rolled her eyes. "Except insofar as the entire country's dragon population is becoming twitchy and hypersensitive and—"

"I do not mean to dismiss your concerns, but our task at hand, when resolved, will be the biggest help in rectifying all those issues. So, it seems wise for us to focus on that and leave diplomacy to those, like Fitzwilliam, who have a taste for it."

"As much as I would like to, I cannot fault your logic. We certainly have enough problems of our own here." She leaned back, massaging her temples. "I checked Lydia's room this morning and the trunks had been opened and rummage through."

Darcy nearly dropped his coffee cup.

"I wish I had made an inventory of what precisely was in the trunks. I cannot make out if anything was taken from them or not. Talia is big enough that she could have gotten the trunks open had she wanted to—I did not have them locked. With her penchant for threads, there are any number of things she could have found appealing."

"So it could be anything from signs of your sister's presence to evidence of dragon-hoarding."

"Essentially. Though, if one did not trust the staff, it could be a sign of theft by one of the maids as well. But I rather doubt that."

"You suspect your sister is about?" He placed his cup carefully on its saucer.

"I have spent hours in the woods and found absolutely nothing pointing to them. Rustle has done the same from the air, and there seems to be no sign. I do not know what to think."

"Perhaps we ought to recruit the forest wyrms' assistance? I brought an ample supply of beetles, and your uncle will certainly acquire more if necessary."

Her shoulders twitched a bit. "Beetles would garner an unusual level of cooperation from our friendly wyrms. They do not appear to have a great deal of sense, but as they seem to think with their stomachs, we ought to play that to our advantage. We might also ask Talia directly about the trunks—a little later in the morning when the sun has warmed the ground. She usually does not come out until then."

"Having dealt with pucks for some time, I came prepared with a stock of wool and silk, and a few buttons thrown in for good measure just in case."

Elizabeth laughed, exactly as he hoped she might,

and pushed a pair of large open books across the table toward him. "I have several chapters on lindwurms for you to read. Naturally they are old and contradictory. This one declares they are rather stupid creatures, intent on eating as much horsemeat as they can get away with, apt to digging pits to trap their favorite prey."

"And no horses have gone missing recently in Hertfordshire, I imagine."

"Exactly. This one, suggests they are wily, secretive souls, not prone to communicate with people and apt to be dangerously aggressive toward other major dragons, attacking them during their sleep, in the safety of their own caverns."

"Do you believe that?" He balanced his chin on his fist.

"Not even remotely."

"Are you telling me these books are worthless?" Darcy rifled through a few yellowed pages.

"I wish I could, but there are shreds of truth in each." She slid a sheet of paper out from under the largest book. "I have tried to list out what each says and sort between truth, falsehood, and what is possible, based on the lindwurms I have personally met and the observations Papa recorded. He may be frustrating on many fronts, but I do trust the accuracy of his reports."

Darcy squinted at the sheet—many, many lines of tiny handwriting. She was nothing if not thorough.

"I would like your opinions on what I have noted. But first, you should see these." She pushed her chair back and reached for the paintings.

He helped her lay them out on the morning room table, entirely covering its surface. Different sizes, different frames, but all with an almost eerie similarity.

"These have come from all parts of the house. The one on the upper left is from the room Lydia stayed in. The bottom row are all from the large drawing room. I am not sure there is a great deal of thought given to where they are hung, mostly where there is room on a wall to place them. But if you look closely, I think they represent a progression that might be significant."

The one from Lydia's room was certainly the most primitive, both in style and composition. "The painter's skill grows—to a limited degree—with each painting, and the symbolism becomes somewhat more refined. But each one seems to repeat." He pointed to similar elements in each painting.

"Yes, that is what I saw, too. Look closely at this on the bottom, hidden in the rocks on the path. I think this is dragon script." She rang her finger along the edge of a painting.

"By Jove! You are right. The word is 'sanctuary' or perhaps 'haven'?"

"That is how I translate it as well. The word before though, is 'it brings' or perhaps road, path, or way? I am not sure."

"And this?" Darcy pointed to more scratching hidden in the clouds at the upper left corner.

"I had not seen those." She pulled a quizzing glass from the middle of another book and peered closely into the clouds. "Does that say 'giver'?"

"That might be one way to read it, but if these are characters as well, not just random spots, it could also read 'wise one' or 'deliverer.'"

She fell back into her seat and threw her head back. "What good is it to include such hidden meaning if one cannot even tell if the characters are there?"

"Have you been examining these—"

"For nearly a month now, and they are making me daft. Each time I think I am getting close to sorting it all out, I find—like you just pointed out—something more I overlooked. I have never felt more stupid than I do staring at these."

"Perhaps you are crediting the painter with far more than he deserves." Darcy tapped his lips with his fist.

"What do you mean?"

"To my eye, it seems that this painter has had no formal training at all—completely self-taught. Georgiana tried to talk me out of hiring a painting master to teach her. Told me she could teach herself from a book she had found in the circulating library. I allowed her to try and her efforts came out looking very much like this. You can see the distorted perspectives and the failure of pleasing composition in all of these. In fact, I have to wonder if the same book Georgiana used might have been used here as well."

"Forgive me if I am a mite muzzy this morning, but I fail to understand the implications."

"I see a bored creature with little occupation. Unlike a proper estate dragon, he has no business, except to remain undetected. I know lindwurms do not have a reputation for intelligence." He pointed to a line on Elizabeth's list, "But if he has nothing to do but stay hidden, and he has a lively mind, this seems the sort of thing an intelligent creature would do to entertain himself and while away some tiresome hours."

"I suppose he could have gotten Talia to bring him books from the Netherfield libraries until he found something interesting." She chewed her thumbnail. "Shall we go outside and meet Talia? She may be able to shed some light on the matter. Besides—it is hard to believe I am saying this—but I would very much like to get away from books and studying for a little while."

She escorted him out to the garden, the sunshine a welcome friend. Just how many rabbits did the puck keep in her hoard to do such damage to the kitchen garden—and how was Bingley to manage when he and Jane returned to take residence?

No doubt the puck would find a way to persuade him to believe it was perfectly fine this way. But it really would be so much better for someone who heard dragons to take the estate. They could make an agreement with the puck to restrain her hoard to this garden plot and plant another that she would restrict the rabbits from. All very neat and simple. The situation as it stood, though, had the potential for some very unpleasant outcomes.

Elizabeth pointed to a tall holly bush at the edge of the garden and sat down on a sunny patch of ground that looked like it had specifically been cleared for the purpose. He sat beside her, trying not to grin. There was something rather exciting about the opportunity to meet a new dragon that made him feel like a child again.

She placed a tin plate of vegetable trimmings in front of her and tapped it several times. "Good morning ,Talia. I have brought a friend to meet you."

After several minutes, a long, red nose peeked out from a burrow under the prickly holly leaves, sniffing the air. It pressed further until one shining black eye appeared, surveying the surroundings.

Even though dragons were predators, only a few were actually at the apex of the predatory ladder. Knowing that one was prey definitely affected smaller dragons' personalities. They dare not proceed with the arrogance of their large cousins.

Finally, she poked her head out sufficiently to flare her hood to its full extent and hiss. Posturing and nothing else—it was after all important to clearly demonstrate how big and fierce one was when meeting new associates. Darcy tried not to laugh—it would be considered rude, but the predictability of the minor dragons was amusing.

"Talia, this is Mr. Darcy, my friend—and April's friend and Rustle's friend—I would like him to be your friend as well."

Talia cocked her head and blinked at Elizabeth, hood relaxing halfway. Was it that Elizabeth had honored her by presenting Darcy to her, instead of presenting Talia to the larger creature? Or was it the offer of friendship—which usually implied the presentation of a gift that caught her attention. Did Elizabeth even know herself? He probably should ask later.

"I would be honored to be part of your acquaintance." Darcy slowly, very slowly reached into his pocket and presented a sliver of dried meat, laying it on the ground half the distance between him and the puck.

She crept forward, one eye on Darcy, the other on the meat. Elizabeth nodded her encouragement. Talia jumped forward and back, grabbing the offering in a single flick of her long tongue. She gobbled it down and licked her face and lips. Just how long was her tongue?

"Good." Talia inched toward Elizabeth until she leaned on Elizabeth's knee. Any closer and she would be sitting in Elizabeth's lap like a pug or a very funny-looking cat.

Apparently, this was an understood sign that she wanted a scratch. Elizabeth obliged until the creature all but purred with pleasure.

"Darcy has a gift for you, if you will be his friend." Elizabeth pointed to Darcy's pocket.

He withdrew a ball of the softest, fluffiest wool he could find.

Talia's eyes grew large, and a tiny dot of drool appeared at the edges of her mouth. "Wool?"

"Yes. It is very warm and soft wool. I would very much like to give it to a friend." He extended the wool toward Talia.

She sniffed at it, her eyes crossing in greedy pleasure. Quincy could be that way about buttons. For a hoarding dragon, their hoard was a direct route to their heart.

Talia sat back on her haunches and scratched behind her frill, eyes never leaving the wool. "He is your friend?" She tapped Elizabeth's knee with her tail.

"Yes, he is. A very fine and loyal friend."

Darcy pressed his lips hard—now was not the time to grin like a boy. But certainly one could be excused when one's betrothed complimented him so.

"He will not hurt my hoppers?"

"Certainly not." Darcy shook his head slowly. "I told my Friend cockatrice, Walker, he was not to bother the Netherfield rabbits."

Talia's tongue flickered in and out, and she glanced skyward. "Saw him hunting yesterday. He stayed away. That is good. You can be my friend." She sat and reached for him with both front paws.

"I am honored." Darcy placed the ball of wool in her paws.

She accepted the gift with open-mouthed glee, rolling over on her back and turning the ball of wool over and over with all four feet, pressing her face into the fibers, sniffing, and even licking it.

Netherfield: Rogue Dragon

Elizabeth shuddered a bit—she was trying as hard as he not to laugh at the pure visceral delight. After several minutes the euphoria subsided, and Talia disappeared into the burrow.

Elizabeth tapped the plate, and the puck reappeared. "I have a question for you. Tell me the truth, I shall not be put out with you whatever you should say."

Talia's hood rose a mite as she rose to tip-toes.

"My sister's trunks, in the room upstairs, were you in them?"

"Not me. Nothing I want."

"Are you sure? She has pretty shawls and stockings." With that tone of voice, Elizabeth managed to make them sound tempting even to him.

"Too much trouble to unravel."

"Have you any idea who would go in my sister's trunks?"

"Warm-bloods? Wyrms like long things, perhaps them."

Wild wyrms in the house? That would be rather odd. But what was not odd about the current situation?

"Might the blue one want them?"

Talia's hood fully flared, and she hopped back, tail lashing. "No. No. No. He cannot go in the house." She paced before the rabbit hole, teeth bared.

Darcy reached into his pocket for his snuff box and flicked it open as he pulled it out.

Talia's hood slicked back, and she stood on her back legs sniffing and licking the air, drool pooling at the edge of her mouth.

"Thank you for your assistance. You have been very helpful." He offered a beetle.

Talia savored it nearly as much as she had the blue wool. She was nothing if not appreciative.

Once she finished her treat she scuttled up to Darcy and stared into his face, one dainty paw resting on his knee. "I do not understand the blue one. He says he does not like you, does not trust you. He is wrong. You are friend."

Darcy slowly reached to scratch between her wing nubs. She arched her back to accept.

"Do you know why the blue one says that?" Elizabeth's voice was barely a whisper.

Talia sat up and shook, rather like a dog, starting at her nose and ending at the very tip of her tail. "Stupid." She pushed the tin plate into the burrow and disappeared into the darkness.

Darcy helped Elizabeth to her feet.

She dusted her skirt. "I am perplexed. First he does not like me, now he does not like you? How can he possibly know you?"

"I did stay at Netherfield for some time. Perhaps I did something to offend him then?"

"There is no point in speculating. I have owed him a response, and I am going to offer it to him now." She marched toward the house.

He hurried after her. There were moments one could see why Bennet might find her vexing. "Do you think it wise to ask so provoking a question?"

"No, probably not, but it is precisely what a dragon would do. That seems to be the best option we have. At the very least, it will continue the conversation and might even provoke him into granting us an audience."

That look on her face! There was no stopping her, so he bit his tongue and followed. She was probably right, even if he had misgivings. Was this what life would be like with her?

Challenging for certain, but that was not a bad

thing. It was probably very, very good.

Halfway to the house, an odd sound, part song, part screech echoed from high overhead. Elizabeth stopped as though frozen by a cockatrice's scream, staring skyward. Colorful specks dove and darted through the clouds.

"A mating flight," she whispered.

"Come, I see a bench near the cutting garden. We can watch from here." He took her elbow and led her, her eyes never leaving the flight.

"April is there, up high, higher than the rest. You see there—the two rose colored ones cannot match her. The purple one—that is the male. You can see he is a little bigger and a bit faster, too." She pointed.

"I have never seen such a flight before. Have you?" He slipped his arm around her shoulders—how could he resist?

"Occasionally. Fairy dragons have lived in the Longbourn woods for generations. Several springs I have been privileged to catch a mating flight as it happened. April would often watch with me and explain what I was seeing. One year Papa was with us. He had never appreciated April so much as he did that day. When we got home, he had me write notes on what we had observed. Later he used those notes to write a monograph on fairy dragons. He was very disappointed when the Order did not see fit to publish that paper. Fairy dragons were not considered important enough to be worth publishing about."

"Does he still have the monograph?"

"I believe the original is still in his library."

"Do you think he would be willing to allow me to read it? If Georgiana is to befriend a fairy dragon, I should like to know as much as I can about them."

"I think that would please him." She pressed her head to his shoulder. "Watch now as the leading female circles above the male—no! Pray no!" She jumped to her feet.

"What is wrong?"

"Those shadows? Do you not recognize the profile?"

He squinted into the bright sky. "Falcons?"

"They prey upon mating flights. The fairy dragons are too preoccupied to notice the danger." She pressed her fist to her mouth. "I have seen so many ... many ..." Her voice trailed off.

"Wait, look!" A pair of dark spots raced toward the mating flight, his thundering heart matching their pace. "Walker!"

One spot became a blur, swooping down on the marauding falcon. A brief scream and the bird was impaled on Walker's talons. He dove to the ground, quarry secured. Rustle replaced Walker, flying sentinel, watching over April.

"Rustle, too?" Elizabeth murmured through her fingers, tears pooling in her eyes. "They are without a doubt the finest of creatures. Cockatrice often prey upon these flights."

"He would not permit harm to come to his Lairda April."

"Sometimes I think the dragons will never cease to surprise me. Just when I think I know what to expect, they do something like this that totally changes my understanding of them. I am not sure even Lady Astrid will believe this."

"It would not surprise me if Cait had her part as well, perhaps in helping to watch for the event itself. For creatures that are by their nature solitary, those three have become a very effective little flock. A flock that seems to include fairy dragons as well."

"Who would have ever thought? I will have to write this down. It is too important to risk forgetting."

A triumphant squawk filled the sky.

"The male has caught her now," Elizabeth leaned into his shoulder. "April shall have her clutch."

What she did not say, but her eyes spoke for her, was that she wished April might allow her to be part of that.

Chapter 5

THREE DAYS LATER, Elizabeth and Darcy stood shoulder-to-shoulder in the dark, dank cellar, staring at the scratches on the floor. Deep slither tracks framed the words, marking the creature's girth—roughly what Darcy could circle with his arms. If accepted dragon lore was to be believed, then it was probably fifteen to eighteen feet in length. But that was only a guess.

"Am I reading this correctly?" Darcy pointed at the wispy dragon script highlighted by the dancing candlelight. "The man is not to be trusted. He carried a Dragon Slayer."

"That is how I read it as well." Elizabeth crouched down and stared at it again, but the fresh perspective did not alter the meaning.

They returned to the light and relative warmth of the house. The chill humidity of the cellar was not conducive to clear thought. Still in a bit of a fog, they meandered to the breakfast room. Who could have predicted the lindwurm's response?

Darcy poured two cups of hot coffee, and they sat down in the restorative sunshine pouring through the large windows, away from the piles of unfinished work, books and paintings littering the table.

"How could he possibly know you carried the Dragon Slayer?" She wrapped both hands around the coffee cup, thawing her icy fingertips.

"Longbourn realized it before the hatching night." Darcy frowned into his cup.

"You think Longbourn would have told him?"

"No, but I wonder how Longbourn knew."

"I suppose one of the local minor dragons saw it and told him. They are supposed to report alarming news to him. What could cause greater alarm amongst them than that?"

Darcy dragged the back of his hand against his mouth. "I do not like the notion that my every move is spied upon by unseen dragons."

"It is an excellent incentive for one to remain on one's best behavior, though." She snickered and sipped her coffee.

"That is one thing we must see to—Pemberley must keep a proper census of the wild dragons on her land and maintain good oversight of them."

"I completely agree, and since we can teach it to her so young, we have an excellent chance that it will become second nature to her, unlike Longbourn, who cannot seem to be bothered with such mundane tasks. Generally, he thinks very little of the small dragons on his land. They are a bother to him." Keeping a very young dragon might indeed have some distinct advantages.

"The minor dragons are no different to a man's tenants if you think about it."

"That is a very good way to understand it. Not that I think it would make sense to Longbourn. Crusty old thing is entirely set in his ways. That aside, though, how else could the lindwurm know about the Dragon Slayer?" She looked toward the ceiling and chewed her lower lip.

"The only other possibility is that he must have seen it for himself."

"Where did you keep it?"

"In the barn, buried in a bale of hay."

"He could not have seen it in the barn. The horses would have alerted everyone to its presence."

"The only time I removed the blade was when we left the ball to find Pemberley in the forest."

"He had to be in the forest, then, with Pemberley and Longbourn." Elizabeth rose and paced the length of the sunbeams on the carpet and back again, pressing her temples hard.

"There was a great deal of dragon thunder that night. Do you suppose it might have been Longbourn and the lindwurm challenging one another?"

"Is it possible the lindwurm stole the egg from Longbourn? That might be what they were fighting over, and she hatched in the midst of the process."

"My horse was especially unsettled as we rode through the woods. I thought it was merely the noise and the storm, but the scent of the lindwurm might have caused it to bolt. The dragon could have easily detected the sword then. Quite easily." Darcy rubbed his chin with his fist. "With no other context to understand why I carried such a blade, the creature could have rightly deemed me a dragon hunter."

"Perhaps he thinks you have returned to complete the task." Elizabeth perched on the edge of her chair. "That does put all this in a very different light. Very different."

"If the lindwurm thinks I am a threat, would it be best for me to leave?"

She set her cup aside and laid her hand on his. "There has been plenty of opportunity for him to have acted upon a perceived threat, and he has not. If you think about it, he could have demanded you go, threatened—"

The windows rattled as a huge black shadow descended, pecking at the glass.

Elizabeth jumped, almost tripping over Darcy.

He flung the window open. "Walker!"

Walker swooped in and landed on the back of Elizabeth's chair, back-winging for balance. "Come, you must come now."

"Cait?"

Walker squawked ear-splitting, terror-inducing, tones.

A shiver coursed down Elizabeth's spine. "Tell me exactly what is going on."

"Your father has a nesting box for her in the study, but she has been pacing in and out and will not settle into it. She waddles like a duck, hunched over her belly which your father says is very hard—not as it should be. She has not eaten yesterday or today and has hardly drunk. Her feathers are dull and drooping—"

"That is not good, not at all. I will leave as soon as I gather my things. In the meantime, tell her she must drink water, as much as she possibly can, and tell my father to have Hill prepare warm water and bring the hipbath into the study."

Walker blinked several times as though forcing his thoughts into a semblance of order. "Drink water, warm water, hipbath."

"Yes, exactly."

Walker launched toward the window, nearly clipping Elizabeth with the edge of his wing. Poor creature—only extreme distress could explain such clumsiness.

"I will ready the curricle." Darcy disappeared before she could comment.

Later she must thank him for that. She ran to her chambers for her carpetbag and threw in her commonplace book containing her extensive notes on egg binding. From there she made her way to the still room for a bottle of witch hazel, a tin of pure lard, and a jar of lemon juice and egg shells she had prepared after talking with the poulterer.

Darcy met her at the kitchen door in Bingley's curricle. The weather was ideal for the sporty vehicle that took much less time to ready than the coach. More importantly, it was designed for speed. In the hands of a skilled driver, nothing could get her to Longbourn more quickly.

Darcy proved a very skilled driver. Did he race curricles for sport back in Derbyshire? If not, perhaps he should.

They arrived at Longbourn house far more quickly than she would have imagined possible, and never once did she fear the curricle was in danger of overturning. It might have been good fun had their errand not been so urgent.

The Bennet's coach, driven by Uncle Gardiner, pulled behind the curricle as Darcy was handing her down from the seat.

Netherfield: Rogue Dragon

"Lizzy, dear! Whatever are you doing here? I had no idea you were coming! You have brought Mr. Darcy, too! You are most welcome, sir." Mama trundled up to her.

"There is a matter we must consult with Papa upon. It came up rather unexpectedly; otherwise, we would have given you notice." Pray Mama was not in the mood for protracted conversation!

"You are certainly welcome, but your timing is most awkward. I fear Kitty and I were just on our way out. You see, we are to call upon my sister Phillips. She has invited us to tea …"

Elizabeth looked over her shoulder. Rustle perched nearby, softly persuading Mama of the urgency of her departure. Persuasion might not be his strongest suit, but he was definitely sufficient to the task.

"Pray do not concern yourself, madam. Your hospitality is well-known, and I would not dream of you disappointing your most gracious sister." Darcy bowed slightly from his shoulders. It would not hurt to add his persuasion to Rustle's.

"You are most kind, sir, most kind. Perhaps I should go back in and ask Hill—"

"There is no need, Mama. I will see Mr. Darcy is made most comfortable." Elizabeth pressed Mama's shoulder to turn her in the right direction.

"You are such a dear girl. Very well. Kitty! Kitty! Hurry along now. We must not disappoint your aunt." Mama kicked up a small cloud of dust shuffling to the coach.

Kitty met her there, and Uncle helped them both inside.

"This certainly makes things much easier," Darcy muttered beside her.

"I certainly will not complain for it." Elizabeth patted her bag and turned toward the house.

Mary met them at the door, pale and wringing her hands. "I am so glad you are come, Lizzy. She is in great distress, like a woman in travail. Can help her?"

"I hope so." Elizabeth pushed past.

Collins paced the corridor outside, crossing in front of the study door, making it very difficult to enter. He mumbled something under his breath—probably something very stupid, and cringed as an unearthly shriek started from within the study and permeated the entire house. Maybe he was not entirely dragon-deaf after all—but one might have to be dead to not react to that sound.

Definitely best that Mama and Kitty were well away.

Another scream. Elizabeth's skin prickled, the hair on her neck stood up, and she shivered. Yes, Cait was indeed in distress. She dodged around Collins and scurried into the crowded study.

At least Papa had moved the piles of books against the walls, leaving an opening around the nesting box space, near the center of the room. While the effort to tidy was welcome, it did force everything together into the small island in the middle of the room almost too tight for her to work.

Cait, belly distended, hopped from the edge of the nesting box near the hearth, to the low windowsill, to the short footstool and back again. She waddled like Lady Lucas days before her youngest son was born. Papa stood just out of the way, brows tightly knit, eyes locked on the disheveled cockatrix.

Walker perched on the family dragon perch near the nesting box, acknowledging Elizabeth and Darcy with a nod. "She is here. You will not die. I promise you.

Let her help."

Cait looked up at him and screeched again, wings extended back as though diving.

Elizabeth covered her ears, the sound as heart-rending as it was terrifying.

"Help." Cait waddled two steps toward her.

Elizabeth rushed to her. Cait wrapped her wings around Elizabeth and collapsed with her head on Elizabeth's shoulder. She smelt oily and dirty which Cait never would have permitted under normal circumstances.

"So much pain. More than the last time," she whispered in Elizabeth's ear.

"Let me carry you to the nesting box. I will examine you and determine what to do next." Gracious, Cait was heavier than she looked! Elizabeth staggered a bit but managed to ease Cait into the nesting box and arranged her in the hay. "Papa, see the hip bath is prepared in case we need it."

"How warm should the water be?"

"Let Walker determine it. Make it as hot as you can comfortably tolerate—it should make you very relaxed and sleepy."

Walker bobbed his head.

Elizabeth stroked Cait's ruff smooth. "Mary, open my bag and give me the tin."

Mary jumped to obey.

"Now Cait, I must feel for the egg and check for swelling. I fear it may not be very pleasant, but I shall be as gentle as I can. Can you control yourself?" Elizabeth popped open the top of the tin.

"No," Cait threw her head back in a deep grimace.

"Then I must wrap your talons so that you do not injure me. I cannot help you if you lacerate my hands.

Have I your permission?"

"Do it."

She caught Mary's eyes. "I need feed sacks and bandages, quickly."

Mary dashed away. Did she really need to wait to be told?

"While we wait for her, may I feel your belly?"

Cait nodded, and Elizabeth ran her fingers over the matted feather-scales of Cait's abdomen. A single large bulge. Very large. Heavens, just how large was a normal cockatrice egg? Why had no one thought to include that piece of information in any of the dragon lore? It would have been very useful to know.

Mary returned; Darcy and Papa helped her wrap Cait's talons whilst Walker perched nearby, carefully out of striking distance, whispering what must have been soothing things in dragon tongue.

"Now I will check for the egg." Elizabeth coated her fingers with pure white lard and carefully probed for the egg. "Yes, I feel it. Perhaps all it needs is a bit of lard to slide free. Let me see what I can do."

Cait squawked, and Darcy barely caught her as she reflexively pecked toward Elizabeth's arm.

"Pray do not bite me! I am sorry it is uncomfortable." Elizabeth pulled away. "But no, this is not going to work."

"I shall die!" Cait thrashed her wings, driving Darcy and Papa back.

"No, we must merely take another direction. Trust me. This will work. I have it on very good advice. Mary, soak a pad of bandages in witch hazel. I will put that on your swollen tissues to reduce the swelling and make room for the egg to pass. Darcy, pour a small glass from the jar in my bag—shake it first."

Netherfield: Rogue Dragon

They handed her what she had asked for.

"Now, while we wait for the swelling to reduce, you must drink this."

"It smells like a hen house." Cait pulled her head away and nearly knocked it out of Elizabeth's hand.

"It is an extract of egg shells—a medicine that will make it easier for you to push the egg out." Elizabeth held the cup up.

Cait dipped her beak in it. "It tastes foul. I will not."

Walker hopped from his perch and stood beak-to beak-with her. "You will do what Lady Elizabeth says, and you will do it without arguing." He plucked a single old tattered feather from her ruff and held it out to her.

She hissed at Walker and returned to the cup, guzzling down the viscous white liquid in a single gulp.

"Very good, that was very good." Elizabeth scratched under Cait's ruff. Under normal circumstances, it was far too intimate a gesture for the proud cockatrix to tolerate, but for now, it seemed to relax her just enough that she laid her head on Elizabeth's shoulder, breathing hard in her ear.

"The bath is ready." Papa called from across the room.

Walker perched on the edge of the copper tub, dangling one wing in the water. "The temperature is right."

"Pray help me carry her." Elizabeth turned from Darcy back to Cait. "I need you to soak in the water for a quarter of an hour. Then we shall dry you off and return you to your nest near the fire. The egg should pass in a quarter hour after that, half at the most."

"You are not just telling me because it is what I want to hear?" Cait snapped over Darcy's shoulder as they placed her in the warm bath.

Elizabeth massaged her tight abdomen in the hot

water as a thunderous roar shook the house, rattling the windows.

"Longbourn is in the cellar!" Papa shuffled toward the door.

Darcy intercepted him. "I shall deal with him. You are needed here with Cait."

Papa tried to argue, but Darcy disappeared down the hall.

Enough was enough! Longbourn might be estate dragon, but there were limits to that privilege that he needed to understand. At the very least, he was not going to continue to bully Elizabeth and jeopardize Cait and her egg.

Darcy followed the roaring and found the cellar door. Interesting how the kitchen staff was nowhere to be seen. Perhaps that had been Rustle's doing, or perhaps Rumblkins was proving himself useful. Either way, it was welcome. He paused a moment to light a candle, then plunged into the cellar's darkness.

His eyes were slow to adjust, but as Darcy made it to the base of the stairs, he could make out Longbourn pacing the length of the cellar, bowing slightly so as not to knock his head on the beams. Clearly the space had not been dug with a dragon in mind—or perhaps it was for a smaller wyvern, a female perhaps? Yes, this would fit a female nicely. Perhaps the original Longbourn had been female.

"What are you doing here?" Longbourn snarled.

"You will keep your voice down and stop making such a distraction." Darcy kept his voice level and firm as Elizabeth did when directing Longbourn.

"I have not given you permission to be in my territory. I banished her. She is violating my sovereignty. The Blue Order declared I have the right to decide who might be here and who cannot." He stomped for emphasis.

Dust rained down from the beams above them.

"Be assured, we will both leave as soon as the situation permits us to do so."

"There is nothing important keeping you here."

"Cait is in distress trying to lay her egg. Elizabeth is helping her. We must stay until Cait is safe." Darcy bit his tongue. Patience was the key here. Patience—hopefully not more than he could muster.

"That is no business of mine. I did not invite Cait here. I do not want her."

"She is here on behalf of the Blue Order so that Collins can become accustomed to dragons."

Longbourn grumbled deep in his throat, scratching the packed earth of the cellar floor. "I do not want him, either. I do not like him. I would just as soon see him eaten."

"That would distress your Keeper, Mary."

"I have never wanted her."

"I know you want Elizabeth, but you cannot have her."

"And that is your fault." Longbourn breathed venom-laced puffs in his direction.

"No, it is yours, and you well know it." Darcy retreated up two stairs.

Longbourn extended his wings and roared again. "I accept no blame."

Darcy backed up several more stairs until he was eye-to-eye with Longbourn.

"Do not think you can win dominance here, little

man. You are nothing to me."

"I have already won, you crusty old lizard."

"You have won nothing! I am the apex dragon here."

"No, you are not." Darcy reached into his pocket and withdrew a leather envelope.

Longbourn sniffed and snorted at the envelope, nearly butting it out of Darcy's hand.

Opening it, Darcy revealed half a dozen silvery-green scales.

Longbourn roared again.

A heavy body slammed into Darcy from behind. He clutched the bannister for balance. "Collins?"

"What is in your hand that has made him so angry?" Collins trembled, pointing at the head scales in Darcy's palm.

Could the man possibly have worse timing? "Get out of here."

"How dare you order me about! This is not your house. It is mine." Collins tried to stand straight and puff out his chest. Fool—trying to play the master here but unable to muster more presence than an uncertain adolescent.

"Not yet, and if this dragon has his way, it will never be."

Longbourn stomped closer, turning his foul breath on Collins.

"What is it … he … saying?"

"This is between you and I, Darcy. Collins has no business here." Longbourn pushed Collins with his nose. "Leave."

"He wants you to leave." Darcy's lip curled a mite.

"I have a right to know what is going on." Did the man really have to whine?

"And I have a right to eat trespassers." Longbourn snorted spittle that landed on Collins' black jacket.

"Longbourn says you look like a good snack."

Longbourn thumped his tail hard on the floor. "That is not what I said! If you are going to translate, then be accurate."

"I am not your assigned translator. I can say whatever I like. The Order does not require my accuracy."

"Tell Collins I do not want him here."

"No." Darcy turned his back on Collins. "He will be master of this house soon enough. You must become accustomed to him."

"I do not want him." Longbourn breathed, hot and pungent, into Darcy's face. "Make him go."

"No. Have you forgotten?" Darcy waved the scales under Longbourn's nose. "I am the dominant dragon."

Longbourn screamed and stomped like a little boy throwing a tantrum.

"You, a dragon?" Collins stared and blinked hard. "What are you talking about?"

"You need to ask Cait. She will explain. It is a principle all Keepers must understand." Darcy tucked the scales back into the envelope.

Longbourn huffed in Collins' face.

"What is the magic in that envelope making him submit? I must have it." Collins grabbed for the scales.

Darcy snatched the envelope back and tucked it in his coat pocket. "There is no magic. Walker and Cait took his head scales in a dispute, marking their dominance over him. As my Friend, Walker gave them to me, establishing me as dominant over Longbourn. I doubt you shall ever demonstrate dominance over much at all, Mr. Collins. I would suggest you aim instead for competence."

"I am a gentleman. I am not accustomed to submitting—"

"Of course, you are, you pandering dolt. I have watched you kowtow to my aunt."

"She is above my station."

"And so is Longbourn."

"He is a ... a creature. He does not have rank."

Longbourn swung his head toward Collins and bared his fangs. "Pendragon declared that we do. A King of your kind accepted our rank, so you must as well."

"You have not read the histories, yet?" Darcy dragged his hand down is face.

"Histories? Those are fairy stories for children." Collins dropped his voice to near a whisper. "Just tell me how you have conquered it."

"Not conquered. We have established the order by which we shall live. The key is respect, Mr. Collins. That is where it begins. Does it not, Laird Longbourn? I respect you, and you respect me. Dominance only tells us who has precedence."

"I do not respect a Collins."

"And I do not expect Collins respects you, either." Darcy raised an eyebrow to Collins. "But perhaps you both might learn something. Cait is in an excellent way of teaching you both if you will be teachable."

They both grumbled and muttered but did not outright deny the possibility. That was a start.

The warm water soothed Cait's tension. Her head drooped on Elizabeth's shoulder, and she snored softly. Definitely an improvement over shrieking.

Netherfield: Rogue Dragon

Mary hid a giggle behind her hand, not a happy sound so much as a tension-relieving one.

"Should she be doing that Lizzy? I would think it a bad sign," Papa murmured, wrapping his arms over his chest in that authoritative, condescending way he had. "She does not look well at all."

"As I understand it, the relaxation is good for her. It will make it easier for the egg to pass, especially when the solution she drank begins to work."

Papa wrinkled up his mouth but said nothing more.

"I am certain it is a very good thing that she is restful. Laying should not be so very difficult," Walker said with a sideways glare.

It was nice someone in the room had confidence in her. Hopefully it was not misplaced.

"The water has cooled. I fear she will take a chill. Mary, towels please." Elizabeth extended her hand.

Mary scurried off.

Elizabeth bit her tongue. Was it too much for her to have seen the hip bath and thought ahead to bring towels when she had gone for the bandages? Obviously the answer was yes, but it was frustrating nonetheless.

Mary returned breathless, a sloppy pile of towels ready to fall out of her arms.

"I will lift her from the bath. Dry her off, and I will take her to the nest."

"But I do not want to hurt her." Mary scooted back several steps.

"She is no different than a travailing woman. You will not hurt her, but getting a chill might undo all that we have accomplished."

"Do as she asks, Mary," Papa muttered, not looking at either of them.

He had been happy enough for her advice and

intervention when he did not know from whence her wisdom had come, but now he knew ... Stubborn old lizard—just as bad as Longbourn.

Elizabeth's arms ached while Mary meticulously dried Cait's lower body, feet, and magnificent tail feathers. After far longer than it should have taken, Elizabeth lugged Cait back to the nesting box and settled her into the clean hay.

"Walker, come talk to her again as I check on the egg. Mary, keep watch and make sure she does not peck at me whilst I do."

"I cannot do that!" Mary's hands flew up, shaking impotently in the air.

"Is it better that I risk losing my hand to a stray reflex? I need you to step up."

"No! I cannot."

Papa shouldered her aside. "I will do it."

As long as she had help, it did not matter from whom it came. She applied more lard to her fingers. "Yes, yes that is better. Some of the swelling has subsided, and the egg has definitely moved. You are making progress, Cait, you are doing very well."

Cait's eyes opened halfway. "I am?"

"Yes, yes, it is very close. Perhaps a wee push, just a little one? Can you muster that?"

"I do not know. I am so tired." Her head lolled back into the nest.

"Here, I will rub your belly as you push so you do not have to try very hard. Just a little—yes, like that. I feel it! A little more and the egg ... you have done it Cait! The egg is laid!" Elizabeth grabbed a towel and took the egg from the nest.

She hurried to the window and held it in a sunbeam. No traces of blood on the shell. Excellent! The shell was sound, lightly green with flecks of gold, firm but not brittle. But so very large! No wonder Cait struggled so.

Papa extended his gnarled hands. It was tempting to be spiteful, but it would serve no greater purpose. She handed him the egg.

He took it reverently. "I have never seen one newly-laid. They become rounder and glossy as the days pass."

Walker hopped to him and examined the egg, nudging it with his beak. "It is even larger than the last one. Her last clutch was only one egg. I do not expect another this time, either. It will hatch sooner than most."

"How soon? As I understand, cockatrice eggs take a month full to incubate." Papa tapped the still soft shell with his fingernail.

"Cait's usually hatch in a fortnight, especially the large ones. Our first clutch was of average size and hatched in the usual time. But as the eggs have gotten larger, they spend less and less time in the nest."

"Do you wish assistance in finding a potential Friend?" Papa asked softly, a little hopeful. There would be some prestige in matching a newly-hatched cockatrice, especially one connected to Walker and Cait, with a Friend.

"No." Cait lifted her head and peered at Papa. "It is already decided. Elizabeth is my first choice—"

"Elizabeth?" Papa staggered back, pressing the egg to his chest. "The egg is clearly male. What would Elizabeth do with a cockatrice? They are not a woman's companion."

Elizabeth winced.

"We are companions to whomever we choose." Cait snapped her beak. "Perhaps I should insist …"

"No, I will not share Pemberley with another of our kind, particularly another male." Walker did not exactly growl, but it was close enough.

That was a reason worth respecting. Not that Elizabeth really wanted another baby dragon to be responsible for when Pemberley's infancy and youth might last nearly all of Elizabeth's life.

"Then Colonel Fitzwilliam. He will do well for our chick." A little of Cait's usual spirit returned to her voice.

"He is in London right now, but Darcy will inform him. I am sure he will be here directly."

No doubt they had already decided this well ahead of time. What purpose did they have in this little charade in front of Papa?

"We shall have a room prepared for him." Papa masked his disappointment well, but it was still clear in the stoop of his shoulders.

"Will Longbourn have him?" Mary looked over her shoulder as though he might appear in the study at any moment.

"Longbourn has no choice. Cait is here by request of the Blue Order. He cannot interfere with anything regarding her." Elizabeth placed the egg back into the nest under Cait's feathers. Dragons did not sit on their eggs like birds, but bird-types often spent time sitting on the eggs as a protective, maternal gesture, declaring to other dragons that this was protected territory, not an invitation for a snack.

"Is that not perhaps a stretch of the Blue Order's rights?" Mary asked. "Should we tempt Longbourn's temper that way? Perhaps it would be best for you to take Cait with you to Netherfield now that her life is in no danger."

"Cait is here for your benefit, Mary, translating for your husband. Without her, he has no way to hear the dragons, small or large. The Order knew she was due to lay her clutch, so taking care of her and the egg was part of the requirements placed on Longbourn."

"Mr. Collins will be fine without her. She can go to Netherfield. It is just a matter of a fortnight, is it not?"

"You really do not understand, do you?" Elizabeth sat on the floor beside the nesting box and hung her head. "He requires her presence as a part of his sentence."

"Elizabeth is right." Papa stood beside Mary, his voice soft and grave.

"What are you talking about?"

Elizabeth braced her elbows and pressed her forehead on her palms. "When Collins stumbled into Rosings' lair in Kent, the crime—"

"What crime? That is not a crime!" Mary threw her hands up. "Why is everyone so intent—"

"It is among the Order. And that offense carries with it a capital sentence." Papa's words hung in the air.

"That was commuted." Did Mary realize what scolding tone she used? Best leave the explanations to Papa.

"Not exactly. He is on probation. He has a year to be inducted into the Order—or not."

"What do you mean, 'or not?'" The color drained from Mary's face.

How could she not understand? She had heard the pronouncements just as Elizabeth had.

"If he is not deemed worthy, or at the very least not a hazard to dragonkind, then the Order will not allow any threat to dragonkind to remain." How did Papa manage to pronounce such news with so little feeling?

"Who is to determine what makes him a threat?" Mary fell into the nearest chair.

Cait chirruped. "My testimony will be a part of that consideration. At the moment, I think very little of him and his high-and-mighty opinions. Your plan to send me away reeks of one who wants to get rid of supervision and go her own way. It is not in either of your favor."

"This is ridiculous."

"Your opinion does not matter." Elizabeth knotted her fingers together. "When one deals with dragons, there is a high price for the relationship. I am sorry the connection is one you do not like and perhaps do not even value right now. I am sorry it has been thrust upon you so unwillingly. But perhaps you can keep in mind, it did permit you to catch the man you wanted, and that probably should count for something."

Mary's jaw dropped. "Are you suggesting—"

"No, I suggest nothing. I merely recommend that you should carefully consider all aspects of your situation before you form opinions too quickly." Elizabeth rose and shook out her skirts. "Keep Cait warm and bring her a large meal and plenty of water. I shall check on her soon." She stalked out, not really sure where she was going.

Stubborn, stubborn, stubborn, the entire lot of them: Papa, Mary, Collins, Longbourn. Could they not see what was at stake and what disaster they were risking by their obstinacy? One of them had to bend a knee soon, or something tragic was going to happen. But how to make them see?

Elizabeth touched her shoulder. If only April were here. She was as obstinate as the rest to be sure, but she was willing to see reason. Only recently she had admitted there were advantages to being warm-blooded. No dragon ever wanted to admit such a thing. Perhaps if she were here to show them a way—but April was not here to help her. She was alone.

Perhaps that meant she needed to do something about the situation herself.

Elizabeth fell into a hall chair, arms wrapped tightly around her waist. The wooden frame creaked, and the back thumped against the chair rail. Even the furniture was complaining about her.

All told, she was as stubborn as the rest. Mary had scolded her for it. Papa had outright berated her for it. Cait had reproached her thoroughly for the same when Elizabeth insisted Longbourn was the only possible dragon who could be persuading Mary—or who could have tried to persuade her about Collins.

While it was by no means certain, Cait did have a point. Longbourn was not the only possible culprit. Why Longbourn would have allowed such a dragon into his territory and into the cellars was difficult to conceive, but it was—just barely—possible.

Just enough to make it reasonable to offer him an apology.

After all, it would be what Elizabeth would want if accused of such an egregious wrong.

Maybe it would serve as an example to the rest of the family that it was time to become more tractable. Even if it did not, at least it held the promise of making Longbourn easier to deal with. If, of course, it did not make things worse altogether which seemed equally likely.

She pushed herself up from the creaky chair and

headed toward the cellar.

"And I do not expect Collins respects you, either." Darcy's strong voice greeted her at the top of the cellar stairs. "But perhaps you both might learn something. Cait is in an excellent way of teaching you both if you will be teachable."

"Yes," she picked her way down the narrow steps to Darcy's side. "Cait is a very good teacher and has taught me some important things as well."

"Is the crisis past?" Darcy reached for her hand and held it tightly.

She had been wrong; she was not at all alone. "Cait and the egg are safe and well."

Longbourn stepped closer to the stairs and leaned toward her face. "Then you can leave."

"I need to teach Mary how to take proper care of your teeth. Or perhaps, Mr. Collins, you might be amenable—"

"I will not have the dumb one touching me!" Longbourn's tail pounded the cellar floor.

"I ... I do not think it ... he likes that idea." Collins pressed himself against the far banister.

"He is only being stubborn. Very, very stubborn."

Longbourn glared and drew a deep breath.

Elizabeth lifted her open hands. "We all have been very stubborn. We will get no further solving any of the problems facing us by being so."

"What are you demanding of me now?" Longbourn leaned in toward her, eyes narrow.

Her heart pounded painfully against her ribs. She sucked in a deep breath; maybe that would quell it. "Nothing. I do not ask anything of you, except perhaps to listen."

"Why should I listen to you?" Longbourn folded his

wings along his back, rather like a child crossing his arms and pouting. But he was no longer stomping and snarling. That was a good sign.

"I come to offer an apology."

"Apologize to a creature?" Collins snorted and stomped. "How can you think of such a thing? It is unseemly."

Elizabeth whirled on him. "Not when I have been wrong."

Longbourn snapped a warning in Collins' direction. Collins jumped back two stairs. Longbourn sat back a little, his tail making long, slow arcs along the cellar floor. Darcy edged a little closer, pressing his shoulder to hers.

"I am listening." Longbourn settled on his haunches.

"We," Elizabeth glanced back at Darcy. He met her gaze, eyes dark and warm and strong beside her, "we believe that there is another major dragon, a rogue, nearby. So there is another who could have tried to convince me to accept Mr. Collins."

"A dragon tried to persuade you to accept my offer?" Collins' jaw dropped. It would have been enormously funny at any other time.

"Indeed one did," she hissed.

"And you still refused me?" Now was not the time for this conversation.

"It violates a fundamental law of the Blue Order, as well as simple common sense, for a dragon to try and persuade a hearer, especially his Keeper." Usually that tone of voice ended conversations.

"You were so dead set against me even that could not have moved you?"

"Have I not made it entirely clear to you, sir, that

nothing in heaven or on earth would have moved me to accept you? Longbourn scooped me up like prey, wrapped me in his wings and breathed venom on me, and still I refused to accept you. Does that not make it clear enough?" She probably should not have, but she stomped. It was rather satisfying, though. No wonder Longbourn was so fond of it.

"It tried to kill you?" Collins turned very pale. "I knew they were not to be trusted."

"I can see why you detested him," Longbourn muttered.

"Would you really have wanted me tied to such a man?" Elizabeth glowered briefly at Collins.

"Mary seems to like him well enough." Longbourn's brow ridge wrinkled.

"Mary is very different to me; she has other priorities."

Collins harrumphed.

"I am not certain I am one of them." Longbourn dragged his claws in the dirt.

"That has to change. I will do everything I can to instruct both of them in better Dragon Keeping. If you will permit me."

"You said you had an apology to make."

"I do." She pulled her shoulders back and looked Longbourn straight in the eyes. "I am deeply sorry that I accused you of trying to use draconic persuasion upon me when trying to convince me to marry Mr. Collins."

"You do not believe I did that?"

"I ... I do not think so. I still have many questions without sensible answers, but no, I do not think you did. I am sorry I accused you of doing so. You have been my friend for a very long time, and friends do not behave so toward one another, even when they are very bad-tempered and do not get their way. Will you forgive me my error?"

"Will you tell your father and your sister that you were wrong? And the Blue Order as well? You accused me of heinous behavior before the entire Conclave. It was humiliating."

Elizabeth sighed heavily. "I had not realized how difficult that must have been. You are entirely correct. I will submit a formal apology to be presented at the next Conclave so that it is as public as my accusation."

"And you do not believe I would do such a thing to you?" He leaned his head in very close.

"Look me in the eye and tell me—would you even consider such a thing?" She touched his cheek.

"I like having my way, but there are limits to how far I would go for that."

"I believe you."

The tip of his tail thumped softly. "Scratch my ears." He shoved his head toward her, nearly knocking Collins off the stairs.

"I cannot believe you apologized to that creature when you should apologize to me." Collins nose wrinkled as he snorted.

Elizabeth reached for Longbourn's itchiest spots. "I understand how I wronged Longbourn, sir, but how exactly did I wrong you?"

"As I see it, she spared you a very unhappy marriage," Darcy grumbled, not looking at Collins.

"And I led you to a wife who not only wanted to marry you, but somehow seems to think well of you. I ask you again, how have I wronged you?"

Collins muttered something that did not deserve attention.

"Now, it is time for your first proper lesson in Dragon Keeping. They are always itchy and like nothing better than a proper scratch. See here, behind his ear—with your permission, Longbourn—" he grunted not quite affirmatively, but he did not growl, and that was good enough. "Like this."

Darcy elbowed Collins hard, and he capitulated, none too happily, until Longbourn began to respond to his clumsy ministrations. An oddly satisfied look crept across Collins' face. The man would never make a truly good Dragon Keeper, but he might do well enough for the Order to make him a Deaf Speaker and live out his life tending to Longbourn. That would be sufficient.

Chapter 6

DARCY STEPPED BACK and scratched his head. Who would have imagined Elizabeth's simple apology could make such a difference? Once she assuaged Longbourn's bruised ego, he proved far less disagreeable—which was certainly not the same as being agreeable. The contrast to his previous manner, though, made him seem utterly pleasant. With Elizabeth's approval, Darcy brought Mary and Bennet into the cellar conversation, and their stubbornness softened as well.

The disgruntled wyvern reluctantly agreed that Elizabeth was no longer banished from Longbourn estate and she might come and go freely from the house and grounds. That alone was a huge breakthrough but not without cost. She had to promise to instruct Mary and Collins in Longbourn's preferences—something neither appeared very interested in learning. Though Bennet still seemed quite put out with Elizabeth, he did agree to speak with her and permit her the use of his library. Small steps, but enough to make the entire affair feel like a victory.

They returned to Netherfield late that night, too spent for words. Elizabeth leaned heavily on his shoulder as he guided the curricle along the moonlit road. Without the morning's urgency, the ride proved peaceful, even soothing, her quiet warmth as welcome as any conversation.

With his last few coherent thoughts, Darcy penned a quick letter to Fitzwilliam, telling him of Cait's invitation to befriend her chick. No doubt, that would bring him to Netherfield in short order. He gave the missive to Walker and collapsed into bed.

Darcy slept well into the next afternoon. As he made his way down the grand stairs, Nicholls met him with news. Miss Bennet was under the weather with a sick headache and might not go below stairs all day. He turned around and trudged back up the stairs. Truth was, he felt rather off himself. If she was not going to be about, there was little reason for him to be.

His muscles ached, and his chest felt vaguely raw, as though a chest cold were coming on. Rather like he had felt whilst recovering from their exposure to the venom in the mapmaker's rooms.

Venom exposure?

He pulled a hall chair near and fell into it. The wooden joints creaked in protest. He scrubbed his face with his hands, knotting his fingers into his hair.

There had been traces of venom in Longbourn's breath yesterday, particularly when he became angry. Could that have been enough to cause a reaction? Perhaps they were more sensitive since they had been previously exposed. He drummed his fingers on the back of his head. According to Gardiner, Longbourn also breathed on Elizabeth when he lost his temper and caused her to lose consciousness. Would that render her even more affected by the poison?

He would have to talk to her about it when—no, it could not wait. He half-ran downstairs to order Nicholls to prepare hot water, then back to Elizabeth's room.

"Elizabeth! Elizabeth!" He pounded at the door, leaning heavily on the doorframe, panting to catch his breath.

"I heard you. You need not break the door down!" Her voice was thin and sharp through the offending slab of oak. A moment later, she pulled the door open and peeked out.

Dark circles lined her eyes over very pale cheeks. Her eyes were swollen and red, and it looked as though she clung to the door handle for support. "What do you need, sir?"

"I think I know what is wrong with both of us."

"You are unwell, too?" Irritation melted into concern as she reached for his arm.

"We were both in Longbourn's presence for an extended time and in an enclosed space. I think there was venom in the air."

Her brow creased the way it often did when she was thinking. "He might have been displeased, but he would not have intentionally—"

"Not intentionally, to be sure. But when he becomes agitated, there is often a drop or two of ochre on his fangs. When he huffs, he sprays it into the air."

"I suppose it is possible." She chewed her knuckle.

"Remember how you felt after we were exposed to

the maps?"

She blinked hard at him. "It seemed just a headache and perhaps a cold, but now that you mention it ... perhaps."

"I have ordered hot water for bathing."

"It seems quite sensible." She squeezed her eyes shut and shook her head as though trying to shake loose a thought. "Now that Papa is permitting me back into Longbourn house, perhaps I should search his libraries for some sort of antidote to the venom. As we are a wyvern estate, it seems some ancestor should have identified something."

"Did he not already look, though?" It would probably have been better not to permit the exasperation to show in his voice.

"He did, but I have discovered he has a bias against particular sources. Prior Keepers kept their own logs and notes, but he considers them unreliable forms of information compared to the canon of dragon lore. I may be able to find something he has overlooked."

A searing jolt coursed through his skull. He clutched his temples. "If we are likely to spend more time with Longbourn, I think it a very good idea."

"I hear the maids coming. You should return to your chambers." She glanced over his shoulder and gently pushed her door closed.

She was right, of course, but he hated to lose her company. He staggered to his quarters, the headache growing steadily worse. He barely made it to his room before his knees melted underneath him, and he fell into a chair. This definitely felt like dragon venom.

A team of servants trundled in with a copper tub and hot water in pails and kettles and pots. They labored for a full quarter of an hour to set up the tub in front of the fireplace and fill it. Walker winged his way into the room just as he shooed the maids out. Darcy shed his clothes and sank into the hot water.

"You look like carrion some dog dragged to the side of the road." Walker perched at the foot of the tub, staring at Darcy.

"I feel worse." Darcy splashed water on his face.

"Why the bath? Have you been back to the map room?"

"No, although we need to. We think it was Longbourn yesterday, venom in the air."

"You should tell Fitzwilliam when he arrives. I saw him on the road. He will be here soon. He carried a rather large portfolio—I would imagine the Order dispatched him here."

"Or he is impatient to visit with Cait and her egg."

"It will not hatch that soon." Walker snorted, dipping the tip of his wing into the bathwater. "That is nearly as hot as the one Cait used at Longbourn."

"Do you wish to use the bathwater when I am finished?"

"Lady Elizabeth may have coaxed Cait into a water bath, but I far prefer dust." Walker splashed a bit of water toward Darcy's face just for emphasis.

"How is she today?"

"Greatly improved. A bit sore and tired but nearly back to herself. We both owe Lady Elizabeth a great debt. Cait would not have survived without her help."

"I am sure she would be keen for news of Cait. Perhaps you should go to her."

Walker smirked. "You want me to bring you news of how she fares."

"I would value your opinions. I fear she underestimates risks to her own well-being." Darcy dragged a small towel over his face.

Walker chirruped and flew out, apparently as concerned about Elizabeth as Darcy.

He leaned back in the bath, ducking until the water reached his ear lobes. So, Fitzwilliam was on his way with news from the Order. If the portfolio was large, it could not possibly be good news. Best finish up and dress before Fitzwilliam barged in.

Two hours later, Nicholls—looking a bit perplexed—showed Fitzwilliam into the small parlor lit by the fireplace and a handful of candles. How snug the room seemed with only a small portion lit.

Walker suggested to Nicholls that Fitzwilliam was a very good friend of Bingley, and Bingley would want Netherfield's hospitality extended toward Fitzwilliam even as it had been toward Darcy. Walker managed to get her to accept the persuasion, but it was clear April was much more adept at the task than any cockatrice would ever be—they were unsubtle creatures at best.

Hopefully, April would yet return to Elizabeth. She was a very useful creature to have around. Though he might not admit it aloud, at least not yet, her company was entertaining, even a little endearing. He missed having her about.

He and Fitzwilliam settled into the small parlor to talk. Nicholls brought word that Elizabeth, though improved, would not be coming down for dinner. Darcy requested dinner trays be brought to the parlor. They made small talk until the trays were brought.

"I am surprised to see you. I sent word only yesterday evening." Darcy arranged his dinner tray in front of him. Not a fine meal, to be sure, but far better than anything they had at the public inns. "I know you are anxious for the egg to hatch, but this does seem a bit enthusiastic."

"If it were only that, I would have taken a wee bit more time. Unfortunately, nothing can be quite that simple." Fitzwilliam hooked a small footstool with his toes and pulled it close enough to prop his feet. "I am a little surprised Elizabeth is not here with us."

Darcy explained his suspicions about the venom exposure. "Even so, I still think it worth the progress we made. While Longbourn will never be tractable, Elizabeth's apology did much to smooth the way. I expect his cooperation on at least the most critical matters."

"Welcome news, indeed. I doubt mine will be, though. Perhaps, for the moment, it is best that we talk without Elizabeth." Fitzwilliam tapped steepled fingers before his face.

"I do not like the sound of that."

"Matters have become more complicated than expected. Things could turn rather ugly."

"From you, that is a very worrisome word. What are you suggesting?"

"To sum up the pile of Order documents you will no doubt read later, reports of unrest continue to pour into the Order offices. While the more powerful major dragons do not feel particularly threatened by the possibility of a rogue, particularly one as weak as a lindwurm, the lesser major dragons are calling for assurances that action will be taken."

"Action has been taken. That is why we are here." Darcy pressed the heel of his hand into his forehead.

"The Order fears it may not be enough to quell the lesser-landed dragons." Fitzwilliam balanced one foot on top of the other. "Unfortunately, that is not the whole of it. The emissary from the Eastern Dragon

Federation is indeed missing. Gone without a trace."

"How is that possible? I thought you said the emissary was traveling via dragon tunnel—?"

"She—we have found out that much about the emissary—was and had successfully passed through several of the checkpoints, but she failed to appear at one and has not been seen since. Several wyrms, large and small, were sent to scour the tunnels, and they turned up very disturbing news."

"Evidence the emissary has been harmed?" Darcy clutched the arm of his chair.

"No, thankfully. That would be an entirely different level of disaster. The wyrms discovered branches and tunnels that were not on our maps. The entrances had been obscured, blocked in such a way that one who did not know they were there would not notice them. When the wyrms uncovered them, the scope of the tunnels was staggering—absolutely staggering. We have teams going through them now, but the task will take months at best, perhaps longer."

Darcy's jaw dropped. "That many?"

"The emissary could literally be anywhere in England right now, absolutely anywhere."

"At some point, she will grow hungry and have to come out to find food."

"With all the unrest about a rogue dragon, even though the Order has sent word that an Eastern Dragon has been invited to England and is expected—"

Darcy stood and paced along the fireplace. "Any dragon lower than a major drake—and even some of them, come to think of it—is likely to defend its territory first and heed the Order only after they feel safe."

"Exactly." Fitzwilliam's expression was grim.

Netherfield: Rogue Dragon

"Dragon's blood and fire! If the emissary is killed—"

"We risk a domestic dragon war whilst trying to stave off a war from the Eastern Federation. Consequently, the Blue Order officers—human and dragon—have decided the only reasonable option is to end the threat of the rogue dragon immediately."

"Is that not what Elizabeth and I have been trying to do?"

"There is no more time. An immediate resolution is required." Something about the look on Fitzwilliam's face …

"No, they cannot possibly require that of you."

"Now that you are Keeper to Pemberley, you cannot possibly carry out the task." Fitzwilliam's foot dropped to the floor with a resounding thud.

"We have been exchanging messages with the rogue. It knows I once carried the Dragon Slayer. He is already wary."

"Bloody hell! I am not surprised, though. I knew there had to be something more complicated going on since the creature was not already winding around Elizabeth's ankles, begging to be scratched."

"She does make getting along with dragons look simple and easy." Hopefully, Fitzwilliam could not hear the twinge of jealousy in his voice.

"I am honestly surprised she does not already have an office with the Order. It seems as though they should have worked out a way to benefit from her acumen by now."

"I am sure Bennet and Longbourn are at the heart of that, keeping her close to home for their own ease. If she became an officer, then she would be spending a great deal of time in London and away from

Longbourn."

"Something neither of them would much appreciate." Fitzwilliam leaned forward and braced his elbows on his knees. "I am not sure she should know I have the Dragon Slayer."

"I do not relish keeping secrets from her."

"I am afraid of what she may do if she finds out."

"You are exaggerating. Elizabeth is not inclined to throw herself into that sort of danger."

Was Fitzwilliam coughing or laughing? Maybe both. "You recall what she did when Pemberley hatched? You think it unlikely she would do such a thing again? Do not try to tell me you would forbid her. You and I both know that is impossible. Recall how she took on Cait when you brought her to Rosings."

"I still have nightmares about Cait clawing her eyes out for that." Darcy threw his arm over his eyes.

"Need I say more?"

"What about Wickham and Lydia? Is there no concern that if you hunt the lindwurm they might become collateral damage?"

"I would not say there is no concern, but let us be honest. Wickham is of no account to anyone. His death would not be difficult to cover with an appropriate tale if anyone even noticed. And Miss Lydia," Fitzwilliam blew a sharp breath through the edge of his lips. "I am sorry, but it was her father's responsibility to curb her behavior. His failure has led to this situation, so any harm to her would be upon his head. He should have been paying attention to the signs that she could hear and acted. The Order is not very sympathetic."

"She is to be my sister. I cannot take such a cavalier attitude." Darcy jumped out of his chair and paced.

"I assure you, I will do everything in my power to

protect her. I do not wish to bring grief to Elizabeth, but certainly she can see that there is a great deal more at stake right now than just her sister."

"If it were Georgiana at risk, you would say the same?" Darcy dared not meet Fitzwilliam's gaze.

"You know how highly I regard her. But not even she is worth setting the world into dragon war and destroying everything Pendragon and all the generations since have worked so hard to achieve."

Damn it all! It was difficult to argue that point.

"With what the Order demands of me now, I wonder if I am truly fit to befriend any dragon, much less one of Walker's line. If I am successful in my mission, I will be an anathema to all dragonkind."

"Cait specifically named you as Friend for her chick. That is not an honor one turns down lightly."

Fitzwilliam raked his hand through his hair. "I take no pleasure in any of this, to be sure. There is an excellent chance I will not survive, even if I am successful. Father did not say as much, but he did bring Mother to London and ensured I saw her before I left."

"There must be another way." Darcy paced a little faster. "I am certain Longbourn must be aware of the lindwurm and at least tolerating it which means they communicate somehow. And the maps! If we can get into the map-maker's rooms, we might be able to learn something more. Between the two, we may find some way to negotiate with the creature and prevent bloodshed."

"The map room is poisoned, is it not?"

"Elizabeth believes an unexplored avenue in her father's library may provide useful information toward countering the venom. Being in the library might well occasion us to speak to Longbourn himself. Perhaps he might even have some knowledge of Lydia. I am certain we will find another way. There must be one."

"I appreciate your faith, Darcy, but it is a luxury I cannot afford. I will go to Longbourn with you and learn as much as I can there. But I do not expect to find anything that will dissuade me from my mission."

After a full day of rest and two more thorough baths, Elizabeth ventured from her rooms. Her skin was near raw in places from scrubbing, and her fingers might never stop resembling prunes. But her lungs no longer burned and the lingering ache in her joints had faded.

How would Longbourn react when she told him how sick his bout of temper had left her? Probably despondent and recalcitrant, or stomping off in another fit of temper. He was always one for extremes.

The morning sun hung high in the sky—so much for her preferred early start. The feather bed beckoned her back into its indulgent embrace. Only the threat of a rogue dragon was strong enough to shatter the siren song. She shrugged into a morning gown, pinned up her hair, and headed downstairs.

Men's voices, Darcy's and Fitzwilliam's, filtered from the morning room. Was it silly to miss having Darcy to herself in the mornings? Yes, and probably selfish, too. Much bigger considerations took precedence now.

Darcy scrambled to the doorway to escort her to her chair, carefully tucking it in under the table for her.

Fitzwilliam sat opposite the window, face lined with weary concerns that sleep had not erased. What could have happened in London? "It is a pleasure to see you out and about today, Miss Bennet."

"It is a pleasure to be out and about, I assure you."

"Would you care for something to eat? Tea or coffee, perhaps?" Darcy smiled carved dimples into his cheeks when he spoke, making it hard to refuse.

He set a heavily-laden plate—enough to feed herself and two small dragons at least, and a cup of steaming coffee before her. She sipped her cup—oh, that was very strong!—and nibbled from her plate for a few moments lest she be thought too direct in her conversation. Probably no need to worry given the company, but the long-instilled habit was difficult to alter. "Dare I ask what news you have from the Order?"

Fitzwilliam glanced at Darcy. Something about the expression seemed vaguely conspiratorial.

"Things have naturally become more complicated—as they are wont to do when dragons are involved." Fitzwilliam described the loss of the Eastern Dragon emissary somewhere in the vast tunnel system underneath England. "It is imperative we gain control over this rogue dragon situation as quickly as possible."

"No doubt." Her mind whirled with possibilities. None of them good. "Since we are making little headway in our conversation with the lindwurm, perhaps it is time to seek Longbourn's assistance."

Darcy's brow furrowed with the worried-worn look he often wore.

"I may be of some use with that." Fitzwilliam reached over several piles to liberate a small stack tied with a blue ribbon. "Lady Astrid sent some material for you."

"Let us bring it to Longbourn house, then. Papa and I may study it whilst you help us scour the journals of past Keepers for further information."

Fitzwilliam groaned like a reluctant schoolboy. "I understand it is our best option. Whether or not we manage to find some miracle cure in those cryptic pages, I need to speak to Longbourn himself. Will you help me secure his cooperation? I hope he may be familiar with some of the tunnels in Hertfordshire and perhaps assist us in locating the lost emissary—"

"Or—I imagine—at the very least you hope to extract his promise not to harm the envoy?"

"That is the least I—and the Blue Order—require."

And the least Longbourn could rightfully offer. Pray let his stubbornness be softened today. "I will do my best to convince him to see you, and barring that, I will extract the desired promise from him."

"Forgive me, Miss Bennet, but how does one convince an obstinate dragon?" Fitzwilliam tapped his palms together.

"Name a major dragon who is not obstinate. It is in their very nature. One does not become the apex predator by giving way easily, no? To criticize a dragon for being stubborn is like criticizing a horse for having four legs. But inflexibility does not equate to stupidity."

Fitzwilliam snorted under his breath.

"Even a pigheaded dragon like Longbourn can see how he has everything to lose and nothing to gain in a full dragon war. The lesser major dragons suffer most in those circumstances."

"You are a difficult woman to argue with, Miss Bennet." Fitzwilliam lifted his cup toward her. "She will not give you an easy run of it, will she, Darcy?"

Darcy raised his coffee cup and winked.

Several hours later, Darcy and Fitzwilliam took

turns on the library ladder in Papa's study, one to find books and the other to add them to the abundant stacks of books for perusal. Normally, the books on the floor comprised that part of his collection that did not fit on his shelves. But today, the group also included all volumes that might have material on lindwurms, dragon tunnels, wyvern poison, or young cockatrices—maybe twice as many piles as usual. With four people, a cockatrice nest and the egg, the room had progressed from cluttered to positively smothering.

Elizabeth and Papa sat side-by-side in two wing chairs pulled very close to the fireplace and nesting box. He studied Lady Astrid's monographs while Elizabeth scanned a journal from a Longbourn Keeper, three generations past.

"I am beginning to wonder, Lizzy, if I do not need to make it to London a bit more often." Papa looked up from the monograph and lifted his glasses to rub the bridge of his nose. "Sending your mother and Kitty there with Gardiner yesterday was a matter of convenience, but perhaps we should do it more often, and I should accompany them."

Elizabeth nearly dropped the journal. "Excuse me?" She had leafed through the monograph on their way to Longbourn and found it absorbing, but not normally the sort of thing Papa would spend a great deal of time with.

"Yes, I know, you never thought I would say such a thing, but this," he tapped the monograph, "is making me wonder. This is absolutely fascinating work, fascinating. I wonder how much I am missing by not frequenting the Order Library. It is different to what they used to publish. It might even be worthwhile to resubmit that fairy dragon monograph."

"It certainly might. I know Lady Astrid would welcome you. She is a very gracious and entirely charming soul. Though she could easily make anyone feel quite dragon-dumb, she is so kind and thoughtful, that I hardly feel as stupid as she must think I am." Elizabeth turned aside. The words had just tumbled from her lips, uncensored. She should have thought them through much more carefully.

"I hardly think she considers you so, Lizzy. Gardiner has told me your commonplace book has created quite a stir among the scribes and even the Lord Physician." His tone did not convey approval.

Her cheeks grew hot as she felt Darcy's and Fitzwilliam's eyes on her. "They are only my scribblings about my observations and experiences from the Blue Order business I attended with you."

"You were apt to write everything down. Always scribbling in that book of yours. I know your mother insisted on you girls keeping those books, but none of your sisters ever seemed to take it as seriously as you did. I wonder, sometimes, if you were full young to have been dragged from one side of the country to the other when you should have been in the schoolroom with your sisters."

"As I remember it, you brought me on your business trips because you could no longer hold a pen to write." She clenched her fist, heart pounding painfully. "Not on some sort of capricious whim."

Papa polished his glasses with the end of his cravat. "Perhaps I should have hired a secretary to do that work instead. The Blue Order would likely have paid for it once I was installed as historian. You were exposed to too much, to too many dragons and their

Keepers, far too young."

She shut the journal forcefully and stood, blood roaring in her ears. "I am sorry you feel that way." She dropped the book on the chair and strode out.

Darcy caught her eye on the way to the door, but thankfully he seemed to notice she was in no mind to be questioned and let her pass.

"Lizzy! There is work to be done!" Papa's voice was filled with an all-too-familiar exasperation that came out whenever she expressed an opinion he did not like. It had become so much more frequent in recent years.

"I need air and to walk and think about all that I have read. That is part of the way I work, and I shall not be denied." She slammed the door behind her.

How kind of him to question the most treasured memories of her childhood, the events that shaped her into who and what she was today. Did she embarrass him, or was it that her presence sometimes led to surprises like April's Friendship? He never did like surprises. Or was it simply because she was a woman, and he did not approve of the elevated position the Blue Order offered them? Or maybe modern Dragon Keeping threatened him and his precious dragon lore.

She wrapped her arms tight around her waist. That kind of thinking could be the downfall of them all.

At least Darcy did not seem so hidebound. He read her notes and acted upon them without critiquing or questioning their wisdom because they came from a young woman. He had insisted she come to Rosings to help with Pemberley. Once there, he abided no interference with her ministrations to the drakling. His letters spoke of the trust he place in her.

What would it be like living with a man who valued and relied upon her understanding? The more time she spent with Papa, the more pleasing the idea became.

"Oh, Lizzy!" Mary nearly ran into her. "I thought you were in the study with Papa."

Elizabeth stopped short and jumped back several steps. "I was, but I need to walk and gather my thoughts."

"Longbourn is in the cellar—he thought he heard your voice. Would you—he would very much like to talk with you." Mary wrung her hands in her apron.

One more stubborn, disagreeable male to deal with? Elizabeth dragged her hand over her face. Now was certainly not the time.

"He is worried about you. Somehow he has gotten the notion that you have not been well. He really is very concerned." Mary bit her lip and cringed a little.

What little dragon spy would have brought him that information? At least he was concerned, not demanding something from her. It would have been nice if Mary expressed as much concern. "Pray tell him that I would be pleased to meet with him in his lair."

"But why go so far? He is in the cellar under our feet." Mary glanced over her shoulder toward the cellar door.

"He is correct. I have been unwell. We believe bad air in the cellar is in part to blame. If he is truly concerned for my health, then he will agree to meet me in his lair."

Mary clapped her hands over her mouth. "I had no idea. Do you think it is unsafe—"

"For you, no I do not think so. For Darcy and me, though, yes. We were both exposed to powerful wyvern venom at Netherfield. It seems the least exposure is apt to affect us now. Pray do not explain that to Longbourn, lest there be any more misunderstandings.

I will break it to him myself when I see him."

"Of course, of course." Mary looked a little relieved. "I am certain he will understand, Lizzy. You should know, your apology meant a great deal to him. Things are so different. He tries hard to be more agreeable now that you no longer accuse him of something he did not do. He did not even complain when I scratched his scales the wrong way, or when I did not warm the oil for his hide properly."

Longbourn was not the only one whose attitude had seemed to change. Was it possible Mary was no longer subject to persuasions from a strange dragon and those effects were fading? Not the sort of thing one could ask, though.

"I am glad about those changes, and I will endeavor to remember." She swallowed hard against a little shudder. There were other memories not so easily displaced.

Darkness as the wings enfolded around her. Hot, acrid, burning breath, searing her lungs and great clawed feet closed around her. She reached for the wall for support. Pray Mary never understood such things.

Mary grabbed her arm. "Are you well?"

"I will be fine. I ... I just need some fresh air. Pray, tell Longbourn I will see him soon." She pushed past Mary and half-ran out of the kitchen door.

Gulping in the cool afternoon air, Elizabeth turned her face into the welcoming sunshine. Focus on Longbourn's attitude today—that was what mattered. Nothing could change what had happened, but the future could be different. According to Mary, today he was good-natured and even repentant—the sort of dragon she had always thought him to be. If he met her in the lair, that would indeed show his good faith. He would never be a gentle lapdog or a sweet-natured dear like little Heather, but as long as he was trying, that was good enough.

The hard ground near the house gave way to the softer earth near the garden. The perfume of newly-turned soil and tiny green things just poking out of the earth greeted her. Those should be comforting. If only her thudding heart and aching lungs might agree, and the vague burning on her face and neck subside. That would indeed bolster her faith in him. Perhaps after she saw him ...

"Mrrow."

"Oh!" She nearly stumbled over the long half-furry, half-scaled body that wove around her feet near the garden gate. "Rumblkins!"

"You upset? I saw you from the kitchen. You ought not be alone." His voice was always purry-soft, so soothing to listen to.

She crouched beside him and scratched his tufty cat-ears. "You are a very sweet creature. Perhaps you may be right; it would be best for me to have company."

After April's near constant presence for over a decade, being without a Dragon Friend nearby felt so wrong, like going out without a proper petticoat—something important was missing. Rumblkins was no fairy dragon, but he was sweet and dear and fluffy. She sniffled and dragged her sleeve across her eyes.

Purring in his funny draconic sort of way, he reared up on his long serpentine tail. Bumping the top of his head under her chin, he licked the side of her jaw with his rough, forked tongue. "Where are you going?"

"To see Longbourn."

"Take the long way about." Rumblkins wove

around her and bumped under her chin again.

"Why? He will be waiting for me."

"I saw something interesting in the woods at the edge of Netherfield Park." He pointed with his paw.

"That is quite out of the way. I am not sure it is a good idea."

"It is a very good idea." He licked his thumb-toe and purred.

"Tell me what you saw."

"You must see it yourself."

She sighed and took Rumblkins' fuzzy face in her hands, peering into his dark eyes. There was always a vaguely daft expression there. Sometimes more and sometimes less, but always just a touch addlepated. Were they all that way? She needed to study a few more tatzelwurms to be sure. But among the wildness, there was also a trace of concern and sincerity, perhaps even a little urgency.

"All right, I will come, but we should hurry."

Rumblkins sprang off toward Netherfield Park.

One really should be careful when telling a tatzelwurm to hurry. They were surprisingly fast, even nimble creatures. Though unladylike, she had to run to keep up with him, nearly tripping as she hopped over the stiles. He slowed just as she was ready to call for him to stop and let her catch her breath.

Rising up high on his tail, he pointed his thumbed paw at a clump of trees. "There, I saw it there, just yesterday. It is long and white and smells like Hill's laundry."

Hill's laundry? Prickles rose on the back of her neck and shoulders. Was it possible? She sprinted to the trees and scanned the ground. There, half-buried in a pile of leaves, a long white streak. She sprinted and snatched it out of the pile, falling to her knees as she did.

A glove! A lady's glove. She turned the length inside out. Talons, claws, teeth and scales! There it was, a little 'L' in blue thread, hidden in the long seam. This was Lydia's glove! From the look of it, it had not been out here very long, either.

But how did it get here?

"Was I right? You needed to see?" Rumblkins bumped her elbow.

"Yes, and I shall find you a nice dried cod when we return to Longbourn."

If his purrs got any louder, they might well be heard all the way to Longbourn. She scratched his face, ears, and under his chin until he flopped on his back in exhaustion.

"Did you see who dropped it?"

"No, found it while looking for rats."

She rose and tucked the glove in her apron pocket. "Perhaps Longbourn will know something about this. We should go to him now."

The last bit of the trek up the hill left her winded and pausing to lean against the old, arching hardwoods. Rumblkins' errand had added nearly two miles to her walk, so it was only natural she should be tired, but perhaps she was not quite as fully recovered as she had thought. Rumblkins hopped ahead into the darkness at the side of the hill. Best she wait outside the lair. Rumblings and thumpings followed.

She forced herself closer instead of running away as any sensible creature might do. The only way to manage her fear was to face it head-on. Then it would subside, or at least that is what Uther Pendragon said

Netherfield: Rogue Dragon

about dealing with dragons: the first rational fear subsided when one dealt with them frequently enough.

Elizabeth brushed a few leaves from her skirt.

Longbourn poked his head out of the lair and fixed his eyes on her. "You came."

"Of course, I did. I told you I would be here." Affecting a light, casual tone was far more difficult than it should have been.

"Why did you not come to the cellar? I was making it easy for you. You have been sick."

"Where did you get that information?"

He screwed his lips up in a funny, thinking sort of expression. "The puck with the furry hoppers."

"You mean Talia?"

"There is no estate dragon there. Sometimes the little ones come to me." He turned his face aside but stepped toward her.

He could hide his guilt no better than Samuel Gardiner. "You had her spying on me."

"Not spying. She wanted Rustle and Cait to stay away from her hoppers."

"So she gave you information about me in exchange." It really was rather clever on Talia's part.

"It was not spying." He nudged a large rock toward her. "Sit, you are not well."

"Thank you. I do feel a bit peaked." Gracious! How welcome it was to sit!

"Why did you walk all this way if you are not well?"

"I do not think it is safe for me—or for Darcy—to see you in the cellar any longer."

He pulled back and rose to full height. "Why not?"

She stood and lifted her hands. "You must not get angry with me."

"But I do not like what you are saying. That makes

me angry."

"I can see that, but that is the problem." Her vision blurred, and her nose burned.

There it was, a drop of venom, hanging from his left fang. She rubbed her sleeve across her face.

"What problem?" The tip of his tail thumped the ground.

"When you become angry, your fangs drip venom. I am very sensitive to it now. I can feel it—my eyes, my chest burn, it becomes difficult to take a breath. My skin is hot and prickly. In the close space of the cellar, it made the air bad and made me and Darcy very ill."

A growl formed in the back of his throat. "I have not tried to poison you."

"I am not accusing you. Nor is Mr. Darcy. But see, even now, there is poison on your fangs."

Longbourn touched a wingtip to his mouth and examined the ochre drop. "It is only a little."

"I know that. But it is enough. I am sure Talia can offer you further details of what happened while I was at Netherfield."

His shoulders hunched, and his face scrunched into a pout. Apparently he had already heard.

She returned to her makeshift seat. "I am just glad I am still able to sit with you here. But if you become angry, I will have to leave, lest the vapors in the air make me ill again."

"I do not want you ill."

"Then control your temper. I see no other way." She shrugged and blotted watery eyes with her apron.

He sat down hard near her rock and stared at her. "I do not like this."

"Nor do I. But I am willing to try. Are you?"

His long tail swept across the ground, clearing a

Netherfield: Rogue Dragon

semicircular path behind him as he lowered his head toward her. "I will try."

She scratched his ears. His foot drummed appreciatively as she hit just the right spot. He arched his back and directed her to half a dozen more spots that desperately needed to be scratched.

Finally, he sighed and flopped down at her feet, ecstatically exhausted by the indulgence. Clearly, Mary needed some pointers in how to scratch a dragon properly. Perhaps a full monograph needed to be written on the matter. Papa would be scandalized at the thought.

"Now you are sated, I hope you will be willing to talk of some more serious matters with me."

He leaned his head against her legs.

She steeled herself for the contact. The ill-ease was still there. Pendragon did not say how long it would remain. Perhaps that was so as not to discourage those willing to try.

"Fitzwilliam came with news from the Blue Order. An emissary, sent from the Eastern Dragons, makes her way to London to open diplomatic relations with the dragons from the Far East."

"Why do I care what they do in London?"

"The emissary has become lost. The dragon tunnels have not been mapped as accurately as we had thought."

His ears stood up.

"It is possible she could appear in Hertfordshire, lost, confused and hungry."

"I will not—"

"That is exactly what I am asking of you. Tolerance. Pray be reasonable and think what could come of your actions. You do not need to have her stay here, simply promise me that you will not attack her for encroaching on your territory. Tolerate her if she has to eat and alert us to her presence. Fitzwilliam will see her to London immediately, and she will never trespass again. The Order will be very grateful for your assistance."

"Grateful enough to—" He nudged her gently.

"No, you know Mary is your Keeper now and Collins is her husband. There is no changing that. But it is never a bad thing to have the Order's appreciation."

He snorted hard enough to blow up a little cloud of dust at her feet.

"Have I your promise?"

He muttered and grumbled and scratched the ground with a wingtip. "Will I have mutton if I do?"

"Absolutely. I will arrange for you to have half a dozen sheep if you find the emissary and unite us with her."

"Six fat ones?"

"The fattest ones I can find."

"I will keep watch for her." He tried to sound uninterested, but the promise of mutton was invariably a cause to celebrate.

"What do you know of the rogue dragon? He has been in the Netherfield cellars—we have exchanged a few written words there. I am certain you must know him."

Longbourn inched away and rumbled something noncommittal.

"Why have you not fought him for being in your territory? I am sure he has trespassed at some time. He must have been near to try and persuade me to marry Collins. He might have been persuading Mary's ill-temper, too. Why do you think he would do such a thing?" She bit her lip to avoid adding '*And why do you tolerate it.'*

Half his tail thumped behind them. "Bored."

"The lindwurm is bored?"

"And stupid."

"In what way?"

"He stole the egg."

She nearly fell off her seat. "Pray excuse me? Did you say he stole the egg?" She held her breath. Much as she had a thousand questions fighting to be asked, now was not the time to risk pushing too hard. She would be patient even if it meant her heart would beat out of her chest.

"After the Deaf One brought it to Meryton, he stole it. He wanted to give me the egg instead of salt."

"Salt? You like salt? Papa never told me." She clutched the edge of her stone seat. One more revelation of this caliber, and she would indeed fall off.

"He says the estate cannot afford it. I must stock my hoard another way."

"I did not know wyverns were hoarding dragons."

"Some of us are, not all, but some." Longbourn grumbled under his breath.

No wonder Longbourn was constantly grumpy. A hoard-hungry dragon was nearly as dangerous as one who lacked food. Gracious, if this was true, then Longbourn's forbearance was extreme.

"He calls himself Netherfield."

"Netherfield gives you salt? Why?"

"So I will ignore him. I have my hoard; he lives in peace."

"You agreed to take the egg to be rid of Darcy?"

He snorted and covered one eye with his wingtip. "Stupid creature did not tell me it was ready to hatch. He was to give it to me while you were at Netherfield, but it hatched in the woods. He decided to eat the drakling to make the whole affair go away. I had to stop him."

She slid to the ground and looked him in the eye. "You were in the woods protecting little Pemberley from the lindwurm?"

"Netherfield was no real danger. He was not actually hungry, only trying to protect himself. Stupid, addlebrained thing to do. He hates conflict and hoped to avoid it by eating her."

"You saved her!" She threw her arms around his head and wept into his scaly hide. "I had no idea. I am sorry I did not think you so noble. No wonder you have been so put out. I have horribly underestimated you."

He stretched out one wing around her shoulders in a tentative embrace.

"I will tell Darcy and Pemberley what you have done. They deserve to know." While none of that excused the fits of temper he had shown, at least it made more sense now. Mary, Cait, they had been right. She had wronged him terribly—what a prideful fool she had been.

"I still do not like them."

"I am not asking you to like them. But I would like them to think better of you."

He grumbled and snorted, but she could feel the corners of his mouth turn up just a bit.

"Do you know where Netherfield is? Why did he choose that name?"

"He is French. He knows nothing. He thinks by taking the name he claims the land. Says the estate was given to him or some such nonsense. What can he know of such things? They have no Accords on the continent."

Elizabeth squeezed her eyes shut and forced herself to breathe. Perhaps this really was more information than she could assimilate at once. "Do you know where we can find him?"

"He is supposed to stay on Netherfield Park. We meet once in every moon cycle when he has salt for me. He puts out a bit of salt for me to smell, and I meet him at the stream that borders the two territories. But sometimes he leaves it in the cellar at Longbourn. He is foolish and capricious."

Those were no doubt the times he was amusing himself by persuading Bennets. Clearly he was bored and seeking entertainment. Was he stupid though? No, bribing Longbourn with his hoard showed a certain level of devious—or mischievous, it was difficult to tell—intelligence. "Pray you will tell me when that next happens? It is critical we meet him and invite him to the Order so all may be peaceful and proper once again." Perhaps that was overstating things just a bit. Life with dragons was almost never peaceful and proper. "Does Papa know about any of this?"

"He suspects, but Netherfield does not want to be known. Dragons in France are killed. Men are not to be trusted."

Who could blame him for feeling that way? "Have you told him we are different?"

"He does not believe it."

She squeezed her eyes shut and clutched her forehead. Of course not. Who would, knowing Darcy had carried a Dragon Slayer?

"Has Lydia tried to talk to him?"

"Lydia?"

"I thought she might be starting to hear. Have you

seen her?"

"She has never talked to me. Scratch my back now?"

She leaned over his shoulder full length and scratched between his wings until he all but purred. The dear creature would have a sheep tonight as well. With a way to meet with Netherfield and an ally to communicate with him, perhaps now they stood a solid chance of bringing this whole affair to a happy conclusion.

Chapter 7

WALKER SWOOPED INTO the study, nearly overturning the dragon perch as he struggled to land. Darcy leapt off the library ladder and ran toward him, jumping a stack of books as he went. "What happened?"

"The rogue dragon?" Fitzwilliam tossed a large volume on the desk and met them at the perch.

"Elizabeth!" Walker squawked and flapped. "She went to Longbourn's lair to talk to him and is collapsed on the ground, insensible."

"What has the brute done?" Darcy barely held back from punching the nearest chair.

"Nothing—and Rumblkins confirms." Walker settled his wings across his back but sidled from one edge of the perch to the other. "The tatzelwurm says their discussion was entirely amicable."

Darcy bounced his fist off his chin. "Perhaps she thought being in open air would be safer than the cellars."

"What are you talking about?" Bennet set his book aside and struggled to stand, face wrenched in painful knots.

"It seems she is—we are—highly sensitive to wyvern venom now. Talking with him in the cellar after Cait's crisis left us both unwell. Just being in his presence, even in the open air, might have been enough to sicken her."

"Why was I not told?" Bennet hobbled two steps toward them and grabbed a chair for support.

'Because you would have been no help at all' was definitely not the correct way to answer that question.

"Tell Longbourn we are on our way." Fitzwilliam jerked his head toward the door.

"Bring her here. I will have Hill ready her room."

"No, we will take her to Netherfield. We do not need Collins meddling in this affair."

"I can manage Collins. Even now he is off with Cait, going over the rudiments of dragon introductions. He will not be a problem. You know there is poison there—" Bennet gesticulated a little wildly.

How had Darcy failed to notice how gnarled his hands were? Could he even hold a pen any longer or manage a fork to eat?

"It is confined to the map rooms. She has been at Netherfield for some time now with no issues. The venom in the cellar here could easily contaminate the rest of the house. If you want to help her, we need a preparation of the anti-venom tincture your distant relation wrote about in that journal." Darcy pointed to the maroon cloth-bound volume, balanced askew against the leg of a small table.

"We have no idea if it was even effective. Just a few scrawled notes between butcher's orders and seed

Netherfield: Rogue Dragon

purchases! You would trust her life to that?"

Darcy stomped across the room and snatched up the journal. "Did Elizabeth not say it aligned with Lady Astrid's monographs and several other obscure references?"

"That is not the same thing as knowing—she is forever leaping to conclusions and jumping headlong into things!" Bennet tossed his head and pressed his arms to his belly.

"She is nearly always correct," Fitzwilliam muttered to the floor.

"She is simply lucky. I will not encourage that—"

"I will prepare it."

All eyes snapped to the doorway. When had the door opened? Had she been listening all this time?

Mary leaned against the doorframe, a little pale. "She went to see Longbourn because I told her he wanted to talk to her. You are right. She avoided the cellar but thought being out of doors would be safe. I pushed her to go …"

Enough dithering and discussion. "We will bring her to Netherfield. Come when you have the tincture prepared." Darcy pushed past her, Fitzwilliam in his wake.

Walker flew ahead as they wound their way through the woods to Longbourn's lair.

Darcy gritted his teeth and forced his fingers out of fists. Remember, the dragon did not intend her harm. The disagreeable wyvern had been such a problem that it was difficult not to consider him the villain. But that would serve nothing. They broke into the clearing before the lair, Elizabeth a puddle of muslin on the rocky ground.

"She was scratching between my wings and

collapsed!" Longbourn whimpered, prostrate and nudging her with his nose.

Darcy dropped down beside her. She gasped in tortured pants, her face pale, eyes fluttering.

"Not his fault," she muttered. "On his skin."

"Get her away from here," Fitzwilliam ordered.

"No! First wash the poison away!" Walker flapped his wings in Longbourn's face.

He popped up and sat on his haunches, nosing Fitzwilliam. "I have water. Come." They loped into the cavern.

Darcy propped her up in his lap. She seemed to breathe a little easier.

"I tried to help, but she has no wounds to lick." Rumblkins pressed in close beside him, resting his paws on her leg and trying to force his head under her hand.

He stroked the tatzelwurm's fluffy head. "I am sure you did. You are a faithful friend."

Fitzwilliam staggered back toward them, a large bucket sloshing in his hands. "There is a spring in the lair."

Darcy pulled out a handkerchief, soaked it, and scrubbed her face.

"Get her apron off! If the poison was on his skin, it is surely covered in it." Fitzwilliam pulled at the ties and cast it aside.

Although it seemed like hours, it was probably only a few minutes later. Color seeped back into her face. She scratched under Rumblkins' chin and sat up on her own.

"I will fetch a horse to bring her to the house." Fitzwilliam ran off.

The man could not bear to sit still. He was exactly

the sort of friend one wanted in a crisis.

"I did not breathe venom!" Longbourn called from the mouth of his cavern.

Elizabeth lifted her head as though it was suddenly very heavy and caught the wyvern's gaze. "No one is blaming you. It seems there is enough venom on your skin to affect me."

"You cannot be near me now?" Longbourn's eyes bulged, a note of panic in his voice.

"I ... I do not know."

Longbourn turned in a circle, tail thumping as he went. "What if I bathe? Will that be enough?"

"I ... when I am stronger, we can try."

"No, you do not need to risk yourself," Darcy whispered close to her ear.

"You will not stop me." She glared venom of her own, and he pulled away. "But you may come with me."

"We need to get you back to Netherfield for a proper hot bath. Mary is preparing the anti-venom tincture from the receipt you found. Perhaps that will help you."

"Make sure she brings Heather. We will need her help with Nicholls."

"We will manage all that, but first we need to get you back. Fitzwilliam returns. Can you sit in a saddle?" He helped her to her feet, but she sagged against his chest for support.

"Or die trying," she murmured.

"That is hardly funny."

"You think I was joking?" Only the pleasing little quirk of her brow, which declared her in better health than she looked, kept him from scolding her.

Though weak and shaky and requiring several

attempts, she was indeed able to mount and remain in the saddle well enough for Fitzwilliam to lead the horse back to Netherfield while Darcy struggled to assure Longbourn she would be well. Stubborn creature only settled down when Walker promised to bring frequent word of Elizabeth's condition. Frustrating, but endearing in an odd sort of way.

Even with several hot baths, Elizabeth did not venture from her rooms for four days. Four long, excruciating days during which Darcy could hardly think or function. He pretended to study the books she had laid out for him and the paintings in the house, but nothing stayed in his mind for longer than a few minutes, except worry. Nicholls became so tired of his constant inquiries after Elizabeth that she took to avoiding him. Maddening though it was, he could scarcely blame her. But really, what else was there for a man to do?

On the fifth day, Mary arrived with the tincture, Heather riding on her bonnet which appeared specially trimmed to accommodate the fluffy pink fairy dragon. Darcy took her to Elizabeth's rooms himself.

Voices in the hall approached. Elizabeth pushed herself up from the soft chair by the window where she had been pretending to read. There was no time to waste, but neither her mind nor her eyes seemed to be able to focus for more than a few moments at a time. Why was it taking so long to recover? Worse still, what might happen the next time?

Darcy's sharp knock resonated from the door. How

many conversations, some rather insensible, had they had through that door in recent days? He had even dispatched Walker several times a day to reassure Longbourn of her recovery. Could any man have been more solicitous of her under the circumstances?

The door creaked open. "Oh, Lizzy! We have all been so worried about you!" Mary rushed toward her with open arms.

Elizabeth clutched at the bed post to brace for the contact.

How much her attitude had changed! Was it just sisterly concern, the fact Elizabeth had apologized to Longbourn, or had Netherfield stopped persuading her? Something about the strength of her hold and the high notes in her voice suggested it was a bit of all three.

"I am much improved, thank you, though I seem to be lacking some of my usual energy." Elizabeth fell heavily on the edge of the bed, struggling to hide her lack of breath.

"I am hopeful this will help." Mary pulled a small brown bottle out of her reticule and handed it to Elizabeth. "I tried to follow the receipt in the journal, but there was a mistake in it. That is why it took me so long to finish. The receipt recommended white wine as a base, but it simply would not come together. Finally, I tried sweet oil, and it seems to have worked, but I cannot be sure. The directions say it should be added to hot water to create a steam. I am a bit unclear whether you are to breathe it, or the text seems to suggest perhaps bathing in it? The handwriting was so unclear and the ink so smudged, I could not tell." The words tumbled out in a single breath as though if she did not say them all at once, the opportunity to say them at all might well disappear.

Lydia had taught her that habit.

Elizabeth uncorked the bottle and wafted the scent toward herself. Pungent was the most pleasant word to describe the concoction. She extended her arm, holding it as far away as she could, blinking hard, but a bit of the tightness in her lungs eased. "Let me first try breathing it. There is already hot water on the hob. I will fetch a towel, and we can make a bit of a tent."

Mary brought the washbasin and a small table near the bed and added boiling water and the oil to the basin. Elizabeth leaned over it, head and shoulders covered with the towel to tent in the vapors. She breathed deeply, but choked on the stultifying antidote.

"I am sorry it smells so. I thought I might try adding dried lavender or roses to make it more bearable, but I did not dare for fear it would somehow change the properties." From below the edge of the towel, she could make out Mary wringing her apron.

The sharp fumes burned her eyes until they watered profusely. The steam tore at her throat, but in a cleansing sort of way. "I think that was wise. It is not so bad, really, when one gets used to it. More importantly, I think it is helping."

"Longbourn will be very relieved." Mary sat heavily beside her. "I swear he would have been here himself without Walker's constant reports."

"He is quite dear. How put out is Papa?" Elizabeth peeked out from the towel.

Mary sighed. "It is hard to tell. He mutters a great deal about things I cannot quite make out. I did not tell him about experimenting with the tincture lest he forbid me from bringing it at all."

Elizabeth laid the towel over the basin and pressed

the back of her hands to her cheeks. "The skin on my face and neck feels much better. I am certain I scrubbed them nearly raw after all the hot baths I have taken, but something feels different now, rather like a prickly scarf has been removed."

Mary drew close and examined her carefully, holding Elizabeth's hands near her face. "See where your hands are still rough and raw, but your face is not?"

"Gracious, yes!" Elizabeth tented the towel over her hands and held them over the basin. "Add a bit more hot water, if you please."

Half an hour later, they examined her hands again, the difference unmistakable. The red, dragon-scaly patches had faded, and her fingertips no longer felt like sandpaper.

"You were definitely right to use the sweet oil. This has worked very well. Do you remember well enough what you did that you might write it in my book before you leave?"

"You think it that significant?" Mary's jaw dropped as though she had been offered some great honor.

"Absolutely. Bathing helped, but it was nothing to this. What is more, I think we might be able to make the map room safe with this. It will be difficult, but perhaps with some sort of mask anointed with this mixture—"

Mary grabbed her arm, a little more tightly than necessary. "You are not thinking of trying to do that yourself, are you?"

A cry choked her throat, but she hid it in a laugh. "No, I dare not, but Fitzwilliam might be willing to try. If he built a fire in the room's fireplace, suspended a great pot of water and this oil over it, and let the steam permeate the room—maybe we need to pull the maps and such near the fire, too—but I think it might render them safe. We desperately need those maps right now."

"Do you think there is enough to accomplish the task?" Mary held up the bottle in the sunlight. There was not very much left.

"How long would it take you to make more?"

"Now that I have worked it out? Two, three days at the most."

"Pray then, write me the receipt, then go and make more, perhaps twice, no three times as much, if you can." Elizabeth rubbed her temples hard. Hopefully the headache would not come on full force this time.

"What shall I tell Papa?"

"Nothing until you have told Longbourn of the results. I am sure he will be pleased. You might suggest to him the wisdom in making more. I am certain he will agree, and if Longbourn desires it, Papa can hardly argue."

"Papa is quite adamant that Longbourn must be appeased." Mary stroked her chin and chewed her cheek, contemplating. "I will bring it as soon as it is ready."

Darcy held his breath as Elizabeth made her slow, deliberate trek down the grand stairs. Though she wore only a simple shawl and gown, she was easily one of the most beautiful sights he had ever seen. Running up the stairs to meet her would have been bad form and might have implied he did not think her strong enough to make it on her own. So, he slowly strode up, meeting her halfway—hopefully it appeared that way at least. But Fitzwilliam's snickers did not offer a great deal of hope for that.

She smiled at him and took his arm when he reached her. That was enough to endure any of Fitzwilliam's mocking. She leaned on him a little more heavily than she usually did, but the color had returned to her face and the sparkle to her eye. Though he would probably never stop worrying about her, at least for now, the anxiety could return to a manageable level.

With servants hovering about, dinnertime conversation was limited to the weather and everyone's health, and even that was constrained to matters that did not involve poisoning by dragons. How odd the life of Dragon Keepers was to think those were normal topics. There were definite advantages to insisting all the upper and senior servants were members of the Blue Order.

At last they withdrew to the parlor and could close the door behind them. Was privacy a palpable quality? It certainly felt like it.

She barely sat down near the fire before the details of her astonishing conversation with Longbourn gushed forth.

Darcy leaned forward, elbows on his knees, trying not to let his jaw hang open too much. "You mean to tell me we owe Pemberley's life directly to Longbourn's interventions?"

"It appears so." She bit her upper lip, eyebrows lifting like a shrug. "His story explains a great deal of what happened that night—I have no reason to disbelieve it."

Fitzwilliam squeezed his fist, popping his knuckles loudly. "Forgive me, but I am more concerned that this lindwurm—"

"Netherfield." Something about the way she said the name suggested she had already developed sympathy for the creature.

"Whatever he wants to call himself. I am concerned that this creature would prove such a danger to another major dragon, even if she was only newly-hatched. Clearly he does not have peaceable intentions." Fitzwilliam shot Darcy a knowing look.

Pray Elizabeth did not notice it.

She squared her shoulders and rested her hands lightly in her lap. "I beg to disagree. If he is trying to claim the Netherfield territory, her presence would be a trespass. With no idea of whom she was, her rank, or anything else about her—"

"She is a firedrake! All dragons know the rank of a firedrake!" Fitzwilliam waved his right hand for emphasis, not that he really needed to; his volume alone made his feelings quite clear.

"English dragons do. But can you identify the rank of an Eastern Dragon on sight alone?"

Fitzwilliam stammered.

"I thought not. I will give you a hint. It is in the number of their toes. You might want to remember that when we find the envoy."

"What has that to do with any of this?"

"Can you not see? The lindwurm's failure to properly act upon her rank does not necessarily mean he was prepared to engage in an act of war any more than your failure to identify an Eastern Dragon's rank would. Mind you, I am not justifying it, but it is the way that dragons seem to think."

Darcy narrowed his eyes toward Fitzwilliam. "In any case, I will arrange for Pemberley to send Longbourn a gift of salt to demonstrate our gratitude."

"That would do a great deal in raising his esteem of you both."

Fitzwilliam leaned back in his chair, exasperation clear in his posture. "I am astonished at your father's behavior on so many counts."

"Not providing for a dragon's hoard seems unconscionable." And dangerous—but best not add that just now.

Elizabeth harrumphed as her lips wrinkled into a thoughtful frown. "Strict interpretation of the Accords does permit it in the case of impoverishment or for excessively expensive hoards. But one can hardly call Papa impoverished. Mama has placed many demands on him, to be sure. She expected a certain style of life upon marrying him and placing limits on that has been difficult. But still, it would have behooved Papa to make greater efforts to fulfil Longbourn's hoard-hunger."

"It does explain Longbourn's temperament. Hoard-starvation does make them … ah … cranky." Darcy said the word carefully lest she consider it an insult to her dragon.

"It would certainly give him reason to believe he was entitled to demand me as his Keeper."

"I am astonished you would excuse his behavior so easily." Fitzwilliam folded his arms over his chest as his command tone crept into his voice.

"I am not excusing him." Elizabeth huffed and rolled her eyes, looking a bit like a dragon herself. "Why are you so insistent upon confusing understanding with approval? They are hardly one and the same. Longbourn was childish, petulant, and throwing tantrums. I do not approve of any of those behaviors and have the intention of teaching Pemberley otherwise."

Fitzwilliam snickered. "You will teach a firedrake?"

Darcy winced. If Fitzwilliam did not desist, he was

going to discover another draconic temper very soon.

She planted her foot firmly. "I most certainly will. Babies can be instructed and so shall she be. Already she has very fine tutors in Lady Astrid and Barnwines Chudleigh and her associates."

Fitzwilliam laughed into his hands, so hard he might stop breathing. "You sound like a mother of the *ton* ensuring her daughter has all the correct accomplishments and connections for her eventual come out."

Fitzwilliam was an idiot.

Elizabeth slowly stood. Darcy leaned back—hopefully she would not notice him there. "So good of you to notice. That is precisely what I am trying to do since neither of you seem to understand the critical importance of the process." She took two long steps toward Fitzwilliam and towered over his seated form. "Pemberley will live five hundred years! Five hundred. What kind of influence will she have in that time? With her rank, it will be tremendous. At least five, maybe as many as ten generations at Pemberley will be her Keepers. What more worthwhile effort is there than shaping the kind of dragon they will Keep?" Her fists trembled at her sides.

Fitzwilliam raised his hands, a small gesture of surrender. "Forgive me. With so few dragons of her rank hatched, it is not something one thinks about regularly."

"Perhaps not, but it behooves one to do so. That means understanding how dragons think—which is not at all the way men think—and adapting ourselves to it. That is the advantage we have over dragons: we are nimble and able to adapt and adjust in ways they cannot. Their opinions are formed early in their lives, and they do not change. It rests on men to exercise forbearance and creativity to finds ways to make it all work. That is what brought about the Pendragon Treaty in the first place."

"You have an excellent point." Darcy sneaked a glance at Fitzwilliam.

Fitzwilliam slapped his fist into his palm. "Understanding alone does not excuse dangerous behavior. There have to be consequences—"

"Of course, but they should be tempered with comprehension. One cannot punish a hoarding dragon because they crave their hoard any more than one can punish a hungry man for craving food. Neither will ever change. But one can teach them to acquire their hoard in acceptable ways, or in some cases, even accept a different item to hoard, like Talia with her rabbits. When her Friend died, she did not take to stealing as many pucks do. She found an acceptable substitute. If she can, then others can as well. Understanding their drives and what is possible for them must shape the consequences we invoke. That is the only way we will be able to live in cooperation with dragonkind."

It was not difficult to imagine her standing before the officers of the Blue Order making the same sort of speech.

She and Fitzwilliam glowered at each other until it seemed they would suck all the air from the room.

Fitzwilliam drew breath to speak again, but Darcy cut in, "So it appears that the tincture Mary prepared was as effective as we hoped?"

She did not turn her attention to him, but her posture and expression changed to something grateful. She returned to her seat in a flowing, elegant motion that relinquished none of her power. "The initial receipt was not correct, and she had to make adjustments, but yes, she was able to settle upon a formulation that did work. I believe we can also use it to decontaminate the map room and the maps as well."

Fitzwilliam's entire countenance transformed from combative to fully attentive. "Tell me more."

She quickly explained what she and her sister had devised.

"A mask of some sort soaked in the stuff might work." Fitzwilliam rubbed his chin. "Instead of steaming the contaminated chamber, what do you think of setting up the room next door to be filled with the steam? We could bring the maps there to expose them to the steam, perhaps even wipe them down with rags damped with the mixture?"

"Will that not damage the ink?"

"We could test it on a letter or a painting first."

"If it does not damage them, then it seems a reasonable plan." Elizabeth glanced at Darcy. "Should it not be done by someone not already sensitized to the venom? It appears the risk to both of us is very great."

"She is right, Darcy. Let me do this. At least I will feel somehow useful in this affair." Fitzwilliam stared into the fireplace, rubbing his knuckles over his lips. He had probably not intended to be so open around Elizabeth. But then, it was difficult not to be.

"It is difficult to feel like the only one not associated with a dragon, I imagine." Elizabeth's voice was soft and gentle. "Mary often felt that way before Heather's hatching."

Fitzwilliam grunted, but did not—or perhaps could not—reply.

"Cait's egg will hatch soon. She named you as her Friend of choice for the chick. I am certain that he will find you acceptable and—many things change once one becomes a Dragon Friend."

Fitzwilliam sighed. "I am not sure it is such a good idea. I am not the sort—"

"That will be the dragon's decision, not yours. Just because you are present at the hatching does not mean that the baby will choose you as his Friend. It does help if he takes his first meal from your hand, but it does not guarantee anything. Some will choose not to take a Friend without any rhyme nor reason. April nearly did that after her hatching. She did not like any of the possible Friends presented to her."

Fitzwilliam cocked his head nearly sideways and lifted an eyebrow. He was not often surprised. "You were not among the choices?"

"No, I was merely there to assist my father. But she found me sympathetic when I understood she hated blood sausage as much as I. I suggested a dish of honey instead. At that point, she decided I would do for her, and my father would just have to live with it—and he was not particularly happy with that."

Fitzwilliam snickered. "It is not difficult to picture her saying just that whilst diving for his ears."

"You must be there for the hatching—you would not want to risk insulting Cait and Walker by shunning the event. If he is as perverse a creature as his mother, he could very well choose Papa or Mary as his Friend, just to make their lives even more challenging."

Darcy chuckled. "I do not see your father as the type a cockatrice would favor."

"Nor do I, but dragons see the world differently to us. They are never entirely predictable. You will forgive me, though. I am exhausted." She rose and headed toward the door. "I will see you in the morning."

The door clicked shut behind her.

Fitzwilliam made for the cabinet where Bingley kept his brandy and poured two glasses. "I cannot believe Bennet's Dragon Keeping! He deprives the creature of its hoard so his wife can indulge in fripperies! Worse yet, how could he be aware of the rogue and not say anything to the Order?"

Darcy sipped the brandy. Fruity with oak notes and a bit of spice. Not quite to his taste, but good enough. "I can only imagine he wanted the notoriety of making first contact and even negotiating peace with the creature."

Fitzwilliam dragged a footstool near his chair and sat heavily. "That is one possibility. Another is that he is very much like his daughter and has too much sympathy toward the creature. He may be willing to take some very stupid risks to try to negotiate with it."

"The creature sounds—well, almost like a pacifist, if you think about it. He has never shown any proclivity toward fighting for his territory, only for bribing Longbourn for it." Darcy swirled the brandy in his glass.

Fitzwilliam propped his feet up and leaned back. "That does not make him a pacifist, only lazy. As long as bribing is easy, any sensible creature would do it. But consider where is he getting the salt? Think on it. Unless he has some secret place to mine it, then he must be stealing it, and that mostly likely means smugglers."

"We already found evidence of smuggling whilst searching for the egg."

Fitzwilliam took a deep swallow. "Precisely. Such men will not take losses of their merchandise kindly. Nothing calamitous may have happened yet, but this is a disaster in the making. Sooner or later, the smugglers and the dragon will encounter one another and the result will not be pretty. Blood will be shed, and there will be death. No matter whose blood and whose death, it will escalate and eventually result in war. There can be no other outcome."

Darcy leaned forward on his elbows. "But if we should make contact—"

"You have—did you forget the scribbling on the cellar floor? It has made no difference. The creature has plenty of evidence that Elizabeth is no danger and even a great ally, but still nothing. I am sorry. The Blue Order's ambassador has failed. It is now time for their warrior to manage the situation."

"How are you going to find the creature?"

"As soon as the potion is ready, we will neutralize the poison on the maps. Hopefully that will give us means to locate the lindwurm's lair. If not, I shall start searching the tunnels myself."

"Do not be foolish, Fitz. You cannot kill a lindwurm by yourself, in its own terrain."

"You would be surprised what can be accomplished when necessary." Something about the look in Fitzwilliam's eye pushed Darcy back a mite.

"You have not …"

"No, not I, but in France, once we found ourselves imperiled by one allied to Napoleon. We had a man—one of the Order—who took it upon himself to deliver us from the danger."

"Did he survive?"

"Long enough to allow us to make a record of his tactics. I have been studying them. They are replicable here."

"With the same outcome?"

Fitzwilliam downed the remainder of his glass in a single large gulp. "If that should be the way, it is not entirely a bad thing. With a death on each side—Blue

Order and dragon—the score is even, and war can more easily be averted."

"So you are to sacrifice yourself?"

"Those are not my orders, and no one has expressed a desire for that to be the endgame. But if it is to be so, then it is pleasing to know my demise might serve the cause."

"How can you be so callous about your own mortality?"

"It is a soldier's way. It is a way one survives." Fitzwilliam shrugged. "Elizabeth cannot know any of this. She is far too sympathetic to the dragons to see the situation as it actually is."

"If the dragon is slain, you think she will not find out how?"

"No doubt, she will. If I survive the encounter, I recognize I will be dead to her ever after. I regret that, but it cannot be helped."

"I am still not convinced a diplomatic solution cannot be obtained."

"I once shared that optimism only to see half the negotiation team eaten by a major drake on a French field."

Darcy suppressed a shudder with another mouthful of brandy. "What happened?"

"The entire event is classified. I should not have even mentioned it to you. If word were to get out about it, the Order fears that it would undermine trust in the Pendragon Treaty—not all truly understand it only applies here, not on the continent. What I can say is that without the Treaty to restrict their behavior, French dragons are far and away more dangerous than you can understand. They are apt to turn on one the moment it is in their interest to do so. This rogue truly has the potential to destroy the entire fabric of English society as we know it."

"Dragon's blood! I had no idea they could be so wholly different to our dragons."

"Elizabeth may understand English dragons—and I have no doubt that she does, perhaps better than any other person, living or dead. On that matter, I completely yield to her expertise. But she has no experience, no means, by which to understand what we are facing. It falls upon you to protect her from herself right now."

Two days later, Darcy followed Fitzwilliam as they traipsed through the hall containing the mapmaker's study, trying to identify rooms that might suit for decontaminating the maps. An especially low ceiling in the room across the corridor made it stand out as a particular favorite. But before a decision could be made, Fitzwilliam insisted on testing its usefulness by filling it with fragrant lavender steam, harmless but noticeable enough that they would be able to tell whether the draughts in the room would carry it away too quickly.

Walker had the staff believing that particular wing of Netherfield was haunted and not in want of any cleaning or attention, so they stayed away from the otherwise too interesting flurry of activity. It took surprisingly little persuasion to convince even Nicholls to avoid the area entirely. Perhaps, Darcy and Elizabeth were not the only ones to feel the faint affects from traces of wyvern poison in the hallway air.

When Darcy complained of a headache, Fitzwilliam dismissed him to find Elizabeth and take a walk outside before the effects became too pronounced. He rarely took on such a commanding tone—was that the persona he adopted for His Majesty's army, or was that the person he had always been, but somehow Darcy had never seen?

Elizabeth had resigned herself to studying lindwurm texts while they worked and warmly welcomed the notion of a walk when he found her in the morning room.

A steady breeze blew through the sunshine, each gust taking with it a little of the malaise weighing on his shoulders. Elizabeth's posture suggested she experienced the same. Yes, a walk had been a very good idea.

Talia peeked out of the rabbit hole to greet them, happy that Elizabeth had returned to offering a daily plate of vegetable trimmings. What an amusing little creature she was, wholly different to Quincy in so many ways and yet so like him in others. Perhaps it might be good to invite a puck to live at Pemberley. Pemberley would benefit from the acquaintance.

Talia rubbed up against Darcy's leg with a pleasant 'good morning' and offered to introduce her current favorite hopper. Elizabeth immediately accepted, laughing that she had never been introduced to a rabbit before. How easy she was among dragons of all shapes and sizes—English dragons. Even after all of Longbourn's transgressions, she was so ready to forgive him, make exceptions for his uniquely draconic motivations. Fitzwilliam had a point: her greatest strength could, in the current situation, also prove her greatest weakness.

After meeting Talia's hopper, they continued into the woods. Like most dragon woods, tall hardwoods arched up overhead, providing a dense canopy—or at least it would be dense later in the spring when all the leaves had filled out. For now, it was only dense enough to cast a dappled shade not a deep one. Rich, spongy loam hushed their steps, lending a soft stillness to the region. Some might consider it romantical, but it was the sort of ground that would muffle the sounds of slithering, too. Not the sort of thing that most lovers thought about while ambling with their beloved.

Perhaps not the sort of place they needed to be right now.

Elizabeth stopped at the broken-down folly and sat on the bench—in the middle as he had done not so very long ago. It was pleasing, very pleasing to think she wanted to be near him.

"I am worried about Fitzwilliam." She leaned her head softly against his shoulder. "He has not seemed like himself since he arrived."

"He is often like that after visiting with his father." Why did Elizabeth have to be nearly as observant with people as she was with dragons?

"Lord Matlock is rather intimidating, I grant you. I would certainly rather not meet with him. But still, Fitzwilliam seems—disconnected, perhaps?"

Darcy shrugged. Pray she did not ask him a direct question he dared not answer.

She turned her face upward, toward a pale blue sky, currently devoid of flying creatures. "With April ... away ... I think I understand him a bit better than I have before. He is surrounded by Dragon Mates on all sides, both in his family and among the Order. He hears but has no Friend of his own. Think about how many individuals highly placed in the Order are in that situation—practically none. It must be incredibly isolating and lonely. I am sure it makes him question his own suitability. No wonder he was so ambivalent about befriending Cait's egg."

"I suppose." That much was entirely true. Pray he could continue to avoid any falsehood with her.

"I am certain of it. He will be better after the hatching. I have often seen that chicks, particularly those of the same sex, take after their parents. Walker is fond of you. Fitzwilliam shares many of your qualities. Walker's chick should find him agreeable."

"You make this all sound so very simple."

"It really is not that diffi—"

Two familiar forest wyrms poked their shaggy heads out of the deadfall near their feet, their yellow eyes wide and agitated.

Elizabeth fell to her knees near the wyrms. "What is wrong? Has someone threatened you? Come close. You are safe with us."

"No, no! It is not safe here, not anymore!" The little female wove in circles around them, looking to and fro for something fearsome.

The male rose very high on his tail and looked Elizabeth in the eye. "We are all in the gravest of peril!"

"We must flee! The blue one ... he says we must all be on guard for our lives!"

Darcy sprang to his feet, casting about. "Where is he? Has the lindwurm threatened you?"

"No, no!" The female hid behind Elizabeth's skirts.

"Not him. He is our friend now! He has promised protection."

Elizabeth carefully placed a hand to either side of the male's face, encouraging him to focus solely on her. "Protection from what? Is there a new dragon in the vicinity? Has a strange dragon—perhaps of a kind you have never seen before—appeared in the territory?"

By Jove! The last thing they needed was the Eastern

Netherfield: Rogue Dragon

Dragon envoy suddenly arriving among them.

"No, not a dragon!" The male hissed, tongue flicking as he wove back and forth, rather like an Indian cobra. His mane, matted with leaves and forest debris, stood out, resembling a snake's hood.

Elizabeth leaned down and whispered with the barest of musical lilts, "What then?"

That had a calming effect on the wyrms.

"The danger is not a dragon." The female pressed into Elizabeth's skirt.

"Then what? Answer and you may have a beetle." She glanced at Darcy's coat pocket.

He withdrew the tin and held it in their sight. The object helped them focus.

"Now, tell us. What is the danger?" Elizabeth stroked the female's head.

The wyrm leaned into Elizabeth's hand, uttering contented sounds that were difficult to name. "A man. A man with a sword."

No! No! No! Stupid, stupid creatures! Why did they meddle in what they did not understand?

"What kind of sword?" Her words came in a breathy staccato.

"A Dragon Slayer!" A shudder coursed down the length of the male wyrm. "There is a Dragon Slayer. In the barn. We have seen it in the barn. There is no mistaking such a blade."

"There is a Dragon Slayer in the Netherfield barn." She stood and stared directly into Darcy's eyes, color draining from her face.

The male hissed and bared his fangs. Darcy edged back. "It is not in my possession. I do not carry such a weapon."

"The newcomer. It is his." The female quivered.

Elizabeth took the tin from Darcy's hand and placed a beetle on the ground for each wyrm. Somehow they seemed to set aside their agitation long enough to relish their duly-earned treat. But it came back on them as soon as they finished.

She folded her arms over her chest, her voice full of authority. "I promise you, on Longbourn's honor, no harm shall come to you because of that sword. It will not taste dragon blood, not so long as I am here."

The wyrms wound around her ankles, rubbing their cheeks against her petticoats. "You are friend."

She crouched to pet them both. "Indeed I am. You can trust me."

They circled her one more time, then disappeared as quickly as they had appeared.

Elizabeth stood, slowly, deliberately, catching his gaze as she stood. It was the same gaze Rosings used when she was not pleased. Pemberley would probably learn it from one of them as well. "Have you neglected to tell me something?"

"It was not oversight." He held her stare with a resolve of his own that seemed to set her back just a bit.

"Then it was deliberate deception." Icy venom dripped from her words.

"I have never lied to you, and I will never lie to you."

Her brows furrowed, shading her eyes. "Perhaps you and I differ on what constitutes deception. Deliberate omission of crucial information is something I consider deception."

"There has been nothing that occasioned bringing it up."

"Do not hide behind that sort of excuse." She stepped closer, slow and intentional, until her toes nearly touched his. "My father has played this sort of game with my mother all my life. Be assured, I have no desire to continue it in my own home."

"Fitzwilliam—"

"Clearly he is under instructions from the Blue Order—there is nowhere else to have obtained such a weapon. He asked you not to tell me."

That knowing look she wore! How could he make her understand?

"In fact, he did. What do you expect me to do? We are all required to abide by the Blue Order's commands." Darcy slipped back half a step.

"I am quite certain the Order did not explicitly state I was to be kept ignorant of its plans. Or are you suggesting it did?"

He stammered something far less informative than he hoped.

"I thought not." She tossed her head, not unlike the way she had in her first meeting with Cait. "I expect you to treat me like a rational creature and trust me as you claim you do."

"I do trust you. Do not pretend to know my mind for me." He rose up on his toes. Perhaps this was why dragons had the need to feel bigger when confronted.

"Apparently not enough."

"Do be reasonable! You are able to see things from dragon perspectives easily enough. Can you please try to do it for men as well?" He raked hair back out of his face. "You do recall what you did the last time the Order sent the sword into Hertfordshire."

"Just how do you remember those events?"

"You rushed out in the middle of the night to confront not one, but three dragons. One of whom was trying to eat another—"

"A wild-hatched firedrakling that no one was sure could be successfully imprinted. But she was!" Elizabeth bared her teeth, snarling the words.

"You endangered yourself—"

"For the sake of dragonkind! For your dragon!" Her fists shook at her sides "How easy it is for you to forget. I had very sound, experienced-based reasons for what I did."

"You had no experience with a firedrake."

"Now you sound like my father. Need I remind you of the outcome? Pemberley was saved, and you were delivered from a fate you dreaded like death itself. You were not complaining then."

But he was also not profoundly in love with her then, either. Was she not aware of that? "Yes, I realize that, too. But the outcome does not always justify the means."

"You would rather I had stayed behind at the ball and allowed you to carry out the will of the Blue Order without considering better alternatives?"

"Do you not think that perhaps you set a dangerous precedent, deciding which of the Blue Order mandates you will follow and which you will not?"

She winced and jumped a step back. No, she did not appreciate that challenge. "And mindless obedience to hidebound curmudgeons who willingly refuse a complete understanding of a situation is better?"

"You assume anyone that does not agree with you is refusing to see the entirety of the situation." Darcy threw up his hands and paced along the front edge of the folly.

"And you refuse to believe there can be an answer that lies outside the canon of dragon lore."

"That is entirely untrue, and you know it. It is you

who fail to acknowledge the true nature of the situation."

"What are you so certain I have overlooked?"

Darcy drew a deep breath, carefully moderating his tone. Perhaps she might listen this time. "French dragons are not governed by the Accords. Expecting them to behave as English dragons is not reasonable, no matter how much you wish it otherwise. Fitzwilliam has had dealings with them—of a variety we can hardly conceive of here. Believing this does not make me hidebound and narrow-minded."

She huffed and pumped her fists again. "The fact remains. You did not—would not—trust me with Fitzwilliam's true purpose."

"You have already resolved there can be a diplomatic result and will accept no other alternative. You did not exactly present yourself as open to hear other possibilities."

"You seem to see Fitzwilliam's way as a foregone conclusion. When did you give up on me?" The pained note in her voice ripped at his soul.

"It is an alternative that must be considered."

"And without me, it is a foregone conclusion. Can you not see that? Truly, will Fitzwilliam consider anything else? Forgive me, but who else will negotiate with Netherfield? You are hardly likely to strike up a casual conversation with him."

"You think so little of me as a Dragon Keeper? I thought I had earned your respect."

"By your own admission, you do not excel in those arts that allow you to make friends easily." Elizabeth stood very straight, her voice dropping to near a whisper. "Do not expect my help in luring him into a trap."

"I would never ask that of you."

"But Fitzwilliam might have. Keeping the knowledge of his purpose from me could readily have been part of trying to use me against my will."

"He is not the sort of man—"

"One who would encourage you to lie to me, to distrust me, is exactly the sort who would do such a thing."

A cockatrice screeched above them. Walker dove between them and landed on the bench. "The egg! Bennet says the time is very near. You must come."

"Pray inform Fitzwilliam. I will ready the curricle." Darcy reached his hand toward her. "Come with me, please."

Elizabeth stared at him. "No."

"But Cait—"

"Cait's welfare is not in jeopardy now. My father has attended more hatchings than any living Order member. His help will be far more useful than mine."

"Cait will want you there."

"I am weary of being pulled this way and that because some being more powerful than myself wants me to do so. I need time to gather my thoughts and clear my head. It seems I have a great deal of thinking to do. Things are not at all what I thought they were." She turned her back on him.

"Elizabeth, it is not as you think."

"Oh, I think it is exactly that. Excuse me."

He reached for her elbow, but she pulled it away and turned down the path that led back to the garden. Her shoulders hunched as she pulled her shawl tight across them. Never had she looked less like herself than she did now.

He took one step toward her, but no. There was no purpose to that now. She was certainly in no mind for conversation. Perhaps he would send Walker to her after the hatching. If she was going to listen to anyone right now, it would definitely be a dragon.

Chapter 8

FITZWILLIAM CLUNG TO the side of the curricle, wild-eyed and breathless. Probably with good reason. Bits of gravel and dust flew up behind them as Darcy took a corner a bit too sharply. He had never seen Darcy drive with such reckless abandon. No one had.

"I was given to think that we had time to arrive there a little more safely," Fitzwilliam shouted over the pounding hooves. "Where is Elizabeth?"

Darcy snapped the reins, urging the horses still faster. "She will not attend."

"She found out?"

"You might recommend to the army that wyrms make excellent spies, able to ferret out secrets and convey them to the very person to whom that information will be most relevant."

"Damnable creatures. All mouth and stomach and little brains." Fitzwilliam clutched his hat. "Do you want me to talk to her?"

"If you befriend the chick, you will be occupied for several days at least sating his hatching-hunger. It is possible she might be ready to talk by then. But she may never speak to you—or me—again."

"I am sorry—I did not mean for this to come between you and your betrothed."

If she still was that at this point. He had promised he would find a way out for her if she desired it. Now that the banns had been read, it would be incredibly difficult, maybe impossible. But he would not hold her to a marriage she detested. "The time for talk will come, but for now, we must deal with the urgent matter of a hatching egg." Darcy stopped the carriage at the front door of Longbourn House.

Mary met them at the front door and hurried them to Bennet's cluttered, claustrophobic excuse for an office. There had to be some better way to store books than on the floor.

Bennet and Collins stood near the nesting box—what the devil was Collins doing there? No doubt the man would make a cake of things—maybe even teach the chick to despise men the moment he hatched. What was Bennet thinking?

Walker and Cait shared the dragon perch which had been moved to one side of the nesting box. They crooned sounds that were probably encouragements in dragon tongue. They looked like doting parents, so domestic. Not that the tableaux would last long. It was a shame Elizabeth was not here to see. She would probably be able to infer a great deal from just the looks the two shared between them—no, now was not the time to dwell upon that.

"Good, you are come." Bennet waved them in, not rising from his seat near the nesting box. "Where is Elizabeth?"

"She declined to come, fearing that the chick might like her best of the party." Fitzwilliam chuckled, tossing an easy salute toward Walker and Cait.

How easily such disguise poured from his lips. Was that something he had learned as an army spy?

Walker and Cait exchanged creased-brow looks and turned to Darcy. He twitched his head, the traces of a frown at the corner of his lips. Both raised their wings a bit and snapped their beaks. How quickly they fathomed that something was seriously wrong.

"Colonel Fitzwilliam, you need to be here, next to the box." Bennet pointed to a nearby footstool, an air of impatience in his voice.

Fitzwilliam wove his way through the room and perched on the footstool. It was just the right height to place him waist high to the nesting box. Though it probably should not bother him, Darcy did not like the way it put Fitzwilliam below Collins, allowing Collins to peer down at him.

"Have you read the material I sent you on hatching?" Bennet sounded like a tutor Aunt Catherine had hired for them when they had stayed with her one summer—cranky and demanding.

"Thrice. And I have taken notes."

"Excellent. But I would expect no less from an officer of His Majesty." Bennet pointed to Fitzwilliam's cravat. "You have a flannel under there for the chick?"

Fitzwilliam fumbled at his neck, finally giving up and tearing the knot out of his starched cravat. He produced a faded flannel cloth that had been tucked under the stock supporting his cravat. "Here."

"Keep it in hand to clean the hatchling. Giving him your scent will help him recognize you. Mary, you have the chicken?" He waved at the doorway.

Mary pushed in with a plucked whole bird on a wooden platter. Bennet pushed a small table near the dragon perch. Walker and Cait set upon the chicken, shredding it in moments. Good thing there had been no feathers, or the room would be awash in them, floating about as the pair cast them aside. Not an attractive sight by any stretch, but fascinating. Sometimes it was easy to forget how formidable even small dragons could be. Pity the creature that fell under their beaks and talons.

"Look!" Collins pointed at the nesting box.

The mottled grey-green egg wobbled. The shell stretched and wiggled a bit like a tall jelly. The needle-sharp tip of a beak poked through.

Darcy held his breath as it disappeared inside the egg. He counted silently. At ten it had not reappeared. The mantle clock ticked loud minutes, and the egg stopped moving all together. That was a very bad sign. If the chick was not strong enough to break through the shell, it would not survive outside the egg. The kindest thing was to allow it to pass in peace within the confines of the shell.

"Will not someone do something? Should it not be breaking out by now?" Collins reached for the egg.

"No, you must not interfere!" Bennet slapped his hand back faster than Darcy thought him able to move.

The egg rocked hard, as though startled by the sounds. It rolled end-over-end toward Collins' edge of the box. Somehow Collins caught it as it tumbled out.

He held it up, mouth agape, face pale, and hands trembling.

"Just put it back in the box." Bennet pointed frantically, probably afraid Collins might drop it.

The egg cracked down the middle and fell away in two large pieces. A matted, bedraggled chick stood in his palm. He turned jet black eyes on Collins and squawked, "Hungry!"

Collins stared at it with such a peculiar look. "What is it saying?"

"Hungry!"

Collins ran a finger gently over the chick's wet, matted head. "I do not understand."

"Hungry!" The chick screeched, pawing at Collins' palm. Hopefully his talons were still soft or Collins' hand might be shredded.

Such a plaintive, desolate sound. A lump rose in Darcy's throat. Beside him, Mary began to weep. Did the voice of a young cockatrice induce sorrow the way an adult's induced terror?

Bloody hell! That would be the sort of thing Elizabeth would want to know. Damn it all, she should be here!

Collins' eyes filled with tears. "I would like to help, but I do not understand."

Fitzwilliam edged around the box and nudged Collins with his shoulder. He carefully took the chick into his hands. "The chick is hungry."

Mary crowded in and pressed the tray of meat toward Fitzwilliam. With his free, hand he grabbed a handful of slivers and offered one to the chick.

The baby gobbled it down, flapping its wet wings to shower Fitzwilliam and Collins with egg slime.

"May I clean you?" Fitzwilliam applied the soft

flannel to the baby's face.

The chick leaned into his ministrations, crooning.

Collins slipped from the room.

Bennet murmured soft encouragements to the chick and Fitzwilliam as he fed it a larger piece. They were in good hands. Best see what Collins was about.

Collins leaned heavily against the wall just outside the study door, face in his hands.

"Are you well?" Darcy asked softly.

Collins gulped several ragged breaths. "The way it looked at me."

"What do you mean?"

"The creature—the baby. Its eyes. As though it—he—knew exactly what he wanted, needed and how to communicate it. As if I should have understood." He clasped his hands and extended them toward Darcy. "I would have helped had I understood. The grief! They feel! The creatures, the dragons, they feel, as we do. I never realized. They are not just clever animals."

Darcy suppressed the urge to slap his forehead. The bigger issue was that the man was finally grasping the nature of dragons, not that it had taken him this long to accomplish it. Darcy bit his tongue and set aside the first three things he thought to say. "You are absolutely correct."

"How easily the colonel managed, cared for the creature, just because he could understand what the chick was saying. It was truly communicating, speaking to him."

"You will find it far easier to deal with Longbourn now that you understand."

"Yes, yes, you may be quite right." Collins blotted his eyes with his sleeve. "That is one too, no?" He pointed behind Darcy.

Darcy looked over his shoulder. Rumblkins spring-hopped toward them.

"Yes, he is. His kind is called a tatzelwurm. There are more of them who live in the barns at Longbourn. They do not usually live in homes." Or with Friends who could not actually hear dragons, but now was definitely not the time to try and explain that sort of thing.

"I believe I may owe it—him—an apology."

Darcy crouched and extended a hand toward Rumblkins. "Are you willing to hear Mr. Collins? He has something to say to you."

"Why should I listen to him?" Rumblkins turned half his body away from them.

"Mr. Collins, it would behoove you to present a good will offering, a bit of dried cod from the kitchen perhaps—"

"Or a dish of cream." Rumblkins turned toward them and licked his lips.

"Better yet, a dish of cream would be very welcome."

"Yes … yes … of course. Lady Catherine is always more amenable after a few compliments. Why would not a … a dragon be so as well." Collins trundled down the hall toward the kitchen.

Darcy dragged his hand down his face. But then again, dealing with Aunt Catherine was not so different from dealing with a dragon. Perhaps she was a good model to use.

How Elizabeth would laugh to hear that, but she probably would agree. How would he explain the transformation that had just come over Collins? Would she even believe him?

Rumblkins laid a paw on Darcy's knee. "She said this was important. I do not know why she left this behind." With his other paw, he laid a long, dirty glove on Darcy's knee.

"She left this somewhere?"

"No, we found it. In the woods. She thought it was important, but left it at the lair in her apron."

He held the glove up by one finger. It did not seem the right shape to be Elizabeth's. "Whose is this?"

"A sister's. I do not remember which."

Darcy's heart thudded hard against his ribs. "I will ask Mary, surely she will know. Thank you very much." He scratched under Rumblkins' chin.

Collins shuffled up with a saucer of cream. He crouched next to Darcy. "What should I do?"

"Put the saucer down and talk while he takes the cream." Darcy rose. "Pray listen to him with kindness, Rumblkins. What Dragon Mates know easily is difficult for others to learn."

"Mrrow." Rumblkins glanced from the cream, to Collins, and back to the cream. Apparently his stomach won the conversation. He pressed his nose into the cream.

"Ah, yes, well then," Collins straightened his jacket and drew a breath long enough to fuel a very long speech, just as he would have done addressing Lady Catherine. Good thing there was plenty of cream.

Darcy excused himself and returned to the study.

Mary leaned against her father's cluttered desk, watching as Fitzwilliam fed the ravenous chick. "The chick's name is Earl."

Darcy snickered into his hand. "I am not sure if Uncle Matlock will be pleased or not having a chick so named for him."

"You think that is the colonel's intent?"

"I think it well within the bounds of his sense of

humor."

Earl had fluffed out as his feather-scales dried. His head, wings, and torso were covered with mottled green-gold down. His serpentine lower half bore soft-looking dark grey scales, wrapped firmly around Fitzwilliam's wrist. Though his beak and talons had a soft, translucent sheen, they had dried enough to be useful in shredding his meal.

"Earl is rather cute, all told." Mary mumbled. "In the way all babies are cute, I suppose."

"Cockatrice are not cute—or at least I would not risk telling one that. You would go much farther calling him impressive." Darcy glanced at Walker. Did he just wink at them?

"I will remember that." Mary's eyes twinkled a little like Elizabeth's.

"Rumblkins just brought me this. It was found in the woods. He seemed to think it very important. Would you happen to know to whom it belongs?" He handed the glove to Mary.

She turned it inside out. "Great heavens! It is Lydia's!"

"You must meet Darcy, my young Friend." Fitzwilliam cradled Earl in the crook of one arm and waved Darcy over with the other. Cait leaned down from the perch to offer Earl another gobbet of meat. He would have to stop eating soon, his belly was distended and his eyelids were drooping.

Bennet moved aside so Darcy could stand beside Fitzwilliam.

Huge baby eyes turned on him. "Darcy?"

"Yes, Earl, I am Darcy. Walker is my Friend." Darcy stroked Earl's fluffy head. Perhaps Mary was right. He was cute after all.

Walker squawked approval from the opposite side of the room.

Darcy offered a sliver of meat. Earl swallowed it slowly, his head lolling into Fitzwilliam's chest as he did.

"I was not sure we would ever get enough food into him." Fitzwilliam stared at Earl with something between wonder and pride. "I never knew a creature so small could stuff himself that much."

"I believe your mother used to say that about you." Darcy chuckled, twitching his brows just a bit. "I imagine your father will have something to say about his name, though."

"I merely offered it. Earl chose to accept it." Fitzwilliam winked.

"Tell your father that." He held the glove toward Fitzwilliam. "You need to see this. Mary says it is Miss Lydia's. Rumblkins found it in the woods."

"So, she is here?"

"It is the first real evidence to suggest that she is."

Fitzwilliam glanced around for a chair and sat. "Is it torn? Are there signs of violence?"

"It does not seem so."

"Perhaps she is still alive. We must begin searching immediately."

"Would it not be wiser to see the maps decontaminated first? I expect the time it would take would be more than amply made up for in the time saved searching."

Fitzwilliam glanced down at Earl who snored softly against his chest. "I suppose you are right. I must go back to Netherfield, though."

"It would be better for the chick to remain here." Had Bennet been listening the whole time? Probably.

Despite his other physical limitations, his preternatural hearing was still as sharp as ever it was.

"Come to Netherfield with us. You can watch over him there whilst we fulfil the Order's business." Fitzwilliam made that an order, not a suggestion.

Bennet scowled and opened his mouth—for protest no doubt.

"There are many book collections there. You can help us identify the volumes that are of particular value." Darcy nudged Fitzwilliam. Sometimes bribery was more effective than demands.

Fitzwilliam nodded with just his eyes. "When we have decontaminated the maps, your assistance in deciphering them will be invaluable."

"I think he is right, Papa." Mary and Mr. Collins came up behind Bennet.

"But Longbourn—"

"He will be fine, I am sure." Mary laid a hand on Bennet's shoulder.

"With Cait's help, we will be able to manage." Collins' tone was so changed. Who would have thought those words had come from him.

"They can send for help if there is any problem. I will drive you back myself if necessary." It must be difficult to put himself in the service of such a man. The things the Blue Order could require!

"Very well, but only until the chick is past his hatching hunger." Was Bennet pouting now?

"Walker, pray would you find Elizabeth and inform her of our plans? I do not think this a good time to surprise her." That, of course, was an understatement of draconic proportions.

Walker muttered something about not being a messenger bird, but for his Lady Elizabeth, he would oblige, and flew off.

Elizabeth pulled her shawl tighter over her shoulders as she turned off the garden path. Talia would insist on introducing more hoppers, and her current mood hardly rendered her obliging. The folly was a far better destination. The forest wyrms were unlikely to appear, and she could have quiet for her own thoughts.

How could she have been so misled? Darcy said he trusted her, yet he would keep such information from her? That was precisely how Papa treated Mama. Of course, he justified it because Mama could not hear dragons, and the Blue Order required secrecy.

Had the Blue Order instructed Fitzwilliam thus? Did they hope he might use her against Netherfield? It would not be entirely unlike them to do so. How dare they try to manage her like the dragon-deaf! Perhaps Mary's concerns over the Order's behavior were very sensible after all.

How like the military they were, always quick to turn to the sword for an answer. But it was foolish and short-sighted. How much better if all could be made to see reason. To resolve this without bloodshed—why did they have so little faith it could be done?

Why did Darcy have so little faith in her? And this was the man she was going to marry? How would that ever work? What point in hoping for a marriage of the mind and soul when he would not turn to her with the truth at such a time as this? No, this would be no more than a typical marriage for advantage and connection.

At least there would be little Pemberley to love. Perhaps that would be enough.

Elizabeth paused at the folly, her feet too heavy to move. The path continued deeper into the woods behind the structure. Why had she never noticed it before? Perhaps it might lead somewhere useful, and if it did not, that was just as well, too. She needed to spend time away from everyone—man and dragon—lest she lose control and say something very untoward.

The subtle path proved challenging to follow as it wound into the deep woods and into a rocky terrain studded with rounded hills. How long had it been here and what sort of creature made it? It lacked the typical marks left by larger game. In places the track looked more like scaly slithers than anything else.

This was the sort of landscape wyrms loved—so many holes for them to hide in and explore. Not just wyrms, other smaller dragons liked it, too. The unique karst landscape meant Hertfordshire hosted an unusually large population of wild dragons compared to the rest of England. Perhaps, there were some who lived here who might help her. Though it was difficult to meet wild dragons, it was possible if one was patient and could manage a proper introduction.

She scanned a small clearing near the hillside for dragon signs. Those could be slither trails among the rocks, and that shiny bit looked like a lost scale. The skeleton of—well something small and previously furry—lay near a few bushes. Multiple wild dragons might well live here.

A scraggly tree offered shade to a boulder near the center of the outcropping. She sat there, still and silent. Surely the dragons would smell her. But if she remained non-threatening, their curiosity usually won over their caution, and they would come to investigate. It merely required sufficient patience.

Her shadow grew steadily longer, and her bones ached from the hard stone perch. Maybe just a little longer, but not much. She needed to leave herself enough time to get back to the house before sunset.

There, wait! Slithering, the unique sounds of scales over rocks just behind her, approaching with caution. Excellent. All she had to do was be quiet and still and—

A wyrm shadow appeared! Exactly what she—wait. Why was it growing so very large? Chills coursed down her neck and shoulders. How could a rock wyrm cast such a long—rock wyrms did not have arms!

She turned very, very slowly.

The creature was blue. The bluest dragon she had ever seen. Bluer than the blue pa snake she had met at the Order offices. He was the blue of a peacock feather, his back a little darker, his belly a touch lighter.

He rose up on his tail until he stood eight, maybe ten feet tall. It was difficult to tell for certain while she was seated. A long, squared face sported both a wild blue mane—more hairy than feathery, and a long white whisker mustache at the end of his nose similar to Longbourn's. Fangs, stained and not at all cared for, poked out just below his nose—not bared to be a threat just yet.

His huge round eyes glittered bright yellow in the sunshine, well-formed for seeing in near-total darkness. Two long, powerful arms defined where his neck ended and shoulders began, ending in paws that looked more like hands. Four lithe toes, with one opposing the other three like a thumb, bore daunting talons, useful for digging and for dispatching prey. No wonder horses were terrified at the mere scent of a lindwurm. They would stand no chance against one.

"You call yourself Netherfield, I expect." She rose on jellied knees. At least she kept her voice level and strong. That was something

"You are trespassing on my territory." The gruff, gravelly tone sounded more like a child's affectation than his real speaking voice. Trying to be intimidating, no doubt.

"This is not your territory."

"I have taken its name. No other dragon claims it. The minor dragons give way to me. It is mine." He spoke the last three words with particular force, a little spittle flying with each.

"That may be how it works in France. But here, there are rules about what territory a dragon claims. You have not followed them."

"I will have this place." He slithered closer to tower over her—a particular tendency among males and dragons trying to prove themselves right.

"It is not impossible—if you work with the Blue Order. Since the proper claimant to this Keep has not been heard from in quite some time—"

"He gave me this land."

Is that what "giver" in the painting referred to? "Then you may present your claim—"

"I hold the land. It is mine. If anyone challenges me, I will hold it, with blood if I must." His lips pulled back to reveal formidable fangs.

Good sense demanded she run, or at least back away. But that was also the surest way to trigger a predator's instincts. "That is not an option. Your attitude places you in grave danger."

"I know about the Dragon Slayer. You have a Dragon Hunter under your control. You are a grave danger to me." He leaned down and blew hot breath in her face. She trembled. This was too much like Longbourn …

"He is by no means under my control. I cannot fathom where you got such a notion. You are a rational, reasonable creature and this entire matter can be solved by—"

He swiped at her. Before she could draw breath to scream, she dangled from his paws over the rocky ground. "I will solve it by removing you."

Struggling would do no good, but the reflex was too strong to stop. How ridiculous she must appear kicking and twisting in his grasp. "Harming me will not profit you. If you kill me, you will die. If Longbourn does not kill you, the Dragon Hunter and his kin will stop at nothing to do so."

"I do not need to kill you, yet. There are other means to try first." He pressed her to his chest so tightly she could hardly breathe and slithered toward the hills. He ducked to enter a large cave. What little she could see turned into darkness.

At sunset, a fast-moving storm released its fury upon Darcy in the open curricle just as they pulled up to Netherfield. Surely Elizabeth would greet them with a warm fire and the promise of a hot meal to be served soon. In his mind's eye, Darcy could see her forgiving smile. No doubt there would be a long discussion to follow, in private of course. But all would soon be well. She would be his Elizabeth once again.

Nicholls met them at the door, not Elizabeth. Apparently, she was not returned. This was not the sort of weather anyone should be out in, especially not a gentlewoman without even a spencer to protect her from the chill. But Elizabeth had many dragon friends. Surely one of them would be able to offer her shelter from the torrent.

An hour later, Darcy paced along the parlor windows, staring at the pounding drops that ran down the windows. A few made their way inside to puddle on the window sill. Did Elizabeth have such protection against the tempest?

"You may as well stop pacing, Darcy." Bennet did not even look up from his book as he sat near the fire with several candlesticks behind him for extra light. The table beside him held half a dozen more volumes.

How pleasant that he was entirely content with the current situation. Darcy, however, was not.

"You may as well sit. Pacing is not going to bring her back any sooner." Fitzwilliam nursed a glass of brandy near the fire while Earl slept in the crook of his arm. But the way he rolled the glass between his palms—he was no calmer than Darcy.

"No, it will not." Bennet grumbled as he resettled himself in the wingchair like a cold drake trying to get comfortable. "What is more, you ought to get accustomed to this sort of behavior. She has been doing these things all her life. I doubt you will have any more luck bringing her under regulation than I have."

"What are you talking about?" Darcy faced him, leaning against the window frame. Best keep a little distance.

"Where dragons are concerned, she has been uncontrollable since she first heard them." Bennet slapped his book shut and tossed it on the table.

"That is a very strong description." Fitzwilliam wrenched around in his chair to look at both of them, a hint of amusement dancing in his eyes.

"For good reason! One afternoon when she was five years old, she sneaked out of the nursery and overheard Rustle and Gardiner discussing a Blue Order matter of importing dragon goods. That evening after dinner, her mother could not find her to put her to bed. Gardiner and I found her sitting on the floor of my study with Rustle, discussing what treats dragons preferred as though it were the most normal natural thing. What kind of child—what kind of girl child—sees a cockatrice for what it is and strikes up a conversation instead of running for cover?"

Gracious, what would his daughters be like! Perhaps they needed to employ a nursery maid with a Dragon Friend. Elizabeth would probably see nothing amiss to have a minor drake rocking a cradle whilst a fairy dragon sang the baby to sleep. What kind of a household would they have?

Fitzwilliam snickered into his hand, probably thinking the same thing.

"You think it funny?" Bennet slapped the arm of his chair. "Try raising a child who has no compunction about introducing herself to every local dragon, wild or imprinted. It was one thing when it was limited to fairy dragons and varieties of wyrms. But no, she managed to find a basilisk to acquaint herself with!"

"A basilisk?" Darcy feigned surprise for Bennet's sake.

"The creature had a reputation for ill-temper among the Conclave on the rare occasions he showed up. He generally refused to speak to the Keeper's daughters, and barely interacted with the Keeper himself. But Lizzy?" Bennet slapped his forehead. "The creature tried to scare her off. Instead of having the sense to retreat, she curtsied, introduced herself, and had the foulest tempered dragon in the county telling her stories of the Keep that even the Keeper had never heard!"

Which Bennet was probably all too happy to write down and add to the existing dragon lore. Would Bennet think differently of the matter if she had been his son and heir engaging in such boldness? Darcy dragged his heel across the carpet.

"On that same trip, she managed to befriend, against my express wishes, the most irritating, ill-mannered excuse for a flutter-tuft fairy dragon and brought her into my house to disrupt the delicate balance that must be kept with non-hearing members of the household!" Bennet panted for breath.

"You can hardly blame her for that. Dragons choose their Friends as they will." Fitzwilliam glanced down at Earl.

Had he ever looked at another creature with so much tenderness? Collins was not the only man affected by Earl's entrance into the world.

"Perhaps so, but she has no respect for propriety, for order, for etiquette. Even her initial introduction to Longbourn was on her own terms, reckless and improper."

"Perhaps that is what has made him so fond of her." Fitzwilliam winked at Darcy.

"I have never seen a dragon so insistent upon a Keeper before." Darcy tapped a finger against his lips. "Perhaps that is why—dragon's blood, it is about the salt!"

Bennet leaned into his chair, brow drawing into deep, defensive furrows. "What are you talking about?"

"Now I understand, and it is despicable." Darcy

crossed the distance to the fireplace in four long, purposeful strides. "What kind of Dragon Keeper are you?"

"What are you talking about, Darce?" Fitzwilliam covered Earl with his free arm.

"Instead of providing Longbourn salt to hoard, you convinced him to take Elizabeth instead. That is why you had been so bloody insistent upon her marrying Collins and not seeking her own choice. You could not risk her leaving the estate. Elizabeth became his hoard as much as Talia is hoarding those rabbits in the garden!" Darcy clenched his fists.

"Just wait until Pemberley discovers her own penchant for hoarding—firedrakes are known for it. Then you will not be so quick to judge. Or perhaps your income is vast enough that you may provide whatever she demands. Mine, however, is not."

"It is your responsibility to provide for your dragon's hoard."

"Insofar as I can afford, sir. That is clear in the Accords. Insofar as I can afford. When one has a wife and daughters who do not hear, one cannot explain that the money, which might have provided them with the style of life they believe themselves entitled to, must be diverted to satisfy a hoarding dragon."

"So you frittered away your income on ribbons and bonnets while your dragon went without?"

"Not entirely without. He received a portion every year."

Darcy took another step, looking down upon Bennet. "And Elizabeth? You traded your daughter like some fairytale princess to be sacrificed to a dragon!"

"You have no right to pass judgement on what you do not understand. You, who have never found your income lagging behind your needs, are in no place to condemn me for what I had to do."

"Modernizing your farming and improving your livestock never came to mind, I imagine. Or were they too much effort for you?"

"I will not discuss this matter further—"

When had it started hailing? Sharp pecking sounded as though it would shatter the glass in the center window.

Fitzwilliam jogged to the window and threw it open. Walker tumbled in, wet and cold. Darcy scooped up a pile of towels near the fire, placed there in hopes of just such an arrival.

While Darcy dried Walker, Fitzwilliam prepared a glass of hot water and brandy. "Here, that should warm your bones." He placed the glass on the floor near the window.

Walker picked up the glass with his beak and drained it in a single swallow. "Much better. I could use another glass, though." He hopped to the fire and spread his wings. "Damned hard to fly when one gets waterlogged."

"I was surprised you stayed out in this weather so long." Darcy dried Walker's wings.

Walker turned over his shoulder and looked directly into Darcy's eyes. "I could not find her."

"What do you mean, you could not find her? She is probably in some cave or even in Longbourn's lair, vexing girl." Bennet stared into his lap, muttering.

Walker turned very slowly and leveled a predatory gaze at him. "Do you think me so lax that I would not have checked all those places already?"

"There are dozens of them on the two estates—the hills are full of caves and crevasses that could shelter someone from the weather."

"Yes, there are. I have enlisted the assistance of no less than half a dozen local wyrms and Talia to search them all." Walker spoke slowly, distinctly as one did to a very young child.

"Because wyrms are such reliable sources of information and so likely to do what they promise." Bennet rolled his eyes.

Walker folded his still dripping wings to his back and hopped to the arm of Bennet's chair. "They will do it for Lady Elizabeth."

"Lady Elizabeth? She is now 'Lady Elizabeth' to you? What grand act has she done to deserve that moniker?"

"Yes, she is, and you would be wise not to question it. Other men might take pride in having a daughter so well regarded by dragonkind."

"Would she be so well regarded if dragonkind realized that she was hardly a prodigy? The disobedient girl has been making things up as she went, consulting farriers, poulterers, and nursery maids for her wisdom."

Walker growled, low and threatening. The hair on the back of Darcy's neck prickled. Earl stirred, squawking softly in his sleep. Did Bennet not recognize the danger he courted?

"I would thank you to take that up with her, not with me. I have warned her on numerous occasions that she was treading dangerous ground, but she has ignored me. Now her secret is out, perhaps you will help bring some sense—"

Walker lunged and snapped at the air in front of Bennet's face.

Bennet jumped back, knocking his chair down behind him.

Walker extended his wings and he landed on the floor before Bennet. It was never a good thing when Walker made himself big. "Do you think Cait or I care where her information came from? It saved Cait's life—or do you not seem to grasp that she was at risk of being torn apart from the inside? Would you wish that fate upon anyone?"

"You are exaggerating. The egg could have been broken—"

"To kill our chick? Yes, that is an excellent option. What matter where her insight comes from when she is right?"

"And what about when she is wrong?" Bennet recovered his composure and staggered forward. "So far she has been lucky with her potions for scale mites and talon rot, but one day her unconventional methods will fail, and a dragon will be hurt or die. What then? Will you still honor her or will dragonkind turn on her for her upstart caprice in applying insights learned from lesser creatures to dragons?"

"You think so little of us?"

"Dragons have a reputation for temper for good reason."

"Perhaps because of the constant disrespect we face from you warm-bloods."

Bennet and Walker stared perilously at one another. Did he not realize Walker could kill him with a single stroke of his talons? Perhaps that was where Elizabeth's nerve came from.

Fitzwilliam cleared his throat. Conspicuous, but not ineffective. "You said no trace has been found?"

Walker turned to him and bobbed his head. "None. The only hint came from a rock wyrm who said that he saw her following a path recently created by the blue one."

"The lindwurm?" A cold knot settled in the pit of Darcy's stomach.

Fitzwilliam clapped his hand to his mouth and spoke through his fingers. "That sounds as if he laid a trap for her!"

"The rain has washed away the path, but as soon as the weather clears, the wyrm has promised to show me where it led, but it is difficult to predict how far that will get us. Any tracks the lindwurm might have left will be gone by now."

"They move very quickly and through terrain most major dragons cannot." Fitzwilliam chewed his knuckle.

"You believe it has Elizabeth?" Darcy swallowed hard.

"Considering the French dragons I have known, if it had meant to hurt her, it would have done so and left us evidence to prove its power. Given that it knows about the Dragon Slayer, I would assume it wants to use her to negotiate its own escape."

"Dragon Slayer?" Bennet grabbed for the edge of the upturned chair.

"Demand answers from the Order, not me."

"But Earl—"

"I have promised Fitzwilliam I shall see to his care and find an appropriate Friend if it becomes necessary." A promise Darcy hoped he never need fulfill.

"How could you present yourself as his Friend knowing—"

"Because I insisted." Walker snapped close to Bennet's knee. "Enough of this talk. None of it is useful in finding Lady Elizabeth."

"In this weather, what else is there to do? It is not

as if anyone can go out in the pitch dark and rain." Bennet struggled to right his chair.

"The map room." Fitzwilliam slapped his knee. Earl opened one eye to offer a reproving look.

"We should begin immediately." It was not as though he would get any sleep tonight anyway. "We should have sufficient antidote with what Mary gave me before we left Longbourn."

"This is a foolhardy effort. No one has ever counteracted—"

"How exactly would you know? Have you read every tome of dragon lore in existence? Are you certain it would have been written down if it had been attempted?" Fitzwilliam stroked the top of Earl's head.

What an education that young cockatrice was getting. At this rate, he would likely be even more cynical than his father!

"We are not asking you to put yourself at risk or even for your approval. Only help us read the maps when they are decontaminated. It seems the least you can do to help your daughter." Such a man he would have as father-in-law.

"Leave Earl here with me, you cannot risk exposing him to the poison." Bennet reached toward Fitzwilliam.

"I am not sure I can risk leaving him with you and your hidebound notions. But it seems I have no choice." Fitzwilliam muttered as he rose and carefully transferred the sleeping chick to Bennet's arms.

Chapter 9

PRESSED HARD AGAINST the lindwurm's cool body in the lightless gloom, time and distance lost all meaning. Only the scraping slithers of his scales against the walls of the rock tunnels gave her senses an anchor.

All the creature had to do was leave her in this darkness, set her down and abandon her, and all would be lost. A creature who would snatch her up and take her captive was certainly the sort capable of deserting her. Exactly the sort of creature—warm- or cold-blooded—with whom she had no experience. The sort of creature Darcy and Fitzwilliam expected the lindwurm to be.

What was that? Her eyes must be playing tricks. How could there be a glimmer of light in this pervasive, stony blackness? But no, it was there, growing larger. She fought for a better view, but Netherfield only held her more tightly. Was he humming to himself?

Surely, that was not possible. Dragons were not musically inclined. It was a sort of self-satisfied sound, not so much aggressive as simply irritating, but definitely melodic and vaguely familiar. Had Mary been practicing that melody recently? Yes, she definitely had. Was he dangerous or just vexing? Probably both.

The light grew and flickered, a familiar yellow-orange. A fire? Why would there be a fire in his cavern? He needed neither the light nor the heat ...

"Go with her." Netherfield set her down none too gently and pushed her toward the fire. She stumbled, blinking in the constricted ring of light that barely reached the walls of what seemed only a wide spot in a tunnel.

Odd, this was hardly a proper lair. Dragons liked to be comfortable. These walls were rough, likely to scrape his hide, and the floor too uneven for easy rest. This space had the hallmarks of a temporary shelter, well away from his actual lair.

At the far edge of the firelight, a heap of pale fabric shuddered.

"Lydia?"

"Lizzy?" A dirty face peeked up.

Elizabeth swept her into her arms and glared over her shoulder. "What you have done here is completely untoward. Why would you hold an innocent girl hostage?"

Netherfield reared back, his expression shifting from satisfied to perplexed. But not aggressive, at least not yet.

"You can talk to him?" Lydia scrabbled back as if seeing yet another monster in the room.

"Of course, I can. No different to you." Patience. Now was an appropriate time for patience. After all,

Lydia knew nothing of dragons nor the Blue Order. What a shocking manner to learn of them, even worse than Collins' first encounter. "Is he the first such creature you have spoken to?"

"Not exactly." Lydia leaned in close to whisper. "You will certainly think me daft, but did you know Mrs. Hill's cat speaks, too?"

"Of course, he does. He is a minor dragon. All dragons speak."

"Our housekeeper's cat is a dragon? He did look rather odd when he asked me for a dish of cream. How long have you heard these beasts?"

"As long as I can remember. Mary can hear them, too."

"Ahem." Netherfield coughed and crossed his forearms over his chest. "I believe you asked me a question. Do be good enough to permit me to answer."

"We will come back to this, Lydia. I have a very great deal to tell you." Elizabeth curtsied toward Netherfield. "Forgive my rudeness. Do go on."

"Thank you. The girl is not innocent. I am holding her for my own protection."

"Lydia, what have you done?"

"Why do you accuse me?" Lydia wrapped her arms around her waist and huddled down. "Truly, I have done nothing, not to deserve this."

"If you did not threaten Netherfield, then who did?"

"The deaf one." Netherfield bobbed back and forth as though preparing to strike at prey.

"Wickham did not take you to elope?"

"No. When he came from Brighton, he was certain there was a monster living at Netherfield. He said Colonel Forster gave him leave to try and find it."

"That is why you were practicing ciphers! Wickham dared not write to you about such things plainly! Is that why you came to Netherfield in the first place?"

"Well, no, not exactly." Lydia scuffed her heel along the sandy floor. "Mama is so bossy! Suddenly, the idea came to me: how much fun it would be to have an entire house under my own command. So I went to Netherfield. Not long after, though, I started hearing voices from the cellar."

"You persuaded her to come to Netherfield! You brought her into all this! How dare you?" Elizabeth stomped—granted probably not the most politic response at the moment, but who could blame her?

Netherfield's shoulders hunched like a scolded little boy. "I was lonely. Longbourn did not want her there, so it seemed she would not be missed."

"So you used her for your own entertainment? That is despicable. Utterly despicable—and illegal."

Lydia grabbed for her arm. "You should not say such things, Lizzy!"

"No, you should not." Netherfield hissed, recovering his draconic bearing.

"Did he entice you to come down into the cellar and talk?"

Lydia refused to meet Elizabeth's gaze. "He seemed friendly and lonesome at the time."

"So you invited Wickham to come meet your friend?"

"I did not say my friend was a ... monster! I was lonely, too and thought to make him a wee bit jealous. What is so terrible about that?"

His long nose wrinkled into many folds. "She and the deaf one came of their own accord. I did not invite them." He rustled his coils, a little defensive, a little uneasy.

"They trespassed upon your lair without invitation." Elizabeth covered her eyes with her hand. Dragon's blood!

"I had been told there were rules against such things. Dragons were not to be imposed upon in their lairs." His lip and nostril curled back.

"That is one of the Keeper's responsibilities. But this estate has no Keeper at present." Lydia should have known better, should have been taught better!

"The deaf one wanted to be Keeper of this territory and use the tunnels running under it. He offered a business proposition. But men do not do business with dragons, not even here." Netherfield wove from side to side. "He wanted to use me to his own advantage, to make me a slave."

"We know he is quite dragon-deaf. How could he use you if he could not even talk to you?"

Lydia crumpled into a heap on the floor. How very courageous and useful of her.

"She translated for him."

Elizabeth's breath caught in her throat. Lydia had committed high treason and had no idea of it. If only Papa had paid more attention to her, he would have recognized the signs and intervened before she came fully into her hearing. Hopefully, the Blue Order would be lenient given the circumstances. If they were able to reach them at all.

"When he resorted to threats to gain my cooperation, I had little choice but to detain them here. Why else would I take a babbling addlepate with no sense and fewer connections?"

Lydia shrieked. "That horrible creature killed my Wickham! He will kill both of us, too!"

"You killed Wickham?" A cold chill snaked down Elizabeth's spine. Those yellow-gold eyes belonged to a killer. She had never looked into a killer's eyes before.

He turned his face aside. "I did what I had to do. I will do it again if I have to."

"We are both of Longbourn's Keep. If you harm us, it will be a declaration of war against him."

"Longbourn? You mean there is another monster like this one? On our estate? In our cellars?" Lydia keened, rocking, arms tight around her knees.

"I will explain it all to you. I promise. But not now."

"You betrayed Longbourn. He will be glad to see you punished." Netherfield turned up his nose and tossed his head, a little like Lydia was apt to.

"We have made up since I realized you attempted those persuasions upon me, not him."

Netherfield snatched her up and dangled her over the fire. The brute! "Do not tempt me."

It was difficult to maintain one's grace and composure hanging like a ragdoll. "I am the only leverage you have over the Dragon Slayer. He has experience with your kind. Do you really want to force a confrontation?"

Netherfield cast her aside, just hard enough to send her stumbling into Lydia, but not enough to slam her into the wall which he could easily have done. "No more talk."

Elizabeth huddled near Lydia while Netherfield arranged his coils to effectively block both ends of the tunnel.

In a very few minutes, Lydia sagged heavily against her with the deep breaths of sleep. Netherfield snored softly as dragons were wont to do. With a lindwurm's keen hearing and the encompassing darkness beyond

Netherfield: Rogue Dragon

the little fire, there was no point in trying to effect an escape. She leaned back against the cold, damp stone.

What kind of creature was this lindwurm? Unlike any dragon she had ever known: cold, cruel, hard. Ancient dragon lore, written before the Pendragon Accords, chronicled such things. Modern dragons were not like this.

Was it as Fitzwilliam said? Dragons of the continent, without the protections and restrictions of the Accords, lacked the civility of British dragons. Could he and the Order be right, that the sword was the only recourse when dealing with a calculated killer? A killer! Netherfield had killed Wickham. She clasped her knees to her chest and hooked her chin over them, making herself very small.

It was not hard to justify the dragon's actions, considering what Wickham had threatened Netherfield with. But a British dragon would have brought it to the courts. As a self-made deaf-speaker who had violated multiple Blue Order laws, Wickham would have been condemned, but it would have been a proper judicial action, not—she swallowed hard—a murder.

Fitzwilliam was right. There was probably no other solution. And heavens above—Darcy was right, too. How bloody stubborn she was—as stubborn as any dragon—and now she was trapped in a strange dragon's lair to show for it.

At least she had found Lydia. That was something. As long as they both still breathed, there was hope, if only a very little bit.

Darcy paced the length of his chambers for—well, he

had lost count by this point. Fitzwilliam had begun their decontamination efforts, soaking the maps in the antidote-laden steam. But it would take time for the cure to do its work. So they waited.

Fitzwilliam had bathed thoroughly and fed Earl his next meal. The chick had refused to take it from Bennet's hand which was saying a great deal considering the power of hatching-hunger. Earl did not appear to like Bennet very much. Who could blame him?

What was more, feeding Earl seemed to do Fitzwilliam good. In just the short time he and his Friend had been together, Fitzwilliam was a changed man. It was difficult to put into words what it was, but it was there: the expression in his eyes; the way he carried himself; even the tone he used to address Walker. All had altered since Earl's hatching. If only Fitzwilliam could have the freedom to relax and relish the relationship—bloody timing of it all!

Impotent rays of dawn struggled to penetrate the heavy clouds and driving rain pelting the window pane. Blast it all—they would be hard-pressed to be able to get out at all today if this continued.

Wait, what was that? The tapping was too regular to be raindrops. A bedraggled blue spot clung to the windowsill and pecked at the glass.

He ran to the window and shoved it open. April fell in, tangling in the curtain. His hands shook so hard that sorting her out from the heavy fabric and fringe proved complicated.

"Is it true? Is it true?" She squawked, flapping her wings, splashing rainwater on his face and chest. "I heard—we all did—that Elizabeth is missing!" Who knew that a fairy dragon could scream like an angry woman?

Darcy shut the window and carried her to the washstand for a towel. "Who told you such a thing?" He dabbed her dripping face.

"The wyrms—they all seem to know. By tomorrow every dragon in the county will know! So it is true?"

"I fear so."

She dove for his right ear. "How could you let that happen to her? You were supposed to protect her."

He dodged and covered his ear. "She was angry with me and went off into the woods. We have not seen her since."

"Fitzwilliam has the Dragon Slayer? That is true as well?" She hovered drunkenly in front of his face.

"By command of the Order."

She attacked his left ear. Her ire was so well-deserved that it was difficult to shoo her away. Finally, she stopped and perched on the washstand, panting for breath.

He picked her up and cradled her in the crook of his arm. "We will find her. I promise you. We are cleansing the maps even now. They will aid us in finding her soon. We will recover her."

"You must! You must." She burrowed between his elbow and chest. "I will lay my eggs soon. She must be here with me. She must vet my chicks' Friends and see to it that nothing goes wrong. I ... cannot do this without her!"

Could fairy dragons cry? It certainly seemed so.

Darcy stroked the back of her head, still damp and matted. "I need her at least as much as you do. We will not rest until she is home."

April stared up at him, tiny and miserable. "Is your promise enough?"

"It will be, my little friend, it will be."

Several hours later, fists pounded at Darcy's door. The door flew open, slamming against the wall behind.

"The maps are in the morning room along with a fresh pot of coffee." Fitzwilliam staggered in, Earl nestled in the crook of his arm. Except for the cockatrice chick, he had the look of a man ejected from a pub after too much cheap gin.

"Hatching hunger or wyvern poison?" Darcy scrubbed his eyes with his fists. When had he dozed off?

April launched from Darcy's shoulder and hovered near Fitzwilliam's chest. "I do not smell poison, but the baby's belly is full."

Earl stretched his long neck toward her, blinked, and cheeped. "Who?"

His baby voice was high, even a little sweet, nothing like the sonorous tones Walker produced. But at the rate he was growing, it would not take very long for that to change. Was it possible he had grown noticeably since he hatched—yesterday? Was it only yesterday?

Fitzwilliam offered his other hand as a perch for April and held her close to Earl. "April, may I present Earl, offspring of Cait and Walker. Earl, she is Elizabeth's Friend."

"Who Elizabet?"

April shrieked and zipped away to bury herself under the collar of Darcy's rumpled coat. What was it Elizabeth did to comfort a distraught fairy dragon?

"Someone you will meet very soon. Walker and Cait consider her a good friend as well." Fitzwilliam scratched under Earl's chin.

April twittered—what did one call that sound?—

and shuddered under the point of Darcy's lapel.

"Have we honey or jam in the morning room?" Darcy asked.

"I want tea," April chittered. "Chamomile."

"I will notify Nicholls." Fitzwilliam bowed from his shoulders and closed the door behind him.

Darcy pushed up to his feet. A fresh shirt would be nice, but that would involve dislodging April who was already quite upset enough. Best just get on with things. Clean clothes could be had later.

Darcy's throat knotted as he entered the morning room. The place was simply not right without Elizabeth's bright smile to greet him. Instead, Bennet occupied the seat near the windows that Elizabeth usually used. Little good it did him. Heavy, dark clouds, and pounding rain obscured any useful sunlight as he fixated on a pile of maps littering the table. An abundance of candles had been brought in, filling the room with a vague scent of tallow.

"Here is your tea." Fitzwilliam tapped a teacup on the table near the chair where Walker perched.

"Fairy dragons do not drink tea," Bennet muttered, barely lifting his eyes from his maps.

"Lairda April may have anything she desires," Walker snapped back, wings half-raised.

It was early to be so irate. Just how long had he been sitting here with Bennet?

April peeked out from Darcy's collar and launched herself at Walker with an off-key squawk. She landed just next to him. He covered her with his wing as he leaned down and whispered something to her in dragon tongue. Darcy took the chair beside Walker.

Bennet gaped. Good, he needed to see the influence

his "difficult" daughter had in bringing species who were often predator and prey into such deep friendship.

Walker nudged April toward the teacup. She dipped her delicate beak in, but shook her head hard, slinging drops of tea across the table. "Needs sweet."

Fitzwilliam glanced at the dainty honey server but threw it aside and poured most of the honey pot into the tea. The gratitude in April's eyes said everything. She plunged her face into the cup and drank noisily.

When had the little thing last eaten?

Earl chirruped on Fitzwilliam's arm and was rewarded by a kipper from a nearby dish. When had he started looking so incredibly paternal?

"Blast and botheration!" Fitzwilliam muttered a little more softly than he might otherwise have, probably out of deference to Earl's sensitive hearing, and struck the pile of maps in front of him.

"Dare I ask?" Darcy poured himself a cup of coffee. Strong, black, and bitter—hopefully, it would clear away some of the fog in his head.

"Are you surprised that the maps are not giving up their secrets easily?" Fitzwilliam squeezed his temples.

"Considering they were labeled with a warning symbol clearly declaring them poisoned—" Bennet mumbled, eyes down.

"Just how ancient a rune was it? Are there more than two men alive who can decipher such a thing?" Darcy gulped a mouthful of barely-not-too-hot coffee.

"If you and Elizabeth had not rushed headlong into searching the house but had consulted me on the matter, we would not be—"

Darcy slapped the table. April and Earl jumped and squawked. "No, sir. You sent Elizabeth to Netherfield to search for maps in the first place. You have grown adept at passing blame to others when it should lie with you. Considering you were the one in the region with reason to suspect a rogue dragon, and you did absolutely nothing to alert the Order—"

Bennet rose, but it seemed to make little difference as he remained hunched over the table. "It would behoove you to be careful with your accusations."

"And it would behoove you—"

"Enough from both of you!" Fitzwilliam pounded the table with his fist while Walker screeched for emphasis. "None of this is getting us closer to answers. There is plenty of time to fight later."

"If you cannot conduct yourselves usefully," Walker glared at Darcy, "then excuse yourself so those of us ready to work can continue without distraction."

Bennet sank back into his chair, grumbling under his breath. "What is wrong with those maps?"

Fitzwilliam snatched up several and stalked to Bennet. "Look for yourself, and tell me what you make of them."

Darcy peered over Bennet's shoulder as he turned the maps this way and that. "There is no legend, no marks at all, unless those faint bits are dragon script." Darcy traced the lines with his fingertip.

"I need to examine it more closely. The most ancient versions of dragon script can be difficult to identify." Bennet adjusted his glasses. "I believe these two are renderings of the immediate area of Netherfield and Longbourn. I recognize a few of the landmarks, but I cannot be certain."

"So, what you are not saying is these are utterly useless to us." Darcy scrubbed his face with his palms.

"No, I am not ready to say that, yet. I think I can

cross-reference these to a set of maps in my library made by a long-ago owner of Netherfield."

"I shall drive you to Longbourn immediately." Darcy offered Bennet his walking stick.

"I cannot."

"What do you mean you cannot?" Darcy rapped the walking stick on the floor.

"The weather, it is too wet and slick. I cannot walk in this. The last time I tried, I fell. The surgeon cautioned me that if it happened again, it might well be fatal."

"Can you direct me to this useful volume?" Darcy enunciated slowly and carefully. Sarcasm would not serve his current purpose.

"It is usually kept on the third shelf from the top near the window-side of my study. The maps are bound in green leather with gold lettering, about as thick as your thumb. It is possible that it has been moved, but I have no other book fitting that description."

"I will go immediately." Darcy bowed and headed toward the door, biting back snide words about the condition of Bennet's study.

"Leave Lairda April here with us." Walker pointed to the snoring pile of blue fluff on the table beside the teacup. "We will take care of her."

Darcy nodded and jogged from the morning room, calling for the carriage.

Mrs. Hill showed him in and took his dripping greatcoat. Mr. Collins trundled into the vestibule moments later.

"Mr. Darcy, you are most welcome this forenoon, most welcome indeed." He bowed, stiff and very proper.

Cait squawked as she swooped toward them. "What he means to say is that we are all in an uproar and in need of someone who can manage it." She landed on the edge of the open hall door. "Is it true?"

"The cat—that is to say Rumblkins—came in bearing news that something had happened to Cousin Elizabeth." Collins wrung his hands.

"She is missing."

"Then it is as they said, she is in the clutches of yet another ... dragon?" Collins' voice dropped to a whisper as his face turned as white as the vestibule's woodwork.

"Nothing is certain right now. I have come to fetch a set of maps to guide our search."

A thunderous roar rattled the windows and door. Someone was in an ill-humor indeed.

"You must speak to Longbourn while you are here. Pray sir, it is quite essential." Collins laced his fingers before his chest, nearly begging.

Cait looked over her shoulder toward the kitchen. "Mary is in the cellar with him right now, but it does not sound like she has been successful. He might take it in his mind to confront—"

"Netherfield, the dragon calls himself Netherfield."

"Whomever—Longbourn seems determined to bare teeth against him." Cait flapped violently enough to swing the heavy door.

Two major dragons in battle was hardly something one kept from the neighbors, one of the few things that could make this situation worse than it already was. Darcy pushed rainwater from his face with his palm. "Go to the study and look for a green leather-bound volume of maps whilst I deal with Longbourn."

"Excellent, most excellent. Perhaps I have seen it …" Collins lumbered off.

At least Collins was useful now, a marked change from before the hatching. Something to be thankful for considering the current short supply of good tidings.

"April returned last night and has met Earl. If Walker has his way, they are well on the way to being friends."

"I knew he would be in good hands with Fitzwilliam." Cait preened her ruff. "And, yes, I have also heard what is being said about Fitzwilliam—keeping secrets with wyrms about is nigh impossible."

"You are not concerned?"

"Of course, I am; I am no fool. But Walker has faith in your line, and that is enough for me." She flew off toward the study.

Cait made it sound so simple. All things considered, he should enjoy the fact that one difficult dragon was cooperating with him. With any luck, another might as well. With a very great deal of luck.

He pushed open the cellar door. Cool, dank air rushed at him. Considering the way his eyes burned and face stung, Longbourn was not bearing the news well at all.

Two candles in a wall sconce at the end of the stairs cast wan flickers on a very angry wyvern.

"Mr. Darcy! You are most welcome!" Mary met him just a few steps down, handkerchief held to her face. She handed it to him. "You need this more than I. Pray talk to him. Perhaps he will listen to you." She dashed past him, out of the cellar.

Her retreat was disappointing, but hardly unexpected. Few could stand up against a dragon's temper. He pressed the handkerchief to his nose and mouth. A familiar scent filled his nostrils—antivenom. The pressure in his chest eased.

"Is it true?" Longbourn roared and smacked the floor with his tail, raising a faint cloud of dust. If the creature were not careful, he could seriously damage the structure of the house itself. "Netherfield has taken her?"

"All we know is that she is missing. It is possible she merely took cover from the rain in the hills. We cannot jump to conclusions."

"I will look for her myself. I am not afraid of what I will find in the tunnels like the wyrms are."

"Pray do not." Darcy descended several steps.

"Do you think I cannot rescue her?" Longbourn bugled a challenge.

"I am sure you are capable, but it could drive Netherfield to drastic, even tragic action."

"If he harms her, I will kill him."

"That would be your right, but consider, there is no winner in a major dragon battle. Not only the dragons suffer, but also their Keepers and their Keeps. We must avoid that at all costs." Darcy lifted open hands.

"But if he has hurt her—"

"If he has harmed her, I will help you slay the beast, both Fitzwilliam and I will—damn the consequences. But we have no sign she has been harmed. Muster the little dragons of your Keep to scour the tunnels for any sign of her. When we know where she is, then we can mount a carefully considered rescue. It is Elizabeth's best hope. Will you do it for her?" Darcy held his breath. Everything about his suggestion was against dragon nature. They were neither cooperative nor patient.

Longbourn grumbled and stomped about. "It is the

kind of thing she would recommend. I will do as you ask, but if she is harmed—"

"Let us not consider that for the moment. It will not help."

Hours, or what seemed like hours, passed, surrounded by consuming dark and sharp chill air. Lydia clung to a tattered blanket, snoring and muttering in her sleep. Elizabeth huddled closer to the waning fire. The cold from the stone beneath her had long since penetrated her bones. She might never be warm again. Still the fire was welcome, a tiny hope in an otherwise very black place.

How had the lindwurm started a fire, much less kept one going? And why did he do so? He certainly did not require it.

"Are you in need of food?" Netherfield opened one eye. It had been yellow in the sunlight, but in the firelight it was more amber, with flecks of green and gold.

Her stomach roiled at the thought, but refusing hospitality was hardly a good way to establish rapport, an advantage she desperately needed. "I suppose a little."

Netherfield curled around himself—how did wyrms manage that?—and picked up a small trunk from the far side of the lair. He unwound and placed it near her. "Feed yourself."

She opened the dingy, tattered trunk, staring inside until she could make out the contents. Some jars of—well, it was impossible to tell—a few apples, carrots, a hunk of cheese, and several loaves of bread. She tore off a bit of bread and a corner of the cheese. They smelt fresh enough. She nibbled at the bread. Hard and dry, but not moldy. "Forgive me if I sound ungrateful, but where have these come from?"

"The forest wyrms bring me what I need." Netherfield rested his chin on his forepaws.

Was it possible that they were the same ones she knew?

"In exchange for your protection?"

"For my patience!" he snarled, but something about it felt half-hearted. "They require my tolerance as does everything in my domain."

"Have you really kept my sister here a month?"

"She has no sense of time."

"I thought not. She has never been very good at such things. My father considers her quite silly."

Netherfield huffed through his nose, rustling his whiskers. "He is quite right."

He considered her of little use, but he had not harmed her. How easily he could have disposed of Lydia when he had killed Wickham. Elizabeth wrapped her arms around her knees and balanced her chin on them, making herself as small and harmless as possible. "Lydia says you murdered Wickham, but I am not so sure."

"He is dead."

"You do not sound like a killer to me."

"I will defend myself."

"He tried to escape?"

Netherfield turned his face aside.

"Did he become lost in the tunnels? Or perhaps he fell afoul of some underground hazard? Perhaps in a naturally-formed room off the tunnels?"

"Sometimes the floors in those rooms are very thin, but a warm-blood cannot tell, especially one dragon-deaf. They cannot hear the rock crying out beneath them." Was that a touch of sadness in the lindwurm's voice?

Something about the way Netherfield's mane fell limp over his neck and the tip of his tail did not move, it all felt so sad, maybe remorseful, too. Had he been a familiar dragon, she would have reached out to comfort him.

Fitzwilliam would argue she saw sorrow because it was what she wanted to believe of the creature. But no, certainly it was there, was it not? "You came from France. That is a long way for a dragon to travel beyond his territory. Are continental dragons not as territorial as British dragons?"

"I expect that we are. But not all territory is worth having. You underestimate what Pendragon has done for you—men and dragon."

"Men forced you from your territory?"

"I do not submit to men!" He growled. "I simply did not relish what it would take to hold my land. Some took pleasure in the fight. Others were committed to ideals that I could hardly believe possible. One came from England, proclaiming that a reformation, an enlightenment as it were, could be obtained between man and dragonkind."

English dragons in France? "But you were not convinced?"

"Hardly. What did they know of the suffering that could be wrought by men? There is none alive in England from those days before Pendragon. What would they know of the true affliction men—and other dragons—might bring?"

"So you left rather than fight?" Was it possible this dragon was a pacifist?

"What good is there to fighting? What does it solve?

Until all parties might listen to reason, I had nothing to add to the situation."

"How did you choose to come to Hertfordshire? This is just a small, unimportant territory."

"What better place? The English ideologue told me of it, said I should see it myself and know what he proposed was not some utopia but an actual working society."

Was that the "Giver" noted in one of the paintings?

"He was wrong, though. Men are hardly different here to what they are in France. Not to be trusted. This is why I have you." Netherfield turned toward her and flicked his forked tongue very close to her face, not in the friendly sort of way that Rumblkins was in wont of doing. No, this was vaguely threatening. But was it real or just for show? "I know Longbourn values you. I know the men at both estates value you. So, I value you. As long as you bring me what I want."

"And what is that?"

"My territory." He hissed foul breath in her face and turned his back.

"I am cold."

He threw a heavy mass of dark wool at her.

A man's coat, Wickham's no doubt. The back was torn open—by claws or fangs? It was difficult to tell—and it sported blood stains near the tears. Had Netherfield torn this from Wickham's back during an attack, or had he tried to catch Wickham as he fell through a cave floor? Now did not seem the time to ask. She pulled the torn garment around her shoulders and shuffled a little nearer the fire. What was this creature about, and what did he really want? Perhaps more importantly, what was he willing to do to get it?

Late in the evening, the clouds broke and weak rays of sunset filtered through. With any luck, no more storms would move in tomorrow. But perhaps that would be hoping for too much.

Darcy climbed into the carriage, the mustard yellow book of maps on his lap. He, Mary, and Collins had spent hours searching the study and eventually the entire house, looking for a green volume. They turned up thin green volumes of farm records, an interesting treatise on the influence of field wyrms on crop production, and a genealogy of Dragon Mates in Hertfordshire from the early sixteen hundreds, but absolutely no maps.

Finally, Mary suggested that Bennet might not see colors very well and the volume might not actually be green. Why had she failed to mention that sooner? They widened their search to all thin leather-bound volumes and finally came across the one he now held.

He leafed through pages as the carriage swayed through puddles in the road. Page after page of maps with proper titles and compass directions carefully penned on each. Surely this had to be the volume Bennet wanted. No other book in the house fit the description even remotely.

He trudged inside, guided by voices into the still-occupied morning room. Had they not moved since he left?

"What took you so long?" Bennet rapped the table with his knuckles. "Bring it here. Bring it here."

"It would have helped had you told me the correct thing to look for. This book is hardly green." Darcy slid the book across the table at Bennet. No, it was not polite, but it was better than throwing it at him.

"What are you talking about? It is indeed green." Bennet slapped the cover and dragged it closer.

"There is nothing green about that cover." Fitzwilliam snorted and rolled his eyes.

"It is the color of ground mustard seed." Darcy clutched his forehead.

"No, it is not." Walker pecked at the book cover.

"Excuse me?" Darcy leaned hard on the table.

"Bennet is correct. The book is green." Walker bobbed his head.

April flitted closer and landed near the book, tapping with her long beaky snout. "It is not the color of grass to be sure. But neither is it the color of mustard. It is closer to the color of the stalks that bear flowers which are bad to eat and the beetles that make one sick."

Bennet removed his glasses and stared at the book. "You are certain this is distinctly yellow to you, Darcy?"

"I would bet Pemberley upon it."

"And you, Fitzwilliam?"

"Absolutely."

"And I would swear by the same certainty that the volume is decidedly green as my wife's garden—"

"Where she grows those awful flowers!" April hopped on the book.

"It would seem, gentlemen, we have stumbled upon an interesting finding. Apparently, not only can some men hear dragons, it seems that some can see like them as well, and it is different to other men."

Fitzwilliam gasped and pressed the side of his index finger to his mouth. Darcy glanced his way, but he shook his head.

"An interesting avenue to explore, but for another time, I fear." Fitzwilliam reached across the table to flip open the book. "Are these the maps you were hoping for?"

Bennet replaced his glasses and peered at the open pages. "Yes, quite so." He pulled the book closer. "Bring me that stack of maps ... no, not that one, the smaller one ... yes, there."

Fitzwilliam retrieved a pile from the sideboard and set it near Bennet. "Come to the kitchen with me, Darcy. I am sure you could use a bite to eat."

Fitzwilliam grabbed a candle and headed away from the kitchen. He ducked into the small drawing room and pulled the door shut.

"I imagine this has something to do with what Bennet just noted?" Darcy perched on the arm of the nearest chair.

"I met a dragon hunter in France. He told me the secret to sneaking up on a wyrm-type dragon was in wearing blue. I thought him superstitious or daft. He had spent so much time stalking dragons in caves and tunnels that his mind must surely have been affected. But now, I wonder. Is it possible that lindwurms tend to be blue because the color is difficult for them to tell apart from the rocks, particularly underground?"

"I would never have thought of that, but it might be a means by which smaller ones protect themselves from the larger, especially in territories where there is no other regulation to protect them."

"Go attend Bennet and his maps. I am going to search the house for some coverlet or curtain, something in the proper shade of blue. There are enough rooms here; surely there must be something. When we go after the beast, I want every possible advantage on

Netherfield: Rogue Dragon

our side." Fitzwilliam darted out. His heavy footfalls disappeared into the dark halls.

When they went after the beast. Darcy pressed his fist against the knot in his belly. What would happen to Elizabeth then? Was she still alive? The creature might well intend to use her to bargain for his own safety. That could mean it was a creature of reason and might be negotiated with. Even so, could it be trusted to hold up its part of a negotiation?

No, probably not. If it had lived with no rules to guide it, why would it be trustworthy now? Their best hope lay in Fitzwilliam's plan.

"Where did you get his coat?" Lydia shook her.

The warmth of Wickham's coat had lulled Elizabeth to sleep—probably not for very long. She hardly felt rested when she awoke—only stiff and sore and hungry. "I was cold last night. Netherfield gave it to me." She stretched aching arms.

"I have been cold, and he never gave it to me." Lydia pulled at the arm of the coat.

"The wyrms brought you that blanket." Netherfield lifted his head and hissed softly. "I thought it would only upset you. She has been whining about the deaf one since—"

"You killed him," Lydia snapped.

"Since Wickham ran off into the darkness is probably more to the point." Elizabeth pulled the coat out of Lydia's hands.

"There is blood on his coat! Right there, on the back! It killed my Wickham." Lydia stood and stomped, wane firelight shadowing her pouting face.

"Hush, Lydia, no more accusations. It is not helpful. Are you not hungry?"

"Yes. I am starving. I have been for weeks now!"

Elizabeth dragged her hand down her face. "May we?" She turned toward Netherfield as much to address him as to avoid seeing Lydia's pandering for sympathy.

Netherfield shoved the trunk closer, and Elizabeth opened it.

Lydia grabbed an apple and crunched into it. Elizabeth took a smaller one and slipped it into the pocket of Wickham's coat. What was that already in the pocket? A knife? Yes, that could be helpful. Certainly not large enough to defend against a dragon, probably not even long enough to penetrate its hide, but a knife was always useful.

Wait. There was something else, too. A metal box with a sliding lid. She closed her eyes and ran her fingers over it again. Darcy carried one much like it—was it possible? A fire starting kit? Darcy always carried one. Was it possible that Wickham had also?

"Have a piece of cheese as well, Lydia. You must keep up your strength." As she spoke, she slid the lid back. Yes, this was very similar to Darcy's kit.

"I do not like that sort of cheese. I will have a bit of bread though." Lydia snatched up a small roll. "Tell those creatures to bring more like these. These are at least edible."

"Have you even thanked Netherfield for what he provided?"

"One does not thank their jailor." Lydia tossed her head and turned her back on both of them.

"If one is smart, one does. I appreciate what you have done for our comfort." Elizabeth rose and curtsied.

"You are welcome. I shall have a blanket brought for you as well, if you wish," he said softly.

"You are most gracious." She sat back down and nibbled bits of bread and cheese. They were stale, but it was best to keep one's strength up.

"I will go out and survey my territory now." Netherfield rose up half way and scattered the fire with his tail. Darkness rushed in with the force of a flood. "You will have no need of this whilst I am gone. I warn you, do not try to follow the tunnel walls. There are pits and thin floors and crevasses that will take you without a trace."

Scales slithered against the rock, growing softer and farther away. Elizabeth held her breath, listening, until she could hear them no more.

Darkness unlike any above ground swallowed them. Complete and utter darkness. One could not see a hand in front of her face. One's eyes did not adjust to the unchanging blackness. Thick, heavy, and cold, it enveloped them, held them securely as chains, fraying their good sense and beckoning the edges of terror.

"He will be gone for hours. He always is. But he will return. It will feel like he has been gone forever, but he will return." Lydia's voice moved as she spoke. She probably sat down.

"Are you sure he will be gone for that long?"

"He has been every time. There was one day when he came back very late, but I cannot think of a single time that he returned early."

"Has any other creature ever visited you here? The wyrms he spoke of?"

"What is a wyrm?"

"A small dragon, long like a snake, but with more

of a lion's head."

"Eww, I have never seen such a thing, nor do I want to. No, I have seen nothing of the kind here."

"Good, good." Elizabeth reached forward, brushing her hands across the sandy ground.

"What are you doing, Lizzy? You cannot be thinking of making your way down these tunnels? In the dark? You will die …"

"Ah, here!" Bits of half-burnt wood and a larger branch! She dragged them closer. "I plan on doing exactly that, but not in the dark."

"What kind of magic have you to bring light into this place?"

"Fire." She fumbled with the fire starting kit. Slowly, she must move very slowly, for if she dropped anything, it might never be found again. There, the charcloth, the flint, the fire steel.

"Trust me. He has thoroughly extinguished the fire. There is no way—where did you get that spark?" Lydia's astonished face appeared in the brief light.

It took far longer than it should, but Elizabeth managed to get a small fire started. Somehow, the small circle of light pushed back the abiding darkness. Perhaps she really could effect an escape. "I thought I saw a pile of wood near the far wall. Help me find some green wood. Birch wood, too. I saw some in the fire last night. If there is bark left, I can make torches with it." At least one could in theory. Not that she had ever actually done so, but she had read about it in a tale tucked away in an old journal about what to do if trapped in a dragon lair. It had seemed just a fancy story at the time, but perhaps not. At the very least, it was worth trying.

Darcy and Fitzwilliam slept in shifts in the morning room chairs as evening turned to night and eventually into dawn. Bennet, though, required no such respite. He did not even seem to notice the passage of time, churning through page after page of books and maps. The man's capacity to take in information seemed inexhaustible.

The mantle clock chimed nine times. Nicholls trundled in with a tray of coffee, tea, a plate of kippers, and a rather large pot of honey. April's work, no doubt. But Nicholls came in whistling a happy little tune and left without any further inquiries of what might be required later, so who was to complain if the fairy dragon wanted sweets?

Fitzwilliam tossed a few kippers to Earl and Walker and handed Darcy a mug of coffee. Hot and bitter—exactly what he needed to drive away the remaining sluggish thoughts.

Bennet tapped the table. "I think I have something."

They crowded around the window side of the table where Bennet had shoved four maps together and placed one of the bound maps above them.

"What are we looking at?" Darcy peered over Bennet's stooped shoulders.

"Here is the key." Bennet pointed to a feature on the bound map that seemed entirely unremarkable and much like everything else on that page. "Here is Longbourn house and the lair." He pointed to the far corner of the map. "And this is the border of the two properties. I am certain this hill is the one you can see from the spot where the main road turns into the lane heading toward Netherfield Manor."

Fitzwilliam spilled a drop of coffee on one of the unmarked maps.

"Do be more careful! Stains will not facilitate reading these maps." Bennet elbowed him back. "What you have just managed to drip your beverage on is what I believe to be the same spot on the Netherfield maps."

Darcy's eyes flickered between the two documents. The stream, the larger hill with a smaller one beside it, yes. It required a little imagination, but there was good reason to believe Bennet correct.

Fitzwilliam set his coffee cup on the windowsill behind him and leaned over the maps. "So then, these others represent the lay of Netherfield's lands? I cannot discern much of what is written here." Fitzwilliam hovered his finger over some scribbles. "The mapmaker does not use standard symbology."

"A great deal of this is derived from ancient dragon script. This—" Bennet pointed at an odd squiggle, "is the sign for water. The direction of flow and the depth is reflected in the angle of the mark and the intensity of its color. These marks are indications that the features are actually underground. Again the darker the color, the deeper it is."

"That is why so much of the map is so faint! I had thought it just bad ink!" Fitzwilliam slapped his forehead.

Bennet harrumphed. "Hardly. These are actually very sophisticated renderings, far more so than they look. Most of your assumptions about them are probably wrong."

Dragon's blood! The man looked so smug. Was it not enough that he was right? Did he also have to be so self-satisfied, so condescending?

"It seems then these are the cluster of hills that mark the west side of the park?" Darcy drew his finger along the far side of one page.

"I believe so."

"But this stream—I have never seen it. We should have crossed it when we rode in." Fitzwilliam stroked his chin with his fist.

"I am not familiar with it, either. But these maps are quite old. I think it is possible that the waterway is underground now, or perhaps it was then, too, and he failed to include the proper marking. The depth of color suggests it is very deep, so perhaps that should be indication enough that the water runs underground."

"But you do not know for certain?" Darcy caught Bennet's gaze and held it firmly.

"No, I cannot be sure."

"Of what else are you not certain?"

Bennet grumbled and huffed but eventually pointed out three other significant features that did not appear in the current landscape.

Darcy flexed and released his hands. Better that than strangling Bennet. "So in short, what you are saying is that you are not actually certain we are looking at a map of Netherfield Park at all."

Bennet waved his hands as though that might make a difference. "I am quite certain that we are."

"Except for the fact it lacks two streams, one outcropping, and a rather large crevasse which should be rather obvious to anyone riding the land, of course, this map is Netherfield." Fitzwilliam sneered, shaking his head.

"I have no need of your sarcasm, young man. I have given you my explanations."

"Your speculations at best."

"Nonetheless, these three—"

"Rather four." Darcy pointed at another spot on the map.

"Make that five, no six." Fitzwilliam indicated two more places.

"—are the most obvious places to search for the lindwurm. I maintain these three are the places that would most appeal to such a creature."

"Assuming we have read the maps correctly." Darcy rolled his eyes at Fitzwilliam.

"And that such places even exist in the first place." Fitzwilliam matched his expression.

"Which, all things considered, we have blessed little assurance of."

Fitzwilliam retrieved his coffee cup and drained it in a single gulp. "Which is all to suggest that we are no farther along now than we were last evening."

Bennet threw up his hands and turned to face them. "You make it sound as if I wish these maps to be unclear. I want to see Elizabeth returned as much as you do."

"Useless warm-bloods!" April hovered over the maps, a drop of honey quivering on the tip of her beak. "What are you accomplishing in all this arguing? Can not one of you actually do something?"

All three men began talking over each other, trying to explain the nature of the situation to her in the simplest possible terms.

April landed on the table and sang until their eyelids drooped and they fell silent. "Much better. Since you cannot settle on anything useful to do, I will take matters into my own talons."

"What exactly do you think you will do?" Was

Bennet trying to get his ears bloodied?

"By now every minor dragon on both estates is aware Elizabeth is missing. One of them will know something. I will find it out."

"How exactly will you force them to tell you? I imagine the lindwurm will want his secrets kept." Bennet truly underestimated the power and resourcefulness of a determined fairy dragon.

She turned to Walker. "It is not something a warm-blood understands. But when one is asked a question by one's predator, one tends to answer."

Bennet snorted. "So you intend to talk to flowers and insects? I am sure they will be very helpful."

Walker landed on the table beside her, knocking the maps to the floor with his broad wings. "I shall be able to convince some of our smaller denizens to answer readily enough."

April bobbed her head as though this had been her plan all along. Perhaps it was. She took off. Darcy opened the nearest window just ahead of her. Walker swooped out behind her.

"I do not like the notion of simply sitting around, waiting on what the local wyrms might be saying," Fitzwilliam muttered.

"I have no intention of doing that. There is no reason why we should not start checking the locations we have identified, uncertain though they may be." Darcy turned on his heel and strode from the room. Bennet would probably be offended that he did not take leave, but, considering the things Darcy wanted to say, it was probably for the best.

Chapter 10

IT WAS IMPOSSIBLE to tell how long it had taken her to craft them, but eight shabby-looking torches lay before her, illuminated by a ninth, done in miniature to test the process. The light waxed and waned but mostly waned, threatening to succumb to the demanding darkness. Her petticoat was in shreds, used to bind the beech bark and green wood together, but what matter if it got them out of the cave?

"You cannot seriously mean to do this." Lydia folded her arms and stared at Elizabeth with a derision she could have only learnt from Papa.

"I most certainly am not going to sit here waiting for something to happen."

"You know a way out of these tunnels that we can traverse before these ugly torches of yours run out?"

"No, I never told you I did." Elizabeth stood and gathered the torches. "I am counting on encountering someone in these tunnels who can get us out before that happens."

"Because, of course, these tunnels are as busy as the roads around Longbourn, and meeting someone in here is quite likely." Lydia stepped closer as though trying to block her way.

"The area is frequented by wyrms. There are also fairy dragons—"

"Whom I have apparently been living with for quite some time without ever realizing it. Moreover, to my untutored eye it appears they fly, not slither about underground." Oh, the look of indignation she wore! The deep shadows only made it more poignant. What bothered Lydia more? That she did not know what they were, or that they had been kept secret from her?

"There is at least one puck in the area, and a small basilisk—"

"You know none of that means anything to me. It might as well be an elephant and an ostrich. Even if it did, what assurances have you that they will conveniently appear just when you need them? No, thank you. I shall stay here." She dropped, tailor-style, to the floor.

"I cannot force you to come with me, but I am leaving now."

"You really believe we can escape before it comes after us?" Lydia's expression softened.

"I prefer to take my chances in the tunnels than wait helpless in the dark."

Lydia shuddered and clutched her shoulders. "I hate the dark. I never want to be in the dark again."

"Then come with me." Elizabeth handed Lydia half the torches and waved her toward the far side of the lair.

With luck, the eight torches would provide about two hours of light. It should be enough. No wyrm would use a blind chamber. They always had at least two paths out, often more. If they could just follow Netherfield's tracks, those should lead them out in short order. Of course, the operative word was "should."

Once they escaped, Darcy would probably lecture her about how truly perilous this venture was. He would be right to do so. But if this dragon was as dangerous as Fitzwilliam and the Blue Order thought, was her plan worse than staying with him? What if the worst happened and the torches ran out before they found their way out? Death from dehydration would be unpleasant, but not instant. There was still hope they might be found.

Especially if they had food with them! Little wyrms had a keen sense of smell and demanding bellies. Perhaps it was ridiculous, but could it hurt to improve their chances?

"Lydia, take that cheese and tie it up in your apron."

"But it is nasty. Why should we bring that? The bread is much tastier."

"Not for you, for the rock wyrms." Elizabeth filled the pockets of Wickham's coat with more cheese, apples, and a jar of pickles. Those would prove particularly pungent upon opening.

"Should we not be worried about feeding ourselves instead?"

Elizabeth slowly turned and stared at Lydia, allowing her face to shape into an expression Longbourn had long since perfected.

Lydia gasped and shoved more into her apron, tied it up, and slung it over her shoulder. "I am ready."

Elizabeth counted steps. Some measure of distance might prove helpful, somehow. If nothing else, it was a welcome activity for her racing mind. About two hundred steps away from Netherfield's lair, a small room opened up to their right. Lydia lunged for it, but Elizabeth grabbed her by the back of her dress. She stuck her torch in the entrance. A gaping hole in the floor swallowed the light.

"This must be where Wickham was lost." Elizabeth's voice echoed off the walls.

"The beast pushed him," Lydia whimpered.

"I suppose we cannot be certain, but that is not the story he told me. You do understand, Wickham criminally threatened Netherfield. He would have been prosecuted in court for it."

"How? A court caring for that creature, that brute …"

Elizabeth raked stray hairs from her face. What would the Blue Order do with Lydia? There were rumors that the Order kept homes in remote parts of Scotland and Ireland for those who heard but would not join the Order. They seemed more like fairy tales to keep naughty children in order than actual places, but perhaps, like dragons, those too existed.

Those worries were for another time, though. After they were away from this place.

Several hours later, Fitzwilliam emerged from the barn leading two horses. A comically too-large greatcoat he had found discarded in one of the family rooms, hung over his shoulders. Hardly the expected image of a dragon hunter, to be sure. With full sun today, the garment would prove hot and cumbersome. Still, it was the shade of dark blue Fitzwilliam felt certain would be difficult for the lindwurm to see. No doubt, he had secreted the Dragon Slayer underneath.

Earl was sleeping in Bennet's care at present—besides eating, sleeping was all the chick did. If they were lucky, they would return with Elizabeth before his next feeding, and he would be none the wiser. If they were very, very lucky.

More likely, they would not be—luck rarely ran in Darcy's favor. There was no telling what that could mean. He suppressed a shudder as his guts clenched. The scenarios ranged from merely bad to completely tragic—and the tragic well outnumbered the bad.

"Start with the western sites?" Fitzwilliam handed him the reins of a smart chestnut gelding.

"That is the direction I last saw Elizabeth heading." Darcy swung up into the saddle and patted his coat pocket.

The maps were still there—of course, they were; it was silly to worry they had somehow disappeared. But Bennet had objected so strenuously to letting them out of his possession that he checked his pocket by reflex alone. Hopefully they would be of some use even without Bennet to interpret them.

They pushed the horses hard though it felt a little pointless to rush after all the time that had already passed with the storms and efforts to decontaminate the maps. Would extra minutes, even hours, matter at this point?

Still, they hurried.

"I think that is the rise on Bennet's map." Fitzwilliam pointed to two hillsides in the distance.

"If I recall correctly, the tunnels are supposed to run along that ridge and breach the surface in three places—at the ends and between those hills."

Dense trees shrouded the base of the rise. How

were they to find the entrances amidst those trees—if they were even still there after all the years since the maps were rendered?

Darcy unfastened his watch fob and raised it to his lips. Hopefully, Walker was close enough to be able to hear it.

Fitzwilliam covered his ears and whipped around to gawk at Darcy. "That is bloody well the most awful sound I have ever heard! What the hell was that?"

"Wait until you hear Earl's first full-bodied shriek. I assure you it will be far more dreadful. There is nothing to rend one's soul like a cockatrice's scream. When Earl is a bit older, I will see you have one of these. The whistle is useful for keeping in touch when he learns to hunt on his own."

For a moment Fitzwilliam looked like he was about to argue, but he closed his mouth and turned aside. They scanned the horizon. Walker should not be difficult to spot on such a clear day.

"What is that?" Fitzwilliam pointed.

An oddly-shaped shadow winged toward them. The wings resembled a cockatrice, but long, awkward legs dangled limply underneath.

Fitzwilliam slipped one hand under his greatcoat.

The shadow overtook them, the air above torn by a nerve-rending screech.

"We have word! We have word!" a tiny voice cried. April buzzed into Darcy's field of vision.

Walker dropped two wild-eyed rock wyrms at the horse's feet. Reminiscent of their forest cousins, they were more scaly than shaggy, mottled white, black and blue-grey with horny nubs on their heads for burrowing. Their fangs were longer and black eyes larger than those of forest wyrms.

They dismounted and approached the cowering wyrms.

"What news have you?" Fitzwilliam crouched near them.

The wyrms reared up on their tails and wove as though trying to make out where the voice came from.

Fitzwilliam slipped the greatcoat off his right shoulder, still keeping the sword hidden beneath the other side. "Is that better?"

The larger wyrm nodded. "Where did you come from?"

"Tell them your news." Walker poked the nearest wyrm with his wingtip.

"Is Elizabeth all right?" Darcy dropped to his knees, clenching his fists so he did not grab the creature and shake answers from it.

"Both females are well. The blue one sent us to get them food and blankets."

"Both? There are two?" Darcy asked.

"Is there a man as well?"

"Was." The smaller wyrm edged back as she answered.

"Did he escape?" The effort to moderate his tone lined Fitzwilliam's face.

"No one has seen him." The larger wyrm twitched and hunched into striking position.

"Did the blue one harm him?" Darcy's whisper seemed to calm the wyrms.

"Not know. Blue one did not say."

Fitzwilliam flashed his eyebrows at Darcy. He was right. At this point, Wickham was of little import as long as Elizabeth—and her sister—were safe. "Where have you been taking the supplies?"

The wyrms talked over one another until it

dissolved into gibberish. Walker squawked for silence.

Darcy produced his tin of beetles and gave each wyrm a treat. They gobbled the beetles without hesitation and descended into ecstatic writhing. As they righted themselves, they cast pleading glances his way.

"I have another for each of you if you will take us there."

"Come! Come!" They bobbed and wove about in circles as they waited for the men to remount the uneasy horses.

Following the wyrms, Fitzwilliam turned to Darcy with a raised eyebrow. "Whatever those are, Darce, it looks like I need to acquire some myself."

"Gardiner imports them. I will see you have some. Earl might even like them himself."

"Pray he does not drool all over himself like those wyrms."

"Cockatrice are known for their dignity. Do not fear." Darcy pointed toward Walker with his chin. The cockatrice followed the wyrms like a schoolmaster herding his students.

The wyrms led them north, toward the stream that bordered the two estates, not far from Longbourn's lair. Even with Longbourn's promise to not engage Netherfield, being so close to the wyvern's territory could not be a good thing.

The horses balked as they approached the hillside. Probably a good sign given horses were terrified of lindwurms. They dismounted and tied off the horses.

Fitzwilliam removed a pair of iron lanterns from his saddlebag, lit them, and handed one to Darcy. Neither cast a great deal of light, but in the overwhelming dark underground, they would be enough.

"In there." The wyrms stopped at a fairly large

opening in the hillside, sufficient for a lindwurm. "It goes straight to the blue one."

"Lead us." Fitzwilliam stepped inside the entrance.

"No, no, no. The blue one must not know we brought you." Both wyrms rose up on their tails, weaving around one another.

"Then you shall have no beetles until we find him." Darcy tapped his pocket.

The wyrms looked at each other, twitching and bobbing and swaying. "We wait here." The larger one said as they coiled up, entwined, on a sun-warmed rock near the opening.

Darcy made his way inside. A few steps into the tunnel, darkness enfolded them, a cold, dank blanket, heavy on their shoulders. Only the two flickering lanterns could push it back and then only barely.

Fitzwilliam led the way, one hand holding the lantern high, the other on the pommel of his sword. On the tunnel floor, they could just make out the scrapings made by the belly scales of a large wyrm. The size alone strongly suggested it was the one calling itself Netherfield.

The tunnel walls widened and narrowed, the ceiling lowered and lifted, ebbing and flowing like the course of a stream, never too tight for them to pass easily.

Odd. Was that the scent of wood smoke? This far underground?

"Look!" Fitzwilliam whispered and pointed ahead.

The remains of a fire were scattered across the tunnel floor. To the left, a small trunk leaned against the rocky wall. Nearby, a tattered blanket lay in a heap. What did a cold-blooded creature need a blanket for?

Darcy ran to the far wall and threw open the trunk, heart pounding. "Jars of preserves and pickles? Apples, crumbs of bread and cheese?"

"Look at these footprints." Fitzwilliam crouched near the remains of the fire. "Ladies' shoes."

He was right! But where was she? How could she have disappeared? He struggled to breathe. "She is not here."

Fitzwilliam laid a hand on his shoulder. "I see no signs of a struggle. No bloodshed. Moreover, it is clear she was here. We are close to finding her. Let me see your maps." They spread them on the dusty ground. Fitzwilliam tapped a spot. "This is the place the wyrms led us. See here? The spot between the hills we just passed through."

Darcy squinted in the flickering light. "So, then this is the passage we took, and here is where we are now."

"It seems the passage continues fairly straight through—yes, this is good! Look, the tunnel only splits off once and both of those lead up to entrances. So, there is little chance they could have got lost! Come, we will find them!" Fitzwilliam folded the maps and beckoned him deeper into the darkness.

"Lizzy, Lizzy!" Lydia grabbed at Elizabeth's arm. "Pray stop! We cannot go on like this. We are hopelessly lost!"

"We have no choice." Elizabeth pulled her arm away and trudged on. The cold and the dark were fraying her nerves, too, but they had to be close to an exit. They just had to be.

"We have been walking ever so long now, and we are down to your last torch. We must go back. It should be obvious to even you that there is no way out."

Just as it should have been obvious to Lydia that with only one torch left, there was no way they could get back to Netherfield's chamber. Their only hope was to press on.

"Lizzy, I said stop!" Lydia grabbed at her dress, and Elizabeth fell hard, dropping the torch. It bounced several times, hit the floor, sputtered, and went out.

"Light it! Pray light it!" Lydia shrieked.

"I cannot see it any better than you can. How am I to do it?"

"You found wood to light a fire in the dark." Lydia clutched at Elizabeth's hand.

"It is not as easy as you suppose. I hardly had time to see where the torch landed."

"You blame me for this? You were the one who dropped it."

"Not now, pray hush, and let me think." Elizabeth felt for the tunnel wall.

"Hush? Hush? Why should I hush? This is not a time for silence." Lydia stomped. "If anything, it is a time to cry out for help. How can anyone find us if we are silent? Help! Pray, someone help us! We are here!"

Elizabeth rubbed her temples. "Hush! I cannot think with you shouting!"

"Your thinking is what has got us lost in the darkness! It seems up to me to get us out. Help! Find us please! We are here, against the wall in the dark!"

Stupid, stupid girl! Elizabeth pushed stray hair out of her face. With any luck, she would be able to find the torch. Not that it would be easy, but it should be possible. If she could light it, they would have a few more minutes to try to find their way out. Not many, but it would be something. But perhaps, she should wait to even try until Lydia had thoroughly exhausted herself.

"Help! Help!"

Yes, she would definitely wait—and try to think amidst the noise. Was there some way to call to some of the local rock wyrms? If she could find one, a little cheese would buy its help. Perhaps if she just laid out the food?

She pressed her temples. The darkness made it hard to think, weighing heavier and heavier across her shoulders. The stark reality of their peril danced just behind her. To dwell on that was to surrender to it, though, and she was just not ready to do that. Not yet.

"Lizzy, look!" Lydia shook her shoulder.

Surely, she must be seeing things. Elizabeth rubbed her eyes with her fists, but the yellow-green blob of light, faint but growing, remained.

"Here we are!" Lydia shook her harder. "See, see, I was right! We are saved! Because of me! you see I was right!"

Elizabeth held her breath. That color was cold, unnatural, not the color of fire. It was unlike any color she had ever seen, more like a willow-the-wisp of legend. Every fable declared they existed only to lead travelers astray. She clutched the wall behind her, knees softening into jelly. Since most dragon legends held a measure of truth, this one probably did too, and that could only mean—

"Pray come here! I am sure you are looking for us! Get us out of this awful place!" Lydia stood, sleeves rustling as though she waved her hands.

The light grew larger and brighter, bobbing, maybe as high as Elizabeth's head. She pressed harder against the wall. The tiny knife in her pocket would offer little protection, and she could not run. Is this how the virgins sacrificed to the dragons of old felt? She pressed her fist to her mouth. Screaming was undignified.

A face appeared.

Lydia screamed and fell against Elizabeth who caught her barely in time to keep her from striking her head against the stone.

"Look, I see light ahead!" Fitzwilliam pushed through the narrowing tunnel, Darcy on his heels.

Sunlight blinded them, stopping them just a step beyond the small exit. Blessed warmth penetrated the layer of cold that had followed him from the tunnels. Fresh, sweet air filled his lungs—he never had liked the stale smell of stone.

Darcy closed his eyes and listened: a slight breeze, birdsong, soft slithering and chattering—probably the rock wyrms approaching, in search of their promised treat. But no female voices, no rustle of skirts against underbrush, not a single sound he wanted to hear.

She should have been here, waiting for him, assuring him she was well and everything was going to be all right. He reached behind him for support.

"Darce, look!" Fitzwilliam elbowed his knee.

Darcy blinked until his eyes finally adjusted.

Fitzwilliam crouched several yards from him, pointing at marks in the sand. "These tracks—I am sure they are lindwurm."

Darcy peered over his shoulder. The marks were subtle, subtle enough for any but the most experienced tracker to miss. When, how had Fitzwilliam become so skilled?

"Beetle?" The two rock wyrms hurdled over a large rock and landed at his feet.

"We did not find her." Fitzwilliam folded his arms over his chest and glared at the now cowering creatures.

"She was there! She was!" The small one cried, hiding in the large one's shadow.

"We saw signs that she had been there." Darcy tucked his hand in his coat pocket.

"You see! We did not lie! She was there."

"Do you know where she is now?" Darcy removed his hand from his pocket.

The wyrms slumped. "Have not seen or heard. The blue one passed but only scolded us to bring more food."

"You saw the blue one? When? Where?" Fitzwilliam whipped his head back and forth, scanning the woods.

"After you entered the tunnel. The shadows moved from there to there." The larger rock wyrm pointed with his tail, but the effect was meaningless. "He went this way. He patrols his territory every day. He would have gone there next, then there and there." The wyrm pointed in many directions, but finally stopped facing east.

Listening to wyrms was almost as irritating as trying to converse with fairy dragons. Perhaps a little more so.

"He always takes the same path?" Fitzwilliam stared at them as he did freshly recruited soldiers.

"He becomes angry if anything interferes with his ways."

"Good, good, then we know where to go. Come." Fitzwilliam beckoned.

"Wait." Darcy crouched and produced beetles for each wyrm. "I have kept my promise to you even though we have not yet found her. If you see any signs of her or find her, you are to let us know immediately, and there will be more beetles."

After their post-beetle ecstasy, the wyrms readily agreed. Of course, they would. Anything to sate their perpetually-empty bellies.

"Those are right handy little tidbits," Fitzwilliam muttered as he tromped east.

"No accounting for taste, I assure you; they smell dreadful. But it is difficult to think of anything else quite so efficacious in gaining the wyrms' cooperation."

"There, look. The trail—a fresh one—the wyrms spoke of. I hardly dared believe they would be sensible, but it seems they are."

Dragon thunder shook the trees.

"Dragon's blood and fangs!" Darcy punched at the air. "I told him not to confront Netherfield."

"Bloody hell! It is possible Longbourn caught Elizabeth's scent and is pursuing Netherfield to rescue her. Or …"

Darcy held up an open hand. No need to go there.

"We might be able to use this to our advantage." Fitzwilliam trotted off into the deep woods, following the dragon thunder.

"What do you mean?" Deadfall crunched beneath them as they ran, dodging stones and fallen branches.

"While the creature is distracted, I may be able to sneak up on it."

"You cannot harm it until we have Elizabeth back. If only he knows where she is … we must rescue her." Darcy clenched his fist.

"Trust me, I will do everything I can to recover her. But I also have orders to neutralize the rogue dragon's threat."

Darcy bit his tongue. What was there left to say? Nothing would dissuade Fitzwilliam from carrying out his orders—and perhaps nothing should.

Clearly, though, he had never been in love. Some things were important enough to bring even the Blue Order's demands into question. But that was not an argument he could win now… or perhaps ever.

The dragon thunder increased, booming in a different voice now. Another dragon! No! The two had already met! Once they confronted each other, little save a more dominant dragon, could intervene—and neither he nor Fitzwilliam qualified as such.

"Look, there!" Fitzwilliam pointed through the trees to a place where the forest gave way to a rocky clearing backed by several low hills.

Longbourn loped toward the clearing from the western edge, the ground trembling with each step. The lindwurm rose on his tail, challenging the wyvern's bellow with his own thunder.

So that was what a lindwurm looked like in the flesh. A dark grey-blue, darker than the rock wyrms, with a wild mane, fully fluffed to increase his size. Fangs bared, they must have been the length of Darcy's hand, stained and streaked with neglect. Short forearms waved near his head, toes flexed to show his talons to greatest effect.

Longbourn stopped well out of Netherfield's striking distance, wings fully extended and flapping. He threw back his head and screeched like a hunting cockatrice, his size lending volume and power to his voice that no cockatrice would ever have.

The sound should have driven every other living thing away from their confrontation. At least those living creatures with sense enough to flee fighting dragons. Unlike he and Fitzwilliam, who were compelled to run toward it.

A face appeared beneath the bobbing yellow-green glow, one unlike any Elizabeth had ever seen. A long, very square muzzle ended in a huge, fanged mouth. Ridges along the nose led to close-set eyes reflecting an orangey glow. Bushy eyebrows swept back and met a hairy fringe along the bottom jaw, becoming a mane—more equine than leonine—full and bushy, extending down a very long neck. The side manes met at the back and merged into a pointed spinal ridge that disappeared into the darkness. Very long whiskers dangled from the edges of the nostrils into a very distinct mustache. It might have hopped off one of Lady Catherine's prized chinoiserie cabinets at Rosings Park. Elizabeth gulped and glanced at the front feet. Four toes!

"You are the emissary?" Elizabeth pulled her shawl up over her head and dropped to a knee before the high-ranking Eastern dragon.

"You are Blue Order?" Her accent was odd, each word slow and deliberate; *blue* sounded more like "brue" and the "r"s of *order* all but disappeared, but her meaning was clear enough.

"I am, Emissary." Elizabeth rose, head still bowed. "We were told you had become lost on your journey. Pray, permit me to introduce myself. I am Miss Elizabeth Bennet." She curtsied.

"Erizabet?" The dragon cocked her head. The odd

glowing ball turned with her.

How peculiar. It seemed to be attached to the top of her head. She carried her own light with her? How astonishingly clever. No wonder she was willing to come all this way via the tunnels!

"I am called Shin-dee-a." The dragon dipped her head.

"May I address you that way?"

"Of course. Why else would I tell you what I called?" Shin-dee-a chuckled, a deep-bellied, sonorous, but most of all, friendly sound. "What wrong with her?" She pointed a long foreleg toward Lydia.

"I fear it is a very long story, but in short, she was not expecting to see you."

"Then why she call for help?"

"I promise, I will explain soon, but first, would you assist us in getting to the surface?"

"I get you out. Come." She poked Lydia. "Up, up, time to go."

Lydia sat up and started to scream, but Elizabeth clapped her hand over her mouth. "Be still. Lady Shin-dee-a has come to help us."

"Lady?"

"It is complicated. Come." Elizabeth grabbed Lydia's elbow and dragged her to Shin-dee-a's side. They walked beside her in the odd glow of her ... what did one call that? A bobble?

Perhaps a hundred yards later a sliver of light appeared in the distance. They had been so close to the end. If only Lydia had not—

"I hope it not problem. I hunted here this morning."

"We are honored to have you hunt on our lands. I will introduce you to the local Laird. He will offer you hospitality until the Blue Order comes for you. They have been beside themselves that you have been lost."

"Most gracious, Miss Erizabet. My thanks." Shin-dee-a bobbed her head.

"We are saved, Lizzy!" Lydia ran ahead into the blinding sun.

"Pray forgive my sister."

"Is complicated?" Shin-dee-a snickered.

"I am afraid so."

Elizabeth and Shin-dee-a paused, squinting at one another as their eyes adjusted. In the sunlight, Shin-dee-a was the color of pure red jade, like a carving in Lady Catherine's favorite drawing room, down to the streaks of cream and black in her hide. "Pray forgive my staring, but you are astonishingly beautiful, Lady."

"You never seen one of my kind, have you?" She tossed her head back, and the glowing bobble flew up and over her head, becoming lost in the depths of her red-and-cream-streaked mane.

"I have not had the privilege—"

Dragon thunder roared. Dragon's fire! It was close by!

"Is that a storm coming, Lizzy? Where are the clouds?" Lydia carefully avoided looking at Shin-dee-a.

"No storm. Those angry dragons." Shin-dee-a's brow creased.

Heavens, what an introduction to British dragons this was becoming! "Yes, they are. Pray forgive me. I must deal with this!"

"I was told dragons lived peacefully here."

"Yes, Lady, they do, but this current situation is—"

"Complex?" Shin-dee-a's bushy eyebrow lifted.

"Quite so."

"Is nothing here simple?"

Netherfield: Rogue Dragon

"It is a very unusual circumstance right now." Elizabeth took Lydia's hand. "Pray, stay right here whilst I deal with this matter."

Lydia snatched her hand away. "I will do no such thing! I need to return to the house and tell Papa what has been going on."

"I assure you, he is entirely, abundantly, and clearly aware of all of this and a great deal more."

"Papa knows about the creatures, too?" Lydia's incredulous expression would have been laughable at another time—probably any other time. She slumped against the hillside like a melting jelly.

Shin-dee-a snorted.

"I hate to ask this of you, Lady, but my sister cannot be left unchaperoned right now. Pray might you stay here and keep watch over her?" Another crash of dragon thunder left them all cringing. "I really must manage this situation."

"Is she as ignorant as she seems? I will keep watch on her and wait for you. Go do what you must. Return soon." Shin-dee-a laid down and rested her chin upon her forepaws, patience carved into her features.

Hopefully, Lydia would be so intimidated by her chaperone that she would not attempt to go off on her own. Now that she knew about dragons, she could not be left alone. Leaving her in the care of anyone not a member of the Order was technically a breach of law, but the two dragons screaming in the distance were an even-greater problem and one capable of inflicting far greater harm than Lydia, for the moment at least.

Elizabeth curtsied and ran toward the dragon thunder.

Fitzwilliam signaled Darcy to the left whilst he ran up the rise to the right. Darcy broke into the clearing, not far from the two dragons.

"You have gone too far." Longbourn lunged and snapped at Netherfield. "I have tolerated you and your trespasses, but taking her is too much."

Netherfield dodged back, arching his lithe body into impossible shapes. "I have tolerated enough from you. Your ceaseless tempers and whining demands. You told me I would not be bothered, that this place was safe. You lied to me! I demand reparation."

"I promised you nothing. I owe you nothing. I want you gone!" Longbourn flapped his wings and rose just enough so his feet cleared the ground.

"This territory is mine. I will have it!" Netherfield struck like a snake, but Longbourn back-winged just out of range.

A pale blur tore out of the underbrush and stopped between the dragons, waving a shawl over her head like Talia's hood. "Both of you! Cease this instant!"

What? No! Darcy pelted toward the dragons, skidding to a stop just beside her. "Merciful heavens! You are safe!" He grabbed Elizabeth's shoulders and pulled her toward him.

She bore no outward sign of injury though her pallor suggested cold and hunger. She pressed her cheek to his. "There is so much to tell you—"

"Elizabeth!" Longbourn snorted and landed beside her in a ground-shaking thud. "What has he done to you?" He lowered his head to peer at her eye-to-eye.

Netherfield dropped to Elizabeth's height, belly on the ground. "Nothing! I did not harm her! Tell him!"

Elizabeth touched Longbourn's snout. "I am well."

Longbourn stomped. Several rocks shook loose and rolled down the slope toward them. "You stole her away—you stole what is mine!"

She paused as if considering how to respond. "I am here now, returned—so nothing was stolen."

"He took you unwillingly. That is insult enough."

"I have a right to protect myself! If you had not come—" Netherfield nosed Darcy, driving him back several steps. "All would have been well. Everything was right until you came, and the egg and all its troubles followed."

Longbourn lunged at Netherfield, knocking him away from Darcy. Netherfield lashed his tail and swept Longbourn's feet out from under him. He landed on his back, wings spread. Netherfield rose up on his tail and loomed over Longbourn, fangs bared.

Just how long were that creature's fangs?

Darcy grabbed Elizabeth's hand and pulled her aside. "We must get away from them. They are beyond listening."

She hesitated a moment but allowed him to pull her partway up the hill behind the shelter of several large rocks.

Longbourn lashed his tail across Netherfield's chest. He fell back just long enough for Longbourn to regain his feet. The two circled, growling and hissing, spittle and venom flying. Longbourn leapt at Netherfield, driving him toward the outcropping where Fitzwilliam hid beneath the blue greatcoat. Was it a coincidence, or did Longbourn know Fitzwilliam was there? Just a little closer and Fitzwilliam would be able—

"Ki—yah!"

Darcy covered his ears against the piercing scream as a red blur plummeted from the hillside above, gliding down to land neatly between Longbourn and Netherfield.

They both scrabbled back, gaping at the intruder.

Long and sleek, like a wyrm, but it was not a wyrm. It landed on four legs, then rose up on the hind two, taller than the other dragons. Webbing extended between the front and back legs—that must have allowed her to glide down with such precise control—extending her body enough to shield the two combatants' views from one another. Her head was like nothing he had ever seen before—except in Aunt Catherine's collections. Dragon's blood!

Darcy clutched Elizabeth's arm. "The envoy? You brought her here?"

He probably did not ask that well, considering the look in her eye. "I did not bring her. She found us in the tunnels. I asked her to keep watch over Lydia whilst I dealt with this matter."

"Lydia is here, too? And Wickham?"

"Dead."

The words clumped together and settled as a cold, hard knot in Darcy's stomach. Of all the ways he thought Wickham might have met his demise, dragons had never been one.

The envoy dropped her forelegs, and the webbing folded. She puffed her body half again as large as she had been, towering over Netherfield and Longbourn. "Both stand down. I command." Her voice boomed, echoing off the rocky hillsides, piercing his skull, penetrating as few voices ever had.

Longbourn bared his teeth and snarled, unfurling his wings. He expanded his chest and hovered several feet above the ground. "You are in my territory!"

The envoy bared her own formidable fangs and snapped a little too near Longbourn's throat for comfort. "You challenge?" She spoke slowly, confident and deadly.

Netherfield dropped flat on the ground, paws on top of his head.

Longbourn retreated gradually, folding his wings as he went. Three steps back, he lowered his head partway—above Netherfield's, but below hers.

"You—" the envoy pointed directly at Fitzwilliam. Her tone changed, not quite as threatening, but without a doubt in charge of the situation. "Come out. Speak for yourself."

Fitzwilliam stepped forward and threw off the coat, sun glinting from the hilt of the Dragon Slayer.

Elizabeth sucked in a ragged breath, fist to her lips, and edged back.

Fitzwilliam was a fearsome, handsome man, resembling nothing so much as a fairy tale prince confronting a dread beast ... beasts. Definitely not the image to present to the envoy on her first encounter with the Blue Order.

Netherfield gasped and reared up to face Fitzwilliam eye-to-eye. "Here to finish the job now?"

"What are you talking about?" Fitzwilliam drew the weighty sword. Sunlight glinted from the polished blade, the reflective qualities part of the weapon's intended properties. Forged from a unique blue steel, it could be honed to an edge far sharper than any other metal known and held its edge even against dragon hide and bone. Only a handful of men knew of its existence, much less how to forge such a weapon.

"You have already marked me in Calais,"

Netherfield turned his scarred neck into the sun. "Or have you already forgotten?"

A jagged line, puckered and covered in drawn white flesh, ran from the bottom edge of Netherfield's jaw down to his shoulder.

"That was not me." Fitzwilliam planted his feet and raised the sword.

"Was it not enough I left that place, that I have been no greater threat to man here than I was in France? Are you so bent upon my destruction nothing will satisfy you but my blood?" Netherfield swung a taloned forepaw.

To the dragon-deaf, it would have seemed a fearsome attack. But in truth, it was more a half-hearted show.

Fitzwilliam parried the blow, cleanly slicing off a talon. He could have taken the entire paw. The talon bounced along the rocky ground with a vaguely metallic clank. "I dealt with no dragons in Calais."

Netherfield wove and struck the air to either side of Fitzwilliam. "You did not slay my mate there in the caverns of our ancestral home? I would know that sword anywhere."

Fitzwilliam held his ground. "Many have carried this sword. This is the first time it has been placed in my hands."

Netherfield snapped, far closer this time. Fitzwilliam repelled his attack, sword to fang. He feinted to the left, but the dragon anticipated and drove him back. Fitzwilliam swung and sliced off the tips of Netherfield's mustache-whiskers. Netherfield skittered back, nearly tangling in his own coils.

"And now it has been sent after me again. What has your Order against me?"

"You have killed—"

"Only in self-defense—or has your precious Order stripped that right from us, too?" Netherfield hissed and dove toward Fitzwilliam.

He dodged behind a rock. Netherfield's fang took a fearsome gash out of the soft limestone.

"A school of women and little girls attacked you? You call digging under the foundations of the building and causing it to collapse on the children self-defense?"

"Smugglers did that and blamed it upon dragon-kind!" Netherfield shook his tooth free of the stone.

"An inquiry—"

"A French inquiry! Men there do not recognize dragons. We were declared guilty and hunted down as soon as the claim was given voice."

"What of the captives you have taken here?" Fitzwilliam lowered the sword but only slightly.

"He killed Wickham!" Lydia shouted from the hilltop. "He is a murderer!"

"Do not speak what you do not know, Lydia," Elizabeth shouted through cupped hands. "Wickham threatened him in his lair so Netherfield detained them there to keep Wickham from bringing the regiment upon him. Wickham tried to escape and fell to his death through a thin cave floor. I saw the place myself."

"What does it matter? I have done everything that could have been expected of me, everything a dragon might do to escape the war, came to territory expressly given me to so that I might live in peace. But I am done." He lurched forward and dropped his head in front of Fitzwilliam's feet. "Be done with it. Just make it a quick work."

Fitzwilliam stepped back, lowering the sword

further. "You said this territory was given to you? By whom?"

"What does it matter?"

"It matters a very great deal. There are provisions in the Pendragon treaty by which a dragon may surrender his territory to another without bloodshed. Tell me precisely who it was who gave you this territory and how it was accomplished. It is possible you may have a rightful claim on these lands. If you do, the Order is bound to honor it."

"You are playing with me. Do you find honor in prolonging my death?" Was it possible for a dragon to sound melodramatic?

"I find honor in obeying the letter and the spirit of the law as it has been given us. You have not shed blood—" Fitzwilliam sheathed his sword and hunkered down beside Netherfield, voice turning very soft.

"Forgive, Erizabet." The envoy bowed her head and shoulders toward them. "Sometime a larger dragon must settle matters."

"Dragon diplomacy at its finest." Darcy bowed to the envoy.

Elizabeth turned to him, her expression very difficult to read. "May I introduce ... my betrothed and partner in Keeping Pemberley. This is Fitzwilliam Darcy."

"Shin-dee-a of Eastern Dragon Federation." She bobbed her head.

"The honor is mine ... Lady." He glanced at Elizabeth, and she half-shrugged, half-nodded, obviously as unsure of the title as he. "I fear this might not be the best introduction to the Blue Order and who we are."

"Not at all." She waved a forepaw. "All most interesting. How better to understand you than in conflict time?" Shin-dee-a twitched her tufted ears, mostly hidden by her mane. Her lips rose at the corners as though enjoying some secret joke.

"Gracious!" Elizabeth gasped and covered her mouth. "Look."

Fitzwilliam sat, tailor-style, beside Netherfield's head, one hand on his shaggy mane. Netherfield spoke softly while Fitzwilliam listened, nodding. He looked up and beckoned Darcy over.

Darcy took Elizabeth's hand—she accepted his hand and held it! His throat tightened till he almost could not breathe—and they rushed to Fitzwilliam.

"I have heard his story and am convinced he has a legitimate case to bring to the Order. Apparently after the last Keeper died, the old Netherfield emigrated to France in hopes of fostering a dragon enlightenment of sorts. He relinquished his Keep to this lindwurm who took the name in keeping with British tradition. Of course, the old dragon never informed him of the proper manner to claim the territory, leading to the current misunderstanding."

"Misunderstanding? Did I hear you correctly?" Darcy blinked hard and stared at Fitzwilliam. Was this the same man who had just days ago refused to entertain the idea of a diplomatic solution?

"Yes, you did. Darcy, and I do realize I am never going to hear the end of it. But I am a big enough man to admit, Miss Elizabeth, you were correct—"

She dragged her sleeve over her eyes. "I am relieved, for all of us, but I am hardly inclined to declare this a personal victory. Pray allow me a few moments to speak with Longbourn. Then, I think it is time for all of us to return home and send a great deal of news to the Order." She squeezed Darcy's hand and waved

Longbourn closer.

One eye on Shin-dee-a, Longbourn approached, head held low.

"May I present Laird Longbourn, Lady Shin-dee-a?" Elizabeth gestured at the two dragons. "Lydia and I had become … lost … in the tunnels, and she rescued us. We owe her a great deal." She said the words slowly, deliberately, staring directly at Longbourn. "Laird Longbourn has agreed to act as your host whilst you are with us. Pray stay with him in his lair and hunt on his land. We will send a messenger to the Blue Order directly. An escort will be sent to ensure you make it to the Blue Order offices without further inconvenience."

Longbourn's face wrinkled as though he were thinking hard. "You may stay with me. Come."

That was probably as friendly as major dragons were ever going to be about sharing their territory with another. Shin-dee-a followed him off into the woods.

"Pray Fitzwilliam," Elizabeth called over her shoulder. "My sister requires a chaperone—at all times now. Would you take her to the house with you?"

"I shall care for her as though she were my own." Fitzwilliam saluted, but his eyes were entirely serious. "Miss Lydia, you will come to the house with us."

"With that creature? I will not—"

"I said you will come."

Lydia jumped back several steps. Most people did the first time they heard Fitzwilliam's command tone. She shrank and ducked her head. "Yes, sir."

"Very nice," Netherfield murmured, doubtless meant to be heard by Fitzwilliam alone. "I should like you to teach me that."

"I will consider it." He escorted Lydia and Netherfield away.

Darcy reached for his watch fob. Walker should be alerted. He could not be far off.

Elizabeth stayed his hand. "We should talk without an audience." She nodded toward the woods.

Chapter 11

THE ROCKY HILLSIDE echoed too much, not to mention Netherfield had taken her from there. Neither was conducive to the words that needed to be spoken. Elizabeth needed someplace quiet and secure.

Darcy took her hand, his grip warm and strong. Hopefully, that was a good sign, but maybe he was being a gentleman, assisting a lady in need. They walked several minutes into the woods where the hardwoods cast deep shadows and grew too close together for large dragons to pass.

"I have never seen the Dragon Slayer wielded before."

He edged the slightest bit closer, his shoulder almost brushing hers. "It is not an easy weapon to use. A man must be trained by an expert to have any hope of success with it."

"The training is tailored to the dragon in question?" Granted, this was not at all the subject she had hoped to discuss, but at least they were talking.

"Of course. Each one is very different in their strengths and weaknesses. In my case—dealing with a hatchling—the training I had was minimal. But sufficient to be the stuff of nightmares. I am grateful we did not have to see a dragon's demise today."

"I am as well." She walked several more steps, drawing a deep breath. "Though, I better understand why it might have been seen as necessary."

"You have no idea how I—we—suffered, knowing you were missing, not even knowing for certain he had taken you." His words were halting, even labored.

"I was foolish to go out as I did. Not for the walk after we argued, that was essential, but following the trail Netherfield laid for me, that was foolish."

"He laid a trap for you?"

"I simply walked into it, believing—oh!" She stopped and slid her hand from his. "It seems I am capable of being every bit as stubborn as I have accused you of being. I have been so intractable you did not even think you could talk to me about what was truly important. I regret that more than anything else."

He caught her hand again. "I did not make things any easier. Fitzwilliam insisted you not be told—ordered it, more or less. But that does not mean I was compelled to obey."

"I see how persuasive his orders can be, though." She giggled. "Apparently, he was right. I hate to confess it, but there it is. He thought I would be headstrong and insist on doing things my own way. I have done just that. I am certain my father would have told you the same thing."

"Your father's opinion is of little concern to me."

"He has always said that I was incorrigible and

would one day get myself into a very great deal of trouble because of my refusal to follow protocols and structure. And indeed I have. I walked into a trap and was kidnapped by a rogue dragon."

"I admit that was a bit troublesome." The corners of his lips drew up in the hint of a wry smile.

"Just a bit? You are far too kind. I was foolish and impulsive, exactly as Papa described." She straightened her shoulders and steeled herself. "I completely understand if that is not what you wish for in a wife. I cannot possibly be the sort of influence you desire for Georgiana. I am unlikely to be a credit to you in society—certainly not the *ton* and perhaps not among the Blue Order, either. My opinions are far too decided. What is more, I lack the self-control to restrain my own tongue. I know what we promised to the Order: we are both to act as Keepers for Pemberley, but there are certainly ways to make it work other than forcing you into a marriage with me."

"It is kind of you to have both overlooked my complicity in this circumstance —I should have brought you into our confidence and committed to developing a more suitable plan—and that you have taken it upon yourself to determine not only how I feel but how I should act."

"I do not have the pleasure of understanding you."

"Good. Then perhaps that will force you to actually listen to me." He crossed his arms and stared— no, glared at her.

"I only mean to make things less difficult for you. I know you are an honorable man. You will hold to your word even if you have changed your mind."

"Which, of course, you know so well, you are able to discern it without my speaking a word."

"Any reasonable man would—"

"I am not a reasonable man!"

She took half a step back.

"I do not know where you ever got the notion that I am a reasonable man, but I am not. I have never been, nor do I ever expect to be. I can give you quite a number of people to apply to for confirmation on that point, starting with Fitzwilliam."

"Whatever do you mean?"

"I am a man who hears dragons; that alone is enough to set me apart from the normal, sensible sort. I also happen to like their company more than I like most people. That certainly is not sensible." He took both her hands in his and drew her a step closer. "And I am deeply and earnestly in love with a woman who finds dragons literally throwing themselves at her feet, yet her father is the laziest Dragon Keeper and most decided curmudgeon in all of England. That, I assure you, is not sensible at all. And yet, here we are."

"What did you say?"

"My dearest, loveliest Elizabeth." He led her to sit near a large tree. "What will it take to make you believe the very qualities that make your father most annoyed are those I most admire in you? I do not want a woman who cannot think for herself, who relies upon me for every scrap of information, and to form her every opinion. Yes, I would like you to do me the honor of talking with me and sharing your thoughts with me, but I relish your ability to leap from one specialty to another, drawing connections and conclusions others would never see."

"And the fact I go brashly charging along after my own ideas regardless of what others think?"

"You are confident in what you know. Sometimes

that might be a bit overwhelming, but now, I think you will also be more respectful of what you do not know and take that into consideration as well."

"You see, I am not—" She pulled away and braced herself to stand.

"Stop it right now!" He grasped her upper arms. "You made a mistake, and yes, it could have cost us everything. It was a serious one. I do not forget that now, nor will I ever forget it."

Her eyes burned, and she stared at the ground.

"You are not accustomed to making mistakes where dragons are concerned, are you? I would wager you probably have never really made one before?"

"No, I have not."

"Then I am glad you have made one and a very serious one at that."

"So that I may be properly humbled into my place."

"So that you might be more cautious and willing to accept a partner with a different perspective on these draconic adventures of yours."

She looked up and stared into dark eyes that could not possibly have been more sincere.

"I do not want you to change. I have never wanted that. I know our life together is going to be challenging. Little Pemberley alone will more than ensure that. No one has raised a firedrakling in centuries. You will be writing the book on the matter in a very literal sense. How could I not want to be part of that?"

"But I am so very, very difficult."

"Is not anything worth having apt to be difficult?" He looked over her shoulder and nodded.

Walker landed beside Darcy, and a chittering ball of blue fluff zipped past.

"You best listen to what he is saying!" April scolded,

hovering in front of her face. "The man has been beside himself since you were taken."

"He has been only slightly more distraught than she." Walker nodded toward April.

Elizabeth extended her hand. April perched lightly on it. "You have come back?"

"It seems I cannot leave you alone!" April pecked her hand, but it was a half-hearted effort at best. "Where is my cloak?"

"Back at the house. There was no point to wearing it without you. I will put it on as soon as we get there." She stroked April's soft head. "I am glad you have come home."

"Then you know how Darcy feels. Declare him your mate, and be done with it. Truly, it is not a bad thing." She hopped to Elizabeth's shoulder and cuddled into her neck.

A tear dripped down her cheek and another. How she had missed her constant companion. Was this truly how Darcy had felt, too?

He met her gaze without hesitation.

Merciful heavens! It was!

"I wish I could make your father see you as I do. But he is set in his ways and will probably never change. I am sorry that is the way of things. I only hope someday you might see yourself as I do, and it will be enough." He traced the crest of her cheek with his fingertips.

She leaned into his hand as his other arm slipped around her waist. April hopped off her shoulder and clung to the tree trunk nearby, singing sweetly.

His lips found hers in a kiss that lingered as his fingertips caressed her throat.

"Pray, are you convinced now that I still intend for

you to become Mrs. Darcy?"

"You have almost persuaded me, sir, but not quite yet."

"Fear not. I am a persistent man and am not easily dissuaded."

Darcy suggested a leisurely route back to Netherfield. No doubt, a great deal would need to be accomplished, and their moments alone might be few and far between in the coming days. It seemed wise to relish them now whilst they could. Happily, Elizabeth agreed.

After a dinner, of which "tense" was the very kindest word to describe, the Netherfield party retreated to various corners. Cait had accepted the temporary keeping of Miss Lydia with, perhaps, a little too much relish. Miss Lydia, with Cait closely following, stalked off to her chambers, clearly annoyed and possibly even disgusted not only with the talk of dragons around the dinner table, but that their presence was welcomed there. If one took her seriously, her storming and shouting was troubling and could be viewed as a great danger to the Order. But those who knew her best seemed unconcerned, so, at least for now, Darcy would hold his peace.

Mary and Collins joined Bennet and Fitzwilliam in the cellar for a brief introduction to Netherfield. Fitzwilliam suggested Netherfield wished to apologize for his untoward behavior. Was it a show to gain favor with the Order or was it sincere? Fitzwilliam seemed to believe the latter, which for now, was good enough.

Darcy and Elizabeth, who had the care of the sleeping Earl, made their way to the small parlor they favored. Lit only by the fireplace, it beckoned them inside like an old friend. He pulled the fainting couch near the fire—very near—and offered Elizabeth a blanket. Though she had not complained, it was clear she relished the opportunity to be near warmth and light. He shuddered just a little. To be trapped in total darkness—that was truly cruel of Netherfield and would be difficult for Darcy to forgive him for.

She bade him sit at the head of the fainting couch with a favorite book. She curled up beside him, Earl pressed against her chest and April against her neck, tucked the blanket around her legs, and closed her eyes. He wrapped his arm over her shoulder and held her close. Yes, it was not only highly improper, it was also a touch too warm, and a bit of an awkward angle for his shoulder, but nothing could have compelled him to move. Finally, the world seemed the way it should be.

Loud footfalls in the corridor made him jump. He must have dozed off—according to the mantle clock nearly an hour had passed. He wiped his eyes with the back of his hand and sat up a little straighter but not enough to disturb Elizabeth.

Fitzwilliam strode in, his steps halfway between stomping and storming.

Bennet followed him at some distance. "Astonishing, truly astonishing, the stories he has to tell. Lizzy. Lizzy!"

"Hush! Do not wake her." Darcy craned his neck around to glower at Bennet.

"Do give the woman some rest. She has, after all, been at the center of ,not one, but two diplomatic coups today." Fitzwilliam pulled a wingchair close to the fire and fell into it.

"These stories need to be recorded before they are

forgotten." Bennet leaned on his walking stick as though waiting for someone to offer him a chair.

Fitzwilliam ignored the silent request. "Given the relish with which Netherfield told them, I doubt he will be reluctant to repeat them."

"But if the Order decides against—" Bennet shuffled toward a chair at the edge of the firelight.

"What exactly do you think the Order is going to do? No council member, dragon or human, wanted to see his demise. They reluctantly accepted the notion only when it appeared there was no alternative. Given the preliminary word Walker has already brought, there is a great deal of relief that the last resort was not necessary, after all."

"You did an excellent job of brokering an understanding." Bennet tapped his walking stick on the carpet.

"The effort began well before I was dispatched. Without Elizabeth and Darcy, I doubt we would have ever come to this point."

Bennet grumbled something about obstinate and headstrong under his breath.

"I have been asked to provide a complete report on the matter." Fitzwilliam glanced at Elizabeth who still appeared to sleep. "I intend to let them know the entirety of the role she played, including her assistance to Cait and encouragement to me to befriend Earl." He looked a little longingly at the chick sleeping in her arms but knew better than to risk disturbing either of them.

"What has the chick to do with any of this?" Bennet waved toward Earl.

"Have you not noticed the change in Collins' attitude toward dragons since he attended the hatching?

Moreover, I find I see the world differently having Earl declare me his Friend. It makes me wonder if dragons are not the only ones to imprint at a hatching."

"Stuff and nonsense. That is not part of dragon lore. You are simply being sentimental. Probably another of my daughter's influences."

Fitzwilliam rolled his eyes. "I am going to suggest Elizabeth write a monograph on the topic. I know many would be greatly interested in it."

"You are just trying to vex me now. I know you are all agog over her way with dragons, but how close to disaster did we all come? In no small part because of her refusal to obey proper protocol. Is no one going to take seriously the risks she took and the danger she placed us all in? Someone must rein her in before it is too late."

"I find it immensely interesting that you would reprimand her for failing protocol when you yourself have been so very lax." Fitzwilliam leveled that gaze on Bennet, the one he had developed to put spoilt young officers in their place.

Bennet sat forward in his chair, sputtering. "What are you talking about?"

"Need I list everything I will put in my report to the Order? Very well, I will start with your failure to provide your dragon with his appropriate hoard as well as your failure to apply to the Order for relief when you found yourself unable to do so. Was that pride sir? Or will you claim that you did not expect the Order would come to your assistance?" Fitzwilliam leaned back in his chair—a casual posture that was anything but.

"I did not violate—"

"Not the letter of the Accords, to be sure. However, one might argue you did exactly that when you suspected the presence of a rogue dragon and did not immediately report it. Shall I speculate the reason, or will you care to tell me?"

"I do not have to answer to the likes of you. Remember, you are talking to an officer of the Order!" Though Bennet tried to don a cloak of indignancy, it slipped off his shoulders quickly. Even he did not really believe his own protests.

"I am certain there will be a full inquiry made over the situation, and your presence in London will be required."

"How dare you spread slander against me!"

"There is no slander in the truth. I will only report the truth as I know it and allow them to determine what is to be done with it. Have I spoken anything so far that is not fact?"

Bennet muttered into his chest. "I had no proof there was a rogue dragon in the area."

"I did not say you did. I said that you suspected. Did you suspect or not? Longbourn—"

"He knew of Netherfield! What of him?" Bennet pointed roughly in the direction of Longbourn's lair.

"So now you would blame your dragon for failing your responsibilities? That is deplorable, sir." Fitzwilliam tsk-tsked under his breath. Now he was just taunting Bennet. It was not attractive even if the man had it coming. "I think it quite likely Longbourn will be absolved of any responsibility in the matter, especially considering Netherfield was sating the hoarding-hunger you so neatly ignored."

"You have never kept a dragon. Truly, what do you understand? Leave these matters to those who know of what they speak." Bennet shambled from the room.

The door shut rather more loudly than etiquette

declared it should. Elizabeth stirred against Darcy's chest. "Would you like to take Earl? He is rather a substantial young thing." She lifted him off her chest and drew a deep breath.

Fitzwilliam hurried over and settled him in the crook of his arm. Earl opened one eye, cheeped, and nestled into his favorite place.

Elizabeth cuddled back against Darcy as he pressed his arm against her waist. "I confess it is pleasant to be able to breathe unencumbered again. He is a very dear, though heavy, creature. I am honored you would trust him to my care."

"Netherfield took right to him; it was rather remarkable to see them greet one another. Earl curled up and slept right on his snout for a few minutes until it became difficult for Netherfield to talk without disturbing him. Quite the scene, I am sure you can imagine." Fitzwilliam scratched under Earl's chin.

"I can indeed. I am sure Papa will want me for his scribe tomorrow." She rubbed her eyes with thumb and forefinger.

"I would not put too much on those plans. I expect Walker will arrive first thing with a summons calling us all to London immediately."

"I am relieved they took Netherfield's application for admission into the Order with such aplomb. Do you think they will give Netherfield this land?"

"No, I doubt it. With what has occurred between Netherfield and Longbourn, and without a proper Keeper to manage his acceptance into the Order, this would be a very poor choice of territory. That being said, I know there are places befitting a lindwurm that could be assigned him. Most of them are north of London and well away from Longbourn."

"I suppose that would be for the best. But Papa will mourn the loss of his acquaintance." She stared at her hands and chewed her lip. Her shoulders tensed against Darcy. "Do you really need to report—"

"Would that I did not have to. Truly, I regret this duty, not because I have any fondness for him but because I know that it cannot but hurt you. But whether he chooses to recognize it or not, he contributed significantly to this unfortunate affair by his own failure to follow the protocols and rules he is so fond of quoting at you." Fitzwilliam's lips wrinkled—there was a great deal more to his opinion that he was keeping to himself. Probably a wise choice.

"I hate that you are right, but when you lay it out like that, I can hardly argue. I am worried for him, though. What might the Order do? If they remove him from his post, I can hardly imagine the effect it will have on him."

"He has been negligent, to be sure, but there has been no bloodshed, so I would be surprised to see harsh judgements."

Elizabeth stared at her hands. "It is just ironic he is under scrutiny for the very things he has judged me for."

"Once we get back to London, I expect your presence at the offices will be in high demand. Walker already mentioned Sir Edward and Lady Astrid want to speak with you regarding all that has transpired. He is particularly interested in your interventions for Cait, and she, well, you know Lady Astrid. She is interested in everything. But that is for the morning. For now, my young charge and I are tired. I had best get some sleep before he is hungry again." Fitzwilliam chuckled as he rose, cradling the young cockatrice.

Darcy and Elizabeth watched him leave.

"You will stay at Darcy House when we return to London, will you not? Georgiana will be at the house—"

"As will Pemberley! I do not imagine she would tolerate me staying elsewhere."

"I was not thinking of her just now." He held her a little tighter. "You look troubled. What is on your mind?"

She sighed and looked up at the ceiling. "Things have changed. I have changed. You bear much of the blame for that. I am not who I was before we met. It is difficult to say exactly how, but I am different, and I simply do not belong here anymore."

"Here, as in Hertfordshire?"

"Yes. I used to have patience: with Longbourn and his temper; with my father and his peculiarities; and with Mary and her reluctance to step up and take responsibilities. Even with my mother and Kitty and their rather silly ways. It all used to seem so normal to me. But now, I find them all so very frustrating. Would it be horrible to say I have on occasion fantasized about knocking their silly little heads together in hopes some sense would shake loose?"

He stifled a chuckle. She might not appreciate it.

"All of that is to say, I could not live here again, not with any sort of contentment. You and your dragon, sir, have ruined me for lesser things, and I fear I cannot go back." She looked up at him with a sort of serious playfulness that he could easily become accustomed to. But beneath the playfulness, there was something a little uncertain, even insecure. "I find it difficult to see myself as anything besides your wife."

"We have that in common. But if you ever have

doubt, I expect there is a rather large collection of dragons who will testify to the same to reassure you."

"Are you teasing me, Mr. Darcy?"

"Absolutely and without reservation. Have you a problem with that?"

"Only that you are not kissing me."

"Permit me to remedy that immediately."

The next morning, Elizabeth and Darcy scurried to return the morning room to something more usable for their party. They remove paintings from the morning room table and stacked books high on a small corner table, sufficiently out of the way to be ignored for now. After papers and maps were tucked into a drawer in the sideboard, everyone could be accommodated, at last.

Papa sat near the book table, his eye on several volumes for further study. It would probably not be difficult to convince Bingley to allow him to borrow them, especially with a little persuasion from Heather who was very good at that sort of thing.

Lydia sat at the far side of the table, pouting, but serving herself generously. Making up for her privations under Netherfield, no doubt. Cait perched on the sideboard behind her, dedicated to not letting Lydia out of her sight. That was worrisome. If Cait was so diligent, she must consider Lydia's running away a serious threat. The sooner they could get Lydia to London and into the hands of the Blue Order, the better.

Collins sat next to Fitzwilliam and Earl, offering the chick bits of kipper and ham from his own plate. Was this a normal reaction for the dragon-deaf who had witnessed a hatching? Were there any recordings of it in dragon lore?

Mrs. Hill had demonstrated it was possible for the dragon-deaf to befriend a dragon after a fashion—had that ever happened before? Surely it must have. All it would take was a clever and persuasive dragon and a sympathetic person. Might it be possible for Jane to befriend Talia in the same way? They both had such gentle personalities; they would be good for one another. It should not be too difficult to persuade Jane that Talia was a rabbit.

"Are you well?" Mary whispered in her ear.

"Forgive me, just a little lost in thought." Elizabeth took a bit of jam for her toast and passed the pot to Mary.

"Little wonder, it has been an astonishing few days, has it not?"

Walker swooped in through the open window and landed on the back of Darcy's chair, a large satchel strapped to his back. "The Order requires your immediate presence in London, preferably by the end of the day. All of you."

"We cannot possibly leave in such short order. We have not even made arrangements for a place to stay." Papa did not bother to turn around and look at Walker.

"The Gardiners await your arrival. The Order asks—" the way Walker spoke the word made clear it was not a request, "that Miss Lydia be chaperoned at Darcy House and that the Collinses might assist in the effort."

Fitzwilliam chewed his lower lip. "They are being rather particular, are they not?"

"You are requested to accompany Longbourn,

Netherfield, and Shin-dee-a through the tunnels to ensure a safe arrival at the Blue Order offices. Earl may accompany you."

"How generous of them." Fitzwilliam pushed back from the table and swallowed the last of his coffee. "I have my marching orders and will get on with it immediately. Will you bring my trunk for me, Darcy?"

"What am I, some sort of prisoner? Have I no say in the matter? What if I do not want to go to London?" Lydia crossed her arms and settled into her chair as if she had no intention of ever moving.

"I thought you were always in want of a trip to London." Elizabeth looked at Papa.

"Perhaps, but not now."

"You will accompany us to London." Bennet stared at the slice of toast he buttered.

"I do not know who these Blue Order people are, but they do not control me. I shall not go to London." Lydia's face wrinkled into a defiant snort that had often settled matters at Longbourn.

Fitzwilliam slowly approached her, man and dragon making way for him as he passed. "My dear girl, you are not just a prisoner, but you are a criminal of the worst order according to our laws—laws which became yours the moment you first heard a dragon speak. You have no choice in coming to London. Your only choice is whether you shall go in a coach with your family or you shall be dragged there via the underground tunnels in a dragon's arms. Decide now."

Lydia shuddered, a show of half-drama, half-dread. "I never want to be underground again. It is horrid and unnatural."

"Then see to it you give your sister and Darcy no trouble, or you will be taken directly to the Order offices to stay in an underground chamber until your hearing."

"Hearing?" She lost the color in her face. "You cannot be serious."

"Do not test him or the Order," Elizabeth hissed in a whisper. "He does not exaggerate."

Lydia clutched at the tablecloth, voice squeaking. "What will they do to me?"

"I do not know, but your attitude will determine a very great deal. Good day." Fitzwilliam bowed from his shoulders and turned on his heel.

Collins leaned across the table toward Lydia. "They are not unreasonable, Miss Lydia. But they are very serious about their rules."

"You, too? You are part of this madness?" The horror on her face was almost laughable.

A very odd look came over Collins' face. "Not in the way your sisters and father are. But yes, after a fashion. Perhaps, it would be wise for us to return to Longbourn to pack."

"Shall I pack for you, Papa?" Mary set her napkin aside and stood.

"There are books I need to pack myself." Papa leaned hard on his walking stick, struggling to stand.

"I shall come, too!" Lydia jumped up and dashed toward the door.

Elizabeth beat her to the doorway, blocking her exit. "No, you have a trunk already packed upstairs. If there is anything else you need, Mary can bring it."

"There are several things I simply must have—" Lydia rushed to Mary's side.

Cait cocked her head. "Do not worry. I shall keep watch over her. You deserve a few moments of peace before it all begins."

"Mary?" Elizabeth caught her sister's and Collins' gaze.

"We will keep her in order." Mary held Lydia's arm tightly.

Elizabeth stepped aside and they left, Cait flapping after them.

Darcy refilled Elizabeth's cup. "I do not envy Cait's task."

Elizabeth returned to her seat and scrubbed her face with her palms. "Perhaps Collins will make an impression on her."

"One might hope—not expect mind you, but hope."

"Do you think I will be deemed disagreeable if I insist that Lydia, Mary, and Collins ride in Papa's coach to London? Even if they will stay with us at Darcy House, I would very much like to greet Pemberley and Georgiana without them."

"I am entirely in favor of the idea, though, I confess my reasons are not nearly so noble."

Her eyes twinkled just a bit. "Who said all of mine were?"

By the time their carriage pulled into the mews behind Darcy House, the sun had begun its dip behind London's tallest buildings. Georgiana, Pemberley, and Slate and Amber, the house staff drakes, tumbled from the cellar steps to meet them even before they rolled to a stop.

Darcy handed her out of the carriage and into a two-way embrace: Georgiana on one side and Pemberley on the other, winding her neck around Elizabeth's waist almost until she could not breathe.

"Walker did not tell us very much, only that the

whole matter had come to a good conclusion, and you would be back today." Georgiana turned to Darcy and took his hands.

"We will tell you what we can, but the important new is that everyone is whole and hearty, and the rogue is seeking the protection of the Order." Tension slipped from his shoulders, and a special warmth filled his eyes.

"Is it true that Fitzwilliam befriended Cait's chick?"

"Indeed he has—a lovely young fellow, to be sure. You will meet him soon, no doubt."

"He is a quite a changed man for it, too." Elizabeth scratched behind Pemberley's ears. "Not in essentials, to be certain, in that he will always be the same. But you should see the way he looks at little Earl. It is something to behold."

"How wonderful!"

April peeked out from Elizabeth's hood and shook her feathers fluffy. "My clutch will come soon. You shall be a Friend to one of them?"

Georgiana's eyes filled with tears that coursed unchecked down her cheeks.

"Another fairy dragon? I like them! They tickle my nose and sing pretty!" Pemberley spread her wings with a happy little flap.

Another dragon in the household? Just what they needed—

"I think it a wonderful thing." Darcy slipped his arm around her shoulder and scratched under Pemberley's chin with the other hand. "A household cannot have too many dragons."

Elizabeth bit her upper lip and squeezed her eyes shut, but it did not really help. Tears trailed down her cheeks. He was right. A home could not have too many dragons, and a home built by a man who said that was precisely the place she belonged.

Chapter 12

THREE DAYS LATER, Elizabeth sat in the antechamber, waiting to be called into the office of the Minister of the Blue Order Court: Nicholas Shillingham, Baron Dunbrook. Two days ago, when they had first waited here to give testimony to Lord Dunbrook, the room had seemed far more intimidating. Large enough to accommodate a dragon of Longbourn's size, the ceiling stared down at them with frescos depicting the establishment of the Pendragon Accords. Built into the surrounding walls, mahogany benches backed with high mahogany backs could hold a large cadre. Mirrored wall sconces above the benches poured light on wall frescos illustrating the formation of the first Blue Order court and the first Ministers of the Court who held office. Surrounded by giants of Blue Order history, it was easy to feel very, very small.

It was the kind of place Papa would normally find fascinating. He had been fascinated by it, two days ago. But not today.

Lord Dunbrook's summons and the ensuing inquest had surprised Papa. He had justified all he had done as sensible and correct. When Lord Dunbrook began to question everything, he became visibly rattled and even contentious. So much so that Lord Dunbrook sent her and Papa out while he continued questioning Darcy, Lydia, Fitzwilliam, Mary and even Longbourn himself.

Dunbrook was the sternest-looking drake she had ever seen: deep stony grey, his face appeared chiseled into a permanent scowl with a voice to match. Lord Dunbrook made a perfect match to him. Tall and broad, wearing a traditional judge's wig, his shoulders barely fit through the door, but probably that was more about the way he carried himself than his actual size. Had he learnt that from his dragon?

They both boomed out questions that sounded like gunfire, and no matter the answer given, their expressions insisted it must be wrong. Their manner did not change whether dealing with victim, suspect, or witness. Moreover, they did not limit themselves to a polite number of discreet questions. Nothing seemed off-limits, including a few things Elizabeth would just as soon not hear. Perhaps that was why it was said Lord Dunbrook's wife lived separately from him. He must be quite the joy at home.

When they had been dismissed from questioning, Elizabeth returned to Darcy House and immediately went to bed, not rising until afternoon the next day. Uncle Gardiner said Papa did not leave his room until today when it was time receive Lord Dunbrook's decision.

Papa shambled toward her, leaning heavily on his cane. He stopped half a step from her and stared at her with such an expression. "I told you. I would have made sure you would have been happy with Collins. I promised you that." He sounded so hurt, even betrayed.

The little girl within withered and fought back tears. "He is better off with Mary."

"I had no intention of condemning you to a miserable marriage." He leaned over her until she felt smaller still.

She stood and increased the distance between them. "How would you have accomplished that?"

"I would have made sure of it."

"I will be happy in my marriage with Darcy. Is that not sufficient?"

He grumbled, trudged back to the other side of the room, and resumed pacing. Apparently not.

Huge wooden doors, carved with the crest of the Blue Order's judicial branch, swung open, slowly, grudgingly. Fitzwilliam appeared and beckoned them inside. He looked satisfied enough, but it was difficult to discern what that might mean.

A blue-uniformed bailiff showed them where to stand: Elizabeth beside Darcy and Fitzwilliam, all to the right, facing Lord Dunbrook's imposing desk; Papa beside Lydia on the left, Mary and Collins slightly behind them.

Longbourn lingered slightly behind the desk, near the tunnel that had admitted him, shifting his weight from one foot to another. He only did that when he was uncomfortable. Given the way the drake

Dunbrook stood beside him, a wary eye fixed on the wyvern, it was easy to guess why.

Lord Dunbrook banged a gavel on his desk. Elizabeth and Mary jumped. "Testimony has been given regarding the complaints against Historian Bennet, and judgement shall be rendered."

Darcy slipped his hand into hers and squeezed tightly. Dear, dear man.

"Historian Bennet, you have been derelict in your duties as a Keeper, both in caring for your dragon and in the larger responsibilities of keeping watch over the safety of the dragon state. Longbourn's needs have been neglected. You have compromised Blue Order security by failing to report the possibility of a rogue dragon and neglecting to train your dragon-hearing daughter appropriately. As of this moment, you are relieved as Dragon Keeper at Longbourn."

Longbourn grumbled and muttered, rocking side-to-side a little harder, but the look on his face suggested he agreed with Lord Dunbrook. Papa bowed his head and swayed over his cane. Mary gasped and leaned hard into Collins' shoulder.

Elizabeth clung to Darcy's hand, struggling to conceal a sigh of relief. Though harsh, the judgement could have been far worse—not that Papa or the Collinses would recognize that, at least not right now.

"Mrs. Collins, you and your husband will be assigned a Blue Order steward. He will instruct Mr. Collins in the proper administration of estate matters. Mrs. Collins, you will immediately take on all dragon-keeping duties under the supervision of your steward who will ensure the needs of Laird Longbourn are properly met. Your steward's Dragon Friend, another cockatrix, will assume the translation duties Cait currently fulfills."

Collins ran his finger along the inside of his cravat and cleared his throat. "How long will the steward be with us?"

"For your entire tenure as Keeper, if necessary. Bailiff, take them to meet their steward." Lord Dunbrook waved the bailiff into action and turned toward Longbourn. "You are to make regular reports to the Order regarding the state of your Keep. For the first two years, a messenger from the Order will be sent monthly to collect your report and to ensure you fulfill all your Keep duties, including wild dragon censuses and attending all Conclave meetings."

Longbourn pawed the floor and huffed.

"I will take that as agreement," Dunbrook said. "You may be dismissed, for now, but do not fail to attend the Conclave."

Longbourn snorted and disappeared down the tunnel, his heavy footsteps echoing behind him. Clearly, he did not like being held accountable for his own duties. Still though, he seemed to take the news well enough to suggest he would cooperate, especially if it meant he would get his salt.

"You, young woman," Lord Dunbrook turned to Lydia who stood, quiet and pale, beside Papa. What had Dunbrook said to her to elicit such good behavior? No doubt it was frightening—and probably true. "You have proved yourself ignorant, even willfully so, and a danger to dragonkind. Moreover, you are not trustworthy, making it impossible to leave you alone for even an instant. You will be committed to a Blue Order girl's school in the north of England until you reach majority at age twenty-one. If at that point you are still deemed a danger, you will be condemned as a career criminal and assigned to a managed home in Scotland for the rest of your natural life."

Lydia glanced at Elizabeth as if to confirm Lord Dunbrook's power over her. When Elizabeth nodded, she covered her mouth and whimpered.

"If however, you prove yourself tractable to the teachings of the Order, at the discretion of the school masters, at the age of eighteen you may be permitted to come out to the Order and be introduced to suitable young men in good standing with the Order and married accordingly."

"Oh, yes!" Lydia clapped and bounced on her toes.

"But only if you prove yourself learned, changed, and trustworthy."

Lydia shrank back.

"Until you are deemed no longer a danger, a guardian drake will be assigned to be with you at all times. You are remanded to the custody of your sister Elizabeth and Mr. Darcy until such time as you are transported to school."

Lord Dunbrook waved toward the tunnel, and a blue-green minor drake skittered in. She was leggy and lean—probably a very fast runner—standing about three feet tall on all four feet and probably as tall as Lydia if she rose on her hind feet. Her nose was long and sharp. If she had glasses balanced there, she would have looked very much like a governess. Something about the way she carried herself suggested she was well-prepared for the task.

"This is Auntie. She will take you to the parlor where you may wait. You would do well to consider her your governess for the time being."

Lydia's jaw dropped. "I am too old for a governess."

Netherfield: Rogue Dragon

Auntie circled her, sniffing as she looked Lydia up and down. "Perhaps too old, but not too wise. If you have any desire to prove you can live without a chaperone, then you had best start now. Do you play the pianoforte?"

Lydia edged back. "I have had a few lessons."

"Then we shall make good use of the time. The parlor has a pianoforte. You shall show me what you know."

"You play?"

"She is quite the proficient," Lord Dunbrook murmured, his eyes twinkling as Auntie opened the door. "When she is at the Order, she is much in demand for concerts."

"Stop gawking at me, girl, and move on. Clearly, there is a great deal of work to be done to polish you properly." Auntie poked Lydia's back until she headed toward the door.

"A dragon governess?" Fitzwilliam whispered in Elizabeth's ear.

"Perhaps Auntie might be available when our children are of an age to need one." Elizabeth winked up at Darcy who sniggered under his breath.

Lord Dunbrook turned back to Papa. The hard lines of his face softened a bit. "You have served the Order as an officer faithfully for many years, and your service has not been forgotten. Since you will no longer have Keepers' duties, the Order invites you to dedicate yourself to full-time service as Historian. You may have the use of an Order townhouse and its staff, along with a stipend of three hundred pounds a year if you choose to do so. Further, you may select a secretary, human or dragon, from amongst candidates Lady Astrid will provide."

"My wife and remaining daughter?"

"They may live in town with you under the watch of the house staff."

"She may be pleased at the prospect." Papa murmured more to himself than anyone else.

"Think on it. You may have two days to make your decision. You are dismissed."

Papa trundled off, his steps a little lighter than they had been.

"That was generous of you, sir. Thank you." Elizabeth curtsied to Lord Dunbrook.

"While he has not been a good Keeper, that is not the only way to serve the Order. His other skills are valuable. It would be foolish to cast them aside." Lord Dunbrook rubbed his palms briskly. "As for you three, somehow you made a coup out of what should have been a diplomatic disaster. Envoy Shin-dee-a was very impressed with how you handled what she called 'an extreme test of the Order's character.' You managed to turn what might have been a violent confrontation into a peaceful settlement, powerfully demonstrating the Order's commitment to its principles. Consequently, talks have begun to establish a formal relationship with the Eastern Dragon Federation. Well done, very well done."

"Thank you, sir." Fitzwilliam bowed.

"What is to become of Netherfield?" The words just slipped out before she could catch them.

Darcy flinched. He was probably right. That question was no doubt out of order. Poor man would need to become accustomed to such bold statements tumbling from her lips for there was little hope of stopping them.

"I cannot say at this time. He has applied for

conditional admission into the Order and requested the Netherfield territory. I will make recommendations after the hearings are complete, but the Conclave must render their vote on the matter. Lady Astrid will help you prepare your statements for those hearings. She awaits you now." Lord Dunbrook nodded a dismissal.

Walker and April greeted them just outside the antechamber.

"Earl is well in Lady Astrid's care, but he is growing hungry and insists only you can feed him properly." Walker smirked just a bit.

"That is his way of saying no one else is willing to feed him enough to sate his hunger. Mother used to say the same of me and my brothers when we came home on school holidays. Swore that we must not be fed at all whilst we were in school. I will visit the kitchen and join you shortly." Fitzwilliam jogged off down the corridor.

"I had thought Earl's hunger would abate by now. April's and Heather's hatching hunger only lasted three days." Elizabeth stroked April's head. How pleasant to be able to do that again.

"A cockatrice chick is much larger and thus more hungry." Walker looked a little proud. "In a se'nnight or so, it should fade."

"I think Fitzwilliam will appreciate the respite." Darcy chuckled.

"It will not last very long." April poked Elizabeth's ear with her beak.

"What do you mean?" Elizabeth craned her neck, trying to look April in the eye.

"Whilst we are here, you should see about procuring a proper nesting box. I will be laying soon. I do not fancy the sort of rough kit your father assembled for his study. A box, properly finished so it is not rough under my feet and has no sharp corners for you to knock your knees upon, with plenty of soft hay, not the coarse, prickly kind, but the smooth, sweet-smelling variety."

"So soon?" Darcy raised his eyebrows.

"It is not soon at all, but exactly the right time." April puffed a bit, looking very proud.

"Then you shall have whatever you require." He bowed deeply.

Elizabeth cocked her head with mock severity. "You shall spoil her, you know. Then where will we all be?"

April flitted to his shoulder and cuddled his cheek. "Whatever do you mean? I have always been sweet and charming and ever more shall be so."

Three days later, Elizabeth hurried in from the mews to what she had dubbed the ladies' parlor, and shut the door behind her. On the ground floor, the parlor windows looked out on the mews. She could watch Pemberley playing outside with Slate and Amber or simply enjoy the already blooming garden. On gloomy days, the pale blue walls and ivory ceiling seemed to bring sunshine inside. Paintings on every wall provided blossoms even when the garden did not. It was the sort of room she would have designed herself had she the opportunity.

April flew from her shoulder to the nesting box near the hearth to rearrange the hay again. Silly dear was never quite satisfied.

"Gracious, Lizzy! You look like you are running

from a rogue dragon yourself!" Aunt Gardiner looked up from the fainting couch near the window where she and Phoenix sat cuddling Earl. The young red fairy dragon had taken an immediate liking to Earl and was preening his head feathers whilst Aunt Gardiner read to them both from *A Young Dragon's Primer to the Pendragon Accords*. Actually, it was an excellent source for both young dragons and young people. No doubt, she read it to the children in lieu of bedtime stories these days. The little dears could not get enough of dragons, it seemed. Unlike Lydia.

Elizabeth sighed and fell into an overstuffed chair near Aunt Gardiner. "More like a rogue sister, but yes, the effect is rather the same."

"Dare I ask?"

"Now that you are a full member of the Order yourself, you may ask anything you like, and I am free to answer." Elizabeth smiled broadly. If there was anything to be pleased of at the moment, it was that she could fully share everything she loved most with the woman closest to her.

"Do tell, then."

"I suppose the most important thing is Colonel Fitzwilliam's defense of Netherfield is going well, as things go for dragons, of course."

"Humor me, my dear. Only being recently introduced to them myself, I cannot quite discern what you mean by that." Aunt Gardiner scratched under Phoenix's chin, then Earl's.

"All in all, large dragons tend to be more competitive than cooperative. So, when asked to compromise, they become rather cranky. It is understandable considering that when one is an apex predator, one assumes one will have one's way in all things. When required to set aside that right, they become grumpy even when they recognize it is in their best interests. So, if one can learn to look past the cross dispositions and the occasional snarling and snapping, discussions go more smoothly." Elizabeth blew a stray curl from her forehead. "But it is rather exhausting."

"You make it sound so very droll and ordinary, rather like dealing with a room full of small children whom one does not need to regard very seriously, instead of creatures who could cause the downfall of the kingdom." Aunt glanced down at Earl, one eyebrow raised.

Gracious, she had a way of putting things! "It all makes a great deal of sense if one can just think like a dragon."

Aunt snickered hard enough to make Earl open one eye with a rather reproving look. "That is perhaps your greatest asset, my dear. Few of us seem to be able to manage the knack."

"Perhaps, but it does little good when dealing with my sisters."

"What happened? I thought Mary was finally coming around."

"She is, I suppose, both she and Collins. I am grateful—a bit astonished, to be sure—but grateful." Elizabeth rubbed her temples. "In anticipation of the Conclave, which they must attend as Longbourn's Keepers, I have been trying to teach them proper etiquette for greetings and introductions. Collins, it seems, has a faulty memory at best and cannot manage to keep straight—well, much of anything at all. Mary tries to correct him but is constantly confusing the rank order of the larger minor dragons. They both understand the issue of size, but the role of horns and venom and frills seem to escape them."

"The way you throw up your hands makes it seem as though it is all very obvious. But those details are not nearly as clear as you might think."

"If one just considers which dragon has the greater advantage in claiming territory, it is very obvious."

"Again, to one who thinks like a dragon, I am sure it is. But you must have some mercy on those of us who do not—yet."

Elizabeth threw her head back and stared at the plasterwork vine-and-fairy-dragon pattern circling the ceiling. "I know you are right, and if it were just Mary and Collins, I would probably be far more patient, but Lydia? I am beginning to sound like my mother, complaining about my nerves!"

"Fanny, by the way, is quite pleased to know Lydia will be off to finishing school where she might receive proper introductions and marry well."

"'Might' being the operative concept. It will all depend on her tractability which I completely doubt at the moment."

"What happened?" Who knew Aunt's eyes could open so wide.

"At the hearing today, the matter of Wickham and his demise came up. How she carried on! Not even Auntie could bring her under regulation. I thought, for a moment, the dear drake was actually going to bite her. Not that I would blame Auntie if she did! The scene Lydia caused! It nearly derailed the entire proceeding which would have meant presenting the matter in detail to the full Conclave instead of the special council. Lydia does not understand the crimes she has committed and that the council is offering her great leniency because of her ignorance. The Conclave would likely hold her accountable and …" Elizabeth shuddered. "Truly, I just want to shake her." Energy coursed through her limbs, itching and twitching until she had to spring to her feet and pace.

"So, what happened in the special council hearing?"

"Lydia explained how she and Wickham had been living in a hermitage they had found on the Netherfield property—we can discuss all the problems with that at another time, for those are things dragons hardly consider an issue—and had been looking for Netherfield's lair. Needless to say, that did not sit well with Cownt Matlock or any of the rest of the Council even though they had already decided not to prosecute Lydia." Elizabeth flung her arms wide and waved her hands. "Then she began carrying on over how Netherfield had killed Wickham—you know how she can be. She worked her way into full hysteria and took much of the Council with her. Auntie finally dosed her with laudanum and dragged her off, leaving it to me to calm not one, but six major dragons and convince them all not to be done with Netherfield simply because it would be more convenient than sitting through the special council."

"Surely, they would not have done such a rash thing!"

"I like to think so, but matters did become quite heated. To be entirely honest, it was frightening when the council dragons began arguing with their Keepers. Once Lydia left though, reason began to return. They listened to Netherfield's testimony about Wickham and what I had to say about it, as well. I think the final sticking point is removed now. I expect they will recommend he be accepted into the Order. They even have a territory—well away from the coast and known smuggling tunnels—in mind for him. A small one, but it will be sufficient."

"And a Keeper?"

"They have not said, but it should not be difficult to find one. Netherfield is a rather docile creature, a pacifist if you will. As long as the Keeper is literate and well-read, I think he will be a content and compliant member of the Order." Elizabeth fell into the nearest chair.

"I am sure Lydia will settle down a bit once she becomes used to everything around her. Perhaps I will have a talk with her, with your permission, of course. Only just coming into this myself, I think there is some sympathy I can offer her that might be helpful to assuage her feelings of ill-use."

"I am sure Auntie will be grateful for any assistance you can offer. She has a reputation as an excellent governess for unmanageable daughters, but at times, it looked at though she may have met her match in Lydia." Elizabeth tapped her fist against her lips. "How is Mama?"

"You must come over for tea as soon as there is a spare moment. She is quite happy. You are to be married, most advantageously to Mr. Darcy. Mary is married to Mr. Collins. Jane, of course, has Mr. Bingley. Lydia is to be sent to school, and now she and Kitty will live in London, something she has always dreamed of. Despite your father's uncertainty, I am convinced it will be a good thing for them all. We will introduce both your mother and Kitty into society here and keep watch over them. Your mother will be kept agreeably occupied while your father can spend his days at the Order offices devoting himself to his duties as Historian. In many ways, I wish this had happened much sooner."

"Perhaps it is all for the best. So much has changed in so very short a time. Is it wrong to say how very much I have enjoyed certain aspects of it?"

"You mean Mr. Darcy?"

Her cheeks burned. "I can hardly imagine a better man or Dragon Keeper. But there is more than that." She rose and stood near the window, tracing the edge of the mullions with her fingertip. "I do not know how to explain. The past few months we have been so deep in dragon matters. I have never felt more at home, more useful. It is like I have found where I belong. But now that matters have finally resolved, things will return to the ... mundane."

"Raising Pemberley is going to be mundane?"

"Hardly. She will be as much a handful as Lydia, though in some ways much easier to deal with. But I know I shall miss being about the business of the Order, involved in something larger than myself. I know I am to be mistress of a great estate, and that should be sufficient for me, managing my own home and family, but ... what kind of woman am I that I am not certain it will be, that I may want something more?"

Phoenix twittered and buzzed toward them. "Come, come! See what April has done!"

April cheeped from the nesting box.

Elizabeth hurried to the hearth. "My gracious, and with no word of this to us! You have been very busy this morning."

Three glistening eggs lay in the middle of the nesting box. Two were half the size of a chicken's egg, vaguely blue, mottled and streaked. The third was much smaller by comparison, it probably would not hatch, but that was not unusual for a first clutch.

"How beautiful they are!" Elizabeth knelt beside

them.

"I will sing to them. You will talk to them as you did to me whilst I was in my egg." April rolled the eggs in the hay, arranging them to her satisfaction.

"You remember that?"

"Your voice was the first sound I clearly recognized. Being shell-bound was very dull. You talked a very great deal, but it was entertaining." April hopped to her shoulder. "That is how I knew to listen to you once I had hatched."

"That and the honey I offered you."

"I well knew your good sense by then."

Phoenix hopped into the nest and extended a wing over each egg. "They will be my Friends, too. I like them very much already."

"As well you should, my Friend." Aunt tickled under his chin, and he twittered happily. "They will do well to have so fine a protector as you."

Phoenix looked very proud of himself, with an expression a little like Mr. Darcy. How her betrothed would laugh to be told he resembled a fairy dragon, but Phoenix would think it rather a compliment to be told he took after Darcy.

Chapter 13

SEVERAL MORNINGS LATER, dawn finally made its way across the sky and Elizabeth no longer needed to pretend to sleep. Who could expect anyone to sleep soundly on the eve of such a momentous occasion? Unless something untoward happened, Netherfield would be accepted by the Conclave, the first foreign major dragon to be admitted in recorded memory. At least, that is what should happen.

Dragons could be unpredictable, though. Even when things went as desired, it often did not happen in the expected manner. Unexpected was not necessarily bad, or so she had tried to convince Papa. Now was the time to back up those bold words with her actions.

During her last visit, Aunt Gardiner had brought over the blue silk gown, now altered to fit Elizabeth as though it were made for her. The color was perfect: a serious but not somber shade of blue, happy enough to make her smile. The fabric caught the light just so—

subtle but striking. It was probably a little vain to enjoy a gown so much, but Aunt Gardiner was right: there was something about being properly dressed that made a day such as today easier to face. Elizabeth dismissed the maid and made a final twirl in front of the mirror. All that could be accomplished in one's dressing room had been done. She squared her shoulders and strode into the corridor.

Best check on Pemberley and make sure she was ready for Rosings to escort her—

"You look very well this morning, Lizzy." Lydia cut her off as though she had been lurking in wait, arms folded and lips pursed. "I do not wish to go to the dragon meeting."

"Pray forgive me, Miss Bennet." Auntie scurried up behind her. "She is quite adept at slipping out."

Elizabeth clapped her hand to her forehead. "Are you using the servants' corridors again?"

Lydia tossed her head.

Auntie snorted and snapped. Gracious, she had impressive teeth!

Elizabeth sidestepped Lydia and addressed Auntie. "I will have the servants' doors near Lydia's chambers nailed shut for the remainder of your stay. Slate and Amber will keep watch over those corridors." Turning to Lydia, she pulled her shoulders back in her most draconic posture. "I have no patience for your tricks and neither does my household. If you cross Auntie one more time, I will take you back to the Order offices and have you locked in a cell until such time as you are taken to school."

"You would not do such a thing." Lydia stomped. "I cannot believe what has come over you, Lizzy. You are not even mistress of this house, yet! Aunt Gardiner was so understanding; she said you would be, too. Why must I attend the meeting today? With all the dragons of the kingdom? It sounds quite awful."

"The Conclave is the heart of dragon government, a key element of the Blue Order." Elizabeth rubbed her temples with her thumb and fingers. "In the upper gallery, there are observation rooms with windows that look down over the Conclave floor. Aunt and Uncle Gardiner will take you there. You will not have to be close to the dragons, but you must go."

Lydia pouted and pressed her back against the wall. "I do not want to go. I do not like these scaly creatures. I do not like their society."

"I am sure the feeling is mutual." Elizabeth sneaked a glance at Auntie who tried not to snicker. "But unless you want to die a spinster confined to the north of England with little money and no society, I suggest you reform your opinions. This will be a good way to begin." Elizabeth stomped away and down the stairs.

April met her halfway down, landing on her shoulder. "You do not look very pleased. Is it the stupid one again?"

Elizabeth sniffed and rolled her eyes.

"You should spend time with my eggs instead. Georgiana is reading them stories from *Tales of English Dragons*. They are very entertaining."

"I am glad my recommendation meets your approval." She cuddled April against her cheek.

April sang a few notes, and a little bit of her tension eased. "They are waiting for you in the parlor. Go to him. He always makes you feel better."

She was right, perceptive little creature.

Darcy met her at the parlor door. Gracious, he cut a fine figure in his best suit. It was not as though she had never noticed before, but today he was particularly dapper. Was it wrong to smile in approval?

Well, if it was, then so be it. He smiled back and anything that put that expression on his face could hardly be bad.

In the room behind him, Fitzwilliam laughed with Georgiana, probably at something Earl had just said or done. The sweet little creature was in his favorite spot, the crook of Fitzwilliam's arm, chittering and warbling his draconic version of baby talk. It was difficult to decide which was dearer, the chick or Fitzwilliam's response.

"The carriage will be ready in just a few minutes. Will you join us?" Darcy offered his arm and laid his hand over hers. "Rosings just came to fetch Pemberley for the Conclave."

"As crusty as she can be, I am a little surprised to find her being such an attentive brood mother."

Fitzwilliam snickered. "Do not think too much of her. There are ulterior motives involved. She is tired of ill-mannered "younger" dragons misbehaving during official proceedings and has it in her craw that if Pemberley demonstrates proper behavior, then others will be apt to follow her lead."

Georgiana giggled. "It sounds like something Aunt Catherine would say."

Darcy's shoulders twitched as they usually did with any mention of his aunt. "It is a shame we cannot do the same for junior keepers."

"Mary and Collins have been assigned a steward to assist them. Perhaps the same might be done for Anne." Elizabeth offered a half-wink that restored Darcy's smile.

"It is an excellent notion, but unless it becomes

policy for the Order as a whole, I fear the de Bourgh ladies would never accept it." Fitzwilliam winked back at her.

"I will take your good humor as an excellent sign for the proceedings this morning." Elizabeth sat near Fitzwilliam and Georgiana, Darcy next to her.

"I am choosing to look at things that way. When Cowent Matlock settles a matter, most dragons are apt to defer."

"With good reason. One does not argue with a huge ancient firedrake without a very good reason—"

"And a small army of dragons in reserve." Fitzwilliam guffawed. "I am convinced it is the right decision. Moreover, Netherfield brings unique value to the Order. He is a wealth of information, able to quote the lineage of nearly every major French dragon line and all of the ranking ones. I am sure the Order has no such Records."

"Forgive my ignorance, but what use is that information?" Georgiana glanced between Fitzwilliam and Elizabeth as though she could not quite decide who was more likely to answer.

Elizabeth extended her hand toward Fitzwilliam.

He nodded, a twinkle in his eye. "Dragons can be quite clannish and if lines of relation can be drawn, those connections may be the foundation of new treaties. The right connections could ultimately help bring the protections the Pendragon Accords offer English dragons to the continent."

Darcy snorted into his fist. "You sound like you are becoming a diplomat."

"There are worse businesses to be about." Fitzwilliam shrugged.

"That is not what you used to say. I recall you once

called them—"

"I am well aware of what I once said, but things change, Darce, things change." Something about his expression, his tone, seemed wistful, even a touch melancholy.

What could Fitzwilliam be repining when his mission had been such a grand success? The housekeeper peeked in to announce the carriage. Those questions would have to wait.

Darcy handed her out of the carriage in front of the Blue Order offices. Would she ever grow accustomed to the fact such a place resided behind such a mundane façade? Probably not. Darcy offered his arm and escorted her to the blue-painted front doors that swung open at Fitzwilliam's knock. Blue-liveried footmen recognized them immediately. They had been spending a great deal of time at the offices recently, so it should not be surprising but somehow, it still was. Darcy and Fitzwilliam might take it for granted they would be recognized when they went to great places, but a girl from a small country town did not even if her father was Historian of the Order.

The footman directed them to wait near a cluster of hall chairs for a robed and hooded Bondsman to escort them to the court room at the deepest level of the Order offices. Odd how the heavy, even cumbersome and quite antiquated official robes lent the Bondsmen an air of authority. The deep hoods, obscuring their faces, did the same. Perhaps revealing the burly but pimple-faced youths who served in that role would undermine their control. She bit her lower lip so as not to giggle. Who could expect Lords and major dragons to submit to mere youths? Such scandalous thoughts as was capable of!

How many steps was it down to the Order's gathering floor? At least one hundred and fifty, maybe as many as two hundred steps, not including the landings where not a few took advantage of small chairs to catch their breath. One day she would remember to count.

They paused upon reaching the court floor. The Bondsman scurried off to ready their places. Though the room had changed little since her first Dragon Conclave, today it felt far less threatening. The round room, as large as four substantial ball rooms together and as tall as a five-story house, still echoed, cool, dank, and dark as a pair of cockatrice flew around the perimeter lighting the wall lamps, first those at the floor level then slowly moving their way up the three balcony levels. With all the torches and mirrors, it would soon have as much light as a typical ballroom though its population would be anything but typical.

Ten tunnels opened into the room from all directions. There was room for two more, but that space, considered the front of the round room, sported the raised platforms with three rows of chairs: the gallery where the Order officials would sit when the Conclave assembled. To the left rose the judge's bench for the Minister of the Blue Court, Lord Dunbrook, and to the right, the desk for the Chancellor of the Order, the Earl of Matlock, who would preside over the Conclave.

Between the two tunnels to the right of the Chancellor's desk, a smaller gallery with five rows of chairs stood on a platform about a foot-and-a-half high. When they had last attended, a gated witness box had stood in this place. The Bondsman ushered them to sit in the front row, Georgiana between Darcy and Fitzwilliam. Earl snored in the crook of Fitzwilliam's arm as Georgiana cooed over him.

Darcy glanced at Georgiana, an odd, warm look in his eye. He had never expected to see her at such an event, much less to see her happy and excited to be there. Now that she was, he somehow seemed content, even complete, as Elizabeth had never really seen him before. He leaned into Elizabeth's shoulder. Perhaps her presence with him was part of that completion as well. She would like to think it was.

Keepers and dragons trickled in, a little like beans pouring into a basin, so few at first it hardly seemed possible it would fill, then suddenly there was hardly any room left. In the balcony galleries above, Dragon Keepers took their places by rank. She made out Mary and Collins almost directly opposite them on the highest level. On the floor above that, shadows moved behind a large window. That must be where the Gardiners sat with Lydia. Ironic, how Lydia was given a privilege open to few non-Keeping members of the Order, yet she probably despised it.

Liveried attendants escorted major dragons of every shape to their places on the floor, carefully arranging them to keep tensions to a minimum. What a puzzle it must be sorting out how to preserve rank order while ensuring individuals remained separated from those whose proximity would spark violent reflexes. Just the thought of working out the correct height for the platforms for the rearmost dragons so they could see the proceedings yet not have their heads above the larger dragons in front of them made her head ache.

Teams of Bondsmen with large curtains strung between tall poles stood ready to separate dragons if it appeared any were becoming too tense with one another. Another job she did not envy.

"Look there!" Fitzwilliam pointed to the tunnel nearest the judge's bench.

Four Bondsmen escorted Netherfield to a gated and locked box next to the judge's bench. Had he wanted, Netherfield could certainly have broken free, but with so many large dragons so close, it was very unlikely he could make an escape. If he even tried, the Conclave would not be merciful. He seemed content to settle into the box and watch the spectacle, catching Fitzwilliam's eye, nodding as he did.

A hush settled over the room, the kind of heavy, unnatural sound that set one's nerves on edge. The sort of sound a forest made—or rather did not make—when a large dragon was walking past. Bondsmen with gold-embroidered Blue Order crests on their chests and feathered turbans in place of hoods appeared from the near tunnel, more of an honor guard than an escort, three on each side of Shin-dee-a. Her bright red hide shone in the candlelight, probably oiled just for the occasion. She smelt of exotic spices, warm like ginger and cinnamon, but not nearly so commonplace. The Bondsman settled her near their gallery.

"You look warm and well-fed." Elizabeth rose and curtsied deep, pulling the edges of her cloak over her head.

April peeked out from the folds of Elizabeth's hood, wings over her head, bowing.

Shin-dee-a chuckled deeply. "Pleasing to see you, Erizabet. I very well treated, thank you. Barwines Chudleigh most gracious, even sharing me her cavern. Her salons most interesting ... Lairda April, surprised to see you here."

"I come as Earl's nursemaid." April pointed at him with her wing.

Shin-dee-a laughed heartily. "Can you sing large dragons to sleep, too? Most handy skill at such a gathering."

April chuckled and twittered softly. Shin-dee-a's eyelids drooped. Whether it was real or feigned was difficult to tell, given the envoy's gentle sense of humor.

Fitzwilliam choked on his laughter. "I have had the same thought. Look! Pemberley arrives." He pointed to the tunnel opposite the Officers' Gallery at the center of the back wall, the most prestigious entrance for Conclave attendants ... and the most noticeable.

Rosings paraded in, regal and assured as only an ancient firedrake could manage. She extended one wing over Pemberley as they walked, both sheltering her from too much attention and making clear her presence was no accident or oversight. For her part, Pemberley did a remarkable job of maintaining her composure, except for a brief moment when she peeked under Rosings' wing and grinned, waving at Elizabeth, but surely that was too adorable to bring much censure.

"Your family dragon arrives." Shin-dee-a pointed at Longbourn who took his place among the lower ranked dragons. That was one of the differences between English and Eastern dragons. Instead of Keeps, Eastern dragons were attached to particular families.

A gong sounded, cutting through the room's roar, and another eerie hush fell. Baron Dunbrook, the Minister of the Court, gold ormolu scepter held high, led in the parade of Blue Order officials, robed in blue, gold, and ivory. Papa hobbled in at the end of the line, leaning heavily on his walking stick.

When was the last time she had seen him in his official robes? If only Mama could see him, looking so official and important—how proud she would be. Or would she be embarrassed that he was at the end of the line? It was difficult to say.

The officers took their places in the gallery.

Lord Matlock, blue robes resplendent with heavy gold trim, mounted the steps to his desk. His somber expression fitted the gravity of his office, but it was far and away lighter than it had been when he had called her into his office to discuss the matter of Netherfield.

Once she and Darcy married, she would be connected to him. How strange it would be to consider someone so far above her as family. Then again, Lady Catherine would be her family as well, so perhaps one would make up for the other.

Lord Dunbrook raised up his firedrake-topped staff and rapped it on the large brass plate in the floor just behind the judge's bench. Sonorous tones resounded off the stone floor and walls, reverberating deep in Elizabeth's bones—the kind of sound it was difficult to tell whether one felt or heard. She struggled not to clap her hands over her ears to block some of the noise, not that it would have helped much. The dragons with the most acute hearing snapped and snorted and stomped. The Bondsmen watched, ready to jump in to prevent aggressions until the sound faded away. Perhaps it was time to craft a new gong that would be less objectionable to all? Papa would probably have a fit to hear her suggest such a thing.

As the room came to order, Lord Dunbrook opened the Conclave by reading a summary of the Pendragon Treaty and Accords, as much an act of ceremony as a reminder to agitated dragons of the behavior required of them. Sitting at the judge's bench, he rang a high-pitched, desk-top chime three times.

"The Dragon Conclave of England is now in session."

A brief roar of assent, then silence.

Lord Matlock rose. "We are privileged to welcome a most honored visitor into our midst: Shin-dee-a, envoy of the Eastern Dragon Federation."

Cownt Matlock slowly rose to his full height, his head above every other on the court floor and strutted toward Shin-dee-a. His blue-green hide shone in the candlelight, oiled and polished for the occasion, orange eyes glittering bright. Ears pricked, wings held just slightly above his shoulders, tip of his tail flicking lightly, he was relaxed and pleased, completely in his element.

He stopped about six feet from Shin-dee-a. She stood on her back feet, extending her forearms to spread her gliding wings, and puffed her body, making herself as large as possible. Each movement was slow and deliberate, a formal greeting, not an act of aggression. Cownt Matlock extended his wings and raised his head a moment to tower over her, then lowered his head to match her height.

It was not a standard greeting, to be sure. According to dragon lore, this sort of meeting had never occurred before. But it contained all the necessary symbolism for the Conclave to understand the honor and deference given and received by both parties.

"Envoy, you are welcome among us. Enjoy our hospitality. Learn who we are, and allow us to come to know the Eastern Dragons."

Shin-dee-a trumpeted an odd trill in a pentatonic Eastern scale, but the overall sound was melodic and welcoming. "I accept your invitation and bring greetings from the Eastern Dragon Federation. Is our hope this be first of many meetings and start of warm friendship among our kinds."

Cownt Matlock bugled back a friendly sound, but the final tone was a warning note to the British dragons. He expected exemplary behavior from the dragons of the Conclave and would tolerate nothing less.

From her place on the floor, Barwines Chudleigh rose, wings extended, and bellowed her welcome. Others followed her example until the room shook with the cacophony. The sound died down, and Chudleigh turned to face the Conclave. "A salon will be held after Conclave for you to meet the envoy. Inform the Bondsmen if you wish to attend."

Cownt Matlock voiced a sound of approval, nodding to Chudleigh and Shin-dee-a as he returned to his place.

Baron Chudleigh, Secretary of the Order, stood just in front of Lord Matlock's desk. He unfurled his scroll. "The French dragon, known in England as Netherfield, presents himself for membership to the Blue Order."

The expected murmur rippled through the room.

"Who sponsors this request?" Lord Matlock's voice boomed. How long had it taken him to perfect that draconic resonance?

"I sponsor him." Longbourn's voice echoed from the rearmost ranks.

Elizabeth whipped around to see Longbourn. He stood tall but shifted from one foot to the other as he scanned the Conclave. How had Fitzwilliam managed to garner Longbourn's cooperation?

Salt. It had to be salt. Now that his hoard was known, Longbourn's cooperation would likely be guaranteed for some time to come.

"And I," Fitzwilliam stood, straightening his jacket and pulling his shoulders back. Though certainly not a dragon's voice, his carried, low and confident, across the cavernous room.

Now that was unexpected. But if the man sent as executioner now sponsored Netherfield, how could the Conclave object?

"Although his immigration into England was not conducted according to strict legal channels, Netherfield did receive permission from the previous holder of Netherfield Keep to reside in that territory. During his time in the territory, he largely obeyed the spirit of the Pendragon Accords and proved himself a reliable dragon citizen."

Darcy rose and cleared his throat. "With the singular exception of engaging in persuasions among the dragon hearers at Longbourn and Netherfield."

Elizabeth drew breath to speak, but a quick look from Darcy begged her trust. She pressed her fingers to her lips.

"How plead you, Netherfield?" Lord Matlock asked.

"Guilty, but ignorant, sir." Netherfield hung his head and clasped his forepaws before him, as contrite as little Samuel Gardiner caught in a transgression. "No such restriction on persuasion exists in France. I had no idea it was considered a criminal offense."

"Upon learning of the injunctions, he has obeyed them scrupulously." Fitzwilliam glanced back at Netherfield.

"I have, most attentively. I do not wish to be the source of any controversy or conflict." Netherfield hung his head.

"His ability to get along with Longbourn in the

neighboring estate attests to this fact." Fitzwilliam gestured toward Longbourn.

Lord Matlock waved Lord Dunbrook forward. "The court has thoroughly examined the case and Netherfield himself. What is your recommendation?"

Lord Dunbrook approached Netherfield, somber as befitting the situation. "The court submits the opinion that Netherfield be provisionally accepted into the Blue Order and assigned a territory in the north, surrounded by reliable Keeps ready to assist his assimilation into English dragon life."

Of course, such a statement could not go unchallenged, but that was to be expected whenever there was opportunity to display a show of dominance. For the next three quarters of an hour, the lower dragons challenged Netherfield's worthiness while Matlock, Chudleigh, and Dunbrook stood their ground in favor of his acceptance. Eventually Cownt Matlock called for a vote. A few dissented simply because they could, but the resolution passed, and Netherfield was called from the witness box.

Under the direction of several Bondsmen, he approached Cownt and Lord Matlock, head very low, whiskers scraping the ground.

"By the consensus of the voting members of the Order, we recognize you as a provisional member and assign you the Keep, to be known going forward as Netherford. Your name is now 'Netherford' to always remind you of where you belong and for what you will be responsible." Lord Matlock declared.

"Do you accept these responsibilities and agree to abide by the Pendragon Treaty and Accords for the rest of your life?" Asked with such a growl, how could anyone refuse?

"I do." Netherford murmured into the floor.

Cownt Matlock tapped the back of Netherford's neck with a claw, loosening several scales which would be kept by the Order, a sort of signature attesting to the contract just formed.

"There is one further matter to be settled: that of a Keeper." Lord Matlock scanned the audience in the gallery. "Several volunteers have stepped forward to offer themselves for the service."

Of course, they had. How many younger sons would be able to resist the opportunity to become established in an estate as a full Dragon Keeper, with little or no expense to himself? All cynicism aside, it was a wonderful opportunity for any young man. Unfortunately, too few younger sons—or daughters—had been trained up to be proper Keepers, especially for a dragon like Netherfield—rather, Netherford—who would need an extraordinary amount of direction for at least a decade.

"At the request of Netherford, we name Richard Fitzwilliam as Keeper to Netherford."

Fitzwilliam's jaw dropped, and his forehead creased deeply, almost as though he expected at any moment to be told it was merely a joke his older brothers were playing on him. Darcy clapped his shoulder and nodded vigorously. Had Darcy been consulted on the matter? Considering the way Darcy usually responded to surprises, probably so.

"Step forward, son." Lord Matlock smiled a very genuine smile.

Netherford turned toward Fitzwilliam and looked him in the eyes. "Will you be Keeper to my estate and help me to establish myself as a proper member of the Order?"

Fitzwilliam rose, his knees trembling, but Elizabeth was probably the only one who noticed. He passed Earl to Darcy and stepped forward, slowly, deliberately, to Netherford's side. "I had no expectation."

"That is part of the reason I asked for you. You have no motives for me to question. Besides, we have a great deal in common. You were in France, too."

"Indeed," Fitzwilliam bowed his head. "I am honored to accept the appointment, and all that it requires."

Matlock gestured for Fitzwilliam to kneel beside Netherford and place his hand on Netherford's head. Matlock laid one hand on Fitzwilliam's head and the other on Netherford's. "Your lives will be linked for all time. Fitzwilliam, your progeny will serve as Keepers. Netherford, you will hold the territory on their behalf, and your offspring will hold it for them after you. This relationship is not just for now, but for all the future generations. With that in mind, I name you Dragon and Keeper. Let the Records show this new bond."

Applause began in the galleries and drifted down to the floor. Dragons bugled, and the room dissolved into chaotic effusions.

Elizabeth chanced a quick glance at Darcy. His eyes glistened, and he bit his lip though his smile still crept through.

The celebratory din died away, and Fitzwilliam took a step back.

"Stay where you are, Fitzwilliam. Mr. Darcy, Miss Elizabeth Bennet, approach the Chancellor." What did Lord Matlock have in mind?

No one had apprised them of any charges being brought against them. They had no opportunity to prepare a defense. That was not according to the established protocols. She swallowed hard. Darcy passed Earl to Georgiana and offered his arm, the creases along his eyes revealing as much bewilderment as she felt. She took it gladly.

As they approached Lord Matlock, Cownt Matlock arranged himself beside his Keeper. Both of them? What could they possibly have done to require them to face both Matlocks?

Lord Matlock clasped his hands behind his back and glanced from them to the dragons in the audience and up to the balcony galleries behind them. "Over the past several months, the dragon state has faced perils unseen for centuries, and you three have managed to be in the thick of it all."

Over Matlock's shoulder, Papa glowered directly at her. Elizabeth gulped.

"An egg stolen from its Keep, a drakling wild-hatched, then sick to near death, deaf-speakers brought into the knowledge of dragons, a rogue dragon, and a lost foreign envoy—"

"It was not their fault that I became misdirected." Shin-dee-a called. "In fact, they were quite—"

Cownt Matlock growled a soft warning.

"It is not lost on the officers of the Order the role you have played in these events."

Breathe. She must remember to breathe. Swooning here and now would be anathema to the dragons—to show such weakness before them. She might never regain their respect after such a display. No matter what Matlock declared, she could endure it in order not to lose her standing among the dragons. Cold air ached in her chest as she forced it in and out.

"It is time that it be officially recognized and dealt with according to the ancient traditions of the Order."

Lord Matlock waved at someone behind his dragon.

Lord Chudleigh appeared, carrying a small stool upholstered in blue velvet with the seal of the Order embroidered in gold thread. Lord Dunbrook followed behind, bearing a substantial sheathed sword. Enamel work along the sheath depicted the Pendragon crest.

The Pendragon sword? Elizabeth's knee threatened to buckle.

Lord Chudleigh placed the stool on the floor before Lord Matlock as he unsheathed the sword and held it upright before him for the Conclave to see.

The blade itself had been worn with time, no longer sharp as it once was. Bits of rust stained the blade, but the hilt and pommel were brightly polished, inlaid with blue gems matching Lord Dunbrook's staff. It could be none other than the Pendragon blade.

"The Pendragon Order recognizes your meritorious service to the Order. Richard Fitzwilliam, step forward and kneel."

Fitzwilliam obeyed.

"By the power conferred to me by Uther Pendragon through the Blue Order, I make you Knight Bachelor of the Pendragon Order." He tapped Fitzwilliam's shoulders with the sword.

Cownt Matlock extended his wings to cover Fitzwilliam and Lord Matlock.

The dragons remained oddly silent as if waiting for Cownt Matlock to reveal them once again.

Cownt Matlock folded his wings and Fitzwilliam stood, eyes wide and face a little pale. The corner of Lord Matlock's lips turned up though, enough to crease the corners of his eyes, as broad a smile as he would ever offer in such company. "Fitzwilliam Darcy, step forward and kneel."

Fitzwilliam winked at Darcy as they passed one another. Darcy appeared to ignore it as he knelt before Lord Matlock, but the barest twitch of an eyebrow betrayed him.

"By the power conferred to me by Uther Pendragon through the Blue Order, I make you Knight Bachelor of the Pendragon Order." He tapped Darcy's shoulders with the sword.

Cownt Matlock received Darcy, and he stepped back to Elizabeth's side.

"Miss Elizabeth Bennet," Lord Matlock gestured to the stool.

Had she heard that correctly? He had called her name? Darcy nudged her, and she stepped forward, lightheaded and unsteady. Kneeling on the soft stool was a welcome relief from standing.

"What does a kingdom do with a woman such as yourself?" Lord Matlock asked. "You present us quite a conundrum, Miss Bennet."

"Perhaps to you, but not to us." Cownt Matlock bumped Lord Matlock aside with his shoulder. "He may have his piece in a moment, but we will have our say first." He beckoned with his wing. Barwines Chudleigh slithered from her place to settle beside Cownt Matlock. Barwin Dunbrook flanked his other side.

"Over the last ssseveral monthsss, your contributionsss to not just dragon lore, but to dragon medicine, dragon relationsss ... nearly all things pertinent to usss has become obviousss." Chudleigh wove slightly as she spoke.

"Your services are needed by the Order." Cownt Matlock pulled his head up high and puffed his body. He was about to say something very significant. "By decree of the dragons of the Council, we create a new officer of the Blue Order and appoint you to serve in that role: Dragon Sage. As such, you will be responsible, with the Chief Scribe, for reforming the education of all Dragon Mates, both Keepers and Friends, and for consulting with the same in all matters of draconic difficulties."

Elizabeth stared slack-jawed. "Sage? There is no Dragon Sage."

"There will be once you accept your possst." Chudleigh's tongue flicked Elizabeth's cheek, a soft nudge reminding her of where she was.

Elizabeth glanced back at Darcy. He stood stiff and straight, but his eyes said everything she needed to hear. "I accept."

"Of course, you do." Cownt Matlock murmured, dismissing Chudleigh and Dunbrook with a flick of his wings.

"May I continue now?" Lord Matlock sounded stern, but his posture seemed more amused.

"If you must." Cownt Matlock shuffled aside.

"As I said, you present us quite a conundrum, Miss Bennet. You flout convention at every turn, and yet, as our dragons have already recognized, you seem to have an unfailing ability to think like a dragon and understand the real needs of a situation, proving yourself time and again. By the power conferred to me by Uther Pendragon through the Blue Order, I make you Dame Commander of the Pendragon Order." He tapped her shoulders with the sword.

Cownt Matlock enveloped them with his wings. "We have been observing you for a long time. These accolades are long overdue. You should have been dedicated to Order service years ago."

Cownt Matlock folded his wings back, but it was

several moments before she found sufficient strength to step back between Darcy and Fitzwilliam. The room erupted in an ecstatic roar. In the gallery behind Lord Matlock, Papa shook his head, clearly befuddled by what had just transpired. But his face was soft, not so much displeased as bewildered.

On Lord Matlock's instruction, they faced the Conclave. "Sir Richard, Sir Fitzwilliam, and Lady Elizabeth."

Pemberley waddled from her place beside Rosings directly to Cownt Matlock, and the room stilled. "This mean she my Keeper now?"

Elizabeth rushed to her side and wrapped her arm over Pemberley's shoulders. "Not yet dearling, but very soon."

"No! I waited! I patient. I learn letters. I learn pencil. I learn gliding. I promised learn, I learn. Now I want Keeper!" She lifted her front foot but stopped just before she stomped. The little dear had more self-control than Lydia. She looked up balefully at Matlock. "Please, may I has my Keeper now?"

Whispers rippled back and forth across the room, drifting down from the balconies above. The human voices Elizabeth could pick out seemed rather scandalized. The dragons repeated the question amongst themselves as though it carried great weight and merit. Human ceremony, especially regarding betrothal and marriage, made little sense to them.

"I will consider your request." Lord Matlock strode to the Officer's gallery and conferred with several officers. He returned with the Blue Order Bishop at his heels and waved Darcy to join them. "The first question is, can it be done?"

The bishop wrung his hands. "Have the banns been

read?"

"Yes."

"It is still forenoon." He chewed his lower lip. "The ceremony can be conducted in the Order chapel behind us. Under the circumstances, I think it can be accommodated."

"The bigger question—how do you feel about it, Elizabeth?" Darcy crouched beside Pemberley, "I understand what you want, but you must remember that yours is not the only opinion of import in the case."

"I want her." Pemberley wound her neck around Elizabeth's waist. "I very patient like I promised."

"Yes, you have been. Barwines Chudleigh has told me you have worked very hard in all your studies. I am very proud of you, my dear." Elizabeth scratched under her chin.

"Tea has already been ordered for my sssalon after the Conclave. We could make a sssort of wedding breakfast for you of that, to celebrate after the fashion of your kind," Barwines Chudleigh whispered, her tongue tickling Elizabeth's ear.

"It is, of course, your choice, but after the anxiety of the recent months, I think it would be a very good thing for the Order's morale to see their heroes wed in the presence of the Conclave." Lord Matlock clearly held a strong opinion, but he was trying hard to appear mild and open to their preferences—not succeeding well, but trying.

Elizabeth giggled. "A sort of happily-ever-after to end a dragon fairy-story?"

"Rather like that," Matlock winked just barely, looking remarkably like Fitzwilliam.

"I suppose everyone we would wish to invite is already here. And we had talked about how to accommodate dragon guests for the wedding breakfast." Elizabeth shrugged at Darcy.

He took her hand. "I would just as soon not wait another day to make you my wife."

"Might our families attend us in the chapel?"

"Of course." Lord Matlock summoned a Bondsman and issued a flurry of instructions. "The request of young Pemberley has been granted. You are all invited to attend the Darcys' wedding breakfast following the Conclave, hosted by Barwines Chudleigh."

Elizabeth clutched her forehead. Perhaps this ending was becoming a little too farfetched for even a fairy-story.

In very short order, Elizabeth stood at the back of the Blue Order chapel with Papa. Except for the absence of windows, it resembled every other chapel she had ever known. Workmanship was probably the biggest difference, with all the mahogany woodwork carefully carved in even, geometric patterns, polished and cleaned. What was not covered in wood bore bright white paint. Neither dust nor cobwebs marred any surface—they would have been quite noticeable with so many candles lighting the interior.

The two families quietly talked among themselves, at least insofar as Lady Catherine was capable of speaking softly with Lord and Lady Matlock. Clearly, she did not approve of anything that was happening. A wedding with dragons?

Lady Matlock did not approve of her disapproval. Collins tried to wade into the situation, only to set Lady Catherine off further, earning both a scolding from Cait.

Near the front of the chapel, Walker extended his wings, trying to block Pemberley's and Earl's view of the bickering. How little Pemberley had pleaded to attend the ceremony that would make Elizabeth her Keeper though she really had no understanding of what was actually happening. The bishop tried to refuse, but even he could not resist her baleful looks and soulful pleading.

Fitzwilliam laughed as he made small talk with Georgiana and Pemberley and played with Earl, pointedly ignoring Lady Catherine's unpleasantness. She seemed determined to have someone attend to her and rose, puffed and bustling like an angry dragon, and headed toward Fitzwilliam. April launched from Elizabeth's shoulder and hovered near Lady Catherine, singing softly. She stopped and then returned to Lady Matlock, yawning.

"Your mother will regret missing your wedding," Papa muttered, not meeting her gaze. He shifted his weight from one foot to the other and tapped his walking stick on the wood floor.

"April will persuade her that she attended a ceremony and a breakfast hosted by Lady Matlock that was everything she could have wanted for her daughter." It was very kind of Lady Matlock to offer the ruse to mollify Mama, for it would mean she had to admit Mama and Kitty into her acquaintance.

Papa harrumphed under his breath. "I am sure that will placate her, especially if your Aunt Gardiner reinforces it."

Elizabeth half-turned her back on him. It was far more pleasant to watch Mr. Darcy talking with the bishop. Darcy's smile was handsome and contagious, much better to dwell upon right now. "It would be entirely appropriate for you to say something kind just before you place my hand in Mr. Darcy's."

"I always wanted you to stay at Longbourn with me—as much as Longbourn did." Papa shuffled a step toward her.

"Even though I did little beyond confound and frustrate you at every turn?"

There it was, that annoyed grumbly sound he always made when she vexed him. "Must you always make things sound so very bad? I confess, your ways are difficult for me to accept or even understand. I know I have been vocal about that. But what you would expect of a historian who treasures the traditions of our Order?"

She shrugged. It was a better alternative than telling him such excuses were hardly becoming.

"I am proud of you. The dragons esteem you in a way unheard of in all the annals. You have a rare gift with them. Perhaps I should have recognized that more."

It was not actually an apology, but it was more than he had ever said. That should mean something, but it was difficult to tell if it really did. Something to think upon later.

The bishop called the little group to order and signaled Papa to escort her to Mr. Darcy.

Papa might be reluctant to express his esteem, but the party who waited for her was not. Fitzwilliam, Georgiana, Pemberley, Walker, even little Earl watched her approach with such anticipation. Pemberley flapped, just a little, as if it might hurry them along. Georgiana tried to soothe her, stroking her head, but it only made her flap harder.

Papa relinquished her to Darcy and sat with the

Gardiners and Collinses.

The bishop opened the Book of Common Prayer and read, "Dearly beloved, we are gathered together here in the sight of God, and in the face of this congregation, to join together this Man and this Woman in Holy Matrimony …"

Pemberley waddled closer and closer until she pressed her head against Elizabeth's waist.

The bishop did well, only raising an eyebrow at her, but not missing a beat in his reading. Only a man who had spent many years in the presence of dragons could manage such a feat. He placed her hand in Darcy's and enjoined him to speak.

"I, Fitzwilliam Darcy take thee Elizabeth Bennet to my wedded Wife, to have and to hold, from this day forward, for better, for worse, for richer for poorer, in sickness and in health, to love and to cherish, till death us do part, according to God's holy ordinance; and thereto I plight thee my troth."

She responded in kind.

The bishop looked at him expectantly. "The ring?"

The poor man went absolutely white.

Walker swooped toward them and Darcy extended his arm for him to land, more from reflex than conscious thought. He was hardly capable of that at the moment. How could he have possibly forgotten a ring? Would the bishop declare them wed without one? Would Elizabeth ever forgive him such a blunder? Where could he possibly—

Walker nudged his hand with his head. How could he possibly look so smug at a time like this? He dropped a small object from his beak. "I went back to the house and found this. It was your mother's. I hope it will do."

Blood roared in Darcy's ears as he gulped in a ragged breath. How could he thank Walker enough for this?

Without looking at it, he slipped the ring on her finger. It was a wee bit big, but that was easy enough to sort out later. "With this ring I thee wed, with my body I thee worship, and with all my worldly goods I thee endow: In the Name of the Father, and of the Son, and of the Holy Ghost. Amen."

Elizabeth's lips formed a perfect "o" and her eyes glittered, staring at the ring. The wide gold band was familiar: a pair of firedrakes together clasping a domed blue stone in raised filigree. Mother had worn it on special occasions, a gift from Father's mother upon Darcy's birth. Had Walker any idea how excellent his choice was?

"I pronounce that they be Man and Wife together, In the Name of the Father, and of the Son, and of the Holy Ghost. Amen. I present to you Sir Fitzwilliam and Lady Elizabeth Darcy."

The next several hours passed in a blur of greetings, introductions, and congratulations that began at the Barwines Chudleigh's wedding breakfast but seemed to spill out and span every level of the Blue Order offices. Knights of the Blue Order were not made every day, Dame Commanders even less often, and the creation of a new office entirely? Unheard of! Everyone, human and dragon, seemed compelled to offer their good wishes and even to begin plying Elizabeth with questions.

Poor woman was nearly overwhelmed by everyone, requiring both of her knights to step in and extricate her from seekers. Was that why Matlock had made them? It was unlikely the only reason, but it was amusing to consider.

By the time they escaped their well-wishers, no time remained to return to Darcy House. They rode directly to Cheapside where the Collinses and the Gardiners had put together a small wedding breakfast. With Cait and the cadre of fairy dragons to persuade Mrs. Bennet and Kitty of the elegant wedding breakfast they had just attended at Matlock House, Mrs. Bennet soon praised Aunt Matlock's generosity and hospitality in welcoming Elizabeth into their family. Surely attending the actual events could not have made Mrs. Bennet any happier.

More importantly, the warmth in Elizabeth's eyes suggested she was genuinely happy for a small intimate gathering to celebrate with those closest to her. As long as they were now married, who was he to complain?

At last, they returned to Darcy House, retreating to their favorite parlor for warm cider, roasted apples, and toast. Perhaps it was a plain sort of thing to do, but after a day such as this had been, something ordinary felt very welcome.

They sat close on the fainting couch, staring into the fire, draining the last of the cider. Surrounded by the smells of the fire, apples, and her subtle perfume, a lazy comfort spread through his limbs. He put out most of the candles, leaving the room small and intimate around them, cozy and inviting. Exactly right.

He slipped his arm over her shoulder and pulled her close. "This was certainly not the day I expected."

"Are you disappointed?" She cuddled into his side.

"Hardly. Merely a little surprised. When one deals with dragons, one does not expect for things to go exactly as one might dream." He pressed his cheek to the top of her head.

"They do usually make things complicated."

"I expect that is a word we shall revisit often."

"There is one thing I have found very helpful when things seem complicated."

"What is that, Mrs. Darcy?"

"Often things seem much clearer if one tries to think like a dragon."

"Indeed, is that so?" He nuzzled the side of her neck, growling slightly. "Are you perhaps recommending now would be such a time?"

"It is a good place to begin." She winked at him.

And it was.

Epilogue

THREE WEEKS LATER, Elizabeth and April ushered a crowd into Darcy House's largest drawing room. Most of the furniture had been pushed against the walls to accommodate the gathering. As twitterpated as April was over the hatching, it was easier to move into a larger room than to try and to convince her to restrict the attendees.

Papa, with Drew, his new secretary—whom Mama thought a rather large dog—insisted on being there. Lady Astrid had expressed interest in publishing his fairy dragon monograph at last, so he wanted to refresh the section on hatching with new observations. April did not object, and the reasoning was sound, so it was hard to deny them.

Walker, Slate, and Amber had to be there as they were part of the household. The hatchling who would hopefully befriend Georgiana would need to accustom herself to them as soon as possible. Though Earl and Fitzwilliam would not be living with them, they would be regularly in their company, so an early acquaintance made sense there, too.

Was it really necessary to have Auntie—and Lydia—there, though? It was not as if they were going to be with them for very long, nor were they likely to see each other with any regularity, but April thought it appropriate.

With Georgiana, Lady Astrid, and Bylock, they now had seven people, five drakes and two cockatrice in the room. Good thing minor drakes were rather companionable sorts.

Walker was not fond of so much company and kept to himself near the windows. His excuse was to ensure they were guarded against predators that might disturb the hatching. No one dared insult his dignity by suggesting the closed windows were sufficient to the task.

Papa sat near the fire, directing Fitzwilliam in shaving slivers of blood and treacle pudding into a pan of broth simmering on the hob. Lady Astrid and Georgiana helped the drakes rub soft flannels over themselves to give the hatchlings their scent, then rubbed the same cloths over their throats and hands. Papa said it made it more likely for the hatchlings to stay and choose a Friend. Naturally, the hatchlings would ultimately do as they pleased, as all dragons did, but anything that might make the process easier was welcome.

"Historian Bennet says you should give these your scent and Walker's as well, then give them to Fitzwilliam and Earl." Georgiana brought them a pile of flannels.

Her cheeks were flushed prettily, and she could hardly subdue her smile. It was difficult to believe she had ever been the dragon-fearing child Darcy had once described. His eyes shone as he took the cloths. If pride could be palpable, his was.

The only one in the room who did not seem to share in the warm feelings was Lydia who hunched on a hard stool near the far side of the fireplace. She did not do well when she was not the center of attention. Auntie insisted she attend to gain a better understanding of the bond between dragon and Friend. Lydia had brought a book—a lavishly illustrated bestiary that took up her entire lap. She stared resolutely at its pages, not answering any inquiry directed toward her until everyone simply ignored her. Ah well, it was probably the best anyone could ask for, given the circumstances.

"The eggs, they are moving!" Lady Astrid cried and hurried to the nesting box.

Georgiana took her place along the adjacent side. Elizabeth positioned herself between them while the drakes stood in a ring just beyond.

Papa and Fitzwilliam prepared saucers of broth and sausage and brought them near the box.

Two of the three eggs in the center of the box wobbled and rocked. The tiny third one lay on its side, resolutely still. Elizabeth moved it to the far corner, out of the way.

Both mottled eggs cracked near the top, exposing the inner membrane. Georgiana clasped her hands tightly before her. She had been warned to let the hatchlings escape their shells on their own. Lady Astrid leaned over the box, hands clutched behind her back. Perhaps she was as excited as Georgiana.

A sharp beak poked through the egg nearest Lady Astrid. April paced beside it, trilling encouraging sounds. The chick seemed to respond, forcing its head through the shell, a rather surprised look on its tiny face as it blinked in the room's muted light. She quickly pulled her wings from the shell and flapped herself free of it, sending egg slime flying in every direction. Lady Astrid offered her hand to the hatchling for a perch and reached for a flannel.

"You are the absolute perfect image of a fairy dragon, just like the illustrations in my books." Astrid cooed as she dried the deep blue chick. It fluffed into a perfect fairy dragon dandelion.

The chick turned her head this way and that, cheeping prettily. "Hungry?" She said it so politely, so sweetly.

"Of course." Lady Astrid offered her a saucer of broth.

What a truly ladylike little thing. Nothing like the greedy guzzles most chicks usually indulged in after hatching.

"May I call you Verona, for you are the true image of what I imagined a fairy dragon to be." Lady Astrid had a rather vivid imagination if this was what she imagined after having known April.

The chick lifted her head and seemed to consider the notion carefully. "Verona. Yes." She returned to her meal as Lady Astrid stroked her back.

"Lizzy! Lizzy! I think something is wrong!" Georgiana pointed to the other egg.

A silvery white beak, followed by an egg-slime covered head, very pale, silvery, almost white, burst forth. With a little squawk, the chick threw off the egg and hopped and flapped, screeching until most of the goo was gone. "No wet!" it cried.

"Clean her off." Elizabeth spoke into her hand. Hopefully it would hide the giggle. The chick certainly had strong preferences already.

"Come here. I will make you warm and dry, little one." Georgiana knelt beside the box, making her nearly eye to eye with the chick.

The chick spread her wings and offered them to Georgiana who already seemed expert in drying and fluffing. "Better!" She cheeped and hopped into Georgiana's hand, such a happy, peaceful little thing cuddling her palm.

"Have you ever seen a white fairy dragon?" Georgiana asked, stroking the chick's head.

"No, I did not realize they could be white. She is quite extraordinary. Go ahead and offer her some broth."

A large book hit the floor.

"Ouch! Stop that!" Lydia snatched her hand away from her lap.

Elizabeth rushed to Lydia. The tiniest fairy dragon Elizabeth had ever seen stood on Lydia's knee, pecking her hand and dripping goo on Lydia's gown.

"Hungry! Hungry now!"

Fitzwilliam pressed a saucer into Lydia's hand.

The black and red chick tipped her beak into the broth and spat it at Lydia's face. "No! Hungry!"

"Honey, hand me the honey!" Elizabeth reached over Lydia's head as Darcy passed her the honey pot. "Here, this will please you." She placed the open pot on Lydia's lap.

The chick thrust her head in the pot, guzzling loudly.

"She is just like you." Elizabeth looked at April.

April flitted to Lydia's knees and examined the chick. "She is very tiny."

The chick pulled her head out of the honey, beak dripping, and pecked at April. "Mine. Hungry."

"Yes, you are hungry, but you are not alone and must be ready to share." April chided as she preened the chick.

"Lydia, dry her off." Elizabeth handed her a flannel.

Clumsy and a touch annoyed, Lydia scrubbed away the slime. "You are actually a pretty little thing, but I thought only two of the eggs were to hatch."

"You were wrong." The chick pecked at Lydia's hand, drawing a tiny dot of blood.

"Ouch! Do not do that!" Lydia snatched her hand away.

"You should not say very stupid things."

"Well, they did not seem stupid to me."

"Then perhaps you should think about them a bit more before you say them. More sweet."

Lydia shoved the pot toward the chick.

"Do not argue!" a tiny voice cried. The white chick nestling in Georgiana's elbow shook her head furiously.

"You are like me and prefer peace." Georgiana stroked the chick's head. "If you are agreeable, I shall call you Pax."

A happy cheep confirmed her name.

Papa shambled up to Lydia and peered over her shoulder. "She is so tiny. I am not sure how she broke through the egg."

Fitzwilliam crouched down and picked up pieces of shell. "It looks like it fell from the nest and cracked."

Papa dragged his gnarled hand down his face. Pray he did not make a stupid remark about dragons who should not have hatched. The little one might peck his eyes out.

The chick pulled back from the honey and jumped on Lydia's hand. Lydia held her up to eye level and stared at her. They seemed to share a conversation in blinks, facial twitches, and the occasional chirp.

"You are too small to fly off on your own." Fitzwilliam knelt beside Lydia.

"I could if I wanted to." The chick pecked toward Fitzwilliam and flapped her tiny wings for good measure.

"Of course, she could. She is as good as any of those bigger ones, better because I am sure she is far more determined." Lydia nodded at the chick and glowered at Fitzwilliam.

"I am not so sure."

The chick hopped toward him, hopping mad as it were. "You should not say such things about me."

"No, you should not." Lydia drew the chick into her chest and stroked between her wings. "Calm down, Cosette—"

"What did you call me?"

"In French it means 'little thing.' You are a little one. But that is no insult, for the littles can be quite surprising." Did Papa catch the glance Lydia threw his way?

"Cosette? It will do." She nodded and warbled, quite loudly for her size.

"Your voice certainly is not small." Fitzwilliam rose. "What will you do?"

Cosette scanned the room then looked up into Lydia's face. "You have more sweet?"

"As much as you wish." Lydia smiled with the same wide-eyed sort of gaze at Cosette as Collins had been wearing since Earl's hatching.

"Then I will stay. With you." Cosette backed up against Lydia's chest, wings spread, challenging.

"No, no, no. Not another!" Papa slapped his

forehead.

Auntie peeked over Lydia's shoulder and licked the top of Cosette's head. Cosette shook her head and pecked at Auntie's tongue. "She is my charge, and it is my say, not yours, Historian."

Lydia pulled Cosette close to her chest and guarded her with the other arm. "I do not care what either of you say. If she wants to stay with me, then she shall."

"I suppose it is good I agree with you." Auntie glowered at Papa.

"It seems to have happened again," Fitzwilliam whispered to Darcy. "First Collins, now her."

"I would not have believed it of either of them, but perhaps it is possible people imprint as much as dragons." Darcy's eyebrows rose.

"It is certainly an interesting theory—one I am sure Papa will not like. But it will make for an interesting conversation with the Lord Physician."

"She seems very like her brood mother. Rather a scold, I think." Fitzwilliam pursed his lips, hiding his characteristic grin.

"Georgiana would be terrified of Cosette." Darcy turned toward Georgiana who was deep in admiration of her peaceable Friend.

"Which is why Cosette managed to find the one person in the room who would not be." Elizabeth tittered. "It is going to be an interesting Friendship for certain. One can only imagine what those two are going to get themselves into."

"Considering who they are related to, one shudders to think." Darcy laid his hand on her shoulder and shook his head.

All told, he was probably right.

For more dragon lore check out:
Dragon Myths of Britain
At RandomBitofFascination.com

Read the rest of the series:

Jane Austen's Dragons Series:
Pemberley: Mr. Darcy's Dragon
Longbourn: Dragon Entail
Netherfield:Rogue Dragon
A Proper Introduction to Dragons
The Dragons of Kellynch
Kellynch: Dragon Persuasion

Acknowledgments

So many people have helped me along the journey taking this from an idea to a reality.

Debbie, Anji, Julie, Ruth and Raidon thank you so much for cold reading and being honest!,

And my dear friend Cathy, my biggest cheerleader, you have kept me from chickening out more than once!

And my sweet sister Gerri who believed in even those first attempts that now live in the file drawer!

Thank you!

Other Books by Maria Grace

Fine Eyes and Pert Opinions
Remember the Past
The Darcy Brothers

Jane Austen's Dragons Series:
A Proper Introduction to Dragons
Pemberley: Mr. Darcy's Dragon
Longbourn: Dragon Entail
Netherfield:Rogue Dragon
The Dragons of Kellynch
Kellynch: Dragon Persuasion

The Queen of Rosings Park Series:
Mistaking Her Character
The Trouble to Check Her
A Less Agreeable Man

Sweet Tea Stories:
A Spot of Sweet Tea: Hopes and Beginnings (short story anthology)
Snowbound at Hartfield
A Most Affectionate Mother
Inspiration

Darcy Family Christmas Series:
Darcy and Elizabeth: Christmas 1811
The Darcy's First Christmas
From Admiration to Love
Unexpected Gifts

Given Good Principles Series:
Darcy's Decision
The Future Mrs. Darcy
All the Appearance of Goodness
Twelfth Night at Longbourn

A Jane Austen Regency Life Series:
A Jane Austen Christmas: Regency Christmas Traditions
Courtship and Marriage in Jane Austen's World
How Jane Austen Kept her Cook: An A to Z History of Georgian Ice Cream

Behind the Scenes Anthologies (with Austen Variations):
Pride and Prejudice: Behind the Scenes
Persuasion: Behind the Scenes

Non-fiction Anthologies
Castles, Customs, and Kings Vol. 1
Castles, Customs, and Kings Vol. 2
Putting the Science in Fiction

Available in e-book, audio book and paperback

On Line Exclusives at:

www.http//RandomBitsofFascination.com

Bonus and deleted scenes
Regency Life Series

Free e-books:
- *Rising Waters: Hurricane Harvey Memoirs*
- *Lady Catherine's Cat*
- *A Gift from Rosings Park*
- *Bits of Bobbin Lace*
- *Half Agony, Half Hope: New Reflections on Persuasion*
- *Four Days in April*

About the Author

Six time BRAG Medallion Honoree, #1 Best-selling Historical Fantasy author Maria Grace has her PhD in Educational Psychology and is a 16-year veteran of the university classroom where she taught courses in human growth and development, learning, test development and counseling. None of which have anything to do with her undergraduate studies in economics/sociology/managerial studies/behavior sciences.

She pretends to be a mild-mannered writer/cat-lady, but most of her vacations require helmets and waivers or historical costumes, usually not at the same time.

She writes gaslamp fantasy, historical romance and non-fiction to help justify her research addiction.

Contact Maria Grace:

author.MariaGrace@gmail.com

Facebook:
http://facebook.com/AuthorMariaGrace

On Amazon.com:
http://amazon.com/author/mariagrace

Random Bits of Fascination (http://RandomBitsofFascination.com)

Austen Variations (http://AustenVariations.com)

White Soup Press (http://whitesouppress.com/)

On Twitter @WriteMariaGrace

On Pinterest: http://pinterest.com/mariagrace423/

Made in the USA
Columbia, SC
29 April 2024